Book one of the *Eramus Pon* novels

Eramus the Coward

Vincent R. Hagman

This novel is dedicated to the little mandos

CT, ES, ET, & RJ

who are already smarter and tougher than I'll ever be

ACKNOWLEDGMENTS

My thanks to the many friends who believe in me not only as a writer, but as a person, most of whom have never actually read a word I've written.

Special thanks are due to: Kev, my brother, for enduring an early draft, and for pushing me in the right direction; Big Ern, for his sound logic and ideas during a crisis; Mary V. and my sister, Liv, for feedback and criticism which improved the book along the way; Jon and company, for keeping me smiling; the Churches and the Gonzaleses, for always getting me out of the house and into trouble, and most importantly for accepting me as I am; the Juarezes and the Lucs, for opening their homes to me and for feeding me; and the BCC, my brothers in arms who've never surrendered in a street fight, no matter who started it.

And, finally, to my great friend, Tanya, who has always believed in me and encouraged me, who listens to me when nobody else will, and who is probably still wondering what happened to the horses.

PROLOGUE

Eramus Pon squinted down into a valley of evergreen treetops glowing crimson in the setting sun. Chimney smoke, the first sign of a real fire he had seen in more than six days, curled up toward the first indigo sleep star twinkling at the sky's eastern edge. He regarded his tattered cloak and worn boots, not exactly presentable attire, nor what he had once imagined a man in the Information Regiment wore.

A rattle of dead leaves was his only warning before biting wind whipped under his wool cloak, reminding him that he couldn't feel his fingers because of the cold. He had expected to spend another solitary night nestled among a cluster of spruce trees before he had spotted the smoke. He lowered his head against the unkind wind and cautiously descended into the valley.

Although he had been somewhat lost in the woods for the last four days, he had kept a loose pace with the refugees on his way east to Keltivar. He stopped and listened for the defeated, shuffling footsteps far below, and wasn't disappointed when they came into earshot. He crept down the rest of the way, thankful for a narrow footpath he found.

A rangy sixteen-year-old Uuslefin with light hair and blue-gray eyes, Eramus could easily pass for Oshlemin, one of the reasons his Uncle Reginald had selected him for the Information Regiment. *Blend in. Avoid eye contact. Conceal your emotions.* Three warnings for the boys off to risk their lives, and one more they came up with on their own: *deliver the message.*

He waited for the Seehlan refugees and subtly eased into their procession, ignoring the concerned scrutiny from hundreds of light blue eyes set in pale, papery skin, confident that he could separate from them at any time. *Blend in.* Their clothing, once as soft blue as a spring sky and as white as billowing clouds, had since been stained by spattered mud and trail dust. He recognized a handful of them and nodded unspoken greetings. He had once shared a campsite with a man and his three daughters. The youngest had spoken a little Oshlema, the bled amalgamation of old Oshlemin tainted by dispersion and ease, and Eramus had learned how they had been banished from their own land, land they had owned for centuries, simply for believing in the Seehli.

The refugees pressed on, winding through the center of a small village, the southern side ringed with military tents around the coals of a single campfire. Chainmail and sandy hair herded the disconsolate flow like livestock, ensuring they wouldn't stop.

Eramus rubbed snot from his runny nose and glued his eyes to the trampled ground. *Avoid eye contact.* The gray evergreens stitched onto soldiers' tunics below triangles of midnight blue ebb stars meant he was in Fushlem, on Count Sevelah's land, but exactly where he wasn't sure. What he did know was that the Fushlemin soldiers were called Filthies. They had earned the nickname for volunteering to drive Seehlan straight through Oshlem.

"Ignorant!" shouted a high-pitched voice from atop a rocky perch off the main path. A robed Geflin missionary waved a three-fingered hand over the refugees, his other gripping the white wood of a simple amulet around his neck, his constricted pupils judging them. "There is no return to the Seehli! There is no return!"

Eramus trembled, though not from cold this time. The amulet reminded him of his father's last day. The knight who had ordered the execution had worn an amulet like that. Anger simmered within Eramus as he contemplated striking the missionary. Instead he glared at the man, despising and resenting him for the consequences of his faith.

"A good Hamaln does not solve problems with violence," Loghemit Pon tells him. "When something you don't like happens, you have to accept it. You have to pray to the Hamal for understanding and the wisdom of Second Awakening." His father

2

serves one bowl of soup for himself. Eramus gets no supper tonight for punching another boy who taunted him, who called his mother a mushroom head. Why isn't his father angry? Why doesn't he care? This is the first of many nights Eramus goes hungry. He doesn't like onion soup anyway.

"Shut up," a Filthy muttered at the missionary. The soldier spun his finger in the air signaling the last of the long line. The Geflin missionaries Eramus had encountered behaved frantically, fanatically, their apparent sole purpose to berate refugees. Though unwelcome in Oshlem, the missionaries sprouted up like weeds.

Cold, hungry, and without the means to change any of that, Eramus shuffled along, head hung low. His feet ached from walking all day. An invigorating drink could ground and refresh him, help him to forget the long journey ahead, if only for a little while.

He jingled the few silver coins he had, barely enough for a night's lodging and a wedge of pigeon pie once he reached Keltivar. He was most likely more than three days from the Hereton Road, still the most direct route through Oshlem despite its unpredictable safety, and more than twenty days from Keltivar. He considered the threat of robbery. He asked himself what good his coins would be then.

Up ahead lay a single story tavern of stacked logs and hard mud, its chimney blowing the same smoke he had seen earlier, a sign of warmth in the muddy, miserable little village. He steered toward the glow of lamplight under the front door, hoping for a bench on which to rest his sore feet, and for cheap ale to mellow his numb face. To the right of the entrance hung an arrow in a bloody circle, a death warning to any Seehlan brazen enough to set foot in the establishment.

As Eramus pushed the heavy door open, pleasant warmth and the bittersweet aroma of oat heavy pottage and burning mutton washed over him. Scuffed wooden boards underfoot surrendered comfortingly to his weight. Shadows flickered along the walls and ceiling as moths fluttered too close to hanging oil lamps. He flipped his hood back for a better view of Filthies arguing at the bar, old gamblers hunched over the hearthside table, and a young man seated at a nearby table who stared at him.

"Lunken, yah," the overfriendly young man said. He held the

bent neck of a lute in his left hand, the teardrop base settled firmly on the floor.

Eramus was no stranger to taverns. They had been his father's second home, and he half expected to see Loghemit Pon passed out on the bar. Instead, one of the Filthies glanced at him, his interest fleeting at best. The soldier's dour lips hadn't lifted into a smile since the surrender almost two years earlier. Chainmail had worn through the shoulders of his tunic, and the top of his left ear was conspicuously missing.

"In Grihm it is considered rude to ignore me," the arrogant young man pressed, his handsome jaw of blonde stubble distracting Eramus from his furtive assessment of the tavern interior. Eramus and the young man were close to the same age, though hardly similar in any other way. The young man's long, muscular arms, hardly those of a lutist, disappeared into cinched leather bracers. He wore an ostentatious vest of black leather armor sewn through with metal rings and held his shoulders back, his angular chin up, the fancy crimson tunic beneath his vest screaming of flaunted wealth. His mismatched eyes—one piercing green and one clear blue—separated him from the typical sea-green of most Oshlemin. Eramus had never met someone with different colored eyes. He couldn't help but gawk at the oddity.

"I'm still in Fushlem?" he asked in accented Oshlema. The young man slowly nodded, and Eramus reciprocated the old greeting, noticing the flicker of firelight across the pommel of the sword hilt on the other's belt for the first time.

The door swung open and a gust of cold misery blew inside. Head down, another Filthy shoved his way toward the bar, a bruised mess beneath his forest of beard.

"I beg pardon," Eramus said as he stumbled a bit. The soldier barely slowed, chuckling under his breath before joining the others to raucous shouts and backslapping.

"Sit for a time," the friendly young man suggested with a wave of his palm as he leaned the lute against a table leg. "Conversation would be a blessing on this night." He slid his wooden cup of golden liquid across the table. Eramus froze with indecision, his mouth watering at the thought of something to dilute his weariness from the road, his keen mind considering what it would cost him.

He snatched up the cup, as tall as the width of his hand, but the young man seized his wrist before he could bring it to his lips.

"*Gohlay-gohlay*," the young man firmly said.

"*Gohlay-gohlay*," Eramus slowly repeated, wincing at the other's crushing strength.

"It means 'could be happy'. Like going one way or the other but you want to go the right way for you."

"Aren't they one and the same?"

The young man shrugged in response and released his wrist.

The drink's piquant tang crippled Eramus's pride. He gulped the cup's contents down, the liquid blazing his sinuses with sweet melon flavor and a bitter aftertaste, an exotic drink for such a barren locale.

"You're not supposed to drink *glistas* that fast," the young man advised. "Every full cup contains three swallows. Remember. Please, sit. My name is Rammun." He flicked his thick, bejeweled fingers in the air for the barkeep.

"*Glis-tas*?" Eramus asked. "I've never heard of it."

"*Glee-stas*," Rammun corrected. "Fermented from the *glis* orchards in the Barony of Medar."

"All the way down here?"

"Sure. There's demand for it in Oslah so occasionally a couple barrels make their way to Grihm. There's no other reason to stop here."

As Eramus sat on the hard wooden chair, he licked *glistas* off his upper lip, reveling in its sweet distraction from the road's aches and irritations. Tonight he wouldn't hear the wails of hungry refugee children and breathe the stink of unwashed bodies. *Gohlay-gohlay*. Perhaps he could enjoy relative peace and quiet, at least for a little while.

"I am Eramus."

"You know…" the young man said as he scratched his jaw, "Eramus is almost like Rammun. Maybe we are brothers." His smile was infectious. "You look like your head is in another place."

"Just thinking about the day."

"Hm. You speak pretty good Oshlema."

"Really?" In Uuslef, Eramus had picked up pieces of the common language from visiting merchants, traders, and his uncle's transient workers. He had gleaned much more of it during his time in the service, chatting with other travelers, shopkeeps and the like on his routes through Oshlem, though every region seemed to have its own inflections and stresses on words and phrases.

Rammun shook his head and laughed, revealing perfect white teeth. "No."

Eramus laughed back, the aftertaste of the *glistas* still tickling his throat. Normally he would be concerned that someone had so clearly identified him as a foreigner, but Rammun's only real interest appeared to be in conversation, and Eramus needed to blend in if he hoped for anonymity. Besides, he didn't want to leave the warmth of the tavern behind. He wanted to forget the cold and his loneliness, if only for a little while.

He brought his focus back to the moment, searching his mind for appropriate conversation topics. He couldn't discuss Uuslef or the clandestine Information Regiment. He couldn't offer opinions about Oshlem, lest he mistakenly incriminate himself. He would have to mention the coming winter or the wonders of *glistas*.

Rammun. Eramus repeated the boy's name in his head. An Oshlemin with a sword and one blue eye. It was common knowledge that Count Sevelah paid a hefty sum for dead Seehlan priests. It wouldn't be farfetched to believe that Rammun earned a good living hunting them down.

Pressure on Eramus's leg startled him.

"That is only the damn dog," Rammun said.

Beneath the table, growling playfully, a tan puppy shot through with streaks of black wrestled with Eramus's boot. The pup's ears flattened and his bushy tail slapped the chair when Eramus scratched the coarse fur atop his head.

"What's his name?"

"I will not give him a name."

"Why not?"

"If I name him, I have to take care of him. I have enough trouble looking after myself."

More *glistas* came in a small jug with a second cup. Rammun uncorked the jug and poured while he briefly explained the traditional Medarn custom of drinking from the small wooden cups. Eramus took a quick swallow this time, leaving what he thought were two more. *Glistas* sounded like a drink he couldn't afford.

"Good," Rammun said with a slight nod as Eramus set his cup on the table. "Now you are part of a tradition."

"Where did you learn all of this? Are you from the barony?"

Rammun studied him after that, as if weighing a decision. "No. My mother had an interest in things Medarn. Plague took her when I was still young."

"What about your father?"

"He was never part of my life. Mercenaries adopted me after my mother died. They taught me respect." He tapped his sword hilt. "They showed me how to use this, how to make my own rules."

Seeing the missionary outside had dredged up painful memories of Eramus's father's death. It had taken him years to accept what had happened, and that acceptance had only brought anger and emptiness with it.

"You look sad, Eramus."

"What?" *Conceal your emotions.*

Rammun held up a calming hand to Eramus's surprise. "I once fought beside a man for weeks. He used to tell me to smile all the time. The more he told me, the less I wanted to smile." He pursed his lips. "But you look sad, Eramus."

The Filthies at the bar laughed in Eramus's direction when he took another measured swallow. He kept his back to them, took another swallow of *glistas* while the dog nipped at his feet. He could feel his anger building despite the soothing effects of the drink. He wanted to stand up and call them Shlems, an epithet he had heard his uncle use, but he couldn't muster the nerve to shout the insult in a tavern full of Oshlemin.

"They're probably going to rob you," Rammun said, giving voice to his worst fear.

Eramus froze in his seat. "What? How do you know?"

Rammun twisted a glittering topaz ring on his finger. "That *kuvos* who bumped you…he tried to do the same to me when I arrived in the village."

Kuvos was an Oshlemin profanity that even Eramus knew. Rammun's conviction indicated honesty, and Eramus had seen evidence of a physical altercation on the Filthy's face. Had Rammun really done that? Count Sevelah's soldiers were the law in Fushlem. They were bound to retaliate sooner or later. Rammun had put Eramus at risk just by asking him to sit down.

Eramus clutched the coins in his waistband pocket, his fingertip straying down to the wire-handled dagger hidden in his boot. He had never used it, even when he had been robbed weeks ago. It was an advantage against one man, maybe two, but not against armed soldiers. He would have to leave soon to catch up to the refugees. He couldn't risk being confronted outside and alone. He swallowed the rest of his *glistas*, searching for an excuse to depart, but Rammun quickly refilled his cup.

One of the old gamblers threw more wood into the hearth, and the heat washed across the tavern. Eramus wiped perspiration from his forehead with his fingertips. Losing a few coins wasn't his only concern. He also carried a sealed document inside his tunic, bundled in a plain handkerchief. The Filthies might not be able to make sense of it, but their captain would surely identify its intent.

His legs refusing to obey his command to move, Eramus sat and stared at his hands around the small wooden cup. They were strong hands, rough and masculine from shoveling and building for his uncle's city contracts. They were the hands of a man, even if he was still a frightened boy inside.

The din of the tavern faded into the background of his hearing while Eramus considered what being captured could mean for him.

A distant voice. *"Eramus? Eramus? Did you hear what I said? About the soldiers?"*

"They won't bother me," Eramus finally responded with no better answer. He drank one third of his *glistas* like he had learned. "I can't stay much longer anyway. I have to get moving."

And he hadn't meant to stay, but the more he missed his father and mother, the more he thought about how he would never see them again, and the more *glistas* he drank, and the more Rammun refilled his cup, and the sweeter the drink tasted on his tongue, under his teeth, and in the back of his throat.

The hilt of Rammun's sword jutted up from his intricately tooled and studded belt. The ring Eramus had admired earlier was one of many Rammun flaunted on his fingers. They might have been the same age, but Rammun was clearly much more self-reliant. He also emanated something Eramus never had: confidence.

"Are you a lutist?" Eramus asked, nodding to the lute still

leaning against the table leg.

"No. My mother used to sing to me when I was very young. I pull at the strings when I miss her." He quickly tucked the instrument away. "More?" He put another full cup in front of Eramus and he couldn't refuse. He felt better than he had in a while, even if he was drinking with a dangerous man. Rammun was pleasant enough, generous with his wisdom and with his *glistas*. Eramus admired him and envied him at the same time.

He sighed, wishing he could tell Rammun about his reasons for traveling through Oshlem in the first place. He wanted to complain about sleeping under trees where rodents nibbled at his fingers and bugs crawled on his face, and how every snapping branch could be someone out to cut his throat just to steal his boots. He wanted to tell him how much he hated his uncle because deep down he thought that the man might be right about him only being one more strong back with a shovel. He wanted to tell him that he was more than just another nameless member of the Information Regiment, that he was better than his father's mistakes, and that he intended to prove it by establishing his own reputation. He wanted to tell Rammun that his mother was gone, too, and that he missed her, but that she had gotten lost, had been hurt or worse, and always intended to come back to her son. He wanted to tell him about how he pretended the plight of the refugees didn't concern him until he thought about the good people he had met along the way.

He wanted to talk about how he didn't want to get up some mornings, and it wasn't because of the cold.

Instead all he muttered was, "Good *glistas*." The *glistas* was very good. It suffused his face with tingling warmth and stole his worries. He wanted more. He enjoyed observing the tradition Rammun had taught him, and he intended to carry that bit of culture around with him if he took nothing else away from this night.

After a while he lost track of time. He sucked in deep breaths and blew them out with greater concentration than usual. He pictured himself back in Uuslef, in the house he hated, where he was safe, lonely, and underappreciated by his uncle. Eramus thought about how good he felt in this tavern, and he finally understood that his father had succumbed to drinking to cope with his own powerlessness. He must have known that Eramus's mother would never return, despite what he told his son.

"Good *glistas* helps a man appreciate life," Rammun said, filling Eramus's cup.

"Yes! That's exactly what is the truth. I mean..."

"And a dog, too," Rammun said as he dribbled *glistas* into his palm and held it under the table. The puppy noisily lapped it up, his excited tail smacking Eramus's leg.

Eramus leaned over to pet the puppy and ended up on the floor, laughing hysterically. The puppy's cold nose wet his face. He hugged the animal close. "Good dog." Tears moistened the corners of his eyes until he wiped them away.

Rammun loomed over him. "You are on the floor, Eramus." He was, and the idea forced another half-laugh, half-cry out of him. A strong, calloused hand gripped his and hauled him upright. He breathlessly collapsed back into his chair, overcome with emotion. The puppy jumped up and down, eager to play. As Eramus scratched his ears, he thought about the refugees outside, cold and hungry. They were people like him, only different. He leaned his head back and took a deep breath, wanting to explain that to Rammun.

"It's not fair," he slurred.

"What?"

The tavern swayed. "A minute." Eramus found it increasingly difficult to maintain his concentration. The time had come for him to say farewell to Rammun and to find a suitable tree to sleep under, but the thought of moving from the chair to the door was too much.

The Filthies burst into prolonged laughter when he clutched the table for balance. "Fucking Shlems," he cursed under his breath. He lowered his forehead onto the cool, smooth tabletop and let his eyelids drop.

"Eramus? Eramus?" Rammun mumbled something else he couldn't understand.

Heavy heels on wood. Jingling chainmail. Sweat, oiled steel, and leather.

"Friend of yours?" a gruff voice asked. More boots.

"Where's he from?" Another voice.

They were asking about him. His head lay nestled in the warmth and comfort of his arms. They would see that he was in no condition to be bothered and they would leave him in peace. He could hear them somewhere past the heavy sound of his own labored breathing. The pup gnawed on his boot. He didn't mind. The puppy was just having fun. Maybe Rammun would let him have this puppy. He had said he didn't want to be responsible for it anyway, and Eramus was tired of being alone.

"He came in off Frehm," Rammun said in a much more serious tone than he had used during their conversation. "He's an apprentice sign maker."

Feet shuffled. Eramus could smell their bad breath. He wasn't from Frehm and he didn't know anything about making signs. Why had Rammun lied? Eramus would never go back to Frehm.

Then wood creaked and groaned and cold air swept in as footsteps splashed in the mud outside. Eramus decided to wait a while and let his head clear, at least until the soldiers settled in to their tents. He didn't want trouble. He didn't want to have to use his dagger. He didn't want people to know how much cowardice his father had instilled into him, how he couldn't even talk back to his uncle.

He hated his life back in Uuslef, hated remembering his father whenever he saw his uncle's face, hated having to work so hard for so little, hated being criticized for his father's failures, hated hearing that his mother cared more about losing herself in mushrooms than anything else. Loghemit Pon had chosen to drown his problems, and Vina Pon had never been fit to raise a son, and Uncle Reginald seized every opportunity to point out their shortcomings.

That didn't stop Eramus from loving his father, from remembering his kindness, his scratchy cheeks and his deep voice. That didn't stop Eramus from thinking about when his mother used to kiss him goodnight, even if he had imagined most of those times. That didn't stop Eramus from pretending his mother and father were back in Uuslef, dancing arm in arm while they prepared dinner like they used to, eagerly awaiting his return.

But reality always caught up to his imagination. His father was dead. His mother was gone. Nobody cared about him. The road was a rough, unpredictable place but at least he felt a semblance of freedom out here.

He didn't want to live in Uuslef when his term of service ended.

He didn't want a constant reminder of everything he had lost, of what he could never have. *Gohlay-gohlay*. Why couldn't he start fresh? Why couldn't he go the right way for *him*? Why couldn't he be successful or even happy with a future he made for himself?

He focused on the crackling of the fire and thought about buying his own pair of traditional wooden *glistas* cups. He didn't have the money now, of course, but he could hire out as a laborer for a couple of days once he arrived in Keltivar. His uncle's contact would be able to recommend him. He pictured himself in his own tavern, clearing space and setting out his jug and cups, fielding questions about local news and sharing what Rammun had taught him.

An annoying nudging on his shoulder interrupted the fantasy. He slowly lifted his head to see that the warm and dry tavern was empty except for the barkeep. Eramus had fallen asleep. He eyed the rushes in front of the hearth. It would be a good place to sleep out the night, safe from cold and damp, from moaning winds.

One glance at the old barkeep's somber expression explained to Eramus that he wasn't wanted. He didn't even try to barter for a place on the floor. Better to save his coins.

He stumbled outside into icy, sobering air. His breath puffed out in white clouds, dissipating like the fog blanketing his thoughts, a moment he spent awed under a dome of twinkling indigo sleep stars. The door closed behind him and a heavy lock dropped into place like a thunderclap. Regret and fear flooded him now that he was outside. He should have tried to convince the barkeep to let him stay.

Shivering, he pulled his hood over his head and tucked his shaking hands inside his cloak, following the hundreds of footprints stamped into the mud. He didn't see anyone outside at this hour. He should have left with Rammun. They got along pretty well, and Eramus trusted him for some reason.

The wind kicked up and Eramus remembered the warmth of the tavern's fire. The rest of the boys in the Information Regiment talked about so many things they wanted, about all the plans they had. Eramus hadn't given his own future much thought before tonight. He considered his own list, and at the top of it was a set of traditional *glistas* cups, followed by a magnificent hearth inside his own tavern filled with barrels of *glistas*. He could do that. He could earn a living in Keltivar. He would start with ditch work and stone hauling, introduce himself to his employer and leave a good impression, prove his reliability, maybe earn enough to share rent on a small room. He thought about how long all of that would take. Five years. In five years he could have everything he wanted. Maybe he would buy a sword and learn how to use it, too. *Gohlay-gohlay*. He could be happy.

Clothing rustled. Had he imagined the sound? He stood perfectly still and listened. Familiar laughter startled him. The Filthies had waited for him.

His legs reacted instantly, and before he knew it his self-preservation instinct had him running with full strides, even with the *glistas*'s lingering effects.

When he peeked back over his shoulder to see if they were chasing him, his foot slipped into a hole and wrenched his ankle so hard that momentum was the least of his worries. He thrust his palms out to break his fall, sliding on cold mud until he slammed onto his chest with a splat.

The Filthies surrounded him immediately, roughly hoisted him up.

"Hold him," one said. Eramus struggled and clawed with his fingernails but the three of them were stronger than he was and his muddy hands couldn't get a grip.

One of the Filthies turned out his pockets and ripped off his belt. Another one clamped a sweaty hand over his face. He couldn't breathe. The more he twisted and jerked, the more forceful they became. He no longer cared about what little money he had. His main concern was that they would find his message.

And find it they did, though only by accident. One of them had already stripped it from him, thinking it no more than a handkerchief, until the weight of the wax seal caused it to slip and fall. They would know nothing more than that the seal indicated importance, but he would be a dead if they discovered his mission.

"A good Hamaln does not solve problems with violence."

His father's words echoed in his head, but his adrenaline and fear drove them away. He stretched for his dagger. Better to live as an outlaw than not to live at all.

The Filthies restrained him, grabbed his blade, and threw him down onto the mud. He pushed himself to his hands and knees, squinted up at their silhouettes against the sleep stars, blamed himself for not leaving with the refugees when he had the chance, wondered how a man like Rammun would act in these circumstances.

"Are you Seehlan?" one of the soldiers asked, a ridiculous question for someone who didn't look anything like a refugee. But when Eramus didn't respond, a stinging slap hit his face.

A man's weight pressed down on him and a headlock cut off his air. He fought but his assailant's leather pads prevented Eramus from finding a vulnerable spot. His strength faded as air became his only concern. Moving proved difficult. He pushed back a bit, knowing the effort was futile. The man squeezed harder on his throat until black spots filled his vision. Tears dripped down his cheeks. He let go of his own weight, thought about the warm, safe fire back at the tavern.

The soldier released him. He twisted onto his back, inhaling life in short, excruciatingly beautiful breaths, hoping for a respite to gather enough strength to make a run for it.

"Where are you from?"

Laughter. "He's crying. Probably pissed hisself."

Eramus ignored them, and instead remembered a promise he had made to himself after his father's public execution in Frehm. He had promised himself he would never die a coward like that.

He sucked cold night air into his lungs, thinking of how much he hated his uncle for forcing him to watch his father's death, for the insensitive way he treated Eramus, for the snide comments he made about his mother and father, the way he stained the few happy memories Eramus had of them.

Gloved hands lifted him back onto his feet. The road stretched before him as clear as anything he had ever seen. This was his chance for escape, his opportunity to prove to himself that he could survive on his own.

But he had forgotten about his injured ankle. It bent under his weight, and then another kind of pain ripped his scalp as he was flung forward by his hair. He twisted, hoping to stop his momentum, and ended up smacking into an unyielding pine tree. His body wouldn't listen to him. Something inside him poked into his side, saturating his breath as he leaned against the tree and panted.

Then one of the soldiers kicked him in the stomach and he collapsed to his knees, unable to prevent red drool from pooling onto pine needles beneath him. His crotch warmed as he wet himself, and he forgot about his promise.

Blood dripped onto his sleeve. He couldn't figure out where it came from. Why wouldn't they take his money and leave him alone? It dawned on him that they couldn't find it. He fished into his waistband and pinched the coins with numb fingers until they came loose. "Here," he said, but the coins slipped from his fingers when one of the Filthies came closer.

He stared at the coins as they settled in the mud. Silver. The cause for all of this, the cause for most problems. It was just money.

His eyes moved from the silver as something ripped through the undergrowth and burst from the woods. The puppy from the tavern charged into the road, barking furiously. One of the soldiers stumbled back, startled. He lost his footing and slipped, falling hard on his side with a shout.

The pup bared his teeth, growled low in his throat as he filled the space between Eramus and the Filthies. Good dog.

But the Filthies didn't care. One of them kicked the puppy, and he yelped and rolled several feet away. The pup fought to get back up, his high-pitched whining hurting Eramus's ears. Eramus couldn't stop himself from crying, from praying to the Hamal to stop the pup's suffering. The Hamal, as always, responded with silence. If they had heard his prayer at all, their assistance would come in the way of wisdom, not action.

"Kill the mangy beast," said one of the soldiers.

Eramus tried to block out the noise as he clawed through the mud and pine needles on his belly, tried to forget what the soldier had said. Tried not to think about how the puppy would die for helping him.

His cowardice surfaced as he considered his own life. Maybe he could hide in the trees. He couldn't stop the Filthies anyway. They were going to do what they were going to do. He crawled slowly, painfully, mud and blood bubbling on his lips, pain grinding through his ribs.

The toe of a boot settled onto his backside and nudged him onto his face. He had lost touch with reality again.

He rolled onto his back, too tired to struggle anymore. He still couldn't catch his breath, his side filling with sharp pain whenever he inhaled. The soldier's silhouette hovered over him, blocking out the night sky. Eramus ignored him and looked to see if the puppy still lived.

Instead his eyes were drawn to an apparition stalking through murky pools of shadow. Shirtless, indigo starlight reflecting across the steel of his sword, Rammun crept ever closer. He hammered the first of the unsuspecting Filthies in the back of the skull with the pommel of his sword, knocking him unconscious with a resounding crack. By the time the others reacted to the sound, Rammun had the point of his blade leveled at another one's throat. The sword didn't waver. The same could not be said of the soldier.

"Oshlemin odds, yah?"

The man with the bruised face clenched his fists. "That's the second time you've interfered with me. I'll personally see to it that you hang, scum."

"You interrupted my sleep," Rammun said. He pulled his sword back to let his temporary hostage retreat.

Eramus heard their voices somewhere far away. He still had trouble breathing and he wanted to rest. The Filthies were right, though. Interfering with them was a hanging offense. Rammun had a sword but the odds were against him and these men were trained fighters with Count Sevalah's authority behind them.

But Rammun had tangled with them before. Neither of the Filthies attempted to arrest him, especially not the one with the bruised face.

Rammun lowered his sword. "Take your man and leave. Now."

The Filthies hustled over to their fallen fellow and draped his arms over their shoulders. He moaned in semi-consciousness. The soldier with the bruised face continued to glare at Rammun.

Eramus wiped the mess from his face. He wanted the Filthies gone. He had to find the sealed message and be on his way to Keltivar. He was too embarrassed to do anything else, too afraid that if he didn't leave now, circumstances would worsen.

The Filthies were almost out of sight, on their way back to the tents in the village.

"Wait," Eramus said. He had his hand on the message that had been casually thrown aside. It was wet and dirty but the wax seal remained. He tucked it back into his tunic as the Filthies slowed. *Deliver the message.* The final warning was never about the job. It was about staying alive to finish it.

He thought about his mission. He thought about the brave puppy putting himself in harm's way to protect a friend. He longed for courage like that. He had always felt like his father, powerless to stop bad things from happening. Now would be a good time to ask the Hamal to show him how to be brave, so he prayed to them for wisdom to soothe him, to calm him, to strengthen his resolve and fortitude, to show him what to do.

"A good Hamaln does not solve problems with violence."

The next thing Eramus knew, he collided with muscle, girth, and chainmail, wondered why he had charged at the soldier, yet instinctively understood that his mind and body had demanded the action. He grappled with the soldier for a few seconds before he was flipped over, his ankle screaming at him. Once more he stared straight up at the stars, and this time they were dazzling enough to hurt his eyes. He found he couldn't breathe. He had made the wrong choice. His father had tried to warn him. He passed out.

When he lifted his head, things were different. People had moved.

Rammun sat near a still, facedown form while the puppy licked his hand.

Eramus crawled on his hands and knees to the fallen soldier. The man's head had been hammered into the mud, but his bruised face was still recognizable.

"I think he's dead," Eramus said stupidly, stating the obvious.

"He is."

"Did you kill him?"

"He pissed me off."

The other Filthies were gone, most likely rousting their fellow soldiers. He had to run. They would issue a warrant for his arrest. He would be a wanted man in Fushlem now. This would be the price for his cowardice.

He gathered up his belt and his cloak. His head pounded and he ached all over but he wasn't dead. He rubbed his hand along his swollen ankle, hoping he could keep his boot on as he limped all the way to Keltivar. He didn't want to think about the return trip.

Rammun saw him favoring the injury. "Your ankle?"

Eramus nodded.

"Keep moving on it so it doesn't stiffen up. It will swell when you stop. You might have to loosen up your laces a bit. In a few days you'll be as good as you're going to be, but it will change colors and get fat until then. Keep it moving, even when you're not."

Rammun didn't appear bothered by the dead man, almost seemed to have already forgotten him. Was that how mercenaries regarded human life? No, Eramus suddenly realized, or the man wouldn't have bothered to help him.

"Thank you," Eramus said quickly as his tired mind fully understood the gravity of what had transpired. Rammun could have just as easily minded his own business.

Rammun didn't speak so Eramus decided to go. The Filthies would come after them in force. Eramus intended to be as far away as possible when that happened. He crouched down and let the puppy come to him and lick his hand with a warm, wet tongue.

"It was nice to meet you, Eramus," Rammun said. "You didn't let our differences stop you from having a drink with me."

"Neither did the fact that you were paying," Eramus grinned. His hand strayed to the message he carried. Rammun had to have seen the official red wax seal. "I don't really care too much about all this."

"That's too bad. I choose to fight for what I believe in, what affects me."

"I…"

"It is not my business what you're doing or where you're going," Rammun said. "You were friendly to me."

Eramus's adrenaline was gone. Everything had happened so fast. He shivered, acutely aware of his throbbing ankle and every other bruise on his body. It would hurt to breathe for a while. "And you to me. It's cold. Do you want to share a fire?"

"You had better be off, Eramus. The Filthies will be back with more men who think like them." He casually strolled back into the woods, oblivious to the cold. Eramus was in his debt. Perhaps he could travel with him, find a way to repay him for the *glistas* and the friendship, for saving his life.

"I'm heading east."

Rammun didn't stop. "I'm not. I'm off to the next lucrative

campaign." Eramus had been wrong after all. Rammun was indeed a mercenary.

Eramus still had his message. He would deliver it, fulfill his obligation to Uuslef and the Information Regiment. Then he would resign and go his own way, just like Rammun. He no longer wanted to die for something that didn't matter to him.

"Choose what's right for you," Rammun said as he disappeared into the shadows. "Come on, dog." The puppy spared Eramus a parting glance before following Rammun into the woods.

CHAPTER 1 – FIVE YEARS LATER

Eramus runs through a meadow, chasing Riya Sen. Naked and glistening with perspiration, she rides bareback away from him, her long blonde hair spilling between her shoulders, her horse's rhythmic gallop pounding in time with his warm heartbeat. The horse squeezes into a hollow between two massive rocks, vanishes into the shadows of dusk. Panting from exertion, Eramus slows and cautiously lets his fingers guide him along the rocks. He creeps past dead Filthies, their swollen tongues lolling from their mouths. Rammun calls from somewhere behind, urging him ahead. He doesn't want to go this way. His stomach tightens. The rocks cool to the touch. He no longer sees what lies before him. He doesn't want to go this way. He doesn't want to follow Riya. A wind picks up and stops. Something huge and unseen flaps its wings, the force sucking him in.

He woke to a silence so powerful his ears rang. He wished he could go back into the dream to catch Riya. He clutched the silver ring he wore as a necklace around his throat, his only tangible connection to her. If he slipped the ring onto his finger, she would know he was out there somewhere. She would feel him.

All he saw of her lately amounted to fleeting dreams. He tried to convince himself that he could get along without her, but his dreams revealed his true desires. He reached back for the memory of the day he had recognized his feelings for her.

Her spontaneity surprises him. Giddy from half a bottle of mead, she drags him to the grove and they dance until she collapses from dizziness, cheeks red, uncontrollably laughing even when he falls on top of her.

The hours fly past while they make love to the point of exhaustion. Their naked bodies intertwined in the tall grass, they tease one another until Eramus's horse grazes a little too close to them.

With a huge smile, Riya leaps up, wraps her fingers in the horse's mane, and vaults onto its back. He admires the feminine curves of her body, the way her legs open over the horse, the way the sunlight kisses her smooth skin and strands of blonde hair. She glances back over her shoulder at him with an expression he believes is happiness. For the first time in a long time, he feels wanted.

He left his face buried in the drool on his pillow until sound formed distinguishable patterns. He had no idea where he was.

When he flipped onto his back and opened his eyes, it was to a ceiling of cracked white paint. He rolled over and noticed blankets in disarray on another cot, a pack and gear spilled across the floor. Last night slowly came back to him. He and his friend Hadrius Uln had ridden into the Barony of Medar and rented a room at the Poor Missionary Inn. This had to be it.

He closed his eyes and filled his lungs with air. He had been too tired even to hear Hadrius leave. The man always started drinking early when they had downtime. He would probably be engaged in bacchanalian pursuits at the Courageous Prince, stretching coppers for local *glistas* instead of paying taxes on the Poor Missionary's imported spirits and liqueurs. He had taken his bow but left his quiver of arrows and his short sword. He always had his bow with him. He used it for hunting and fighting, relying on it more heavily than his sword. He only owned the sword because Eramus insisted.

Wind chimes rang outside the second floor window. Children shouted and played in the autumn air. Eramus lay on the cot for a while, watching a spider crawl across the wall, listening to the din of the barony, reveling in a rare moment of calm in his lonely, worry-free life. He reminded himself that Riya wasn't right for him, that he was better off without her, even if he couldn't stop thinking about her.

He also knew he was ravenous for a hearty breakfast. He wasn't a member of the Information Regiment anymore, living on stale provisions or starving for days on end. Now he could afford to quiet his stomach when it cried.

He stuffed his feet into his black boots and belted on his sword, slipping it out of the sheath far enough to study the dark gray crossguard where it intersected with the smooth, polished steel blade. It was a simple enough weapon, reliable and plain. The comfortable black leather wrapping on the handle bore visible stains from the sweat of his palms and flecks of blood from combat. He made his living with this sword now, and for a while he had wanted to add an inscription to it that reminded him of what kind of man he was. His eyes slipped out of focus, lost in the glint of the steel. Who was he? He certainly wasn't a mercenary. He certainly wasn't Rammun. No, Rammun wouldn't profit on the misfortunes of others.

Eramus jammed the sword back down by its round pommel to secure it in its sheath. He armed himself with a pair of daggers next. The more elaborate fighting blade with a carved ash handle and narrow crossguard he secured on the secondary belt around his right thigh, while the older wire-handled thrusting blade from his messenger days he concealed in his boot. Armed or not, he still wasn't prepared for the greatest of the barony's obstacles.

Toh. Good morning. *Fijah.* Breakfast. He repeated the words. His friend Sadir Nom had taught him some basic Medarn vocabulary but Eramus never stayed long enough to master fluency in the language. There was no need. Oshlema was the common tongue. Whenever Eramus visited the barony he wondered why Baron Kent tried so hard to hold onto his own language when there was something simpler and easier right there for the taking.

He opened the shutters to dull blue ebb stars and a shiny white smear of sun higher in the gray sky than he expected. Morning had advanced into afternoon while he had slept, the passing of seasons evident in the russets and golds of shedding trees. White geese wound through rows and rows of *glis* trees in distant orchards, most picked clean of the small yellow fruit. A pair of the Medarn militia brigade in gray cloaks and a young boy and girl, most likely brother and sister, children of a local hunter or tracker, trotted through the streets with a day's worth of wear and tear on their clothing and horses. Eramus had heard that the militia's searches for the baron's missing children were being aided by any with tracking or riding experience.

People milled around the crowded streets, some ducking into shops, some stopping to talk on corners, while others hurried through the foot traffic with their own agendas. Eramus didn't envy those people. He was a peeran now, an independent agent. He took the jobs he wanted, charged whatever he wanted to, and only worked when he needed money. He remembered being under his uncle's thumb, the long, hard hours and the pay that never matched the effort. *"No matter what profession you choose,"* his uncle used to tell him, *"you will never be as successful as I am. Ever."*

Eramus hefted his full coin purse, wondering why his uncle had insisted on telling him that. Eramus and Hadrius had worked a lot recently, saving money for Keltivar's upcoming festival. They would probably take one more job, hiring out as bodyguards on their way up there. They didn't have to work, but they were headed that way anyway so why skip out on extra money?

He shook his head as he recalled the way he used to travel, without money, insecure, alone, barely armed, and afraid. That had all changed the night he had met Rammun, when the mercenary had saved his life. Yes, Eramus Pon had changed considerably in the last five years.

He searched his memory for the Medarn word for afternoon. *Tah*? Was that it? Yes, it was *tah*. *Tah* and *fijah*. The local inns and taverns were a perfect place to practice Medarn. Nobody cared whether it was right or wrong, and there would be no repercussions for defaulting to Oshlema for elusive words.

Eramus tucked his long-sleeved shirt into his leather pants on the way down a set of winding, creaking stairs. The balding innkeeper dusted windowsills in the common room while the cook dozed on a stool, mouth agape, chin resting on his palm, apron stained with tomato sauce and grease. The lone patron, a jobah, sported a shiny circular badge over his left breast. Eramus cursed under his breath, forgetting all the Medarn he had practiced. He could have woken up at any time, come down to eat at any time, and yet it was exactly this time when his path had to cross a jobah's.

"Ah, *tah, melo. Se kift hon di demnuw?*" the jobah asked as he swirled his dark, syrupy drink. His sharp, alert eyes darted to the sword at Eramus's side. It wasn't safe, even for a jobah, to antagonize a man with a sword.

Baron Kent's edict for enforcing the purity of the Medarn language frustrated Eramus at times like these. Jobahs operated directly under the minister, who answered only to the baron. If the jobahs determined violations, including inappropriate use of a foreign language or repeated errors in form, they had discretion and authority to assess fines. The enforcement of the laws annoyed Eramus to no end, but the collection of penalties from violators afforded the treasury to pay for clean, well-maintained roads and other essential public projects. It also created a labor pool for the city because some of the visitors who were fined either refused to pay or couldn't afford the amount and found themselves sweeping, painting, or trimming hedges. Most visitors didn't understand that the income from the fines preserved local culture and funded public works. Eramus might not have either if his friend Sadir hadn't explained the intricacies to him.

"*Tah*," Eramus said, hoping that the jobah's jumble of syllables had been rhetorically friendly. He hadn't even had a full day to let the local conversations settle in. He was no more prepared than he had been the last time he was here.

The jobah leaned forward expectantly. *Tah. Kift?* He had to have been asking about a drink. Eramus groaned and dropped a silver onto the table. It wobbled and settled onto its side. The jobah simply stared while it came to rest near his immaculate, neatly folded lambskin gloves and quarter full snifter. Why wouldn't he just accept the fine? Unlike most visitors, Eramus intended to eventually learn the language. Unfortunately he was typically preoccupied during his short stays and hardly ever had a chance to study with Sadir.

"*Tah, me-low*," the jobah taught, his finger tracing syllables in the air. *One*. Pause. *One, one*. The beats formed a natural cadence.

"*Tah, me-low*," Eramus repeated proudly, taking advantage of the unsolicited lesson. He remembered Sadir's soothing voice reinforcing the language's natural rhythm. The jobah pointed at him. Sir. *Melo* was sir. He wanted companionship for a drink.

Eramus waved off the invitation, considering his next words carefully. He welcomed conversation with his meal if it wasn't with a jobah. "*Rin demfijah*." Sitting for breakfast. *One, one*. Pause. *One, one, one*. The rhythm felt diluted, impure. His use of syllables and timing affected his speech. At least he had remembered to add the "ah" to any word starting with the letter "r" like Sadir had taught him. *Ah-rin. Ah-rin.*

The jobah nodded, his lip curled up in a tolerant grin. *"Rin demf-yah." One, one.* Pause. *One, one.*

Eramus imagined his thinking would benefit with a full stomach. He knocked on the bar to wake the cook. *Knock. Knock.* Pause. *Knock, knock.* Maybe he could get the hang of Medarn after all, he laughed to himself. The cook's bloodshot eyes snapped open and, unlike the jobah, he possessed a more expedient means of negotiating language barriers. He slammed a greasy menu down and helped Eramus's finger point out crude illustrations resembling his *fijah.*

"Ud beda," Eramus added, his hand formed in the shape of a cup. *One.* Pause. *One, one.*

"Beda," the cook grumbled on his way into the kitchen.

The jobah shoved his chair out and stood to his full height. He gulped down the rest of his thick, syrupy drink which could only be Keltivarin Honey, an ironic and expensive choice for a public servant who legally enforced cultural intolerance. Suddenly he was beside Eramus, sliding the silver back to him with a gloved finger, leniently patting his shoulder. The man was thin and graying at the temples, his cheeks rosy from the strong, imported liquor.

"Tah," he smiled. An iron spoon clanged in a pan and the scent of bacon wafted out of the kitchen. The jobah straightened his badge, his symbol of patriotic pride. Despite the circumstances, he had made an effort to be friendly. He could have levied a fine and left without explanation like most jobahs did.

"Tah," Eramus said. He would remember this man's face even if he couldn't remember Medarn. As the sweaty cook carried out a steaming wooden trencher, the jobah casually left the inn, the door swinging shut behind him.

The innkeeper tossed his dusting rag behind the bar and pressed his long, unkempt hair against his scalp with his palms. "Food to your liking?" he asked in Oshlema, catering to his only customer in the jobah's absence. The hard, familiar consonants of the popular language almost offended Eramus's ears after the musical cadence of Medarn.

He chewed his dark, barley-rich hunk of bread and poked at his unorganized pile of eggs, browned bacon, and mashed beans. "The milk would wash this down the right way."

The innkeeper barked after the cook, snapping his fingers for the forgotten mug of goat's milk. Eramus drank most of it down right away. The two of them hovered nearby as he ate.

"Will you need the room for another night, sir?" the innkeeper asked. He motioned for the cook to pull chairs from the tabletops for evening business.

"One more night," Eramus nodded as he mopped up the last of his beans with a bite of bread and dusted off his hands. "My companion…about when did he leave?" He handed the silver on the bar to the innkeeper, along with another from the coin purse secured on his belt.

"Hours ago."

Eramus saluted a two-fingered thank you and stepped out into the cool afternoon air, wrinkling his nose against the stench of a filthy pig wallowing in its own muddy feces alongside the inn. From his affected swagger to the sword swinging at his side, Eramus the peeran attracted more than one interested glance as he hooked his hair behind his ears. He no longer bore resemblance to the timid messenger he had once been.

Medarn chatter bounced all around him, and his mind translated common words. *Leen*. Horse. *Fon*. Money. *Wulo*. Smile. He even recognized a child's sentence. *Demeen shool*. From where is the stranger? *One*, *one*. Pause. *One*. He heard the jobah's voice inside his head saying, "*De-meen shool*." *One*, *one*. Pause. *One*. What was it about the patterns? He would have to ask Sadir when he saw him.

Unlike most baronies and cities, Medar's streets were relatively safe. There were dangerous areas where traveling mercenaries, adventurers, cutthroats, ex-military, and the like would gather, as was true in any barony, but Medar seemed to have less of them, and even less crime. The local magistrate was usually on hand to escort unruly visitors beyond the gates. The citizens were friendly and happy for the most part. They smiled at strangers. In the past, they had even temporarily opened their homes to impoverished refugees.

All that had changed when Sir Jacob and the Filthies had arrived. The knight and his detachment of Count Sevelah's soldiers were permanent visitors now, an occupying force that the citizens resented and didn't understand.

The barony brimmed with activity on the crisp afternoon. A handful of colorful, Keltivarin merchants bartered with a weaver in the entrance of his shop, leaning heavily on Oshlema as a means of conducting transactions. A cooper and his sour-faced sons rolled barrels through the street, calling out to prospective customers. Local farmers arranged colorful vegetables and fruits, such as the late autumn harvest of their allotment of the yellow sugar fruit *glis,* under the awnings of their portable stands. Diverse nationalities and races milled along, peering past armed guards through the goldsmith's tidy window, eagerly avoiding the darkened stoop of the local burial guild's shop, and dodging horse-drawn carts filled with construction materiel.

Foreign vendors flew midnight blue flags with stitched red crosses indicating that their merchandise incurred a foreign goods tax. Recorders paced around the vendors, waiting for a sale so they could log the amount and collect tax revenue. Though the barony only exported palatable yellow cheese, *glis*, and juicy dates, the baron encouraged domestic dependency and heavily taxed foreign goods. As a result, his masons handled all local work and his artisans strove for quality. Property was taxed. The right to operate a business was taxed. Transactions were also taxed, though citizens paid far less to recorders than foreigners did. Between the local taxes, foreign goods taxes, the toll for entry at the city gates, the fines the jobahs levied, and everything else, Eramus imagined the Medarn treasury was overflowing with gold and silver. Baron Kent taxed everything in the barony because he could. The difference between him and most other royal landowners, though, was that he invested the money back into the people and property.

Eramus stopped at a cart to admire a selection of swords among stacks of mismatched cloth bolts, tongs, a rusted candelabra covered in beaded jewelry, and cast iron cauldrons piled on a soot-stained anvil. It was clear from the way the owner's fingers and wrists were weighed down with garish bracelets and rings that she had handcrafted many of the pieces herself. The swords themselves had been stripped bare to blade and crossguard only, but the emerald-burnished crossguards flared in exquisite Keltivarin fashion. He was particularly interested in the superb inscriptions carved and polished along the steel.

"*Tah, melo*," the vendor said cheerily as she brushed wavy black hair out of her eyes. Her natural, pleasant smile and rosy cheeks put him at ease.

"Save it," Eramus said with a glare. "I've had more than enough Medarn for today."

"Keltivarin swords are the best made," she promised in a lighthearted voice, quickly switching to Oshlema without taking offense. "And mine are the best of the best." Eramus couldn't argue with her. The perfectly angled blades soaked in every ray of hidden sunlight and almost glowed from their emerald finishes.

"You must be hard up if you're down here when the festival's only days away."

She shrugged. "I come down here to collect when I can. There are always things to fix up and sell. I'll be heading back soon enough."

"Did you engrave these?" Eramus asked, pointing to the swords with elegant script. "What do they say?"

The vendor turned one to the side and ran her dirt-stained finger along the letters, looking around nervously. "Mind you, this was supposed to be a gift, and—"

"What does it say?" Eramus demanded.

"New Man in Glesk," she said quietly, her expression close to shame. "An uncle commissioned it for his nephew a week before the push. The uncle paid but never collected. I heard the nephew died." She pointed out a pair of initials. "I don't know what they stand for."

New Men in Glesk. Eramus had heard of them before. Arrogant Suraamin men had labeled themselves that after Suraam's declaration of war against Oshlem. They were the sons of small landowners and public officials who wanted their own notoriety. Skirmishes over river traffic rights had existed between Glesk and Suraam for years, but amended treaties had kept the disputes to a minimum. When Oshlem surrendered to Gelofass, Suraam tore up the treaties. Within three years the localized disputes escalated to war. Suraam had marched an army straight down the river, expecting Margrave Valls to surrender when he saw the size of the opposing force. But the margrave had brought his own army, and the Border Wars had begun.

A month into the fighting, the self-proclaimed New Men

boasted that they possessed the means to bring a swift end to the conflict and to force the margrave to surrender. They paid for and recruited one hundred soldiers and attempted to map a route around the westernmost end of the Skytop Mountains through treacherous swampland. They hadn't known about its inhabitants, a community of swamp rangers and trappers called the Dawn Hunters. The New Men made it less than a mile into the swamps before the Dawn Hunters surprised and slaughtered them.

When King Willum learned of the Suraamin strategy to cut through the swamps, he sent a formal summons for reinforcements, and soon enough the margrave's army expanded to include some of the king's own royal soldiers from the capitol of Oslah, as well as detachments from Haulken and Medar. Even now, Baron Kent continued to send soldiers to prove his loyalty to the king. This woman could be hanged for selling this weapon in the barony. She must have thought its value to the right collector outweighed the risk.

Eramus had once wanted glory and admiration himself, but he had seen enough bloodshed since his days in the IR to understand the realities of war. The legend of the Dawn Hunters served as just one of many cautionary tales to those who sought glory.

"Put it away," Eramus warned her. "Or I'll report you to the magistrate."

"It's one of my best—"

"Do it."

The vendor reluctantly complied, muttering as she stuffed it under various linens and leathers in her cart.

"And this one?" Eramus asked, pointing out the other sword with engraving.

"Don't know," she said with a shrug. At first Eramus thought she was upset and didn't want to answer, but then she elaborated. "I can't read Oshlemin. The man who wanted this gave me the letters and asked me to do it. He couldn't pay upon completion, though, so I kept it as a sample."

Eramus couldn't read it either. "You're very good with script."

"Thank you," she replied, eyeing Eramus's sword with professional curiosity. "My brother learned a little from a jeweler and he showed me a few tricks. Did you want something on your own sword?"

Eramus drew the blade quickly and expertly. "What's your name?"

"Trichsaia." Her cheeks flushed and she hooked her hair back over her ear, her fingers slowly tracing the curve of her jaw and settling on the fur lining of her vest. He couldn't seem to look away from her. "People call me Trixie." She held her palms out and carefully accepted Eramus's sword, studying its weight, balance, and edge. "This must have cost quite a bit of money. I guess something like this is important in your trade, though." She cleared her throat, realizing she had said too much. "I can do it, but I'll need the letters from you."

"Put fresh leather on the grip, too. How much?"

Trixie pawed at the crossguard a little too overdramatically, turning it to absorb the weak sunlight. "Without knowing the letters and how much other work I have to do…ten silver. It will take a couple of days. I have other customers ahead of you once I pack up and head back to camp."

Eramus seized the handle. "I don't like your engravings that much."

She pulled the blade back just a little. "I can do the work right, but I need time and good compensation. I have to pay all these taxes on anything I make, you know, and it's only worth it if I can clear a lot."

Without taking his eyes off her, Eramus fingered the smooth ash handle of the dagger belted to his thigh. "Not my problem. Take your hands off the sword or I'm in my rights to remove them."

Trixie quickly released the sword, the blood gone from her face. "I do good letters. You said so yourself."

Eramus studied the Oshlemin engraving again. He had spoken to several blacksmiths and even apprentice jewelers over the last couple months and hadn't been as impressed with their work.

"I'll give you six silver…"

She groaned and threw her hands up in the air.

"I'll give you six silver, and I'll pay the taxes," Eramus finished. "If the work suits me I'll tell others who did it."

Trixie considered before nodding. "Fair enough, but you pay for everything up front. Call a recorder over."

The entire transaction cost Eramus nine silver, three for the tax and six for Trixie's fee. He had barely made a difference with the haggling. The money didn't matter to him. He didn't want to be taken advantage of. He could see where her predicament came from, though. The taxes on any foreign sales in the barony were outlandish. The only reason these vendors continued to stay in business was because they offered something the people in the barony couldn't get anywhere else. It was a tough way to do business, but if there was enough demand for their products or services they could eke out a profit.

Eramus borrowed the recorder's quill and a scrap of parchment and struggled through what he wanted Trixie to engrave. He hadn't put Uuslefin letters down in a long time, and they appeared almost foreign to him. She wisely didn't ask what the finished words meant. The recorder, thankfully, spoke Oshlema. He answered to the auditor, not the minister, and was therefore only concerned with a record of the transaction and the proper tax percentage he collected.

"I'll have it for you tomorrow," Trixie said with outstretched palms and a smile. "And I'll sharpen it for you, too."

Eramus gave her the sword, immediately feeling naked and off-balance without it. He still had his daggers, though, for whatever that was worth, and he let his right hand settle comfortingly on the one he had just used to threaten her.

He headed down the street, thinking a bit about how Trixie had looked at him, or at least how he believed she had looked at him. He passed squat rows and rows of solid brick and wood-trimmed shops on either side, their upper floor windows open to mostly living quarters, and found himself looking forward to picking up his sword for more than just the sword itself, though he wasn't exactly sure what his plan was. *"Trichsaia. People call me Trixie."*

A sign painter, taking a break from his work atop a ladder, wiped his hands on a rag. He had outlined the shape of a shoe on the wooden sign hanging above the cobbler's. By law, all signs had to contain Medarn text. But shop owners and sign painters alike recognized that it was simply good business to advertise to as many potential customers as possible. The butcher's sign had a pig, stables had horseshoes, bound parchment had a thick book, and so on. Only those businesses within close proximity, such as rival inns or bakeries, paid extra to add a unique flair to their signs. The popular Three Brothers bakery, for example, enticed its potential customers with three pious young men sharing grace over a loaf of bread. The sweet aroma of fresh baking bread didn't hurt business, either. They used actual wheat flour and cooked a variety of expensive white breads in a brick oven.

A pair of Filthies passed, chins raised in arrogant smiles, the recognizable brand of the sun on their foreheads marking them as redeemed *duba*. They shouted insults at passerby, shoved an old woman out of their way and laughed. Their mere presence sickened Eramus. *Avoid eye contact.* He kept his hand close to his dagger. He wouldn't let Fushlemin soldiers intimidate him, and he wouldn't let them take him by surprise, either.

Count Sevelah's occupying detachment had taken to braiding turquoise beads into their goatees, rumored to not only represent their loyalty to the Temple of Gefil but also to boast each Seehlan kill, and most of the soldiers had abandoned Hamaln and embraced the return of the Forgotten Prophet. The men resided in the barony as the baron's guests, summoned east by Sir Jacob under the guise of maintaining peace along Hereton Road. Baron Kent had loosely seceded from Oshlem and declared his barony years ago, but he still maintained loyalty to King Willum, and respected the king's wishes enough to allow official status to Count Sevelah's troops, though it was clear from the bristling reactions of locals that these foreign soldiers were despised and unwelcome. To dispute the request of one of Ismah Carleton's knights, however, would have put the baron in an even more unfavorable position. The knight represented the Temple of Gefil, and as such was its official agent. Baron Kent had acquiesced to King Willum by allowing Fushlemin troops into his barony rather than a detachment of Gelofassin soldiers, and this seemed to satisfy the Ismah and the knight.

Roughly the size and shape of a crow, a bird with white wingtips on indigo feathers swooped in from atop a nearby shop and settled gently onto a high branch. A patch of the same snowy white along its wingtips stained its throat, and it glared back at him with yellow eyes.

"Caw, caw, caw."

Eramus tried to ignore it. He passed more buildings, the bird pacing him the entire way, its dirty feet disturbing debris when it touched down on rooftops, its neck craning as its sharp eyes locked in on him. Its feathers appeared matted and stiff, its movements almost too jerky for a living creature. Eramus refused to acknowledge the thing but it was always active in his peripheral vision.

He stopped a little girl from being half-dragged by her impatient mother, and pointed up at the bird. "*Nepa?*" he asked, knowing he'd heard the word for bird before but couldn't recall it. At least he recalled *nepa*, the Medarn word for name. When the little girl gawked at him with confusion he asked again.

She finally answered, "*Rootu.*"

"*Rootu?*"

The mother shook her head. "*Roua,*" she corrected them.

Eramus's gratitude earned the girl a copper. He mussed her hair with the approval of her mother's warm smile.

It was ridiculous to believe that the bird was really following him, but Eramus tracked its movements all the same, repeating the word *roua* over and over in his head as if the litany would somehow discourage it. *Ah-roua. Ah-roua.* The bird hung onto a ledge with its clawed feet and furiously flapped large wings at him. He shouted "*roua*" at it more than once. Eventually, to his relief, the bird slid off the roof and floated away on a draft.

His anxiety left with it.

A pair of old men with wispy hair and black gums for teeth sat in chairs beside a dry white fountain and shared a plate of *glis*. When they finished the oval yellow fruits, they casually tossed the pits into the street. Eramus inhaled the sweet scent. Was the Courageous Prince left or right? He had lost his way.

"Uh…*tah, melo,*" he began, picturing the folding lips and lifted tongue of the jobah. "*Dem* Courageous Prince?" *One.* Pause. *One, one, one, one.* It was all wrong, but how else could he say it? He would meet them halfway, of course. He hadn't a clue beyond using *dem* as an introduction to what he sought. Would they know enough Oshlema to make sense of his question? He waved it off, started again. One of the men ignored him and the other regarded him as an imbecile. "Courageous Prince?"

A head jerked to the left, allowing him to abandon his embarrassment. The clip clop of hooves drew nearer until a Medarn militia brigade, professional bearing and quilted armor under gray cloaks, trotted past. They had no doubt been out scouring the countryside for the baron's missing children. From the scowls on their faces, the search had been unsuccessful. The boy and girl had been reported kidnapped two days ago, the suspects described as pale with blue eyes: Seehlan, and dressed in the patchwork garb of refugees. The guards at the city gate had been very generous with their information last night.

The Courageous Prince's hitching posts were packed with horses of all types. It was a popular inn, one where visitors could depend on reasonably priced ale and infrequent if almost nonexistent appearances from jobahs or militia patrols. It was the kind of place where Eramus felt the most comfortable these days, a place where he didn't have to tolerate scrutiny or judgment. He heard laughter and shouting as he walked up the porch. He shoved the doors inward, his mind again acutely aware of the empty scabbard at his side.

The hot, crowded inn reeked of stale air, bad breath, and spilled ale. A half naked, sweat-drenched, ridiculously drunk man danced on a table, his red headband whipping with his frenzied steps while patrons clapped and cheered encouragement.

A wiry bald man repeatedly stabbed his thin dagger into the bar as the frightened barkeep begged him not to. A network of veins bulged across his arms as he stabbed faster and faster, daring someone to interfere.

A pale Geflin missionary with a narrow mustache and deeply impressed brand on his forehead hunched over a nearby table, chewing on spotted *culipi* mushrooms, laughing hysterically at his enlightened madness. His overly dilated pupils made his eyes appear black and empty, soulless, a frightening side effect of the mushrooms.

Eramus turned his head to the side and spit in disgust, first at the presence of the missionary, and then at his weakness for the mushrooms, which only served to remind him how they had torn apart his family. If he had his way, anyone growing, selling, or using the hallucinogenic mushrooms would suffer severe punishments. They were an illegal commodity in the barony, but easily attainable in a place like the Courageous Prince. It was well known that criminals controlled the *culipi* trade, but the profits and the people involved ensured its continued success.

Baron Kent allowed missionaries in his barony at the request of the knight, but he had expressly outlawed verbal and written interpretation of the *Otauh*. Missionaries violating this law were subject to solitary incarceration. Citizens of the barony, like most of Oshlem, believed in Hamaln, the comprehension of wisdom through the reincarnation of Awakenings under the guidance of the Hamal, the caretakers of the Eternal Fires.

Gefil was a relatively new faith, though its spread over the last several years bordered on plague-like infection. Its introduction originated from a pair of scrolls detailing the departure of the Blood Eagle and its single passenger from the Eternal Fires. The gigantic bird had flown beyond the light of the Eternal Fires only to learn that the passenger had lost his memory along the way. The Blood Eagle no longer had the strength to carry the passenger on the return trip, so instead it explained to the man how he could safely lead only the most devoted of his people back to the Eternal Fires, and how only his true believers could find him. The man had transferred this wisdom to the scrolls, eventually called the *Otauh*, and had never been seen since.

The *Otauh* had been preserved in the archives of a Hamaln temple outside Gelofass for years before a charismatic young priest named Carleton had translated the first of the scrolls. He declared his translation to be the words of the Blood Eagle itself, spoken through the Forgotten Prophet. Carleton gained support with his interpretation of the scroll, and also taught the Gelofassin population the criteria for the Forgotten Prophet's appearance, at which time he would be able to read the second scroll. Carleton claimed that the second scroll contained directions provided by the Blood Eagle to take believers to the Eternal Fires.

Duba, or the redeemed, had grown exponentially over the years. Carleton named this reimagining of the Hamaln faith Gefil, which translated from Gelofassin into "holy knowledge of light." People quickly embraced this new faith which offered a clearer purpose and enabled an active, more urgent path to the Eternal Fires of the Hamal, as opposed to the old way of Hamaln that suggested enlightenment could only be found through comprehensive reincarnation. Gefil was now observed throughout most of Gelofass, and had trickled into Fushlem and even Oslah, to some extent.

Eramus, who had been taught to learn through experience in

First Awakening since he was old enough to listen, did not accept Gefil. He did not believe that the journey to the Eternal Fires could be found in First Awakening. His father had tried to teach him about some of the sleep stars, where they resided in the night sky and what they meant, doing his best to explain to Eramus that only through understanding what they represented could Eramus pass gracefully into Second Awakening. But Eramus had been too stubborn to pay much attention at the time. Now he knew that he still had many lessons to learn, as did his friend Hadrius Uln.

Hadrius leaned against the bar, brown eyes glazed over, dumb smile plastered on his sideburn heavy face, his leather jerkin unlaced at the top to expose a mess of chest hair. He wasn't a particularly tall man, but his rough skin, the cut of his physique, and the thickness of his hands made for an imposing figure. A long hunting knife hung on his right thigh in a leather sheath. Tightly laced boots with a combination of evergreen and bark-colored dye ended just below his knees. His bow rested against his stool, the yew illustrated with complex paintings of forested glens and golden suns, the artwork a gift from one of his former lovers. Eramus couldn't remember much more about the woman than her skill with a brush and her penchant for explosive jealousy.

A redhead sat on the bar in front of Hadrius, clumsily braiding his oily dark hair with intense concentration. Like him, she sported leather bracers and a matching jerkin, though a brace of knives patterned her waist. Her dusky complexion and the fur lining her jerkin pointed toward Keltivarin heritage. The sun reflected off the snow much more brightly in the northern kingdom, and its absence made the winters that much colder. Eramus wasn't surprised to see Hadrius with another woman, though he wondered how long this one would last. His friend's romances burned brightly and briefly, but he always expected Eramus to treat them seriously, and to never mention one woman's name in the presence of another. Discretion wasn't difficult for Eramus because he barely learned their names before they were memories.

"Prophuug, *what do you say*?" Hadrius slurred in Uuslefin. "*I'm getting prettied up right now.*"

The woman's clear green eyes immediately scoured Eramus. She stopped braiding Hadrius's hair. Eramus noticed the awkward bend at the first joint of the ring finger on her left hand. It had been broken, never properly set. That accounted for her difficulty with the braiding. She gulped down the contents of her goblet and snapped her fingers at the barkeep, who was only too happy for an excuse to walk away from the madman with the dagger.

"You Eramus?" she asked. "You want a drink?"

"No." Eramus hadn't drunk alcohol since that night in Grihm, even if he could still taste the *glistas* on his tongue. His father had died drunk, and Eramus had no intention of following in his footsteps.

The barkeep leaned over and the woman playfully slapped his cheek, irritating him. "Fill me up, and one more for the brave peeran."

Hadrius beat his chest with his large fists. *"I'm the peeran."*

She cupped the back of his head and pulled his lips to hers. When they parted she blushed, though she tried to hide her embarrassment by drinking more wine. The dagger at the end of the bar stopped and started up again. The missionary muttered something to himself. The dancing man fell off his table and passed out on the floor to peals of laughter and applause. Eramus missed drinking. A little *glistas* could steal his troubles for a while.

"Where's your sword?" Hadrius asked with a hint of concern. The man didn't miss much, even when drunk. He took a quick swallow of *glistas* from a traditional wooden cup, then waved a finger at Eramus. *"Is that a smile I see on your face? There's only one reason you smile."*

Eramus sighed in irritation, shaking his head. *Conceal your emotions.* He wished he could meet women the way Hadrius did. They flocked to him. *"My sword's getting sharpened and wrapped. Sadir invited us to eat. You want to come along?"*

Hadrius, cup held near his lips, shook his head before the end of the question. He didn't have any obligations. *"I'm not going unless you tell me who is making you smile."* He closed his eyes and guzzled the rest of his *glistas*. Eramus had hoped Hadrius would join him to ease the awkwardness, but his friend was having too good a time with this new woman.

"What's your name?" Eramus asked her. She reached out to ruffle his hair and he gently batted her hand to the side. Hadrius set down his cup and quickly enveloped her fingers in his to divert the slight. The leathery skin over his hands bore old white scars, some that Eramus remembered him getting. Her broken finger appeared fragile and delicate in his masculine grip.

"This is Sylvia," Hadrius said with an unexpected burp. Her lean frame and sensuous neck displayed her feminine side, even beneath her belt of knives and light combat raiment, and the more she tried to hide her crooked teeth when she smiled, the more attractive she became. Hadrius loved physical flaws, and Sylvia had plenty.

"*I'm off to Sadir's,*" Eramus said without another glance at her.

Hadrius roughly embraced him, smacked him on the back. "*Fine. Keep your secret,*" he said as clearly as the *glistas* would allow. "*And don't start any trouble on the way.*"

Eramus maneuvered his way out of the drunken hug and the two clasped wrists, Eramus wincing. Hadrius had the strongest grip of any man Eramus had ever met. He squeezed Eramus's wrist one final time for fun before he let the bloodless white flesh go. Eramus shook his arm to regain feeling, turning his nose at the stench of his alcohol-heavy breath. He would answer his friend's questions when they were back on the road. It would pass the time.

Eramus left the Courageous Prince, inhaling calm, fresh air. He nodded greeting at everyone he passed during his uneventful walk, and ended up doubling back to the Three Brothers Bakery for a good loaf of bread before cutting across a few alleys on his way to Sadir's.

He turned a corner to a dozen or so young Medarn soldiers kneeling in front of a golden-hued brick chapel. The single room sat on an expertly kept carpet of green leaves and blossoming white star-shaped clematis. The soldiers bowed before the outstretched hand of a robed chaplain, a thin golden circlet resting atop his shaven head. He spoke the words of a famous Hamaln prayer, translating it to Medarn as he asked the Hamal to grant wisdom to those gathered before they departed for Glesk and battle.

Eramus kneeled with the others at the holy man's invitation, inhaling the sweet fragrance of the clematis, rubbing the leathery surfaces of the leaves beneath his fingers while praying in his native Uuslefin tongue. He recited the same prayer, intending to aid the young soldiers. The reality of their anxiety and fear would soon test their faith. Those who lived would lose innocence. Some would even resent the baron for separating them from loved ones and friends, but their pride for serving their fellow countrymen would outweigh all.

"'Sacrifice in First Awakening brings about wisdom. It is wisdom which frees us of physical and emotional dilemmas. We are too naïve in First Awakening to understand what wisdom reveals, but there is faith enough in the promise of a Second Awakening.'"

When the prayers were concluded the young men, including Eramus, kissed the sunstone ring on the chaplain's finger and thanked him for the blessing and faith only a man of Second Awakening could grant. The chaplain stroked Eramus's head and reminded him, in Oshlema, to guide others with the limited experience First Awakening had bestowed upon him. Eramus promised to do his best.

The chaplain looked at Eramus again, this time with added scrutiny. "Though the path through First Awakening may not always be clear, it does not mean you are alone without faith. Believe in yourself and wisdom will reveal the way."

"I will try."

"You must love yourself. Do you love yourself, brother?"

"I..." Eramus began, his voice catching in his throat. Hopelessness smothered his soul. What could he love about himself? Why did he deserve love? His mother had left him. Riya didn't care about him.

"Do you love yourself, brother?"

Hot tears leaked from Eramus's eyes. Embarrassed, he lowered his face and reached for the firm warmth and comfort of the chaplain's hand, the unyielding shape of his ring.

"Do you *love yourself*, brother?" the chaplain pressed.

After a moment of silence Eramus finally said, "I cannot."

Surprisingly strong hands pulled him to his feet. His legs wobbled beneath him. He looked back into confident wise eyes nestled in the depths of thick, sun-leathered skin.

"But you must love yourself," the chaplain insisted. "Your brothers and sisters need your example. They need your courage and your aid. They need to learn from you." The chaplain drew Eramus into a gentle but firm embrace. "I love you, brother. Love yourself as I love you."

Warmth trickled into Eramus's blood and strengthened his sense of self worth. If this man could love him, he could love himself. He dropped down to one knee and kissed the chaplain's ring again. The chaplain patted his head and left him there to see to new soldiers. Women of all ages sprinkled wild blue indigo petals at the feet of the young men setting out to protect their way of life. Eramus and the other young Uuslefin men like him hadn't been given the same respect as these soldiers, hadn't been treated with that kind of esteem when Uuslef had drafted them into the Information Regiment. He wiped away his bitter memories and considered the barony's love for its soldiers. They would gain much in their First Awakening.

Full of hope for the young men, bread in hand, Eramus set off at a hasty walk. He hadn't been entirely honest with the chaplain. Within Eramus bled a deep cut of despair, his one defining characteristic, a single trait he despised but could not be rid of. He could lie to the chaplain, but he couldn't lie to himself. He decided in that moment not to talk to Trixie about anything other than the work she had done for him. It would be better for both of them.

Several minutes later, he sat at Sadir's table while his friend stood on his porch, talking in low tones to an older member of the militia brigade while another member searched the home's interior, a mere formality. Eramus couldn't overhear the conversation on the porch, especially while the clumsy man searching the house rattled and banged almost everything he touched. The searching of every residence for the baron's children or any clues as to their whereabouts had become a daily routine.

Raisa, Sadir's three-year-old daughter, struggled to lift a gravy bowl. It tilted drastically, warm brown drippings trickling down her arms. Her mother, Kathryn, hardly seemed to notice. She was more intent on determining how much longer her husband would be occupied and how much longer the search would take. Worry lines had worn away at her face, her smiles reserved for her husband and daughter. Eramus was dubious about many things, but never about Kathryn and Sadir's love and commitment for each other over the years.

"Raisa…" Kathryn said with a hint of irritation when she noticed the mess her curly-haired daughter was making. She was about to stand up when Eramus took the gravy bowl from Raisa.

"*Tustah*," he smiled to the little girl, respecting Kathryn's wishes to speak only Medarn in their home. His politeness encouraged a fit of laughter from Raisa. She noticed how much gravy covered her and she wiped it on her clothes and the tablecloth. Kathryn rolled her eyes. She had seen enough. Eramus calmed her a bit with a wink and helped Raisa contain the mess with a napkin.

Kathryn's patience for her husband's work finally ran out and she left to interrupt the conversation. Kathryn was a good mother, though Sadir had confided in Eramus more than once that his wife's strict choices about how to raise their daughter frustrated him. He had also revealed to Eramus that the two of them had always wanted another child, but had given up after years of failed attempts. Kathryn and Eramus had never become good friends, but he respected her, even if most of his time around her was spent in awkward silence. She had mentioned to her husband more than once that men with swords attracted danger wherever they went.

Raisa, on the other hand, was precious. Eramus enjoyed watching her grow up, being a part of her life, and he would always be there to help her if she needed him. Perhaps Kathryn was right in sheltering the girl, though. The world was full of disappointment and loss. Eramus had learned that firsthand, and he vowed long ago to Sadir that he would never let Raisa grow up alone or without love should anything happen to her parents.

"*Fehfee!*" Raisa shouted, Medarn for father. "*Feh-fee!*" she banged her palms on the tabletop, rattling dishes. At least she wasn't leaving gravy handprints.

Sadir limped back into the dining room, a relieved Kathryn on his arm, his long salt and pepper mustache ending past his chin. The man on the porch signaled to his comrade to end the search, and the men politely excused themselves and departed. Sadir hadn't changed out of his midnight blue jacket and matching boots yet. He took his work as the baron's librarian seriously, one of the reasons Eramus admired him. With so much conflict between people, here was a man with the intelligence and courage to leave a much more fruitful legacy.

Sadir kissed his daughter on her gravy-stained cheek and took his place at the head of the table. With a smile he admired the bountiful spread of wild greens, mutton, a healthy looking dace, steamed carrots, a pile of turnips, and black pudding. He reached over everything for the loaf of fresh white bread sprinkled with pecans that Eramus had purchased from the Three Brothers Bakery. Kathryn politely waited for her husband to tear off a hunk and dip it in gravy before she tucked into her own plate and sipped her *glistas* from a traditional wooden cup.

"*Gohlay-gohlay*," Eramus said as he raised his cup to hers. Though he only drank water, the sentiment was the same. She touched her cup to his and they both sipped.

"*Loneep uld demayha*," Kathryn said to her husband after she set down her cup. *One, one, one*. Pause. *One, one, one, one*.

"*Duli fehnuep*," Sadir said sternly to his daughter. "We can talk Oshlema if you'd like," he said to Eramus, despite his wife's disapproving look. "*Se Medarnep o mols*?"

Eramus scratched his jaw at the foreign words. *Se* for the question, but he could determine that with tone and body language. Something about Medarn. He could translate half of it. He tried to remember exactly what Sadir had said, but the staccato delivery had sounded like one long word. Frustration ate away at him the harder he tried to reconstruct the words in Uuslefin. It was easier for him to speak Oshlema. That was probably why he never learned Medarn.

"Oshlema, if you don't mind," he said with a disappointed shake of his head.

"You're going to have to take the time one day, my friend."

"I know. I was actually hoping I could ask you a few questions tonight." He cleared his throat.

"Is *roua* the word for bird?"

Sadir shook his head. "*Rootu. Roua* means bluebird."

"*Roua*!" Raisa shouted with a smile. "*Roua*!"

Eramus smiled back at her, happy with a name for the bird he had seen. He was disappointed with himself for still not having a solid grasp on Medarn. He had tried to learn it. There just weren't many opportunities to keep up with it outside of the barony. He had studied with Sadir before, even from the popular book *Practical Medarn*, and had gleaned enough to know that Medarn, though spoken differently from Oshlema, was derived from written Oshlemin, as most languages were. Oshlema, on the other hand, had become a mixed, regional pot of language. While most of the common words were the same, terms varied from region to region. Eramus could speak Oshlema, could speak Uuslefin and read a little of it, and could even speak a bit of Keltivarin. He often wondered if some people just had limits when it came to these things. Medarn was much harder to learn than any other language he knew, and even Sadir, who taught it along with the written words of old Oshlemin in the barony school on occasion, never seemed to be able to get Eramus past the basics of rote memorization before impatience prematurely ended the lessons. But Medarn was also the last language he had tried to learn, and he believed that made a difference.

Beside Eramus, Raisa reluctantly chewed on butter-drenched greens. Her father's scolding had calmed her. Kathryn scooped an extra helping of mutton onto her husband's plate. He was a thin man with an appetite for learning.

"Did you pray today?" Sadir asked him.

"We do not pray," his Uncle Reginald used to say when he caught Eramus kneeling to the Hamal. "Prayer is for those who cannot help themselves. Prayer is the weakness upon which lesser men rely for hope and salvation. Prayer was for your father. True men beseech the Hamal for the wisdom to help ourselves. True men do not wish obstacles removed. True men know they must face them again, and they must learn to remove the obstacles themselves."

"Yes," Eramus replied. "With a chaplain and some soldiers off to war." He didn't mention the chaplain's personal words of guidance.

Sadir raised a questioning eyebrow while he examined the food on his plate with disinterest. Food never fulfilled him like his books. "Did you invite Hadrius?"

"He's otherwise involved," Eramus shrugged, well aware of Hadrius's uncomfortableness in pleasant, domestic settings. Eramus could relate. He couldn't remember family dinners with his parents, and often felt as if an unspoken behavioral code existed at these meals and he had no knowledge of it. The chaplain had told him to love himself, but the real truth was that he didn't feel he deserved to. People lived their lives without him. He did nothing more than stand in the way of their happiness.

"Another woman? He just needs to find the right one."

"Could be he's looking," Eramus replied. "He's more and more reluctant to take on risky jobs, and he spends a lot of his free time drinking and talking to women."

"And what about you?"

Eramus cleared his throat, changed the subject. "How much longer will they keep up the search?"

Kathryn glared across the table. He couldn't remember how much Oshlema she spoke, but it appeared to be enough. Her husband took her hand.

"Until they find the children," Sadir said.

Eramus felt guilty for evoking such a strong reaction from Kathryn. Raisa sensed her mother's discomfort and observed her with sympathy. "I heard about what happened from someone at the gate."

"The children are much loved by everyone. It's an unthinkable crime. Hadrius should offer his services. He's the best tracker I've ever seen." Sadir had only been picking at his food. Now he pushed his plate away and walked over to his desk, rifled through stacks of parchment. Huge, overflowing bookcases flanked the desk, and Eramus spotted the cracked leather cover of Sadir's copy of *Practical Medarn* among other volumes. His friend recovered his pipe and tobacco pouch from underneath a mess of scrolls and returned to the table.

Eramus watched him eagerly, waiting for that first strong whiff of enticing smoke that reminded him of his father. Sadir lit his pipe from a candle, the flash of fire casting his features in light and shadow while he ignited the tobacco and puffed out smoke.

"Any leads?" Eramus wondered while he inhaled the sting of floating residue from the pipe. He had tried to smoke a pipe once but it had disgusted him. He loved the smoke that came out of it, though, the strong scent that reminded him of Loghemit Pon and happier times.

"According to one witness, Seehlan carried them off in the middle of the day."

"Do you believe that?"

Sadir looked over the end of his pipe, through the cloud of smoke pooling up to the ceiling. "No reason to doubt it. It's the only information His Lordship has, and he's acting on it. Patrols are out non-stop. The magistrate's men are stretched thin.

Criminals are taking liberties. Just yesterday a man was garroted in the street. The man I was just talking to told me it was over *culipi*."

Eramus picked pecan slivers out of his bread and set them on the other side of his plate to keep his fingers occupied. More about the *culipi*, about what had corrupted a mother enough to abandon her son.

"Love yourself."

"I noticed a Geflin missionary lost in his head before I came here, black eyes and everything."

"Doesn't surprise me," Sadir said over his pipe. "The missionaries we get in the barony are weak-willed, uneducated. As far as I can tell, they only spread anti-Seehlan sentiment and watch out for priests. His Lordship won't allow any talk about the *Otauh*. They don't serve much of a purpose here."

Eramus didn't know if it was the smoke or if he was still tired, but the unwelcome probing of a headache had begun to take hold of him. With the militia focused on the search for the children, the missionary hadn't been concerned about ingesting *culipi* in the middle of the day. And, as was always the case with illegal commodities and profits, violence would eventually ensue. The dead man Sadir had mentioned was an example of that.

"What about the Filthies? Are they helping?"

Sadir picked a hair from inside his lip, examining it closely before smearing it onto the tabletop. "Do you mean Count Sevelah's men? They don't interfere with barony business unless they know without a doubt that Seehlan are involved. Supposedly that's the order from Sir Jacob. They don't care about the people who live here, or about *culipi*. For all I know they're selling the stuff."

A flare of white pain cut through Eramus's skull. He winced and cupped his head in his hands.

"Are you okay?" Sadir asked.

Eramus nodded. The pain had been intense but brief. "Filthies are pond scum."

Sadir cleared his throat. "They're still guests here with His Lordship's permission."

The next words came out of Eramus's mouth before he could stop them. "The ones I saw are *duba*. They stay here while the baron sends his own people off to fight for King Willum. That doesn't seem right." Eramus regretted his accusatory words. His headache had worsened and affected his courtesy. He was a guest here.

Sadir stared from across the table. "In case you've forgotten, His Lordship is still loyal to His Majesty King Willum."

"Alright, alright," Eramus said, holding up his palms in quick surrender. He didn't want to incite Sadir in front of his wife and daughter. He decided not to remind his friend that at least a score of Filthies had been living off the baron's hospitality for the last four years. Sir Jacob had ridden in with them one day and hadn't left.

"*Roua!*" Raisa shouted as she leapt out of her chair and ran toward the window.

Bluebird, Eramus's mind quickly translated. His eyes were magnetized in horror to the aggressive indigo and white form squawking from the windowsill, its beak snapping shut after each vicious call, the sound amplified in the confines of the little house. Its ragged, dirty feathers and unnatural yellow eyes left no doubt that it was the same bird Eramus had seen earlier.

With her napkin in hand, Kathryn gently moved Raisa to the side and shooed at the trespassing beast until it hopped once and flapped away, but not before it glared a warning back at Eramus.

He hoped they wouldn't notice his hands shaking under the table. How had the bird found him and what did it want from him?

CHAPTER 2

Giant white clouds cast moving shadows over everything along their eastern migration. Eramus lounged beside the dry fountain he had passed yesterday. He imagined what its spray would resemble, and his memories whisked him to a moment he had spent beneath a rainbow, close enough to the vestiges of rain to see drops sprinkle on the grass mere feet away. His father had taken him to that spot on a lush green hillside overlooking a valley to lie to him about his mother coming home. Loghemit had struggled with his matches, cursing as a stiff wind extinguished two before the third finally caught and he started his pipe, sucking in several deep puffs before exhaling that first trail of strong tobacco into the air. *"I'm sure life has been difficult without your mother, Eramus. You'll see her soon. She's not herself right now."*

Eramus had been six years old when he had closed his eyes and inhaled that sickly sweet smoke, relieved that his mother would return. He had wondered at the familiarity of the moment, despite the fact that it occurred for the first time. Had he experienced that moment before? Or had that been a dream? He struggled to differentiate his dreams from reality these days.

He hadn't practiced Medarn with Sadir last night. The bird's unexpected appearance had fragmented his concentration. He had excused himself shortly thereafter, blaming his departure on fatigue rather than fear. And where did that fear originate? Within himself, he knew. There could be no other explanation. Even now, he struggled with overwhelming hopelessness. Perhaps it was related to the fact that he knew he would never find happiness in his life. Perhaps he missed Riya even more than he thought he did, and his decision to stay away from her could be the wrong one.

"*Roua*," he said to the old man dozing in a chair beside him. "*Roua. Roua. Roua.*" Heavy snoring answered.

The bird had found him again. It chattered as it hopped along rooftops, its proximity questionable enough for him to stay alert.

Something brushed the top of his hand and he swung violently, blindly, barely missing the stone fountain with his fist.

Chasing the edge of a cloud's moving shadow, a fly harmlessly buzzed away. The bird hadn't attempted to peck out his eyes. Eramus opened his fist, thankful that he hadn't done any serious harm to his hand.

His outburst had incited whispers and glances. The old man next to him continued to snore.

Eramus slid his sword out far enough to reveal the new engraving. Trixie's impeccable work would serve as a constant reminder that Eramus couldn't escape himself, a fact that he had paid to remember. He inhaled the fresh, re-wrapped leather grip while he ran his finger across the polished, sharpened and oiled steel. The woman had done an excellent job, and he felt a temporary pang of guilt for treating her harshly. She had been nice enough. He would keep his word and refer business to her when he could. She had seemed expectant when he had picked up his sword, as if she wanted to talk to him about something else but couldn't seize the opportunity. He had pretended to be oblivious, of course, and when she had told him how she and her brother would be packing up to depart tomorrow, he had shrugged and left.

He eased his sword back into the scabbard and looked up at the clouds, hoping to see what the Seehlan priests could, that something would coalesce into meaning for him. Instead the clouds reminded him of the day his father died.

"*Reality has abandoned me,*" Eramus said in Uuslefin, well aware that the old man couldn't understand him even if he was awake. "*Three days ago I met a man who asked me if I feared anything. I said I didn't. He told me his mother had watched him die. When I told him he still lived, he again asked if I feared anything, and again I told him no. He thanked me for listening and we shook hands before parting company. Our brief conversation could have contained a thousand lies.*"

He scooped up a handful of pebbles. "*But I'm not afraid now.*" He hurled the pebbles at the bird, expecting retaliation, but it only shrieked and scattered.

The commotion woke the old man. He rubbed sleep out of his eyes, pointed to the sky, and said, "*Roua.*"

"Yeah," Eramus replied, spitting at the old man's feet as he left. The bird couldn't hurt him.

He sighed in frustration, his exterior façade of confidence nothing more than a fragile surface. He attributed his superstitious imagination to his separation from Riya. His subconscious deceived him, invented problems only she could solve. Her face leapt into his memory, the sensous slowness in her fingers as she brushed a lock of hair out of her glittering eyes. They were back in her bed on a warm afternoon. Curtains rose and fell with a breeze. They had nothing but time.

The impression of happiness fled as abruptly as it had appeared. He remembered her frequent, hurtful apathy toward him. He had only fooled himself into thinking that she had cared about him, and the feeling left his insides hollow.

He considered breaking his vow to joining Hadrius for a drink, something bitter and strong to help him forget for a while. They could laugh about his hopeless attraction to Riya and the bird that wouldn't leave him in peace.

When he pictured a mug in his hand, though, Filthies converged on him like they had years earlier. He shivered the image away. He hadn't touched a drop of *glistas*, ale, or anything close since that strange and terrible night. It was easier to blame the alcohol for what had happened than to accept his own weaknesses.

He was different now. He carried a sword, had spent years learning to use it. Coping with the emotional aspects of his life had been the far greater challenge. Over time he had learned to suppress happiness, his method for balancing on the precipice of his own well-being. The alternative was to sink much lower emotionally when circumstances exceeded his control or satisfaction.

He still struggled to recognize inevitable waves of despair, to endure them when they smothered his confidence. They always passed, and much more quickly when he had a goal, a purpose to keep himself busy. In the meantime, he felt miserable. How could he love himself when loneliness extinguished any and all flares of self reliance?

He and Hadrius would have to leave the barony soon. The persistent bird and his steeping frustration with the fastidious language chipped away at his patience. He needed change, something he could get when Keltivar's autumn festival commenced in a few days. There would be plenty of boisterous personalities and diverse entertainment. Fun would lift his spirits and distract him from thinking about Riya.

But he couldn't seem to escape the bird. It had returned, pacing him from the rooftops, running clumsily along before launching into the air and swooping onto other buildings, stretching the tolerance of his peripheral vision. The farther he went, the more unrelentingly it heckled him. He shouldn't have instigated it. He tried to ignore it, tried to convince himself that his fear of it originated in his head.

Left. He was going left to the Courageous Prince. The bird flitted onto windowsills and scampered over shingles, eyes trained on him. With no better idea, Eramus broke into a run.

He had only covered a couple of blocks when he noticed a commotion ahead. He broke stride, veering away until he recognized the Courageous Prince. It had been the noise of a gathering crowd that had attracted the bird. It hadn't singled Eramus out, as he had originally thought. His paranoia had gotten the better of him. The winged spectator of the bird had taken to the sky, gliding high above a trio of Filthies shouting at a frightened woman. He cursed to himself. Filthies in groups meant trouble.

He wondered why the Filthies were bothering the woman, but it soon became clear by their laughter that she represented nothing more than their entertainment. They made no effort to arrest her. One of them repeatedly beat her on the arm with a heavy, knotted length of rope, while the others blocked her every attempt at escape. People pretended not to see what was happening or they nervously watched from a safe distance, shielding their eyes against the sun.

The bird feverishly shrieked and cawed in response to the loud smacks of impact, its wild call rippling shivers through Eramus. He took a deep breath. The familiar incident with the Filthies angered him. The terrified woman couldn't escape. He stepped closer and noticed indigo eyes set in a youthful bronze face. She reminded him of Riya, and tension clenched his belly. This woman wasn't a refugee. *"A good Hamaln does not solve problems with violence."*

Fists clenched in frustration, Eramus closed his eyes and allowed his ears to assume control of his senses. He heard the soldiers' wicked laughter and taunting. He had no reason to get involved in an incident which didn't concern him. He turned his back on the woman, only to stare down at his mocking shadow, a bitter, selfish version of himself in retreat: Eramus the coward.

He hated himself. He hated his confrontation avoidance, how his first reaction always leaned toward self preservation. His father had taught him that, but how much of that lesson really came from his father and how much of it was Eramus himself? *The woman was terrified.*

He wouldn't walk away. Rammun had intervened on his behalf, and he owed it to this woman to do the same. Besides, he would never abandon Riya if she were in trouble.

He ignored his pleading shadow and took a pair of long, measured strides toward the Filthies. *This doesn't change anything*, his conscience laughed. *You're still a coward.* He laughed with it. Stupidity didn't amount to bravery. His hands shook.

At his approach, one of the Filthies turned around. The wiry patches of beard on his ugly face reminded Eramus of one of his attackers from years ago, but this man bore the brand of the Forgotten Prophet, as did the Filthies with him.

"Stay out of this," the soldier warned. Eramus counted four beads on his goatee, and wondered how many of those kills had been defenseless women and children.

Murmurs rippled through the crowd. Witnesses would remember that the soldier had given him an explicit order, and then they would forget because the soldiers had never been welcome in the barony.

Eramus was in the process of sizing up his three opponents, regretting his hasty involvement while he read their body language, their proximity to the woman, and the positions of their weapons, when Sylvia strolled out onto the Courageous Prince's porch. Color left her face when she comprehended his involvement, but she expertly controlled her physical reactions, nodding almost imperceptibly to him on her way back into the tavern. *Good girl.* Eramus absolutely needed Hadrius's help, even though Hadrius preferred to avoid direct conflict with legal authority.

Then Eramus received a warning in his head, an impression. *Danger.*

Footsteps from behind almost surely meant that a Filthy had gotten the drop on him, but as he whipped around and unsheathed his sword in the span of a heartbeat, his reflexes honed to attack, he saw the jobah he had met yesterday, palms up as he backed away from the mortal threat of the blade. Eramus could have sliced him open. He squeezed his sword's grip tighter, acclimating his hand to the new leather wrapping while he subtly slid his right foot into a planted position should he need to thrust at the man. Jobahs didn't belong on a battlefield, and that's what this place could become.

The bird passed overhead, and as Eramus drank in the cool darkness of its shadow rippling over the uneven ground, he wondered what had warned him of the jobah's approach.

"Go away, jobah."

"Easy," the jobah responded in Oshlema, the language spilling from his mouth like a bad taste. A glimmer of recognition illuminated erudite eyes. He lowered his gloved hands and shouted over Eramus, at the Filthies. "*Se dupi koray?*"

"None of your business," their leader retorted. The crowd of onlookers had grown.

Eramus tried to translate the jobah's Medarn. The pattern exceeded his capacity. *One.* Pause. *One, one, one, one.* The rhythm had sounded off, even if the words had been correctly delivered. *Se* began a question. *Dupi* meant here. The jobah didn't appreciate the liberties the Filthies had taken with this woman, despite the fact that the incident lay outside his realm of enforcement, too.

Eramus lowered his sword as he glanced from the Filthies back to the jobah, his cheeks flushing with color. He didn't need the jobah getting in his way. He didn't need more trouble. The situation would escalate well enough on its own. "You should go before you get hurt. What are you doing here anyway?"

"My job," the jobah sternly replied.

A bleary-eyed Hadrius stumbled out of the tavern like a bull, his dark hair a mess of ridiculous braids, the imprint of a tabletop stamped on the side of his face from where he had passed out on it. He shook his head disapprovingly. Sylvia hustled out a handful of seconds later and tried to tighten his leather bracers for him. He discreetly waved her away and slipped through bystanders to flank the soldiers. Eramus felt an enormous sense of relief at his friend's involvement.

The woman tried again to run past the Filthies. One of them placed his open palm on her abdomen and threw her back into the center of their human barricade. She remained silent throughout the ordeal, a wild animal on the verge of captivity, desperate to escape at any cost. The bird beat its wings so furiously that Eramus felt the rush of wind.

The jobah, whom Eramus had almost forgotten, remained calm, directing his authority at the soldiers. *"Melo, demlustar demMedarn bubgahep treg shuld, dor dempoh wird."*

One. Pause. *One, one…*Eramus nervously laughed at the jobah's audacity once he understood the words. The man had assessed a fine against the Filthies for their use of Oshlema.

One of the Filthies kicked up dirt, and a fine cloud of dust dispersed into the air. "Fuck you, jobah."

The situation worsened by the second. The Filthies wouldn't back down. The jobah should have fetched the magistrate's men for backup. The older man had the baron's legal authority, but an intangible wouldn't protect him from physical attack. The Filthies would eventually have to answer to the baron for their actions, but anything could happen in the meantime. Eramus weighed his options, none of them favorable. At the very least, he would have to leave the barony or face retaliation. At worst, he could end up imprisoned or executed. He hadn't seriously considered any consequences until now. He couldn't allow this woman to fall victim to the whims of the Filthies. He wouldn't leave Riya alone when she was in trouble. He rubbed sweat from his eyes. This woman wasn't Riya.

Hadrius bumped spectators aside as he moved closer, awaiting a signal despite his misgivings. Sylvia remained on the porch, white-knuckling the railing, her crooked left ring finger jutting out almost comically as she observed.

Eramus could still walk away.

"I'm Ander Carden," the jobah said. "Jobah Carden to you. I

remember you from the Poor Missionary. Speaking Medarn to you would be a waste of both our time. The ugliest of the bunch is named Eamon something or other." Eramus didn't know if Carden expected a reply so he kept his mouth shut. Carden cleared his throat. "Are you willing to get her away from them?"

Eramus swallowed hard and nodded. He could do it. Hadrius would give him the surprise he needed, the edge in a fight. And then what? Antagonize Filthies and answer to a knight, assuming he didn't get himself killed? No. Jobah Carden represented the law here.

"Good," Carden continued quietly, reaffirming that authority. "You have His Lordship's authorization to perform that specific action under my orders, including immunity from language laws. Are you affiliated?"

"No. Peeran."

"Excellent. What's your name?"

Prophuug. "Eramus Pon."

"Well, Eramus Pon, I don't really care so much about that woman as I do about those *kuvos* over there spitting in my face. I take pleasure in heightening the misery in their simple little lives, and in reminding the people in this barony that His Lordship is the law here."

"I never thought I'd hear a jobah use a word like *kuvos*," Eramus said, happy that Carden loathed Filthies as much as he did.

"I hear the same things you do. I have my favorites." He noted the length of Eramus's sword. "Are you any good with that?"

"*Tros bo dow!*" someone from the crowd shouted. A rock sailed out of nowhere and skimmed off Eamon's leg. This incited the bird into another frenzy. *One.* Pause. *One, one.*

"Who threw that?" Eamon demanded, his sweaty face flushed with anger and embarrassment, the brand on his forehead glistening pink and white in the sunlight. One of his fellow soldiers looked a bit uneasy at the crowd's attention.

Raise the sword, Eramus thought, the weight reassuring in his hand. *Swing it. Then you can't take it back.* He hefted his blade, considering how the swordfight could potentially spill into the crowd. Children hung on their mothers's arms and old men sagged with the exhaustion of age. Why wouldn't the mothers and fathers take their children away from the danger? Then Eramus remembered the spectators at his father's execution. The people in the barony wanted to see the Filthies hurt or worse, and that desire outweighed their own safety.

He decided confronting the Filthies unarmed could prevent unnecessary casualties. He sheathed his blade and stepped forward, eyes locked on the thick, knotted rope Eamon had used to splash welts on the woman's arms. When Eramus made eye contact with her, she turned away as if ashamed. Anger rose inside him. What could she have done to deserve this treatment?

"What gives you the right to enter this barony and ignore His Lordship's laws?" Jobah Carden shouted at the Filthies. *Good. Distract them.*

"The right of My Lord Sevalah, His Majesty King Willum, and the Temple of Gefil, old man!" Eamon shot back.

"I can't find Seehlan here, only what pass for soldiers bullying a defenseless woman."

Eramus took another step, ignored the gathered crowd. The background faded to bleeding watercolors, the Filthies a series of heavy lines and edges in the foreground. One of them seized the woman's upper arm while his other hand strayed to his sword. Eramus inclined his head at the soldier, indicating his first move to Hadrius, who reluctantly nodded acknowledgement, jaw clenching, brutish hands curling into iron hammers.

"Oh, yeah," the jobah continued, his needling voice distracting the soldiers. "I forgot. You surrendered to Gelofass seven years ago, right? Doesn't seem like very long, eh, *duba*? You probably like it when Geflin priests read the *Otauh* while they take you from behind. Just lie down and follow orders, right? Orders like hide my sword."

Nervous laughter rippled through the crowd. Losing the Rite War was a sore spot for Oshlemin, especially for Fushlemin soldiers. Count Sevalah's men had served on the front lines, and they had also been the first to surrender. The jobah could manipulate words as well as a sword, and Eramus had thought him unarmed.

The Filthies, especially Eamon, didn't appreciate the insults. He growled through yellow teeth, but Carden didn't let up.

"The stench of your Fushlemin brothers taints our air. You stink, too. Your foul smell reminds me of a rotten outhouse."

"I'll—" Eamon began, his teeth fully bared, veins popping around his neck.

"Oshlemin odds, eh?" Eramus interrupted, close enough to the Filthies now to see their stubble. A shadow slid past his feet as the bird drifted overhead. Carden had superbly engaged the Filthies.

Eamon disdainfully regarded Eramus. He let the rope fall back, his fist tightening over it, his face still burning red with anger. "I told you to leave." He turned his head for a heartbeat, a gesture Eramus had anticipated.

The rope came down hard and fast, but Eramus's hand came up to meet Eamon's fist in mid-swing. The rope snapped forward, stinging into Eramus like a snake, but he held on to Eamon's hand anyway and squeezed. He could have used his sword and cleaved through the man's wrist, but he still hoped to salvage the situation with as little violence as possible.

Hadrius shouldered his way through the crowd and made his presence known. The discomfort of his hangover and the veins bunching along his muscles presented a generally irascible appearance. The other Filthies exchanged worried looks, and the closer he got to them the more they settled into fighting stances. He looked angry enough to rip them apart with his bare hands. No swords had been drawn, though.

Their hands were interlocked, and the outcome of the confrontation isolated to Eramus and Eamon, to who would yield first, with complete disregard for temples or laws. The other soldiers froze in place, unable to move without orders. Even Hadrius had stopped, though Eramus had no doubt his friend could leap onto a Filthy if need be.

Eramus imagined an apple in his grip. He squeezed harder and harder to crush it.

At first the challenge inspired Eamon. His eyes smoldered with hatred. Gradually, however, the overconfidence left his face. It became apparent that he was nothing more than a bully, a man who relied on superior numbers or even a weapon for his victories.

The soldier holding the woman shook out of his trance and released her as he decided he would be better off preparing to defend himself. She bolted immediately, past Carden, to vanish into the gasping, parting crowd. The Filthies watched her go, none of them willing to go through Eramus or Carden to pursue her.

Eamon violently jerked himself free now that the woman was gone. Eramus had sole possession of the knotted rope. He tossed it aside, and Eamon flinched. Eramus couldn't help but chuckle. He wanted to tackle the man, to pin his arms and saw the beads off his goatee.

"Eamon," one of the Filthies said. "Eamon, are we—"

Eamon waved his question off as he backed away, his expression twisted, bitter with impotent rage. His eyes ran over Eramus and Carden, memorizing their features.

"Your fines await you at the minister's office," Carden said with aplomb. "You'll be settling up or the magistrate will issue warrants for your arrest."

Eamon didn't reply. Instead he pointed at them in turn, as if marking them. After slowly backing away from Eramus, he spun around and barreled past his fellow soldiers. They stood confused for a handful of seconds before following.

Someone in the crowd clapped once the Filthies had been driven off, and soon applause swelled throughout. Eramus released a heavy sigh. Nobody had been arrested or killed. Sweat dampened his cheeks and palms, cooling with the soft breeze.

He scanned the rooftops. The bird watched him intently, clearly agitated, as if it somehow understood what had transpired. It launched itself off the roof and retreated on an unseen gust of wind until it vanished into the distance.

Carden stepped up beside Eramus, startling him. The jobah had tucked his expensive gloves into his belt. He shook Eramus's hand, wiping its sweat on his pants afterward, slightly embarrassing him. "Good work, my friend."

A portly man with red cheeks wheezed his way over, his jobah's badge crooked on his vest. He asked Carden something in Medarn as he regarded Eramus.

"Just fine now, Soames, thanks to this young man. Please use Oshlema for now."

The crowd dispersed a bit to reveal Hadrius, out of place now that the excitement had subsided.

"Friend of yours?" Carden asked Eramus.

Hadrius took a couple of steps towards them, ignoring Carden.

Jobah Soames fished writing charcoal and a tablet out of his inner vest pocket. He cleared his throat, seemed to think about his upcoming words. "I'll need your names for the official report."

Hadrius blew out an irritated breath and cracked his knuckles in an intimidating fashion.

"Er...perhaps you could give them to me," Soames said to Eramus.

"Eramus Pon and Hadrius Uln."

"Hm. From?"

"Uuslef."

"Oslef? Wh...uh...Ouslef. I see. Don't get many Ouslefin here."

"No. Uuslef. You pronounce it like Ooo-slef."

"Just take their names, Soames," Carden ordered.

"Right," Soames nodded, furiously scribbling. "Eramus Pon and Hadrius Uln." He quickly peeked at Carden to see if he was listening. "From Ooo-slef."

Hadrius disapproved of their names in any public record, but Eramus accepted what he couldn't control for the time being. They could have provided false names. They could have fled the scene. But Eramus wasn't ashamed of his actions. Perhaps his pride had gotten the better of him. Perhaps he believed this incident would balance his debt to Rammun, would return the favor the mercenary had granted him all those years ago.

"Come down to the minister's office when you have the time. Your money will be waiting, Eramus Pon of Uuslef," Carden said. "Tell them Carden sent you."

Eramus nodded, though he had no intention of ever collecting. He and Hadrius would be gone by tomorrow morning. Eramus knew men like Eamon. The man would retaliate.

"Do you know the woman, Carden?"

The jobah shook his head. He patted Eramus on the shoulder before filtering through the remaining witnesses with Soames, asking questions and taking statements.

Hadrius shoved Eramus. *"I don't know why you do things like that."*

Eramus shoved him back. *"Sometimes people need help."* Hadrius had needed help, had needed a purpose when the Information Regiment had disbanded, and Eramus had helped him.

Hadrius shoved him again, harder this time, almost knocking him over. *"But why do you always have to be the one to help them,* prophuug?"

"*My friend would understand.*"

"*I don't understand. I guess I'm not your friend. My friend said we work when we need money, and we take the rest of the time to spend that money. Don't you remember what happened in Drohm?*"

A little over a year ago, Eramus, Hadrius, Riya, and three of their companions at the time had been on the way back from a job in the south of Antonay. On their return, they had passed through a northern town called Drohm, and had stopped long enough to aid townsfolk to hunt down a group of slavers who had kidnapped some of their wives and children. None of the slavers survived the ensuing fight, and several of the townspeople also died saving their family members. Afterward, the mayor had insisted on taking names for the public record. The same mayor who had begged the peerans for help had later asked them to leave. Riya's presence, it seemed, had made the survivors uncomfortable.

Eramus shook his head and shrugged. As much as he and Hadrius were friends, they still had their fundamental differences.

"*Did you even know that woman?*" Hadrius asked.

Eramus ignored the question and nodded at Sylvia. "*You two getting along?*"

Hadrius furrowed his brow in concentration. "*Don't change the subject.*" His expression eased as he massaged the bridge of his nose with his thumb and index finger. "*She likes strawberries and my hair. She's only been here a couple of days. I asked her to the festival.*"

Eramus planted his hands on his hips. "*I'll find us some work, maybe get us up there with extra money. I'll be back later tonight, after I say goodbye to Sadir. We've been here long enough.*"

"*Next time I'm coming here alone,*" Hadrius sighed, jerking his thumb back at the inn. "*I'll be in there, working on a buzz. Don't do anything else stupid because I'm not coming out until tomorrow.*"

Without another word, Eramus turned down a side street. Hadrius hadn't meant what he had said. He would be upset for a while, but that would be the end of it.

Eramus thought about the woman who had fled. He didn't want to think about how her indigo eyes resembled sleep stars, how she somehow reminded him of Riya.

He followed the flow of foot traffic until he reached the main square, yellowing grass overrunning an intricate mosaic of weathered flagstones. Not a single bird lurked in his line of sight. He nodded in greeting to people he passed, conversing in his limited Medarn until he found Trixie, whose face brightened at his appearance. He met her brother, Tayuron, a humble man with hunched shoulders, and some Keltivarin businessmen who had come to negotiate trade taxes with the auditor. The businessmen had reached the barony with rude, nasty, mostly drunk bodyguards, so when they learned that Eramus was a peeran and he offered to provide protection on the return trip for three quarters the going rate, the men hired him on the spot, provided Trixie and Tayuron joined them. Hadrius would be displeased about the cut salary but Eramus wouldn't say anything about it until the festival began.

The businessmen intended to depart early the following morning, which fit Eramus's plans nicely. He stayed and talked with Trixie, Tayuron, and the businessmen for a couple of hours, listening to their propositions and ideas about what they called exception flow, most of which were a little too complex for him. *Blend in.* They were all very friendly, and the *glistas* jug they passed around made them even friendlier. They offered him a drink once or twice but he politely declined and they didn't take offense.

Trixie smiled at Eramus often, and he found himself returning her smiles with easy smiles of his own. Tayuron used a stick to illustrate the layout of a bizarre, multi-tiered solarium he had once helped to build for a wealthy calex, and soon everyone gathered around to ask questions about how long it had taken and who could even conceive of such designs. The trip to Keltivar would pass quickly with amiable companions like these. Their enjoyment of life and their willingness to share their perspectives reminded him of his father's behavior on summer nights. Before Loghemit had turned to drink for comfort, he had been a good man, a kind man who loved his son. Eramus remembered his father's comforting hand on his shoulder while he snatched glowing insects out of the dark and recited constellation names. Sometimes he would hear his father sobbing, saying his mother's name, Vina, when he thought Eramus slept. It was usually when Loghemit was drunk. It always sounded odd to Eramus to hear his mother's name.

Unable to stay any longer, Eramus bid the men farewell with firm handshakes. Trixie unexpectedly hugged him, her cheeks warming the side of his face, her faint flowery fragrance tantalizing his sense of smell. Unable to stop himself, he brushed her hair out of her eyes like he had seen her do so many times before. Then they both stood there with nothing to say. Her brother finally told her it was time for them to go, and that's when Eramus remembered who he was and how he would always be alone. Trixie and Tayuron were kind, generous people. Eramus wasn't like them. He could never be like them. He didn't understand how to be that way.

He headed to Sadir's for a final goodbye. He thought about his future, something he tended to do more as he grew older. His father had once told him that men reflected more in First Awakening than in any other. Eramus lived on the road, earned his way with his sword, and risked his life for money. Would he still be a peeran a couple of years from now? Would he be alive ten years from now? He doubted his father had expected to die at such a young age. Eramus relished the exceptional freedom and pay his occupation provided. During his time in the IR, he owned little more than the clothes on his back, held little or no money most of the time, and possessed no suitable means of protection.

When he considered a permanent home and a family like Sadir had, a heavy weight pressed down on him. He didn't exactly know how to care for a family. What if he couldn't? He also couldn't answer a simple question: how would he earn a living without using his sword? His only other experiences came from carrying messages back and forth and from his time with a shovel, a common enough profession for younger men with no real skill, a profession that paid next to nothing.

He was so lost in thought that he barely noticed a Filthy slipping back into an alley. Was he being followed? If so, how long had it been going on? He had lost track of his surroundings, a mistake a man in his line of work couldn't afford to make.

He maintained the appearance of still being deep in thought as he kept stride down the street, sharply veering around corners as often as possible to get a good look at the soldier through his peripheral vision. He finally caught a flash from a window lantern.

He recognized the man from the earlier altercation outside the Courageous Prince. But why follow him now? And was he alone? Did the Filthies intend to arrest him? He had been right about their leader, Eamon. The man obviously wanted payback.

Eramus considered his destination. He couldn't lead the Filthies to Sadir's house. He had to shake the pursuit. He only noticed one man tailing him, and he could handle one if he had to, but more of them were probably nearby. Filthies wouldn't act unless the odds were in their favor.

Much to the owner's dismay, Eramus jogged into a curio shop and hustled out the back door. From there he sprinted across an empty lot and emerged onto a street two blocks away. He waited in alleys, doubled back, and walked for several minutes in completely different directions until he was confident he had lost the soldier. By this time street lamps were already being lit.

He considered going back to the Poor Missionary. Filthies were after him. Leaving the barony would solve that problem. He and Hadrius would have to sleep outside the walls for the night.

Paranoia had taken over. Even if the Filthies had been after him, he was free and clear of danger now. If he hurried, he could still make dinner at Sadir's.

When he was a block away, he looked over his shoulder one last time. Nothing suspicious. Breathing hard, he jogged up Sadir's front steps.

"You're late," Sadir said from the head of the table. His use of Oshlema indicated its approval. Eramus wondered if his friend's drawn, gloomy expression had to do with his tardiness. Kathryn kept to herself, not even offering a greeting as she fetched his plate from the kitchen.

"I meant to be here sooner but I lost track of time," Eramus lied as he smiled and tousled Raisa's hair. At least she was happy to see him.

"What's wrong?" Sadir asked. "You're out of breath."

Kathryn nearly dropped the plate in front of Eramus. "*Dush tene*," she said to her husband with concern.

"Just hurried over here, that's all," Eramus said as he patted perspiration along his brow with his forearm. He managed to capture the general tone of her statement, if not the literal translation, and it bordered on interrogation. How should he respond? Should he tell them how his impulsive actions had upset vindictive men, that Kathryn was right about men with swords attracting trouble?

She furtively studied him, eventually ceasing her vigil to return her attention to her solemn husband, whose mood was more subdued than usual. Eramus decided to ask him about it after dinner.

Despite her surliness toward Eramus, Kathryn had prepared an exceptional feast of ham, cabbage, and sugared pears. While Eramus, hungrier than he had realized after shaking his pursuer, cleaned his plate, Kathryn cradled Sadir's hand and whispered endearments. If happiness such as theirs was possible, Eramus could still hope to one day end up with someone who reciprocated his love.

Raisa shouted, clapping wildly as the meal wound down. Kathryn blushed and gathered plates, returning from the kitchen with syrupy *glis*. Raisa laughed and laughed and laughed until everyone joined her.

The first bite of warm *glis* melted on Eramus's tongue and relieved all his anxiety. He ate a couple, until his stomach refused to take any more. He thanked Kathryn for the wonderful meal, Raisa for bringing a smile to his face, and Sadir for opening his home.

Again he thought about the bond Sadir and Kathryn shared, and he reflected on his relationship with Riya. Why had things between them been so strained, so difficult to maintain? He had only wanted to be with her, to be near her. Was that selfishness? Did he demand too much from her? Was she too selfish?

While Raisa helped her mother clear the table, Sadir and Eramus stood out on the porch. Neighbors passed on their way home, and Sadir greeted them in turn by name. Eramus closed his eyes, listening to the soft murmur of distant noise as cool night air tickled his hair. Sadir lit his pipe and the heady aroma stung Eramus's nostrils.

"Love yourself."

"My friend hanged himself today," Sadir said with the subtleness of an ax on a wood block, shocking Eramus out of his complacency. "I found him in his office. I had to tell his wife."

"I'm sorry to hear that."

Silence settled in. Eramus didn't want to say anything awkward so he waited for Sadir to continue.

"I guess he never recovered from his son's death. He lost him a couple of years ago to the fighting in Glesk."

"A shame," Eramus said, shaking his head. "Was your friend a librarian, too?"

"No," Sadir replied with a scathing, challenging stare. "A jobah. A damn good one, too."

Eramus felt his knees weaken. A horrible sensation, like a hundred insects, skittered its way up his spine. "What was his name?"

That look from Sadir again. The man could read people as easily as he read words on a page. "Carden. Ander Carden."

Eramus dropped his head into his hands and groaned, begging for the jobah's death to be coincidence. Carden hadn't behaved like a suicidal man. The wisdom and benevolence he had shared in their brief encounters led Eramus to mourn his passing. They might have been friends after only another conversation or two, surely if Sadir had been present.

But a Filthy had been following Eramus, and that meant more of them could have tracked Carden down just as easily, could have arranged his murder to appear like a suicide. Eramus had put Sadir and his family in jeopardy. He had to leave immediately.

"What is it?" Sadir asked with incredulity, pipe dangling from his fingertips.

Eramus examined his boot tops. "I should go. Now." He swallowed hard, debating if he owed his friend an explanation. "Sadir, I…"

A horse shuffled several feet away.

"Eramus," Sadir said. "Trouble."

Eramus glanced up at the stark light of a naked torch in the darkness. He felt weightless, out of body. He hadn't eluded the soldier after all. In fact, he had led him right to Sadir's, to his family's home.

"That's him," Eamon said, pointing at Eramus, gloating satisfaction on his ugly face. *I found you.* Three more Filthies accompanied him, as well as an armored figure on horseback lurking in the shadows. Oshlemin odds. Eramus reached for his sword.

"Get your family out of here," he ordered his friend.

The horse snorted as its bald, helmetless rider, eye sockets still recesses of darkness, steered it closer. Torchlight played off the rider's combination of blood star red and silver armor, the latter prominent in steel tasset and gauntlets. His surcoat bore the stitched gold leaf of Gelofass floating beside the Blood Eagle. Unlike the redeemed, the Ismah's knights did not light the way for the Forgotten Prophet, but supposedly paved it, and therefore had no need for the brand of the *duba*. The Ismah had dubbed his knights purifiers, but to Eramus they were depraved men who used faith to justify unholy slaughter. Eramus had witnessed their lack of mercy firsthand at his father's execution. Panic set in.

He shoved Sadir behind him. "Go! Get out of here now!" Visibly upset and confused, Sadir ran inside and scooped up his little girl. Kathryn argued with him while he half dragged her to the back door. They opened it to a pair of waiting Filthies. Sadir slammed the door in their faces and dropped the bolt. Kathryn set to shrieking.

Eramus stood sentry, filling the doorway as best he could. He peered into the night, wishing he had persuaded Hadrius to come with him. The Filthies at the back of the house kicked the door until the wood splintered under the assault. They plowed into the house, seized Sadir and his family, and still Eramus hadn't moved. He was too busy waiting for the knight to make the first move.

"That's your father, boy," Uncle Reginald reminds him, as if he could forget. His uncle's sweaty hands hurt his head and he wants to cry. The man ordered cheap wine before the execution's commencement, laughed and joked with strangers about it. Eramus claws at unyielding hands forcing him to watch.

"You. Throw down your weapon and approach," the knight commanded in a tone accustomed to obeisance. The Filthies maintained arm's length from Eramus while he unbuckled his sword belt and tossed it off the porch, his cheeks hot with frustration. He couldn't challenge a knight, especially with Sadir and his family in harm's way. Better for him to surrender, to face the consequences of his actions.

Eamon, bold and stupid enough to wear Carden's lambskin gloves, proving he had participated in the jobah's murder, nibbled on his lower lip as he retrieved Eramus's sword. It was all Eramus could do to restrain himself from lashing out at the gloating dog. He had to consider the safety of Sadir and his family. He had to stay in the moment, in control of himself. He walked off the porch, made himself an easier target.

"Smart one, you are," the knight said, his Oshlema stained with the rolling of every "r." Eramus closed half the distance between them, noting the lack of compassion within the knight's familiar gold-flecked brown eyes.

He stands atop a wagon at the edge of the crowd, hay under his bare feet, as soldiers drag his father, clumsily kicking and clawing, to the town center. A knight sits nearby at a small table, eating his meal as casually as if he is in the comfort of his home.

Eamon prodded Eramus in the back with the handle of his own sword, but Eramus just shrugged him off. The Filthies wouldn't act without orders.

"What's your name?" the knight asked.

"Eramus Pon," he answered coldly, regretting that he had surrendered his sword. The knight flinched at the sound of his name, a reaction he concealed in the span of a heartbeat.

Eamon handed the sword to the knight, who examined it in both gauntleted hands, sniffed the blade's length until his eyes came to rest on the engraving. "You haven't killed anything for a while. What does this inscription mean? Is it your name?"

Eramus nodded. The Ismah's knights had a reputation for being learned men, but he doubted they would have taken the time to study Uuslefin.

"You will answer when spoken to, Eramus Pon," the knight said in a firm tone.

"Yes," Eramus lied, clearing his throat when his voice failed him. In his imagination, he sprinted at the knight and decapitated him with a single slice. "The inscription is my name."

The knight carelessly discarded the sword and it clanged on the ground. He canted his head a bit, his pauldrons and upper vambraces scraping with the subtle shift. His burnished armor could have funded a small border campaign. Every section of plating had been acid-etched with foreign runes. The craftsmanship would have required unerring accuracy and skill from a master in the trade.

"Where do you hail from, Eramus Pon?"

"Uuslef."

"How fortuitous," the knight snorted. He paused, as if reliving a memory. "I knew a Pon once. Any relation?"

Eramus squirmed a bit, fighting back the urge to leap for his sword. "My father," he answered through gritted teeth.

"Hm."

Suddenly Eramus was back in Frehm again, watching his father die, listening as he drunkenly cried and begged for his life while excited soldiers pelted him with stones.

"My captain couldn't tie a noose and my men needed to get a few things out of their system so they used stones instead. Took a bit longer than I expected but everyone got to participate." The knight leaned forward in his saddle, leather groaning with the movement, his horse shuffling under the weight. "Long way from home." He carefully scratched his nose with a metal fingertip and straightened up in his saddle. "I am Sir Jacob, knight of the Blood Eagle, purifier under the Temple of Gefil's holy protection. Now there won't be any misunderstandings about who I am or what I represent." The knight personified ethnic murder, rumors estimating his Seehlan kills in the hundreds. He nodded a signal to the Filthies and they bound Eramus's wrists. He struggled but they outnumbered him and he knew he had nothing to gain even if he could get free. "Your father's irresponsibility led to the deaths of four men, one of them under my command. Apparently you intend to carry on his tradition."

"A good Hamaln does not solve problems with violence."

Eramus tried to launch his body at the knight but the Filthies restrained him. "I demand to know your intentions" he said, ceasing to struggle when he remembered Sadir on the porch, his face pale with fear as he protected his wife and daughter.

The knight smiled, as if he welcomed the demand. "I came here to arrest you for interfering with Count Sevelah's soldiers." The knight looked past him, and Eramus turned to see Raisa peeking out from behind her father's hand. "Bring them forward." While two Filthies kept hold of Eramus, Eamon and another soldier approached the house. Sadir was the only obstacle between them and his family, but there were two more Filthies standing just inside his doorway. They had nowhere to go.

"Keep away!" Sadir growled, as animated as Eramus had ever

seen him. He backed into the doorway, into the Filthies, and braced his hands against the jamb to wedge himself in place, keeping his family behind him. For a librarian, he was particularly brave, his courage and lack of self-preservation inspired by his need to protect his family.

"Stop this, please," Eramus begged Sir Jacob. "You have me in custody. I surrender. Let them go."

The Filthies kicked the back of his legs out and forced him to kneel. They slid his ash-handled dagger out of its thigh sheath before he could try for it. "Shut your mouth," one of them warned.

Eramus averted his gaze when the soldiers beat Sadir to the ground. They dragged a screaming Kathryn down the steps. She clutched Raisa to her chest, the little girl petrified with fear, unable to comprehend why these men were hurting her parents.

"Bring the girl here," Sir Jacob ordered. Kathryn's eyes widened. Sadir tried to get up, but one of the soldiers cuffed him in the back of the head. Stunned, he collapsed, groaning, covering his head with his hands.

Adrenaline burned through Eramus, pumping hot blood through his body. He planted his heels beneath him, coiling to leap, when the cold steel of his own dagger pressed against his throat and sharply nicked him. These men weren't taking chances. Bile rose in his throat. He was helpless, his hands tied in such a way that he couldn't reach his concealed dagger.

Kathryn didn't release Raisa until Eamon smacked her across the mouth. She unsteadily reached for her daughter but received a vicious punch in the stomach for her effort. Raisa's fingers stretched for her mother as she was dragged away. The Filthies enjoyed it all. Sir Jacob's apathetic expression bothered Eramus more than anything. The knight treated the beating of a mother and father as an everyday occurrence. Eramus, on the other hand, was overcome with shame and guilt for his carelessness.

Kathryn yelled at him to do something as she crawled on her hands and knees toward the knight, blood and snot dripping out of her face. Eramus remembered his promise to Sadir, to look after Raisa, and struggled even harder against his captors as they pressed their weight onto him. They had him fast, pinned to the ground, and he couldn't escape. Kathryn screamed louder this time, calling for her neighbors to help them, to fetch the magistrate. Candles winked out. Shutters closed. None of the neighbors stepped outside their homes.

"Are you familiar with the *Otauh*, Eramus Pon?" the knight asked, ignoring Kathryn's screaming as he leaned over and accepted Raisa from Eamon. The frantic little girl's body shuddered with silent sobs. "Hush," Sir Jacob warned her. When she gasped out a sob, he clamped his gauntlet over her face, smothering her.

"Enough!" Eramus shouted, ignoring the knight's authority and advantage. He cared little for his own life at the moment. He couldn't watch this anymore. He wasn't helpless. He could do something about it.

The dagger pressed in harder on his throat, drawing more blood. The weight of another soldier pressed down onto his shoulders, three men now, pinning him in place. He caught the torchlight on his sword only a few feet away. He had been stupid to give it up. He could have given Sadir's family a chance to run, but he had never anticipated this level of brutality.

Raisa's tiny hands came up to pull on the knight's gauntlet but it didn't budge.

"I asked you a question," Sir Jacob said, his tone rising sharply, his piercing eyes commanding Eramus's attention.

"I've heard of the *Otauh*. That's all. Please," he pleaded. "I said I surrender. Let her go. She has nothing to do with this."

But Sir Jacob didn't, and Raisa continued to claw at the gauntlet. Kathryn bawled her daughter's name over and over. Neighbors peeked out of recently lit windows but none left the safety of their homes. They were all just going to watch. They valued their own safety too much to interfere, just like earlier in the day when the crowd had gathered to watch the Filthies harassing the woman.

Eramus coiled his muscles. He could spin away from the blade at his throat, perhaps twist his arm enough to reach his concealed dagger. Then what? His arms were still tied behind him. His mind raced, searching for a way out of this predicament that didn't harm his friend's family.

"Though the path through First Awakening may not always be clear, it does not mean you are alone without faith. Believe in yourself and wisdom will reveal the way."

The chaplain's words echoed in Eramus's mind. Unfortunately he did not believe in himself. Was this a lesson of First Awakening?

"The Forgotten Prophet wrote the *Otauh*," the knight droned on, oblivious to Eramus's inner turmoil and the suffering of the child in his grip. "As his words came from the Blood Eagle, his words *are* truth. His words are law higher than man or lord. I will recite a passage. There is no need to thank me for your enlightenment."

Kathryn begged Sir Jacob to release her daughter but he didn't even acknowledge her. Raisa's arms lowered, the last of her energy fading from her little body. If the knight didn't release her she would suffocate. Eramus panicked but the knight was as calm as ever. Eramus tried to ignore the knight's words but they sliced into his thoughts.

"*'And if my agents deem it appropriate to spill blood for my cause, those of my faith shall support the decision'*. Verse 4. I took the liberty of translating the words to Oshlema so you would understand, though I think even this passage may exceed the limited scope of a man without redemption. Nevertheless, you may still play a role in revealing the Forgotten Prophet."

Suddenly he released Raisa. She tumbled to the earth with an awkward thud. At first Eramus sighed in relief, but when she didn't move his breath stopped. Then Raisa coughed and gasped through tears.

Sir Jacob nodded to the Filthies. "Take the woman and the girl back inside. Bring the man."

The soldiers holding Eramus in place jammed down even harder on him, bending his legs beneath him, eliminating all possibility of escape. One of the Filthies dragged Raisa through the mud by her hair. The little girl shrieked and kicked until the Filthy smacked her senseless. Eramus roared, the sound erupting from deep in his belly, but he couldn't escape the soldiers, and every time he squirmed the blade gouged deeper into his throat, and his muscles burned from compression and strain. Warm blood dripped onto his tunic.

"Help us!" Eramus shouted at the people in their homes. "Call for the magistrate!" Men and women closed their shutters or snuffed their candles.

Kathryn slithered through the Filthies and scooped up her

daughter, stroking Raisa's hair, whispering comfort. Two of the Filthies hoisted the disoriented Sadir to his feet and dragged him away from the house, past Eramus, while Eamon and another soldier escorted a protesting Kathryn and her daughter inside.

"What are you doing?" Eramus demanded as the Filthies hauled Sadir toward a lone fencepost.

"I have decided not to arrest you, but your manners and your obedience leave much to be desired," the knight replied. "As a result, I am obligated to discipline you, to ensure that you understand the severity of disobedience." He nodded at the post. "Tie him there," he ordered the Filthies who were carrying Sadir. They dropped him on his rear, his back to the post, and secured his wrists behind it. He groaned in semi-consciousness.

"What's happening here?" Eramus demanded. "I'm right here. Punish me if you have to."

"What good would that do?"

Leering grins on their faces, *duba* brands starkly prominent on their foreheads, the Filthies collected stones. Eramus finally understood what they intended. He rolled his shoulders and tried to push off the ground but the Filthies were prepared. He felt the blade move up another inch on his throat. If he even flinched his windpipe would open.

"These men serve me willingly, Eramus Pon. They have embraced the return of the Forgotten Prophet. Now you will learn what your interference with their work and mine has caused." He nodded to the Filthies. "Begin."

Eramus watched in horror as the first stone hit his friend in the stomach. The Filthy had thrown it hard and it had struck with a disgusting smack. Eramus squeezed his eyes shut when Sadir cried out. He was being forced to relive his father's death.

"You will watch this," Sir Jacob said. "You will learn."

With great reluctance, Eramus opened his eyes, hoping his compliance would save his friend's life. The sweaty hands on the sides of his head weren't his Uncle Reginald's, but they just as easily could have been. Another Filthy threw a stone at Sadir, though this one only skidded off his friend's thigh. The next blow fractured Sadir's left cheekbone and split his face into a bloody mess. Albeit extremely dazed and disoriented, he retained consciousness.

"Now you will repeat the words of the *Otauh*, Eramus Pon," Sir Jacob said from somewhere in the distance. Eramus had completely forgotten about the knight.

"Now I will repeat the words of the *Otauh*," he muttered senselessly. His strength drained from his body. He couldn't endure much more of Sadir's torture. His own helplessness and cowardice sickened him.

"*' And if my agents deem it appropriate to spill blood for my cause', "* Sir Jacob began. When Eramus didn't respond, the knight signaled to a Filthy, and the man gleefully flung another stone at Sadir. This one cracked his knee. Sadir's head lolled to the side as he mercifully lost consciousness. "Say the words, Eramus Pon."

Eramus searched his memory for words that had floated away on the wind. Seconds stretched to minutes, the circumstances unbearable. *This man ordered your father's death while he ate dinner.*

"*' And if my agents deem it appropriate to spill blood for my cause', "* Sir Jacob said again.

"*' And if my agents deem it appropriate to spill blood for my cause', "* Eramus repeated emotionlessly.

"Very good. Very good. And now the rest. '*Those of my faith shall support the decision'.*"

Eramus recited the rest of the words, forgetting them when they left his mouth. They were blasphemy. He didn't believe in the Forgotten Prophet. Sir Jacob knew that. What was the point?

"Do you doubt my faith, Eramus Pon?" Sir Jacob asked. "Do you doubt my conviction?" When Eramus, too emotionally and physically drained from the ordeal, didn't respond, Filthies pelted Sadir's limp form with more stones, dull thuds against soft flesh. "Do you doubt me, Eramus Pon?"

"No," Eramus said in another man's voice.

The knight lowers his arm and Loghemit Pon leaves his First Awakening.

"Good. My purpose is to eliminate the disease of the impure. I would not remove a blighted branch to accomplish this, but rather the entire tree, from its roots, and burn the soil upon which it failed. Now, Eramus Pon, you must ask how you can serve me, and in knowing when you ask that I serve a higher power."

Filthies chucked their last two stones at Sadir. His body

twitched though he remained unconscious, possibly dead. A huge purple and red bruise swelled on his cheek. The injury would be a permanent disfigurement if he survived. Eramus recalled that the knight had told him something a few minutes ago. Or seconds ago? What was it? He found the words separating in his head, grains of sand in a strong wind.

"How can I serve you?" Eramus asked between clenched teeth, hoping he wasn't supposed to interpret an ulterior message from the knight's ranting. He glanced at his sword, only a short distance away. It wanted Sir Jacob's blood so Eramus could jam it under the knight's nostrils for a whiff.

But Eramus dismissed that stretch of his imagination. Sir Jacob was mounted, protected with full plate armor, possibly unseen defenses. Attacking him would be akin to suicide.

The Filthies dusted off their hands and flanked Sir Jacob. Eramus studied their faces. They bore no hint of remorse or guilt, only twisted pleasure.

"You're going to serve the Forgotten Prophet," Sir Jacob said.

Eamon and another Filthy loitered on the porch. Eamon grinned at Eramus, rubbed his gloved hands together.

"Fine," Eramus said, fighting back his urge to vomit. "Tell me what you want me to do."

The knight placed his palm on his chest. "Oh, it's not what I want you to do, make no mistake about that. The Ismah needs you to find Baron Kent's children." He nodded at the Filthies. "They can't find them because they don't have the right incentive." He leaned forward in the saddle again. "You…you have a reason to look harder than they do. Besides, you will be compensated for your services."

Questions flew through Eramus's mind, but negotiating for answers would be a waste of time. The knight was very serious, regardless of his motivations, but Eramus couldn't understand why he felt compelled to involve himself in the fate of the missing children.

A temporary solution to the problem was simple. Sadir and his family were in danger and Eramus had to help them. Sir Jacob had taken great pains to demonstrate his conviction, but the lives of innocent people were in jeopardy because of Eramus alone.

The knight pointed at Kathryn and Raisa. "Bring them with us.

Inquiries by the magistrate are to be directed to me." Sir Jacob swiveled his cold gaze at Eramus. "I'm sending two of my agents to assist you. They'll be at the eastern wall two hours before sunrise. Follow my instructions or these three will die painfully." Sir Jacob nudged his horse away at a trot, and for the first time Eramus noticed the four foot long massive bastard sword sheathed in the saddle. Like Eramus, the knight hadn't even drawn his sword.

Eamon and his companion escorted Kathryn and Raisa from the house, while the two Filthies who had stoned Sadir untied him and carried his limp form after Sir Jacob. Eramus noticed the man's chest rising and falling with shallow breaths. He still lived. Kathryn wouldn't look at Eramus.

The Filthies holding him down carefully released him. The dagger which had been at his throat, his own dagger, severed his ropes before landing next to him, drops of his own blood staining the edge. The soldiers backpedaled, weapons drawn, as they left with the others.

Eramus stayed on his knees, inhaling deep, calming breaths. He wanted nothing more than to chase them all down, to murder every last man, but they would be ready for that. They would expect that. Moisture clouded his vision.

"We'll see to your friends," Eamon shouted over his shoulder with a chuckle.

Eramus sheathed his dagger without cleaning his blood off it and picked up his sword. He glared after Eamon, entertaining violent thoughts of slicing the grin off his face, but he recognized that the action would have consequences. He spared a last look at the post where Sadir had been tied. Stones, blood, and a mess of footprints surrounded it. He couldn't help but think of the day his father died.

Lightning flashed. Thunder boomed seconds later. The first drops of rain pattered on rooftops. Candlelight appeared in windows, people slowly recovering courage after the threat had passed. But this hadn't been the worst. The worst was yet to come. Ashamed, Eramus turned and left, his head throbbing with frustration, anger, and sadness. A man who brought such pain and suffering to others could not love himself.

CHAPTER 3

A pair of men approached the low, crumbling eastern wall. Even through distant lantern lights and biting rain, Eramus could see the taller of the two was lean and muscular with a pale, joyless expression, his sopping wet cloak frayed at the hem. A short sword hung in a makeshift case at his side. He looked out of place, as if he had been isolated for a while. His clothes and weapon didn't suit his appearance, as if he had gathered his possessions along the way.

Several years older and a few inches shorter, the other man wore black down to his boots, with the exception of something Eramus couldn't quite distinguish across his tunic. The man maintained a bearing of military discipline, chest out, shoulders back.

"Which one is Eramus Pon?" he asked over squishing steps in the mud. He wiped rain from his eyes with one gloved hand while the other hovered near the heavy mace on his belt.

"Every time I tell myself it's better for my health not to ride with you, we get into something even worse, prophuug,*"* Hadrius muttered under his breath. *"I can't keep doing this."*

Eramus had his own misgivings about working with strangers, especially those hand-picked by Sir Jacob, but blackmail was a powerful motivator.

"That's me," he said. He slid off the wall and stood to his full height, still inches shorter than the taller man.

"Who's that?" the man with the mace asked as he eyed Hadrius.

"Sir Jacob only mentioned one man."

"He comes with me," Eramus answered curtly while Hadrius cracked his knuckles. Just hearing the knight's name raised the hair on the back of his neck. "What difference does it make?"

"It's a complication," the man with the mace said as he sized Hadrius up. Apparently satisfied, he jerked his thumb back over his shoulder. "That's Gavrel and I'm Lebon."

"You work for Sir Jacob?" Eramus wondered.

"That's right," Lebon said. "We're under orders."

"You aren't being paid? You aren't mercenaries?" He had hoped these men wouldn't be affiliated with the knight, that this was just a job for them.

"Under orders. You speak Oshlema, eh?"

Eramus crossed his arms over his chest. It wasn't difficult to tell that these men were concealing the real reason for their involvement with the knight. "You're not Filthies but you have orders. Why is that?"

A frown fell over Lebon's face, and his feigned cordiality vanished. "Enough with the questions. We've got a job to do. Let's get it over with."

Gavrel stepped up beside him, pulled his hood back, and stared down at Eramus. A gruesome garrote scar poked out from the faded handkerchief around his neck and a jagged knife line puckered just beneath his left eye. His loosened cloak revealed a clump of skin between his neck and left shoulder, fleshy candle wax pinched together with bent fishing hooks.

Eramus had hoped for reasonable men. What sort of relationship did these two really have with Sir Jacob?

It didn't matter. Eramus had to work with them anyway. He promised himself he would make an effort to get along with them. "Fair enough." He turned to Hadrius. "You packed?"

"You're leaving tonight?" Lebon asked, surprised. He held his gloved hand out in the rain. "Better sense to leave in the morning. The rain could let up."

"Like you said, the faster we get this over with," Eramus said dismissively, "the better off we'll all be. Fewer people on the roads at night. Better way to travel. Faster, too. Where's your gear?"

Lebon tugged his gloves on a little tighter. "We travel light."

They made the short trek to the Courageous Prince. Despite the late hour patrons mingled on the porch. The indigo and white bird waited for Eramus, paced along the roof's edge. He tried his best to ignore it. He glanced back, finally able to make out the Oshlemin evergreen stitched across the front of Lebon's tunic, a fox head over a slanted dagger covering his left breast, the Haulken coat of arms. These were Duke Moritare's men.

"Do you at least have horses?" he asked Lebon, taking the new information in stride. "Something to carry supplies, spare clothing, your gear, water?" Lebon had been observing the bird with more than passing interest. He shook his head. Hadrius wordlessly strolled inside, leaving them to soak up rain. Locals pointed at Lebon's uniform, laughing, taunting him with "*shlem.*" Gavrel flipped his hood over his head, his face retreating into the safety of anonymity. So far he hadn't said a word.

"You'll need horses," Eramus said over the insults.

"We'll get horses," Lebon said as he stared back at the antagonists. He shivered in the cold rain. Gavrel hardly seemed bothered by ridicule or weather. He stood disinterested, as if waiting for an attack before he considered the men as a threat.

"Is he mute?" Eramus asked.

"He can talk," Lebon replied, answering for him.

"Just get some horses," Eramus said. He forced his way through the belligerent men and into the inn, shaking water out of his hair along the way. With any luck the men on the porch would chase the knight's agents away.

Water pooled under the table Hadrius and Sylvia occupied. She closed her mouth into a tight line when Eramus joined them. She and Hadrius grew closer by the minute, and Eramus didn't need his friend distracted at a time like this.

"Ready?" Hadrius asked, glancing out of the corner of his eye. He took a swallow of his drink and set the wooden *glistas* cup on the tabletop.

"Everything's in my room," Sylvia said. She ran her fingers through her fiery red hair. "And I loaded up on a week and a half's trail rations for four, like you asked."

Eramus nodded. "Thanks." He pointed at a mug with brown liquid in a sea of empties. "Cider?"

She handed it to him with warm fingers. He lost himself in endless green eyes until she averted her embarrassed gaze. He drank down bland cider, understanding his friend's physical attraction to the woman.

"I want to come along," she said.

"Really? In what capacity? How do you think you can help us?"

She leaned in, lowered her voice. "I spent three months on the border." She pulled back the top of her jerkin to expose a set of nasty scars under her collarbone and a line of indented flesh. "I went into the swamps, got caught in a snare. I was the only member of my company to make it out alive."

"You're a merc?" Eramus asked, impressed. Not very many people could boast about surviving a Dawn Hunter trap. He concealed his newfound respect for her. The baron still supplied troops to the Glesk side. The people of the barony wouldn't take kindly to a woman who might have killed their sons or husbands, and it was possible that the two men they would be traveling with had fought up there as well. Revealing this part of her past placed Sylvia in immediate danger, and also showed intimate trust on her part. He examined the lean cut of her muscles and the dagger handles jutting out of her brace. She carried herself with a warrior's confidence.

"My father told me there's no shame in earning an honest living."

"This isn't battle. We're not looking for a fight. We're going to be smart and quiet about all of this."

"Money's money," she shrugged. "I'll take a share if there is one."

"I'm not promising anything," Eramus said. He had asked Hadrius to lie to her about who had commissioned the job. As far as she knew, the baron had hired them through independent sources. "Do you speak any Medarn? We may need a translator if we run into patrols."

She self-consciously hid her disfigured finger under the table, an absentminded tell that what she said next wasn't the complete truth. "A little." Hadrius drummed his fingers on the tabletop, distracting her.

"Got your own horse?" Eramus asked.

She nodded.

"I need to talk to him," Eramus said, nodding at Hadrius, who tapped more insistently now.

Sylvia rolled her tongue around in her mouth and stood up. Hadrius playfully swatted her rear end before she sauntered to the bar.

"There's nothing to talk about," Hadrius said. *"We agreed to work for ourselves but now you're a* duba.*"* He knocked mugs onto the floor. *"She's with us or I'm not. I need someone reliable with me."*

The remark stung Eramus, who still struggled with guilt over what had happened to Sadir and his family. *"She's a mercenary who isn't concerned about money?"*

"Now I know two."

"We left Uuslef to make our fortune. We made that choice. Do you regret it?"

"We're supposed to be taking manageable work. Bodyguard work. Village protection. Even the occasional kidnap recovery if the money's right. "

"Then treat this like a kidnapping. Forget about me being blackmailed."

"But it's not just a kidnapping. You agreed to work for a knight. This is how you end up hanged. Somebody's bound to burn me alive just for being a part of this, and I still haven't heard anything about how much I stand to earn."

"I can't abandon Sadir. You know that."

Hadrius reassuringly squeezed his shoulder. *"If I don't stick by you, you'll never make it to Second Awakening."* He sighed. *"But this is the last time. This is the last job. I'm tired of hurting people. I'm tired of being punched and cut and threatened all the time."*

They shared a moment of silent understanding, friends bound by a common past and the experiences they had shared. The support Hadrius offered at a time like this was worth more than anything. Eramus didn't know if his friend was upset or truly intended to follow through on his words.

"What is she to you, seriously?" Eramus asked as he pointed his chin in Sylvia's direction. He had already been impressed with her actions in the short time he had known her. She had proven to be quick, subtle, and reliable.

Hadrius finished his *glistas* and tossed the cup onto the floor with the others, much to the barkeep's chagrin. He flexed, shrugged. Water beaded in his braids. He tugged some of them loose. "*A headache. Something to touch. I don't know yet. She was on the way to Keltivar to see her sister, but when I told her about this she wanted to come along. Things work out, we can go to Keltivar together when this is over.*"

Eramus needed a straight answer. "*It's not like you to plan anything with a woman. Is she going to have a problem taking orders? Those men outside might cause trouble if they find out she fought on the other side. You need to tell her to tone it down. Is she going to get in your way?*"

"*No more than an imbecilic* prophuug. *We'll get the horses and supplies and meet you out front.*" When he joined Sylvia at the bar, she smiled and kissed him on the cheek. They headed to her room, her fiddling with his braids, though her eyes watched Eramus. Barely contained excitement lingered on her face, and he pitied her. She didn't know about Hadrius's whimsical history with women like he did. She seemed to think that her time with Hadrius would bring them closer, but he would quickly tire of her and would leave her angry and hurt. Eramus had seen it too often.

But he couldn't think about that right now. He hoped the worst of this terrible situation was over. He intended to put as much distance as he could between himself and Sir Jacob once he found the children. The knight's reputation as a murderer didn't leave much room for interpretation. What still baffled Eramus, though, was why the knight had insisted that he undertake the mission when so many Filthies were at his disposal.

Just trying to organize any semblance of thought hurt Eramus's head, and Hadrius's second-guessing didn't help. He knew this wasn't the smartest choice he had ever made, but he was making it for someone else's benefit.

He glanced around the inn on his way out, one of his self-taught habits. To his surprise, the woman who had fled from the Filthies, the catalyst for his current troubles, sat at the far end of the bar. At least she was safe. He had never heard her accused of a crime, but he had nevertheless chosen to involve himself, and she had indirectly led him to his father's killer. She waved him over.

"What do you want?" he asked. Dim lighting swirled through her jet black hair and indigo eyes. A loose shirt exposed colorful lumps and bruises along her smooth arms. Her ragged travelling cloak was draped over her pack, and it looked as if she had been nursing the drink in front of her for a while.

"Thank you for standing up for me," she said, jarring him back to the moment. "But I'm not interested."

"What?"

"I overheard you talking. You're going somewhere. I don't want to go, but I wanted to thank you for helping me. Thank you." She looked lonely, weary, as if always on guard, unable to trust anyone. She couldn't hide her emotions from someone like him, someone who felt the same way, who had lived that life during his time in the Information Regiment, who still lived it to some extent. "I don't want to go."

"I didn't ask you," Eramus said. "Conditions will be...harsh." He glanced at the other side of the room to where he had been sitting. "You heard us?" She couldn't have understood the Uuslefin portion of the conversation. When she didn't answer, he asked her name.

She took some time before answering. "Alina."

"That's a nice name. My name's Eramus."

"I know."

"Are you in trouble, Alina?"

She shook her head until he believed her.

"Those soldiers are still out there. They won't forget you."

Her eyes flicked toward the door. "They won't find me. I'm leaving at first light."

She seemed so vulnerable, like she needed to trust someone, like she needed conversation and a little laughter. He wanted to join her, to order warm cider and a couple of bowls of stew. He wanted to be a friend to someone who needed one.

"Watch out for yourself," he said. She looked disappointed as he turned to go. He left her at the bar, wondering why even more guilt gnawed at his gut. Was it because she reminded him of Riya? He suppressed the urge to turn around, to try to convince her to join them.

When he stepped outside the inn he could hear rain beating against the porch's overhang. Gavrel and Lebon waited in the cold and wet astride saddled horses. Patrons leaned over the railing and taunted them, but none mustered the courage to attack. Eramus looked back at the roof. The bird had gone.

"Can we leave?" Gavrel asked in a throaty whisper, his hood

concealing his face. Veins on his forearms bulged as he wrapped his reins tighter and tighter around his hands. An unfamiliar animal skull tattoo stood out on his left forearm.

"Shortly."

Hadrius and Sylvia walked their horses, saddled and loaded with supplies, around the side of the inn. Eramus swung up onto his mare's strong back, the weight of the long day sinking into his bones as he thought about sleep. He pulled his hood over his head to stay dry.

Lebon erupted into a coughing fit. He shivered, huddled in his saddle. "I suppose she's coming with us," he said in Sylvia's direction.

"Yes," Hadrius replied.

"She's my translator," Eramus added.

"I've been listening to gossip," Sylvia asserted herself. She peered into the shadows of Gavrel's hood for a better look at him. "Patrols are riding back and forth from the watchtower."

"East," Lebon said. "Straight down Hereton Road."

"Fine," Eramus said, steering his horse away from the inn. "East it is." The only scrap of information they had about the kidnappers was that they were supposedly Seehlan, and no refugee in his right mind would take a baron's children back into Oshlem.

The party rode single file past the crumbling wall until they arrived at the lanterns of the eastern gate. Despite the late hour, heightened security attributed to the kidnapping prolonged even the most perfunctory searches, though Eramus didn't see the point. Kidnappers could have easily snuck the children past the gate before they were reported missing.

When it was his turn to open his saddlebags, he saw to it that a bit of silver ended up in the guard's hand to ease their egress. He spared one last glance over his shoulder, thinking about Trixie. She would wait for him, at least for a little while. He should have found her, told her, but it would be easier for him this way. She wouldn't understand at first. She would leave, would spare him the trouble of ruining things for himself. He knew any sliver of happiness he found wouldn't last. It never did.

And yet his stomach tightened when he thought of how she would react to his absence. He was a fool. He had barely exchanged a few sentences with the woman, and already he assumed that he meant something to her.

Hadrius led them away from the sizzling braziers and torches on the ramparts, down Hereton Road until it intersected with the Lestwine. Scattered patrols and the weapons men carried were the law out here. Eramus returned his attention to the present.

"North is the best option now," Gavrel said at the crossroads. He pointed east. "The militia would have already checked the Hereton." Weak lights glittered in the distance, torches on the eastern watchtower.

"Kidnappers wouldn't be dumb enough to go north," Sylvia said, shaking her head. "They couldn't have gotten children like that into Keltivar."

"We're not sure who took them," Lebon said as he patted his damp forehead with the hem of his cloak. "What if a man and a woman pretended to be their parents? Then north is just as probable as east. I would even be more inclined to say north because watchtower guards would recognize the children. Seehlan can still apply for asylum in Keltivar. They would have taken their chances there."

Sylvia stubbornly shook her head. "They didn't go north."

Lebon threw his hands up in frustration. "How do you know? Are you one of the kidnappers?"

"The truth as we know it is that Seehlan kidnapped the children," Gavrel said. "They're free to travel either road. Militia might spot the children, but Baron Kent's leniency permits refugee passage." He viciously scratched the heavy scarring along his neck.

Hadrius trotted into the grass a ways, in the northeastern direction of the heavily forested base of the Coronal Range splitting their choices. Heavy clouds and rain obscured moonlight and starlight, revealing little more than an enormous, distant mass of silhouettes and degrees of darkness. "If I needed to hide, I might go that way."

"The Coronals pose too great a risk," Lebon said. "Even for kidnappers." Thick evergreens surrounded the mountains. Horseback travel would be difficult, if not impossible, which steered Eramus to Hadrius's line of thinking.

"Pilgrims used to brave these mountains all the time," Sylvia said. "So don't say it can't be done."

"Yeah, and how many of those pilgrims died along the way?" Lebon snapped. It was rumored that the lake containing the world's first rainfall resided somewhere deep in the mountains, and that to drink from it would grant immortality. Every few years, pilgrims mustered the courage to quest for it. Many died along the way, and those who survived returned emptyhanded.

"Do you think you can find anything?" Eramus asked Hadrius while the others argued. He tried his best to pretend that he and his friend were alone on the mission.

Hadrius nodded. *"Rain's washing everything away, though. I'll need daylight for a good look. I've heard there are plenty of passes and highlands along the range. Anybody could hide if they made it far enough."*

"Fine," Eramus said to everyone, pointing out a stand of rocks encircling a clearing less than one hundred yards off the road. "We'll camp there until the rain lets up, then see if we can find anything at the bottom of the mountains."

"Camp…wh…" Lebon sputtered. He spread his arms to either side, catching more rain. "The militia would have searched in those trees. We gain nothing by going in there. Let's go back and have a few drinks, maybe something hot to eat until it's dry out here."

"The watchtower's half a day's ride as the crow flies," Sylvia argued. "We could ride that way and ask about new information."

"And subject ourselves to suspicion? Not a very good idea, even for a translator."

"I mean that in the interest of casual gossip. I'm not as—"

"We can't spare the time," Eramus interrupted. The rough terrain of the Coronals trumped the hangman's noose. He thought like a kidnapper, asked himself how he would behave given similar conditions. His backward questions only led to one: how had refugees gotten close enough to the children to steal them away in the first place?

He guided his mount onto the bare, packed earth inside the rocky ring off the road and took immediate note of a well-used fire pit. "Don't unpack. Keep your eyes on the road."

The natural enclosure of surrounding rocks diverted the occasional gale but failed to prevent the deluge from soaking them. They tethered their horses while Lebon slogged through the muck, scanning the ground for anything to burn. The last people to stop here had stored a small amount of firewood inside the cover of the rocks. "We should be drinking by a fire. We don't even have shelter."

"This should help if you think you can start a fire in the rain," Hadrius said, handing a tinderbox to him. He produced a small clay jug from his saddlebags next. "As for the drinking, I'll be taking care of that."

Backs against the rocks, hoods pinched over their faces, they all watched Lebon huddle over a bundle of jute tinder, striking flint with the dull edge of Gavrel's short sword. Eramus, too wet to care, wondered about a motive for the kidnapping with Lebon's huffing and cursing in the background. The Seehlan believed in the Seehli, the mother who had birthed them all. She lit a beacon fire for her people, one invisible to this world. The ashes and smoke of the fire supposedly trickled into the sky and formed clouds the Seehlan priests had spent generations interpreting. Why would people like these ever want to kidnap children?

Eramus had worked kidnappings before, and had learned that kidnappers could be from any walk of life. Ransom wasn't the only reason for hostages. Unfortunately an attempt at political leverage by the kidnappers could lead Eramus and the others to dead children. No matter how convincing his story, Eramus would likely face charges if he delivered the bodies to the authorities. Maybe Sir Jacob had already thought ahead, and had sent Eramus in the event that anything untoward had occurred. Hadrius had already mentioned that a job like this could only end badly. Eramus's best option was the safe return of the children to their parents, not to Sir Jacob, who would gain favor from their rescue. Then again, Eramus would make a dangerous enemy if he tried to double-cross the knight.

Sylvia leaned against Hadrius, snuggling under his cloak. They giggled and whispered in the manner of irritating new lovers while they shared the jug.

Lebon shouted in victory as a spark skittered off the short sword and caught the tinder. He shielded the tiny, spitting flame and gently blew into the smoke until it ignited in the dry moss he had found growing under the rocks. He shoved the weak fire under dead branches, leaving it to the rain's mercy, and returned the tinderbox to Hadrius.

"Are you related?" Sylvia asked as she handed the jug over to Lebon, who licked his lips in anticipation.

Gavrel ignored her. His half shut eyes and grinding teeth indicated that he suffered in some way.

"We have the same father," Lebon sighed after a swig. "My mother died in childbirth. My father remarried and had him with the new wife." He offered the jug to Gavrel, who ignored him as well.

"Half brothers," Sylvia smiled. "It's good that you can be together. I have a sister and I hardly see her anymore." Sadness passed over her face. She curled up closer to Hadrius and closed her eyes. He wrapped his giant arm around her. The warmth of the fire soon eased everyone to sleep.

"Sit there and do not move," his father says. Eramus can barely contain the rage in his trembling body. He wants to hit something, to release his anger. Sitting still is near impossible.

"For how long?"

"Until I say so."

Eramus opened his eyes. It had been a long time since he remembered his father calming him down, stifling his reactive emotions.

By the time dawn's first light spilled gray around the Coronal Range, the rain had stopped and dark blue ebb stars had patterned the sky like a twinkling mosaic. The fire had dwindled to a smoking mound of ash. Hadrius slipped free of Sylvia and stood up, his bones popping and creaking. Without a word, he leapt onto his horse and galloped toward the mountains.

"He shouldn't go alone," Lebon said while he wrung out his damp cloak.

Sylvia, disoriented with sleep, sat up and watched as Hadrius grew smaller and smaller the closer he got to the mountains. Eramus sensed that even this short separation bothered her. Then she stiffened, shielded her eyes with her hand, her gaze straying east into the sunrise. "Patrol," she warned. "Three of them. Two are militia."

Gavrel squinted at the riders coming hard and fast. Nobody moved too quickly, but they all checked weapon accessibility before settling into innocuous positions, Lebon cursing under his breath at something.

Eramus watched Hadrius vanish into the forest. The patrol couldn't have spotted him. A disturbed bird flapped up from the treetops. *Roua.* The indigo and white form fluttered back down onto higher boughs.

Hooves pounded mud, louder and louder as the patrol closed in. Gavrel crouched beside the remnants of the fire and hid his face in the depths of his hood. Eramus tried to shake the indelible image of the bird out of his head.

"*Toh,*" a thick-bearded Medarn rider said as he slowed and circled the rocky campsite, his horse's snorting visible in the cold, steam rising from its sweaty flanks. The other rider sported a long mustache. He rested his loaded crossbow across his forearm. The third member of the patrol, a disreputable-looking local, wore his long flowing hair to the side. Bags under his eyes indicated sleeplessness. Dry cloaks and shirts meant they had come from the watchtower.

"*Toh.*" Eramus said with his wave, wishing they would use Oshlema so he didn't have to feel like an idiot first thing in the morning. Recent events had already disturbed him. He needed to forget them for now, and to concentrate on the present.

The man with the crossbow held steady aim, waiting for a mistake. He regarded all of them in turn, his attention settling on Gavrel's conspicuous attempt at anonymity. The local, obviously a guest on the patrol, feigned interest.

"*Se dupi koray*?" the bearded one asked. He inhaled the damp morning air through flaring nostrils, the interrogation no more than routine on his part.

Eramus studied the cadence of the question. The words he could understand hadn't reconciled with Carden's hinted rhythm. Fortunately he remembered Carden asking exactly the same question, and he recalled enough of the context to place its meaning. They wanted a reason for Eramus and the others to be out here. This same simple question had led to Carden's death. The more Eramus recalled the jobah's integrity, the angrier he became. Carden had been a decent man.

Lebon looked to Sylvia to answer the patrol, still believing her to be their translator.

"Uh…" Sylvia mumbled, fumbling for an appropriate response. Eramus let her grasp for words, knowing he wouldn't do any better. He wished the patrol had passed them. If these men saw Hadrius there would only be more questions.

Finally Lebon cleared his throat. "*Poh demmin Medarn, perran demyost,*" he said in the general direction of the watchtower. *Yost* meant east. He might have told them they were going to the watchtower. If Eramus didn't make time to learn the damn language it could end up costing him his life one day.

"*Medarnep woodah,*" the man with the crossbow said. He slid off his horse and aggressively drew down on Gavrel, who tensed at his approach. The local licked his lips in anticipation. Eramus cautiously stepped backwards, raising his hands in a gesture of cooperation. He had witnessed a crossbow bolt shredding open a man's stomach before. None of them would survive at close range, even with light armor. Their only advantage was numbers. The crossbow could fire one shot and took a while to reload. The man on horseback wore a longsword. Suddenly Eramus wasn't so sure about their odds against the patrol. A mounted man with steel reach tilted the advantage in the patrol's favor.

"What did he say?" Eramus asked Lebon out of the side of his mouth.

"That my Medarn is for snakes." His tone lowered. "Watch the third man for me."

"Show us your face!" the local barked in Oshlema, startling everyone. Crossbow lined up a yard from Gavrel. He couldn't miss at that distance. Eramus held his breath, expecting the heavy click of the shot at any second.

Longsword picked something out of his teeth and tossed it aside, but Eramus didn't let the casual manner fool him.

"Let him see your face," Eramus snapped. The patrol's attention had already cost them time, and the situation was quickly escalating.

Very slowly Gavrel exposed his irritated face. Crossbow immediately recognized him. The local leered with excitement, stroking his chin as if he had discovered a chest of gold.

"*O shun fen,*" Crossbow said.

"Uh oh," Sylvia whispered. "Why would they know him?"

"Explain yourself," Longsword growled at Gavrel.

Lebon stepped into Crossbow's line of fire, his cheeks rosy with blood. "We're under orders from Sir Jacob. You can take it up with him. I'm escorting this man to the Duchy of Haulken." Slowly, deliberately, he produced a folded document that reminded Eramus of the IR messages he used to carry. Crossbow snatched it with his free hand and gave it to Longsword, who opened and read it.

The local leaned over for a look. "It's official," he added. He turned to Lebon. "You're going to drag this scum all the way back to Lord Moritare?"

Lebon flashed Eramus a warning glance before he nodded acknowledgement. The Duchy of Haulken lay to the northwest and they were facing east. The patrol must have assumed they passed through from the east a day before.

It occurred to Eramus that he could turn Gavrel and Lebon over to these men and be rid of them. The patrol clearly wanted to arrest Gavrel, for what Eramus had no idea. The broad label of "scum" could have meant anything. He thought ahead, considered consequences for Hadrius's sake. The militia arrested them. What next? Sir Jacob would find out. Harsh consequences would follow. It wasn't worth the risk.

"It's the truth," Eramus said. "We're all together. The rest of us are being paid."

"Shut up," Crossbow ordered. He looked to Longsword. "*Se curin leost?*"

Longsword picked something else out of his teeth. "*Fram gen.*" He sniffed in disgust at the local, disrespectfully flicking the document at him. The local flinched, subsequently recovered enough to review what might have been the knight's orders.

Apparently *fram* meant search in Medarn. The party submitted to a thorough inspection. The patrol didn't steal their money or weapons like Filthies would have, but they did keep the document. When Crossbow and Longsword had satisfied their curiosity, they rode to the barony without another word. The local followed them, glancing back at Gavrel more than once.

"Why the interest in you?" Eramus asked.

"Nothing you need to know," Gavrel said.

"They obviously knew you," Sylvia argued. "Why didn't they arrest you? What did that letter say?"

"Shut it."

"They just don't like him," Lebon said. "Leave it alone."

"I don't like him either," Sylvia muttered.

"Why didn't you ask to have the letter back?" Eramus asked. "We might need it if he's a wanted man."

Lebon scratched his nose. "Letting them maintain their authority keeps him from being arrested."

"Arrested? Arrested for what? You obviously knew that man with them. Give me a reason why I lied for you."

"I didn't know that man, but I know his type. Besides, I didn't ask you to lie. What difference does it make anyway? We'll be gone soon enough. They won't remember you."

Eramus pointed accusingly at Gavrel. "They remembered him, didn't they?" When nobody answered, Eramus stormed off into the wet grass. He needed distance before he lost his temper. He didn't like surprises that put him at risk.

The patrol had dwindled to specks by the time Hadrius returned. Eramus met his friend away from the others. Hadrius read the anger on him.

"What's wrong?"

"I'll tell you later. What did you find?"

"Prints going into the mountains, children's among them. Runoff got through in several places but they're still visible. I had to go in a ways."

Eramus scratched the stubble on his chin. *"They could be anyone's tracks. Maybe a hunter and his boy. There are a lot of young volunteers out right now."*

"Doubtful. Patrols have been out. They're watching the checkpoints. Nobody's pushing into the mountains. It's too much trouble, and I haven't heard about any recent pilgrimages." Hadrius's eyes flashed at someone's approach.

Eramus switched to Oshlema when he noticed Sylvia's red hair in his peripheral vision. "I wonder if anyone was even kidnapped. Did you wonder that, too? I mean, people are talking about it but it could just be a rumor."

"I considered it," Hadrius said. "But there's more. I'll show you when we're there. Something happened recently."

Sylvia gravitated to Hadrius's excited horse and soothed it with gentle words. "I heard a lot about the kidnapping everywhere I went. It's real."

"Your Medarn isn't good," Eramus said. "Besides, it's only gossip."

Hadrius nodded at the mountains. "*I say we go that way.*"

Sylvia bristled at her exclusion from the conversation.

"*A patrol visited us while you were gone,*" Eramus said. "*They recognized one of our friends.*"

"*The shorter one?*" Hadrius asked, avoiding names.

Eramus shook his head. "*The other one. They wanted to arrest him for something.*"

"*Why didn't they?*"

"*His brother had a letter. They took it. And then he lied about what we're doing.*"

When they reached the campsite, Gavrel was monitoring the riders on their way into the barony.

"Well?" Lebon asked.

"Well what?" Eramus snapped. "Now *you* want information?" He sighed, knowing his anger wouldn't do much for cooperation. "Children's footprints. That's our best lead. If the patrols have already searched the roads, we won't find anything new at the checkpoints."

"Agreed," Gavrel said. "Let's get moving. The kidnappers have a head start." He threw his saddle onto his horse, stopping before he completely buckled it to furiously scratch at his scar tissue.

With Gavrel's support and the tracks Hadrius had found, it was much easier to convince Lebon to begin their search in the mountains.

They rode across the open field and walked the horses once they reached the trees. Incredibly tall and wide, the first thirty or forty feet relatively steep and smooth, the Coronals loomed before them.

"The horses will be fine here," Hadrius said as he led his mare into the scattered shadows of the woods. Sharp scents of pine needles and sap hung heavy in the close air. They steered the horses into a natural corral near a carpet of healthy groundcover, piled their saddles and blankets under an enormous evergreen, and broke their fast with salted pork and bread. Eramus grimaced as he swallowed the bread and tore off another bite. He couldn't stand rye, and this was full of it. He stopped in mid chew and spit out the rest. This was the result of delegating supply responsibilities to Sylvia.

"*Show me,*" Eramus said to Hadrius while the others ate. He followed his friend to dried blood spattered on flattened ferns and bushes, one of which had been scorched to its roots. Hadrius pointed out a crossbow bolt lodged into tree bark and turquoise beads trampled into the mud. Filthies.

Eramus squatted for a closer look. *"Can you make sense of this?"*

"Maybe they found the kidnappers. I count nine different sets of prints, not including the children's, some of them barefoot. Rain washed most of it away. There might be something to this kidnapping after all."

"And the fire?"

"Looks like magic maybe. I can't see any place it started."

Eramus cursed. *"This makes everything that much more complicated. Sir Jacob had to have known about this."*

They rejoined the others.

"Now we go up," Eramus said. He threw his bedroll over his shoulder.

"What about the horses?" Lebon asked. He craned his neck to find a suitable way up the mountains.

"What about them? Stay and pet them. I don't care. We go up. If you're coming with us, get your things."

Lebon rolled his eyes. "I only asked about the horses. I happen to like mine. He's a good listener. I'm assuming you discovered something worthwhile?" he asked as he made a show of tapping the spikes on his giant mace. Hardly anyone outside armed services carried bludgeoning weapons quite like his.

"Just tracks," Eramus lied.

As the sun rose higher and higher among the ebb stars, it spilled golden light around the mountains and throughout the deepest shadows. Eramus scanned the canopy. The bird had fled. He closed his eyes, wishing he could see what it saw. A bird's eye view would be an incredible advantage in terrain like this. He exhaled and opened his eyes.

Lebon tightened his belt in preparation for the climb. "Keep alert. Anyone living up there hides for a reason."

"Worried about pilgrims?" Sylvia joked.

"Maybe," he replied with a wink.

A zigzag, nearly vertical furrow hacked through brush appeared to be the only clear way up the first thirty feet. They hoisted one another up in precarious spots, wrapping their hands in thick ivy strands for support, leveraging themselves in rocky footholds.

Eramus assumed the worst was over after they scaled the base, but it only opened onto a steep grade. They were forced to negotiate fallen trees, animal burrows, and slick piles of leaves and pine needles at every turn on their way up the tree-covered mountainside. Eventually they reached the incline's summit and paused, winded, to look down through a natural gap in the evergreens at the Hereton Road far below. Only Hadrius, who had been tracking, hunting, and climbing his entire life, wasn't out of breath.

"This is an excellent position," Gavrel said, awkwardly shifting his shoulders for a better view. "You can see who's coming for a long time, and they'll be tired when they get here."

Hadrius spread his fingers in the dirt. "Good call. Someone spent the night."

"How long ago?" Lebon asked. He leaned over Hadrius, his shadow blotting traces of wet ash and fingernail clippings.

Hadrius glared until he took a step back. "Maybe four days. Rain distorts accuracy." He pointed up at the canopy, which scattered daylight into dappled patches. "And the sunlight that gets through and dries the moisture isn't consistent."

"We need to keep moving," Eramus said. Broken tracks ascended the mountain. Stopping to examine every minute detail along the way would only cost them more time.

"*There are at least three different groups,*" Hadrius said when the sparse, rocky inclines they had been tripping over leveled out. The ground had become much firmer beneath their feet the higher they climbed. Eramus and Hadrius let the others pass them.

"*The same as below?*" Eramus asked.

"*Maybe. I would guess Filthies had the fire. Only they would leave a mess. They came after the first group.*"

"*Chasing them?*"

"*Most likely.*" He pressed down on a unique footprint. "*This is heavier at the toes. Someone in the first group has a custom boot for an uneven right leg. Makes it easier to distinguish his tracks.*" He ran his fingers over small circles. "*Walking stick.*" His hand spread apart. "*The second group was barefoot. Looks like three people.*"

"*Pilgrims?*"

"We won't know until we catch up to them."

Sylvia walked back down to them. Eramus nodded greeting to her, and she dipped her head in response.

"And what about the third group?" he asked Hadrius, who was oblivious to the woman's pining.

"They came later. Four men, fresher tracks." He pointed out individual prints. *"They doubled back, too."*

"That's a lot of people."

Hadrius brushed off his hands and draped his arm over Sylvia's shoulder until they caught up to Gavrel and Lebon. Easygoing terrain stretched for hours. The trees thinned to a scattering of hardier conifers like spruce and pine. Hadrius set a grueling pace, often jogging uphill. The sun had already begun to drop on their left, lighting the entire side of the mountain in golden, dazzling fashion.

Older than the others and clearly out of shape, Lebon panted through a mask of dripping sweat, shielding his face against the sunlight with his hand. He stopped to lean on his thighs and to catch his breath more than once, but never complained.

Trees gave way to hard dirt, rocks, and tenacious pink bunches of creeping phlox the higher they climbed. Even Eramus soon struggled to breathe the thin air. He maintained trust in Hadrius to read the landscape and keep them all moving.

The countryside of the barony stretched out for miles below them. Sylvia pointed out the eastern watchtower, a blurry smear of color with tiny specks populating the Hereton Road between it and the barony, a sprawl of buildings within farming plots.

"It's certainly different from up here," Eramus commented as he gazed at the *glis* orchards and their neatly separated rows of thin trees. "Disconnected." He reveled in the thrill of the altitude, at his separation from the majority of men and their problems, even if his own problems still weighed heavily on his mind. From up here, he felt as if he could face everything, and not just his immediate concerns. For the first time in a long time, he missed Uuslef. He promised himself he would return one day to walk through the house his mother and father had shared when he was young. Right now he wasn't ready to face his uncle, to see the echoes of his father's memory in the other man.

"I see people down there," Sylvia said, pointing out movement far below them. Twice already she had proven the benefit of her exceptional eyesight. Eramus counted five bodies, and he really only distinguished their movement. They resembled nothing more than insects from this height.

"Wouldn't have been too hard to follow us," Lebon grumbled as he wiped sweat from his eyes. "One, two…"

"I have five," Eramus said. "Could be they found our horses. No reason for them to come after us, though."

Gavrel shook his head in a tight motion. "Seven men. Two in the trees."

"Are you sure?" Hadrius asked, glancing back to Sylvia for confirmation. She shrugged. He squinted below until another pair of men appeared. "You're right."

"Well," Lebon panted. "We didn't hide our tracks. If they keep on the main trail they'll get to us eventually."

Their pursuers, and that's how Eramus decided to assess them until he could prove otherwise, certainly complicated the mission. Eramus recalled how interested the local with the patrol had been in Gavrel's presence. He could have informed others, and any halfway decent tracker would have been able to determine their direction from the campsite.

"Whoever they are," Sylvia said. "They're moving quickly. We should go."

They resumed hiking as the trail broke left and ran alongside a ridge. With the protection of the mountain now to their right, none of them discussed the strangers. Exhaustion finally set in and they all agreed to stop and rest.

Lebon sat against a thick bush and closed his eyes. "I haven't marched this much since drills."

Hadrius chomped down on an apple he had picked along the way. After a couple of bites he handed it to Sylvia, who eagerly devoured the rest of it.

"I'm still finding both groups," Hadrius said to Eramus.

"The children, too?"

"Sure, but there's a lot more foot traffic up here now."

"Any chance we'll overtake them?"

Hadrius shook his head. *"They're days ahead of us."*

Mentally and physically tired, Eramus sighed. *"And how's this new companion of yours?"*

"Any woman willing to come along on a job like this is worth getting to know. She already offered us a place to sleep at her sister's. I'll probably stay there for a while after the festival."

Lebon opened one eye in irritation. "Anything the rest of us need to know?"

"I could ask you the same question," Eramus retorted.

Hadrius accepted a waterskin Sylvia offered and took a few swallows before giving it back. "Pilgrims have been known to come this way," he said, shifting the facts.

Gavrel scratched his neck. "Seehlan kidnapped the children and dragged them up here to slip past the patrols." He peered down the side of the mountain, breathing quickly while he dealt with some sort of pain. Eramus was fairly certain that Gavrel had an idea about who was after them. Soon enough the man's problems were going to become everyone else's, too.

They walked on a while longer, until dusk blurred shapes and the top of the sun sank in the west. Sylvia plopped down on her rear, yanked off her boots, and wiggled her toes.

Indigo sleep stars burned in the night sky, sharper and clearer following the rain. Cold crept over them, but they had the ridge at their back.

"We need to be ready for anything," Gavrel said. He and Lebon spread out their bedrolls.

"What do you mean by anything?" Eramus asked. "If you know something…"

"What do you think I know? Men are on their way up. What else do I need to know?"

"What do you think, prophuug?" Hadrius asked as he firmly gripped Eramus's upper arm and led him aside. *"I wouldn't come up here unless I had to."*

"It is what it is," Eramus said. He looked over at Gavrel, who had already struck up a new conversation with Lebon.

Eramus volunteered for first watch. The journey up the mountain had been exhausting, but his thoughts were still racing. He headed down the trail several yards, his eyes gradually adjusting to the darkness. He concentrated on immobile shapes to measure movement. His feet ached up to his back but if he sat down he wouldn't get back up.

The realization that he had been awake for almost two days

suddenly struck him. He paced around, hummed to himself, and wondered if he had made the right decision to hunt down the kidnappers. When it got colder he tucked his hands inside his cloak. When it got colder than that he slipped on his old gloves and pulled his hood over his head. He almost jumped out of his boots when Sylvia relieved him.

"Anything out there?" she giggled, her breath visible in the cold air, her hair noticeably red even in the strong indigo starlight. He was getting used to her, maybe even admiring her little arguments with Lebon.

"Nothing but sleep stars."

"Yeah, but we're still awake" she said, staring up in awe. "I love looking at them on a clear night. I've never seen them from this high up. *Kreest demafen.*"

"What does that mean?"

"It means 'the stars above you'. It's part of a Medarn poem my sister taught me. I can't wait to see her. It's been almost a year. That's the longest we've ever been apart."

"You actually do know some Medarn," he chuckled as he pointed up at a sequence of five stars leading to a larger, twinkling one. "Do you know what that is? That line?"

She shook her head.

He dragged his finger across the stars, stopping at each one in turn to identify it, stressing the Brothers, Felv and Loxias. "You're Hamaln, right?"

"Yes. Do you know that's the first time I've seen you smile? You have a nice smile." She gazed up at the stars with newfound admiration. "Who taught you about all of that?"

"My father," he said, clearing his throat when his voice caught.

His father crouches in the grass, pointing up at glittering indigo lights against a velvety black background. An insect lands on Eramus's arm. He tries to ignore it.

"You must know all of them to truly understand First Awakening," Loghemit says. "The good and the bad, even events you cannot control."

A pinch. The insect has bitten or stung Eramus on his left forearm. He can't tell which. His patience gets him nothing but a slight swelling that will itch. If this is only one example of what life has to offer, the stars hold no value for him. Six stars barely noticeable among thousands more.

On the porch, long hair lifting slightly in the breeze, hollow cheeks forced into a smile, hands twitching, thoughts clearly elsewhere, Eramus's mother watches both of them. He hasn't seen her for three days until tonight. His father wouldn't tell him where she had been. She waves. A daisy rests in the space between her hair and ear. He longs for the affectionate hugs and kisses she used to give him after a day of playing, misses her laughter when his father tickles her. This is Eramus's last memory of Vina Pon.

Sylvia smiled at him. "You love your father a lot. I can tell. Do you see him often?"

"No. He's dead." *He was a coward.*

"That's awful," she said as her smile vanished. Brilliant indigo starlight drowned the green in her eyes, mesmerizing him until he forced himself to look away. *Avoid eye contact.* "My father left to campaign in the east when I was just a girl. He's very successful from what I hear. Even has his own men."

"Does he come back to visit?"

She shook her head. "Not since my mother died. It's been at least ten years."

"Hadrius said your sister lives in Keltivar?"

She nodded. "I can't wait for the two of you to meet her. You'll like her. She has a family of her own. She doesn't approve of how I make my living. Says it's too dangerous for a woman."

"Too dangerous for anyone," Eramus added.

"Maybe."

He wiped his runny nose with the back of his wrist, knowing she expected some sort of response or hint about what Hadrius thought of her. "Your watch," he said.

As Eramus walked back up to the others, he remembered how he and Riya used to look at stars together. He settled onto his bedroll and closed his eyes, hoping to catch a glimpse of her in his dreams.

CHAPTER 4

Mother.
Mother.
Mother.
"…about your mother?"

"What?" Eramus asked as he snapped awake.

"You kept repeating 'mother' over and over," Sylvia said. "Were you dreaming about your mother?"

He didn't remember dreaming about his mother. He didn't remember dreaming at all. "My mother is dead."

"Oh." She gave him the same pitying look she had given him the night before when he told her about his father, but this time he could see it much more clearly. He turned away, gathered up his gear, and immediately set out on the trail. The others hurried to catch up.

They half marched, half climbed for almost an hour. Despite the fact that the sun had yet to rise, their surroundings were visible in the red tint of blood stars. When they found a stream bubbling across the trail from the top of the ridge, they stopped to fill their waterskins. Eramus drank deeply from the cool, refreshing mountain stream, wondering why he had lied to Sylvia.

"I don't really know if my mother is dead," he told her. "But she left my life a long time ago."

"What was her name?" she asked.

Vina. Vina Pon. Her name always sounded odd to him. It made his father cry. Although simple curiosity inspired her question, it had dredged up his personal, private memories, and he couldn't respond. *Conceal your emotions.*

"He doesn't like to talk about his mother," Hadrius said.

"Is that true?" Sylvia asked, more pity on her frown, in her eyes. "Is that really true?"

Again Eramus said nothing. He wasn't sure why he had said anything to Sylvia at all. He didn't need her pity. It reminded him of the times he had gone to collect his father from taverns. The patrons used to look at him like that.

Washing his face and sniffing his nose clean, Lebon combed his thin wet hair over his head with his fingers. Gavrel walked back down the trail a ways to see if they were still being followed. Their early departure should have added distance to the pursuit.

Gavrel quickly jogged back up to them, his slightly flushed cheeks and deformed shoulder leading the way. A racket of snapping tree branches resounded from below. "They're gaining on us. They must have kept on through the night."

While he rubbed his face dry with his hands, Lebon flashed a conspiratorial glance at Gavrel.

Eramus slung his waterskin back over his shoulder, suppressing his rising temper. Any information at this point in time would be more than helpful, and yet these men refused to share their knowledge. "They obviously have an agenda."

Gavrel pointed back down the mountain. "I'm sure they'll answer your questions."

"You don't think their timing is too much of a coincidence?" Eramus asked. "You're recognized on the Hereton and now we're being chased?"

Lebon, calm and cool, slipped on his gloves. "They're opportunists."

"Right," Eramus scoffed. "Opportunists."

While she motioned for the others to hurry, Sylvia absentmindedly chewed on her fingernails. "Let's go. Now. I don't care what they want."

"Up again we go, then," Lebon said with a wink to Sylvia as he tossed up his arms and uncharacteristically took point, his hair still comically wet from his impromptu bath. She shook her head and sighed in response to his cavalier attitude. Eramus shared her concern.

They pressed on until Hadrius discovered the remains of another campsite.

"Really? Is this necessary?" Lebon asked. "They're closing ground on us every time we stop."

"Yes, it is necessary," Eramus said stubbornly. He stood beside Hadrius, hoping to call their bluff, to see if either one of them would talk. "Missing things will cost us more time."

"The rain didn't bleed these tracks much," Hadrius said, waving his hand over them. *"Two distinct sets of child size feet."*

"We're going the right way," Eramus said, patting Hadrius on the back as he spotted the edges of footprints over his shoulder. He had always admired his friend's gift for careful observation. *"We already know that. Come on."*

Sylvia extended her hand to Hadrius. He appeared confused by the gesture, and ended up pulling her close and kissing her forehead.

"Maybe those are the kidnappers behind us," she said as she tugged at the ends of her hair, still in his embrace. "Maybe they hid the children up here and now they're coming to get them."

"That's certainly worth considering," Hadrius said. "But I haven't found anything similar going back down. I would have noticed. Still, we should break off the trail and double back around the other side of the ridge. They may know this terrain and how to ambush us."

"No, we can't do that," Eramus said. "The children are up here somewhere. The last thing I want to do is let those men pass us." In almost any other circumstances, he would have voted to avoid the confrontation. They were outnumbered and he would be fighting alongside people he didn't trust. Unfortunately, his priority was to find the children. Sadir's family's safety depended on every decision he made.

Gavrel and Lebon marched ahead, the former grunting when the latter occasionally raised his voice. When Eramus and the others caught up to them, they were waiting atop the open terrain of a mountain pass, Lebon's hands resting on his waist. He winced at sharp pains in his sides, the attrition of their pace.

"What is it?" Eramus asked when he noticed their resigned expressions. "And no more lies."

Gavrel pointed down the trail. "We're going too slow." He

glanced at his brother, who shrugged. "Time to make a stand."

The undisturbed pass ahead contained valuable clues for Hadrius to read. More foot traffic would compromise all of it.

"They picked a pretty good spot to fight," Hadrius suggested. *"We can control what we want to do here."*

Eramus studied the natural cover of bushes and boulders. Generous maneuvering room narrowed into a choke point. The Coronal Range spread out to the northeast for miles like the twisted back of a snake dotted with flora, shrouded in low hanging clouds.

"What do you think?" Eramus asked Sylvia, hoping her experience as a mercenary could assist in their tactics.

She had resumed chewing on her nails, but she yanked them out of her mouth and hid them behind her back when she realized what she was doing. "No time to fortify. We'll be better off using the terrain to our advantage, unless they know it, too. It would help to know who these men are."

"Last chance," Eramus said with a glare at Gavrel and Lebon. "I've already lied for you. What comes now?" Neither man answered. "Then it's us against them." With grim determination, he pointed out a rocky niche down the way to Sylvia. "Can you use that as a lookout post?"

She nodded and jogged away, her anxiety eased by the familiar subordination of following orders.

Gavrel discarded his cloak, rolled his shoulders and neck as well as he could, his upper mobility limited by his handicap. He wore a sword but Eramus hadn't expected to see him fight.

"You've got a minute to sharpen that," Eramus said, nodding at the dull short sword. He dug into a pouch on his belt and tossed his whetstone to Gavrel.

Lebon hefted his mace, flipping it end over end, catching it easily. He practiced against air with deadly, precise strikes while his brother ran the whetstone against the edge of his short sword.

"Better with that than with your mouth?" Eramus asked.

Lebon smiled. "Miss your mother, eh?"

With a frown, Eramus crossed his arms over his chest. "Now isn't the time."

"I always hear that. Know what I don't hear?"

"I have a feeling you're going to tell me whether I want to know or not."

"What I don't hear is the soothing song of the bastard snowthroat."

"The what?"

"Exactly," Lebon said, pointing at him for emphasis. "Purple or blue with white smeared on their necks, resemble crows a little bit."

"Indigo? Like purple but closer to blue?"

"Right. Like purple but closer to blue. Anyway, we had some walnut trees near our house when we were kids. Those damn birds woke me up every morning with their chatter. They liked to talk after a meal. Then one winter our father cut down the trees for firewood. The birds didn't come back next spring. I haven't seen any for two decades, and then suddenly one of them is sitting on a roof back in the barony and I felt like a kid again. You know, no worries and everything is new and exciting."

Eramus froze, wondering if he had said something during a dream, something that Lebon had overheard and was ridiculing.

Bastard snowthroat.

"Are you aware a bunch of armed men will be here any second?" Eramus asked.

Lebon rubbed a finger over one of the spikes on his mace. "Like I said. Now isn't the time, right? So I waited for the birds after that but they never returned. I thought they were gone."

Hadrius strung his bow nearby, oblivious to Lebon's story. "*Good elevation,*" he said, indicating a higher spot with concealing brush. He nocked an arrow and loped into position.

"I know it doesn't seem important," Lebon continued. "But I miss those birds waking me up. It was something new. Everything feels stale these days, like I've seen it all or something, but seeing that bird again made sense of it all."

Strangely enough, Lebon's words resonated for Eramus. Experiences didn't tend to affect him as profoundly as they used to, and what he thought was the bird's interest in him had given him a new perspective of sorts. No, not a bird: a bastard snowthroat.

He brought his thoughts back to the present. He remained in the center of the pass, cycling potential strategies through his mind. Their pursuers outnumbered them seven to five. Sylvia gave them the advantage of preparation, they had chosen a suitable field of combat, and Hadrius provided ranged attack and surprise, but how long could that last? The fighting could ultimately come down to bloody hand to hand. People would die.

"Awake..." Lebon muttered to himself as his eyes wandered off to the sky with rapt amazement. Eventually his gaze settled back on Eramus, the man's expression shrewd and intensely focused. "Don't worry so much."

"What?"

"I can see it on your face all the time. You worry about everything. Every decision doesn't have to be life or death. Focus on what you can affect and forget about the rest. First Awakening is really just a bad dream. A tour of misery. Questions with no answers, and when you're finally, really awake...it's over."

"And how would you know?"

Face devoid of color, Sylvia hustled back, daggers in hand. "They're coming." She immediately noticed Hadrius's absence and looked around for him. He waved from his cover, then melted into it again.

"Any idea who they are?" Eramus asked as Gavrel gave him back the whetstone. His pulse quickened, his entire body tensing in anticipation. He tried to loosen the dagger on his thigh and it stuck a bit in its sheath. He had forgotten to clean the blood off it. It was too late now. He would have to remember to pull harder if he needed it.

A single daisy stood just off the side of the footpath, its white petals vibrant despite the season. *"Only the best for your mother."* Eramus glanced over at Lebon while he thought about what the man had said, about how he had never expected to see a bastard snowthroat again. He wanted to ask Lebon more about them. He wanted to ask Lebon about other things, too. In that moment he selfishly envied Gavrel, and he wished he had had a brother like Lebon to look after him.

Footsteps grew louder and seven forms, more resembling hungry animals than men, appeared from the trail. Sylvia spun around, her grip tightening on her daggers, her legs spread into a fighting stance.

"*Lunken!*" one of the strangers shouted. Dust stained their dishonest faces. A couple had short swords, the rest heavy sticks.

None bore official markings on their patchwork assortment of clothing and light armor, but the brand of a *duba* had been burned into their leader's forehead. Heavy bags darkened the space under their eyes and some of their hands trembled for no apparent reason. How long had they been awake? Their leader forced a smile.

Gavrel spit to the side. "*Kuvos*," he growled to himself. His eyes locked on them, he tilted his head in Eramus's direction. "They won't be making any deals."

"Who—" Eramus began.

"They hire out to a *culipi* dealer. Look at the way their hands shake."

Eramus thought back to the patrol's interest in Gavrel. The patrol had searched them for *culipi*, and he hadn't figured it out until now. They hadn't found anything, of course, but the local would have reported the encounter to someone. An opportunity for good profit existed in illegal business. That still didn't explain Gavrel's involvement. They were clearly after him. Both sides of the law wanted the man. Eramus had spent years avoiding trouble like his.

"Killing them should be a last option," Eramus said. He didn't need a *culipi* dealer after him, too.

"They don't look like the type to fight fair," Sylvia muttered as she paced side to side, twirling her daggers between her fingers with well-practiced ease. "I don't, either." The strangers spread out to prevent any escape. She looked to Eramus for direction. He shrugged. They would have to react to whatever happened.

"Hardly any protection on the lot," Lebon observed.

"What do you want?" Gavrel demanded in an unfamiliar, booming voice. He lowered the tip of his sword in the earth, his head tilted in a grimace of severe discomfort. Eramus drew his sword as well, hoping threat of resistance would deter the men.

The spokesman glanced back at the others, then said, "You know what we want." His smile melted. "You cut out on a contract."

"I don't have any money," Gavrel replied. "They really didn't tell you anything about me, did they?"

The leader switched his attention to Eramus. "You're outnumbered." His eyes drifted to the ground, to the single, resilient daisy that had every reason not to grow up here, and he smashed it underfoot. He didn't know Eramus, and already he had challenged him, threatened him, disrespected him. Eramus found himself eager to fight alongside Gavrel and Lebon. Now he had an outlet for his frustration about everything beyond his control that had happened. He rolled his sword around with his wrist, ready for action. *"A good Hamaln does not solve problems with violence."*

"Quit talking and let's get at it," Lebon barked. He scratched his crotch with his free hand, held his mace over his shoulder with the other. "I'm going to open your fucking skulls."

The spokesman shook his head. "You had a chance." His men raised their crude weapons, though some appeared less confident than others after Lebon's comment. He pointed his huge mace at each of them in turn.

Gavrel lifted his short sword in his left hand, tucked his right hand behind his back. "I've been waiting six months, and this isn't even worth the effort." He lunged at the men mid-sentence, closing the gap in an eyeblink, shifting his momentum to slice into a femur, whipping his newly sharpened blade deep into exposed flesh on the follow-through, leaving a surprised opponent in his wake. In shock, the victim tested the gash with a shaking hand, his fingers coming away red and wet. Gavrel's accurate, one-handed strikes left no question about his blade precision.

Eramus rushed into action as well, cutting into the opposition's left flank to scatter their sloppy formation while he strove to build off Gavrel's surprisingly graceful maneuvers.

With snapping overhand throws Sylvia released her daggers, quickly filling her hands with another pair from her brace for closer combat. She screamed excitedly in the moment of battle, bloodlust contradicting the shy, nervous behavior to which Eramus had grown accustomed. Lebon fought from the right, herding with powerful swings of his bludgeoning weapon. He established defensive footholds as he advanced, an indication of his military training. Sylvia, however, struck into presented openings, feeding off Lebon's solid position to stab or maim the enemies he knocked off balance. Blood drenched her hands less than a minute into the fight. Despite their personal differences, she and Lebon worked well together.

An arrow hissed out of the brush and buried itself into a man's shoulder. With a shrill scream he clawed at it. His inattention allowed Eramus to stab him through the liver.

Gavrel, meanwhile, crossed swords with one opponent while sidestepping a stab from a second. His blade hardly committed to any motion before he twisted his wrist or utilized his momentum for a better attack angle. He yanked the first man inside his own defenses, slipped his sword arm around the back of his neck, his other arm under his chin, and violently snapped his neck with a clean jerk, quickly engaging the dead man as human shield while he hacked through his second opponent. Eramus couldn't help but admire Gavrel's conservative, brutal technique.

Another arrow zipped across Eramus's line of sight, this one skittering off a boulder onto the far side of the trail, distracting him. A two-handed, overhead attack surprised him. He raised his sword to block, but the hard strike rattled him and his knees wobbled. Sweat stung his eyes, blurred his vision. When he lifted his wrist to wipe his face, someone kicked him in the back and he tripped, losing his sword in the process. He fumbled for his dagger but it stuck in its sheath and he couldn't wiggle it loose with one hand.

In the glare of the sun and his own perspiration, the silhouette of his original opponent loomed over him, sword raised. Eramus feebly lifted his arm, hoping his bone would prevent a mortal wound.

Abruptly his opponent's head burst like a melon, and warm blood splattered across his face when he heard the sickening crunch. By the time Eramus rubbed his eyes enough to see, Lebon had begun to wrench his mace free with a tug. The dead man's broken skull had given way to fleshy brain matter and a mess of spurting red. An eyeball, clumps of blood-sticky hair, and bone fragments decorated the spikes of Lebon's wet mace.

Before Eramus had time to make sense of the grisly scene, a blade sliced a deep groove into Lebon's upper arm, a missed stab at his heart from behind. He snatched his hand back, instinctively dropping his mace as he clamped his palm over the wound.

Eramus reacted with the experience of a trained fighter, leaping to his feet and spinning around Lebon, finally wrenching his dagger free and stabbing in one fluid motion where he anticipated the attacker. The reward came when his blade shoved through leather and speared soft flesh. The man dropped his sword and clutched desperately at the blade. Eramus yanked the dagger out of him and watched him fall to the ground, dead.

When Eramus, out of breath, heart beating in his ears, surveyed the battle, it had already concluded. Six of their attackers lay dead or dying. The seventh, the spokesman, lay curled up, piteously crying, his hands grasping his damp red mess of shirt and stomach as he renounced the Forgotten Prophet and begged for a proper Hamaln burial and Passage of Awakening. Eramus actually considered it until Sylvia remorselessly wiped the flat of her dagger across the man's leg to clean it, and he whimpered at the contact.

"Shut up," she said. She scooped up a handful of dirt and scrubbed her bloody hands with it. Eramus no longer harbored any doubts about her martial competence. She had eliminated two opponents, and had assisted in killing another. If nothing else, Eramus could take solace in the fact that none of his companions had proven to be a weakness in combat.

With an arrow nocked and ready, Hadrius trotted down from his hiding place and checked the bodies for signs of life. Satisfied nobody would get up, he spun the arrow between his fingers and slid it back into his quarrel, hung the bow across his back. He grabbed Sylvia's squirming face in his rough hands and inspected her. She grinned over his ministrations, her filthy fingers settling intimately onto his.

Gavrel stood perfectly still in the center of the carnage, his breathing controlled as if the fighting had never happened.

"I still think I'm better with my mouth," Lebon said to Eramus. He tore a strip off his tunic and cinched a makeshift tourniquet tightly around his shoulder with his teeth. He flexed the fingers of his left hand before snatching up his mace and plucking out pieces of bone and brain, flicking them aside. "Damn. This will take forever to clean…"

"Thank you for saving my life," Eramus said. His adrenaline had begun to fade, his brief fear of leaving First Awakening vanishing with it. He recovered his sword, and this time he properly cleaned the blade of his dagger with a rag and tested it in the sheath. His carelessness had almost proved fatal.

Lebon merely nodded in response. "It appears my journey here isn't over after all." He shoved past Eramus to crouch before the dying spokesman. He thumped him on the arm with the dirty spiked head of his mace. "Did you want a reputation? You're not the first person to try to kill my brother and you won't be the last." He traced the lines of the sun across the brand on his forehead. "You look thirsty, *duba*." Flies buzzed around him, lighting quickly on his mess of stomach. He was too weak to even prevent them from preening themselves. Lebon lifted the man's sticky hands away from his wound to reveal dark blood.

Gavrel's shadow fell over them, but the spokesman, so focused on his pain, didn't notice. Gavrel nodded to Lebon, who prodded at the exposed wound with the spikes on his mace. The man groaned and curled up tightly.

"What's the price on me?" Gavrel demanded.

"Price on you?" Eramus asked. "There's a bounty out on you?"

"F-five gold pieces," the spokesman whimpered. "I have no shroud. I need—"

Gavrel scoffed. "You died for five gold pieces? Not too smart, are you? Who put up the money?"

"I'm Hamaln…please, brother…I'm Hamaln."

"Say the name."

Blood bubbled on the spokesman's lips and he shut his eyes. Eramus didn't like to see someone suffering but they needed answers.

Just when he thought the man was dead, he gasped, "Prince Luc."

Lebon poked the wound again and the spokesman mustered enough strength to swat his hand away. More and more flies settled in the blood. "Say hello to your prophet for me."

"Wait…please…" the leader whimpered. "I only wanted to feed my family." He clutched himself, grimacing in agony as something inside him constricted. His breathing ended with a heavy sigh. Then he lay still. Lebon prodded him to no reaction. Gavrel stormed off. Lebon dusted off his hands and stood, wincing when he tested his hurt shoulder.

"Who is Prince Luc?"

Lebon didn't answer right away, then his eyes flicked to all of them in turn. "He's not a real prince. He runs the *culipi* trade."

"I've never heard of him."

"You wouldn't have. He thrives on anonymity."

Eramus fought down his anger, but couldn't keep the disgust from his voice. "Then these men are only the first who will be after the bounty. You didn't think that information was important?"

"You're in no danger," Lebon replied with little care. "There are no witnesses."

Without thinking about consequences, Eramus shoved Lebon. It was a reaction, nothing more. He clenched his fists, ready to give as well as he got. He expected retaliation and was surprised when it didn't come. Gavrel appeared to care less about the confrontation, but Hadrius and Sylvia watched the two carefully, their hands close to their weapons.

"My brother is not as forgiving as I am," Lebon said. "And he tends to bear a grudge. Calm down."

"You're mixing us into that trouble. In case you've forgotten, the third man in that patrol recognized your brother. He knows our faces now, too."

Lebon gently placed his hand on Eramus's shoulder. Eramus immediately slapped it away. "Don't touch me."

"Calm down. I just saved your life. Hear me out." He hooked his mace back on his belt so the others could see and he muttered, "...clean it later." He inhaled a deep breath. "My brother's in trouble."

"I can see that, "Eramus said, waving his hand at the dead. "Now we're all in trouble. Don't you get it? I don't want anything to do with the *culipi* business. I've got enough problems."

Lebon shook his head. "I really am escorting him to the Duchy of Haulken. We grew up in a village named Kluhm. I have some land there, and a wife." He paused and rubbed his chin with his fingers. "She's ugly but she's good to me and she cooks."

"What—this isn't my problem. Don't you understand? This isn't my problem."

Lebon lowered his voice, spoke directly to Eramus now so the others didn't overhear. "I know you don't care about my problems. Nobody cares about anybody's problems these days, but I don't want my brother to die. You can understand that, can't you? He's too stubborn to stay alive on his own."

The words hung in the air. Eramus wasn't sure how to respond, so he remained quiet.

"I ran off to war when he was young," Lebon continued. "When he needed his big brother most, I chose my duty before him. He made poor decisions after that, and I accept the blame. I wouldn't have let him do what he did. I would have stopped him. Now he's stubborn and foolish but I have to help him straighten things out. Do you understand? I don't care what he did. I'm here to help him. That's what a big brother does."

"What does that have to do with me?" Eramus asked coldly, unsure why he had responded that way. He could certainly sympathize with Lebon's feelings for his younger brother.

"Hate me if you want, but we're all in this together. You can either accept that or we can keep arguing. Personally, I think this ragtag company works well together. All we have to do is stick together for now and then we'll go our separate ways." He joined his brother among the dead, his way of ending the conversation.

Both of these men infuriated Eramus, but it was difficult for him to stay angry with someone as affable as Lebon. The man controlled his emotions and made sense for the most part, even if he was concealing information about his brother. Sir Jacob must have offered the brothers a deal, maybe a pardon or protection in exchange for work. They could be in the same situation as Eramus. But what exactly had the knight asked of them, and why these two men when Sir Jacob had plenty of others at his disposal?

Lebon and Gavrel searched the bodies, talked among themselves. Their efforts uncovered coins, a short sword Gavrel preferred more than his own, as well as a leather jerkin, better boots, and a pair of ugly red greaves. Once he stripped the bodies and outfitted himself, he untied his kerchief and vigorously rubbed the scarring on his neck until a purple mess remained. He laced up his new jerkin and stuffed the kerchief in the space between his tunic and bare skin.

"What now?" Sylvia asked of nobody in particular. She interlaced her fingers with Hadrius's and leaned on his shoulder. "Is the plan to turn back? We can still make the festival. My sister will will roast quail for us and we can watch the sunset from her porch. Have you ever seen a Keltivarin sunset?"

As Hadrius looked down at her, he brushed loose strands of red hair from her eyes, licked his finger and smeared a spot of blood from her cheek. "Quit it with the festival and going to see your sister. We're not turning back until this is over."

"But someone's after us."

"This complicates things, but doesn't change what needs to be done," Eramus said, even though he agreed with Sylvia about potential pursuers. More men might come after them if this group failed to return. Eramus would like nothing more than to sleep for a day and then head to Keltivar for that roasted quail and to maybe seek out Trixie to apologize for leaving without saying goodbye, but he had to press on. He couldn't leave Sadir and his family to the knight's mercy. Sir Jacob had already threatened to execute them if Eramus's mission wasn't successful.

"No bare feet," Hadrius said.

"What?"

"This group hasn't been here before. They're new."

"I guess we can rule them out as kidnapping suspects."

Hadrius stared up at the sky. "Something's wrong. The air's funny, the way it tastes on my tongue."

Eramus shielded his eyes against the glare of a pale sun in an overcast sky of smothered ebb stars, half expecting to see the bastard snowthroat circling overhead. He slid his tongue out, wondering what Hadrius had meant. He couldn't notice a difference. "What? I don't see anything."

"I don't either," Hadrius cryptically replied.

"You two don't ever make sense," Sylvia said, clearly pouting about the visit to her sister's being delayed. "Even in Oshlema."

After a brief rest the party descended the pass onto another mountain, veering right as the trail and the tracks did, eventually ending up well below the tree line. Eramus stuck close to Hadrius and Sylvia. Lebon reprimanded Gavrel behind them, but the younger man retaliated against the verbal assault with short curses.

Their interaction reminded Eramus a lot of his relationship with Hadrius. They bickered but they looked after one another. If Lebon had told the truth, he just wanted to get his brother out of trouble. Eramus would do the same for Hadrius.

A dragonfly zoomed past them, and Eramus marveled at the network of veins running through its wings. He had never seen a dragonfly so clearly before. With everything that was going on, he had to wonder why this particular moment in time had become so relevant to him. Out of sheer curiosity, he licked at the air a bit. It might have been his imagination, but he could have sworn that something about it really was different.

Up ahead Hadrius had stopped to stare at the ground. At first Eramus assumed he was reading the trail, but his eyes uncharacteristically drifted out of focus.

"What is it?" Eramus asked.

"This isn't right," Hadrius replied.

"Are we going the wrong way?" Gavrel asked from up the trail. His thumbs hooked into the belt he had taken from a dead man.

"I can't...I can't tell," Hadrius said. Eramus was shocked. His friend always knew which way to go.

"We can keep going or we can head back up," Gavrel said as he approached them. "I know what's back there waiting for me."

Lebon tugged at his tourniquet, the dried blood on it lending a pink hue.

"How's your shoulder?" Eramus asked.

"Bleeding's stopped," Lebon growled. He quickly cleared his throat. "If nobody else will do it, I'll take a look ahead." He glanced at Sylvia. "Come with me?"

"Not too far," Gavrel warned them. He regarded Hadrius carefully, just as concerned about his behavior as Eramus was. "The tracker's spooked."

That snapped Hadrius out of his trance, though the initial confusion didn't leave his expression.

Sylvia spared a concerned look at him before she vanished deeper into the trees with Lebon.

Eramus squeezed Hadrius's shoulder. "*Hey. Are you okay?*"

"*I'm fine*, prophuug," Hadrius nodded, but his eyes looked glassy, unorganized.

With Hadrius distracted, Eramus decided to see if Gavrel would open up any. "Where did you learn to fight like that? I've trained with ex-military and I've never seen that style." He waited for a response. Nothing. "What were the two of you arguing about?"

"My brother already made you for Uuslefin," Gavrel replied. "He said you used to be spies."

Eramus struggled to keep his cool. The man lacked certain social graces. "Your brother's right. We are Uuslefin, but there are no spies here. Regardless, I don't care much for you or him either."

"He saved your life."

"After you two put me in jeopardy."

Gavrel sighed, even that simple action pinching his scar and irritating him. "But you must be curious."

"It doesn't make a difference to me. You still haven't answered my questions."

"Shall we?" Gavrel asked, indicating the trail. Eramus assumed their conversation to be over until Gavrel spoke up again. "He arrested one of your people on suspicion, during his first enlistment. He didn't know about your regiment."

"Information Regiment," Eramus corrected. The trail turned again, though this time a steep climb took them onto a series of narrow highlands leading toward another mountain.

Gavrel snorted dismissively. "My brother and his men thought they'd caught a Gelofassin deserter, but it turned out to be a spy from your regiment."

"We weren't spies."

"My mistake. I thought your people claimed neutrality."

"We agreed not to fight," Hadrius interjected, clearly upset with Gavrel's insinuations.

"Ah, well, the spy who stabbed my brother's friend must have tripped."

Reality existed within a framework of perception. Eramus shook his head, remembering his experience in Grihm while he had been in the IR. If Lebon and his men had treated the Uuslefin in a similar manner as the Filthies had treated Eramus, it was no wonder the man had fought back. "And the messenger? What happened to him? What was his name?"

"Nobody cared what his name was. They hanged him after they interrogated him, like they did to every other spy they caught after that." Silence hung in the air for a handful of seconds. "Did you even know what messages you carried?"

A cold knot tied itself in Eramus's stomach. Had he known the messenger? If Rammun hadn't saved his life, he would have met a similar end. Stories about messengers who never came home became cautionary tales for every member of the IR. For each messenger lost, the rest taught themselves to be that much more careful. It wasn't until later, after the IR had disbanded, that Eramus had learned that they actually were spies, even if they hadn't known it at the time. A small group of Uuslefin men and women living in Gelofass had sold information to his Uncle

Reginald, who in turn had sold it to an interested group in Keltivar. Eramus and the other members of the IR had been used, but there was no point explaining that deception to Gavrel.

"And what about you?" Eramus wondered. "Men are hunting you. That patrol almost arrested you. It's as if—"

"Stop!" Hadrius shouted, interrupting them. Palm out, he waved his arm in front of him, testing the air. Beneath them the earth had been worn away to the solid rock of the mountain, and the trees seemed to be several yards away on either side, withered and half-dead.

"What is it?" Gavrel asked, scanning around for signs of trouble. It occurred to Eramus that they should have caught up with Lebon and Sylvia by now. He stuck his tongue out again, tasted the air, and this time a clear, metallic hint of what he might have only imagined before soured his tastebuds. What unnerved him more than anything, though, was his friend's odd behavior.

"I can't see anything past that line," Hadrius said, pointing into the distance. The air hummed with raw power. The mountain split in front of them, a sheer drop bridged only by narrow rock.

"We need to hurry," Gavrel said, suddenly worried. "Something's wrong. My brother's in trouble."

"Look," Hadrius said, indicating the ground around them. Nothing, from the withered trees to their own bodies, cast shadows.

"What is this?" Gavrel asked, hoping someone would explain the phenomenon.

"It's magic," Hadrius replied. "This isn't right. We shouldn't be here." He glanced at Eramus. "*We need help with this.*" He didn't say Riya's name. He didn't have to.

Eramus inspected the foot of the rocky bridge, where reality warped into the unknown. If he crossed that line, he surrendered any illusions of control. Powerful and merciless, magic acted on the whim of those who harnessed it. Normal men couldn't defend against it very well, and certainly couldn't comprehend it. Eramus, through experience, had learned to respect it, had learned to fear it, mostly for its unknown qualities.

"I'm going," Gavrel said. "My brother needs me."

"Fine," Eramus said. "You go first."

Gavrel didn't move for a long time, and Eramus hoped he

wouldn't work up the courage to step out onto the bridge. The still soundless air had transformed into a force of its own. "You know something of magic?" Gavrel finally relented.

"Enough to avoid it. We're the only ones who know how to get here. If anything happens to us, we probably won't be found for a while."

"We're not leaving without Sylvia," Hadrius said.

"Or my brother," Gavrel added.

"Then take the lead," Eramus said, stupidly ignoring his own internal warnings. His recklessness could cost them the mission, could leave Sadir and his family helpless against the knight's vengeance, but the only way to find Lebon and Sylvia, and possibly even the baron's children, was to keep moving forward.

The three of them cautiously negotiated the bridge. The ground absorbed the sound of their footsteps while a thick fog swirled in the chasm below. Giant black trees sprouted from the mountainsides at odd angles, their old and ugly branches devoid of leaves. For every step the men took on the bridge, another foot or so of it coalesced into view through the fog. They moved single file, arms spread wide for balance though no wind rose from the depths or buffeted them. Soon the other side of the mountain loomed in front of them, the end of the bridge reminding Eramus of a cemetery entrance. Fog leaked from somewhere beneath them, distorting and obscuring their view.

"Don't go in there," Eramus warned. "We should wait here. Maybe the fog will let up and we can make sense of this."

"I've seen fog before," Gavrel said. He drew his sword and plunged in, concern for his brother outweighing his fear. Admiring his blind courage, Eramus reluctantly followed while Hadrius picked up the rear.

Whispering broke the silence when they had immersed themselves in the fog. The unintelligible, unfamiliar voices urged them on, begged them. Eramus armed himself, as did Hadrius.

Iridescent blue light beckoned to them. They approached the source, a large circle of glowing chalk in a clearing. The fog thinned enough to reveal Sylvia inside the circle, facedown and still, surrounded by other bodies. Eramus looked back to see Hadrius frozen, his mouth open, his face pale and bloodless in shock.

The closer Eramus and the others came, the brighter and harsher the supernatural light bursting off the chalk burned. Sections of a symbol, visible only in portions below the bodies, sizzled white hot.

"Gavrel?" a weak voice called. Lebon tottered halfway inside the circle, his left arm dangling uselessly at his side, his upper body invisibly supported. Panting like a dog, covered in sweat, his ghostly face reflected the circle's nebulous blue light.

Gavrel shouted his brother's name and lunged at the circle, but Eramus and Hadrius had anticipated his reaction and restrained him.

"Don't be stupid!" Eramus hissed. You step foot in that and you'll end up like them."

With a grunt and a shift of his shoulders, Lebon desperately tried to turn his head their way but he couldn't manage even that simple change of direction. The invisible force trapped him like a block of cement. "Gavrel. I'm…I'm…" his voice trailed into horrible sobs. "The woman's dead. Tell the tracker it was quick."

Eramus glanced back at his friend's pale face, at the anguish in his eyes.

"I don't know what it is," Lebon said weakly. "It's got me, though, squeezing my chest, stealing my breath." He forced down deep breaths. "Shouldn't have gone off to war like that. My fault…those…*kuvos* got to you."

"I've always been proud of you," Gavrel said. "You did something for us, for your people. Don't regret that." He squirmed and struggled like a wild animal in their grasp. Eramus had his arm securely locked but without Hadrius's help he wouldn't have been able to hold him.

"We can get him out," Gavrel snapped at them. "What's wrong with you?" He nearly broke free of them in another wild struggle, shouting with desperation. "He's my brother!"

"We go in there, we're dead too!" Eramus yelled back.

"I'm not leaving him."

"You don't have a choice."

Lebon panted more heavily, gasped for breath. "Turn…back." His voice quavered through dry, choking sobs. "I'm sorry. I left. Go…somewhere…far   away…start   over.   You'll know…in…Second Awakening…brother…"

Silence. Lebon collapsed into the circle, his body simply one more among many.

Growling in rage, Gavrel finally managed to wrench free of them, his eyes glistening with tears. He didn't move any closer to the circle. He just stared at his brother.

"Try an arrow," he said calmly.

Hadrius quickly strung his bow, more from routine than anything, and drew back, aimed at the circle. He held the shot for several heartbeats, then exhaled and released the arrow. It split the air until it reached the circle, at which point it immediately lost momentum and fell inside.

"What are we dealing with?" Gavrel shouted in frustration. He plunged back into the fog, toward the bridge.

"*Should I try another?*" Hadrius asked after Gavrel had disappeared. Hadrius hadn't taken his eyes off Sylvia's still form.

"*Waste of an arrow,*" Eramus replied. He walked around the edge of the circle, maintaining a distance of at least six feet. There appeared to be no way around it. They would either have to descend into the chasm and search for a ledge farther inside the mountain, or they would have to go directly through the circle. The latter wasn't an option.

Eramus returns early from catching frogs. Quiet as a cat, he avoids every creak in the floor and creeps into the house to find his uncle sitting in his father's favorite chair. Eramus almost says hello when he notices his uncle caressing a lock of his mother's hair. Loghemit must have left it there. It is all his father has left of Vina, of Eramus's mother. And Uncle Reginald holds it to his cheek and whispers softly. Eramus feels his hands clench into fists, though he's not sure why he's upset. He leaves the house as soundlessly as he entered. He decides not to tell his father.

When they found Gavrel by the bridge, the sun had almost set. Feet dangling over the chasm, with no better plan for the present, they sat in silence, staring into the depths of the fog for a while.

Gavrel finally stood up and brushed off his pants. "I was upset when my brother went off to war."

"What did he mean about someone getting to you?"

He lowered his head. "I let him down." He slammed his fist into his palm. "He didn't deserve to die like that." He glanced at Hadrius, his expression softening. "Neither did she."

Hadrius refused to look back at him. "I'm not staying here. There's nothing we can do."

"So we just leave them?" Gavrel argued.

"There's no way to go forward here," Eramus said.

Gavrel thought for a bit. "There has to be a way around, maybe from another angle."

"We already tried that. Whatever it is, there's nothing the three of us can do."

Their voices echoed into the chasm, drowned in the fog. Not a single cricket, bat or other nocturnal animal could be heard. No wind caressed their naked skin.

"We have to go back to the barony," Gavrel said. "We can ask the knight for more men."

"More men?" Eramus asked. "What will men be able to do about that? What makes you think Sir Jacob will help us anyway?"

"He will. He'll understand that I have to bury my brother."

"Really? He could have sent Filthies for this job. The only reason we're here is because we're disposable. We're motivated to get the job done. He said so himself."

"My brother wasn't disposable."

"I know."

"He mattered."

"I know."

"Help," Gavrel said as he yanked at his short hair in frustration. "If the knight can't help us, who can? I've never seen anything like that before."

Eramus got to his feet, his muscles aching with the effort. "We know someone who has experience with these things, with magic."

Gavrel didn't bother concealing his distrust. "A sorcerer, you mean."

Eramus nodded. "We have to go. We'll come back for Lebon and Sylvia."

Gavrel's head hung low, his profile nothing more than a grotesque silhouette. "Someone made that death trap. When I find the person responsible, I'll kill him. I swear this." Reluctantly, he followed them back across the bridge.

They headed up the mountain despite the darkness of night,

retracing the familiar curves along the trail as damp earth replaced scoured rock and scattered trees soughed with life. Even an owl hooted to confirm that the supernatural danger existed only beyond the bridge. Dawn eventually uncovered the landscape, basking it in stark hues of pink and gray, and it wasn't until then that Eramus realized they had been walking all night.

"You're always so curious about me," Gavrel said. "Why is that?"

"In my experience," Eramus replied, "the less someone talks, the more he has to hide."

"Hm. You know, my brother didn't care for you, but he respected you."

"The feeling was mutual."

Their rapid ascent clipped their words, shortened their sentences. Hadrius never once looked back. He swiped low branches out of his way, hopped over boulders, his beautiful bow, slung over his shoulder, vibrant even among the natural greens and browns and grays on the mountain. Eramus was worried that his friend hadn't said anything about Sylvia.

The trail leveled out once they reached the peak of the mountain pass. "A moment," Gavrel shouted at Hadrius's back. He adjusted the sweaty kerchief padding his scar. "Just so you know, I've never met Sir Jacob. I don't give a shit about his holy mission. My brother worked out some kind of deal with him. Lebon wanted me to start over. I'm going to do it, but first I need to bury him. Can you understand that?"

Hadrius trotted back to them, breathing the thin air as easily as if he had been out for a casual stroll, his expression uncharacteristically angry. "What kind of deal did your brother agree to?"

"Sir Jacob wants us to return the children. That's it." His jaw set stubbornly, his eyes shifted almost imperceptibly as he waited for their acceptance. While he gambled that they would believe his lie.

"You're holding back," Eramus said. "I guess it really doesn't matter, though, does it?"

Gavrel wiped perspiration from his forehead. "No. It doesn't."

With a quick gesture, Eramus stepped in line behind the other two and they resumed their hike. They had been on their feet for hours, making excellent time, and it seemed to go by much faster when they talked amongst themselves. Eramus wondered if Hadrius blamed him for Sylvia's death. His friend's reticence was hardly new to him but he had been acting more aloof than usual since last night. He vowed to broach the subject with him later. For now he decided to let him grieve in peace.

"Since you won't talk about yourself," Eramus said to Gavrel. "Then tell me about your brother."

Gavrel shot him a quick glance, determined the sincerity of the request. "Lebon swore he was living his Second Awakening, put in a First Awakening body by mistake."

"A bold claim," Eramus sputtered in disbelief. "Determiners are trained to identify Awakenings. How would one miss something like that? And if your brother was in Second Awakening why didn't he do the proper thing and donate his wisdom to priesthood?"

Gavrel cocked a grin. "You met my brother, right?"

Eramus chuckled. He really couldn't imagine Lebon with a circlet on his head. The idea alone bordered on comical. "He'll be taken care of in Third Awakening, and he'll be that much closer to his journey to the Eternal Fires."

"But I won't know him anymore. He won't be the same person in Third Awakening. My brother was the only person who cared about me. Now I'm alone."

"We're all alone. I guess that's what First Awakening is. You find someone to care about, people care about you for a while, and then you're just alone again. Maybe the lessons are worth it once you get to Second Awakening. You want to learn a lesson now? Do what your brother asked you. Start over."

"I'm trying," Gavrel grumbled. "But you wanted to know more about Lebon. He was one of the last to surrender. That's how stubborn he was."

Eramus recalled what Lebon had said to him. He had told him not to worry so much, not to put so much weight behind his decisions, that First Awakening was nothing more than a bad dream. Was that true?

They arrived at the familiar killing ground to see the corpses of the dead men baking in the sun, flies already swarming over them.

"Surrender to Gelofass, you mean?" Eramus asked, hoping Gavrel would reveal more personal details about himself or Lebon.

Sir Jacob could have chosen anyone for this mission, and yet he had hand-picked Eramus, Lebon, and Gavrel. Eramus was a desperate foreigner. Sir Jacob was simply using him because he could get away with it. Gavrel, on the other hand, was obviously a criminal and a killer. Perhaps Sir Jacob had selected him for that very reason. Perhaps Sir Jacob only wanted desperate men in his employ.

Gavrel nodded. "He didn't give up until My Lord Moritare sent down the order."

"What order? Wasn't the surrender unanimous? I mean, I know there are still rebels, but…"

Hadrius trotted down the ridge, his face emotionless. They had already covered an incredible distance in a short amount of time, and yet Hadrius continued driving them at a relentless pace.

Gavrel craned his neck back at Eramus, gauging his sincerity. "Parts of Oshlem still refuse to lay down their arms, but His Majesty King Willum assured the Ismah everything's fine. As long as Seehlan aren't within our borders, the Ismah could care less. Margrave Valls and Count Sevalah complied with the terms of the treaty once His Majesty King Willum presented it to them. My Lord Moritare had to be…convinced. Duke Eaves of Antonay, on the other hand, refuses to bow to the Ismah or to convert to Gefil. His army is too strong and his land is too well defended for His Majesty King Willum to force him. He pledges loyalty to the crown, but he may declare himself independent, like Lord Kent did." He sighed in disgust. "Nobody in Oshlem cares about Seehlan. They were just a drain, always begging for help and never giving anything back."

"So the Filthies drove them out."

"That's right, because it was either comply with the terms of the treaty or stay at war with Gelofass. His Majesty King Willum can keep the internal problems quiet as long as the Seehlan are gone. You've seen firsthand what the Ismah does when terms aren't met."

"The barony," Eramus said.

"That's right. The Ismah sent Sir Jacob there in the capacity of ambassador. Lord Kent apparently tolerates him as a gesture of goodwill, and I suppose the Filthies are there because they've sworn loyalty to Gelofass. Lord Kent hasn't. I don't understand all of the politics. Maybe they're keeping an eye on him, to see if he's forming an alliance with Keltivar."

"That's absurd. I saw the soldiers riding to Suraam with my own eyes. Why would he supply troops if he shared an alliance with Keltivar?"

"How would I know?" Gavrel asked. "They're not at war. That's pretty strange to me." He gasped for breath, bent over and unexpectedly vomited. "We have to rest." He wiped his mouth clean.

Eramus shouted down the path. Hadrius flashed a hand signal. He would scout ahead. Eramus waved him off.

"It's conversion to Gefil that bothers everyone," Gavrel said while he caught his breath. "Missionaries and priests get a hold of the children or the people with problems, and fill their heads with stories about a prophet. There's no such person. Nobody's coming to save us. We have to learn our own lessons."

"I know," Eramus said. He dug out the last of their rations, stale bread with rye, and choked it down. "Sometimes it seems like we'd all be better off with the Seehlan gone."

They handed their remaining water back and forth.

"You seem to know a lot about all of this. The politics, I mean."

"You wanted to know about Lebon. That's what he told me. Those are some of your blanks. That's why Lebon went off to fight. My Lord Moritare gave him land after the surrender. Every soldier received tax-free land for service. My Lord Moritare had promised them that before the war, and he kept his word."

All Eramus had gotten was eleven silver pieces, a sweaty handshake, and a pat on the back. Then he was left to fend for himself. He thought about Uuslef on occasion, and found he rarely identified with it anymore. What would happen if Uuslef ever went to war? Would he go back and fight?

He had been on his own for so long now that he had settled into a comfortable groove, a life devoid of serious responsibility, but also a life lacking simple pleasures, such as a wife and family. He thought about Lebon, and how his wife would never see him again. He also thought about Sadir and envied him. Kathryn was good to him, and their daughter was beautiful and happy.

He dismissed his errant thoughts. This mission was about fighting for a purpose. His friends were in jeopardy. If he and

Gavrel could put aside their differences and work together, they would have a much better chance at success.

"Your brother was a soldier. What about you? Were your mistakes connected to *culipi*? That's why those men were after you, wasn't it?"

Gavrel's hollow eyes and near constant frown reminded Eramus of people who expected the worst from life. Eramus could relate because he was one of those people. Yet Gavrel also behaved like a man with nothing to lose. Maybe that had something to do with Sir Jacob's deal.

"I can see it's personal for you. Do you know someone involved with *culipi*?"

My mother. "I asked about you."

Gavrel scratched his shoulder. "Men I worked with for years betrayed me. My brother begged me not to go after them, but now he's dead and my list is getting longer."

"So that's what you're going to do with your freedom?" Eramus asked. "Revenge? Your brother didn't want that. I heard him." As much as Eramus disliked Gavrel, he also understood him. Eramus wanted nothing more than to go after Sir Jacob and pay him back for what he had done.

Gavrel took a minute to respond. "I'll clear my name, like he wanted. That won't stop them from coming after me, though. You saw the trash. There will be much more of it."

"Once we get off the mountain they won't be able to track us."

Gavrel slipped out of his jerkin and rubbed at the scar tissue on his shoulder.

"Are you going to be all right? That looks pretty bad."

"I'll be fine. It just itches more when I sweat."

"How did it happen?"

"The usual. Bad fight. Someone did the best he could with what remained. I've grown accustomed to it. Anyway, where will we find this person you mentioned?"

"She lives in Brudgewan." Riya Sen had been in his thoughts since the first time he had laid eyes on her. Weak was the most appropriate term he could think of to describe himself in her presence. They had lived together for several months, at least until he had accepted her unwillingness to reciprocate his feelings. Parts of those months had been the best of his life, but the sadness and

126

resentment that came with them still clung to him.

"Brudgewan? The roads are unsafe."

A bird whistle rang out from below them, and Eramus answered back. "Time to go."

"You really think she'll be able to help us?" Gavrel asked. He pulled his jerkin back on.

"She has experience with the unexplainable. You were there. What good will a hundred soldiers be against that?"

Neither of them spotted Hadrius from his perch atop a boulder. He leaped down behind them, startling them into action. They both exhaled in relief when they recognized him. "No more breaks," he snapped before jogging ahead.

By sunset they reached the familiar overhang affording them a clear view of Hereton Road. The torches of the watch glowed like beacons. Indigo sleep stars had already winked to life in the rapidly spreading darkness. They practically slid down decomposing leaves to where their horses grazed.

"We've been at it for a long time," Eramus said. "We should get a little sleep at least, then start riding. The roads should be safe enough at night."

"Night's better anyway," Gavrel said. "Too many familiar faces during the day." He stared off into the distance. "I could head out now, you know, and tell Lebon's wife what happened to him. She might even let me live there with her."

"Is that what you want?"

"What I want? No. I have to return some favors. That's not what my brother wanted, though. I'll finish this with you. Then I'll go my own way."

"Fair enough," Eramus said as he settled in. He slept fitfully as his subconscious peppered him with memories of Riya. His anxiety mounted with his anticipation. How would she react? They hadn't parted on the best of terms and they had left a lot unsaid.

An hour later they broke free of the woods and rode northwest to Lestwine Road. It was a refreshing change to let the horses carry them after all the climbing and walking they had done over the last few days. They left the two local horses Gavrel and Lebon had ridden out of the barony, and Gavrel took Sylvia's better-seasoned mount. Eramus placed his hand over his breast, imagining he could feel the ring dangling from the necklace beneath his clothes. He tried not to think about what would happen if Riya wouldn't help them.

CHAPTER 5

The hot summer night is sticky and wet, alive with mosquitoes. Eramus returns to his uncle's home after a long day of catching frogs and exploring the ruins at the city's edge. It is his last night of being eight years old. He doesn't like living here but his father couldn't afford to pay the taxes on their own home once he took up drinking as a full time occupation.

"You're too late for supper," his uncle tells him as he mops up the last of his beans with a hunk of bread.

Though Eramus's mouth waters at the smell of food, he knows better than to beg. It will get him nowhere with his stubborn, cruel uncle.

"Go and fetch your father before that big mouth of his gets him into trouble," his uncle tells him as he wipes his mouth with his hand and stands up from his small table. "I don't look after brats."

Eramus lowers his head and nods obediently, though his hands shake at his uncle's tone. There is no reason to ask where Loghemit might be. Eramus already knows.

He finds his father slumped on a stool inside his favorite tavern. He has not yet passed out, though he is close. The barkeep forces a smile. The other patrons pat Eramus on the head or nod in recognition at him. Retrieving his father has become a common occurrence. Every once in a while, Eramus arrives in time to hear Loghemit telling people how bad luck spoiled his life, how it's unfortunate for bad things to happen to good people.

"Turning nine tomorrow, eh?" old Peter asks him. Eramus nods, unable to hide the excited smile on his face.

"Father," he says, shoving Loghemit's shoulder to rouse the man. His father, eyes closed, smiles at the sound of his son's voice.

Eramus helps him off the stool, leads him out of the tavern. Patrons bid them farewell. His father is well liked, even tolerated when he drinks and speaks his mind.

"Did you get your supper?" his father asks as they stumble down the street.

"Yes," Eramus lies, not knowing why. He is hungry. He is always hungry. He has gotten used to it. He'll catch a few frogs tomorrow. He won't be hungry then.

His father squeezes his shoulder. "Your mother would be proud of you. We were so in love, your mother and I. Did I ever tell you that?"

Eramus feels his face flush. He doesn't want his father to talk about his mother when he's drunk. He will go on and on and eventually start to cry and to call her Vina. Eramus hates to see him cry because it reminds him that his mother isn't coming back.

"I'm proud of you too, son," his father says. The words make Eramus angry, and he doesn't know why. "For being so strong when I can't be. You seem to have First Awakening all figured out." Loghemit straightens up, clears his throat, his tone suddenly stern. "Your Uncle Reginald and I are taking you to Frehm with us."

"Wh-wh..." Eramus stutters. He has never been outside of Uuslef before.

"Your uncle has to hire some men for a big job, and Oshlemin labor is cheap. You're going to have to learn a few things if you're going to earn your food and bed. We leave in the morning."

Loghemit Pon stumbles off and leaves Eramus alone in the street. At least Eramus has his father, and even his Uncle Reginald, as much as he doesn't like him. Eramus decides working for his uncle might not be such a bad thing.

The reek of livestock manure fused to pipe smoke and heavy spice on Lestwine Road. Wagons rattled, men shouted and laughed, and wild children ran underfoot. Eramus had begun to realize that the baron's children could have easily been smuggled past the watchtowers. The guards were well trained and on high alert, but any textile cart or vegetable wagon could conceal two small children.

Eventually the road overflowed with traffic and Hadrius steered them away from simple farmers, unkempt traders, and affluent merchants under armed escort protection. The trio resumed their northward ride on a less popular river path, slogging through green mud and insect swarms for several hours, until they arrived at a deserted bridge crossing into Brudgewan. Unchecked trees and ferns had wrapped around the bridge's planks and guide wires, lending the structure an ancient, natural appearance.

Beyond the bridge appeared a dirt road flickering with dappled sunlight. They wordlessly formed a single file line and maintained a trot. Eramus wanted to study the verdant canopy above them but he could barely keep his eyes open. He shook off the encroaching sleep and rubbed his trail-dusted face with his hands to stay awake. He spied a fisherman and his son on a parallel game trail, poles over their shoulders.

"Anything?" Eramus shouted, startling them.

The boy bashfully lowered his head. His father, wary of the armed strangers, regarded Eramus carefully before responding. His pride overcame his caution and he hoisted up a bountiful hook. "My son sang five gudgeon onto his line."

Hadrius sidled up to Eramus as they rode on. *"Nobody to greet us?"* The last time they had crossed the bridge, soldiers of some warlord or other had detained them and then released them for a hefty fee "in the interest of enhancing their stay."

"I won't question good fortune," Eramus said, relieved that Hadrius was back on reasonable speaking terms again. *"Don't forget the reward for our companion."* Gavrel had fallen several lengths behind, grimacing when he jostled too much in the saddle.

Weather damaged trees lay across the road. Wild foliage overran everything. Giant spider webs connected one bush to the next. Compared to the neat and tidy streets of the Barony of Medar, Brudgewan's upkeep fell vastly short.

"Whoever put that spell up in the mountains is mine," Hadrius growled. *"Don't get in my way."*

Eramus looked over at his friend. The man's knuckles were white on his reins, his jaw clenched. *"Hadrius, I'm sorry about—"*

"*What are we doing here,* prophuug?" Hadrius asked, frowning as he changed the subject, unwilling to discuss what had happened to Sylvia. "*We're dealing with too many variables.*"

"*Sadir needs our help. It's as simple as that. I won't let a friend pay the price for my mistake.*"

"*Too late for that,*" Hadrius muttered, gritting his teeth. He glanced over his shoulder at Gavrel. "*If we get the drop on him, we can surrender him to a patrol. You want to help Sadir, right? The knight won't suspect an ambush. We find out where Sadir and his family are being held, go in strong, rescue them, take them to a safe place, and then finish this other business on our own.*"

"*And where would we take Sadir? Uuslef?*"

"*Why not?*"

"*These aren't just our lives, Hadrius. There's no way two of us can get past a knight and a garrison. And what about him? He's got a stake in this, too.*"

"*I don't care about him. Look, it's worth considering. That's all I'm saying. Don't you remember the pact we made,* prophuug? *We don't work for anyone unless they pay well, and we choose our own jobs. Nothing political. Remember that? I doubt you hear anything I'm saying, because you clearly don't remember any of that.*"

Eramus didn't need any reminders about their agreement. Uuslef had enlisted wide-eyed boys into the IR, and haunted men had returned home in their place. Unable to forget much of what they had seen, many turned to drink, and others took their own lives. Though his time in the IR had inflicted mental and physical scars, Eramus's experiences had also motivated him. He had convinced Hadrius to join him with the promise of freedom and wealth.

"*Do you really want to go back to Uuslef?*" Eramus wondered.

"*No.*"

"*Then trust me that this is the right decision.*"

Hadrius scoffed. "*For you.*"

Eramus wanted to talk to his friend about what had happened, but he wasn't sure what to say.

With a tug on his reins, Eramus slowed up and waited for Gavrel, who caught up via his own leisurely pace.

"Where is everyone?" Eramus asked as the pair eased into a

trot.

"I haven't been here for years. My brother warned me that Lord Harton's paranoia runs things now. He'll have his men close to his castle."

They circumvented one more moss-covered log in the center of the road, this one ripe with a half-eaten carcass swarming with flies. Between the cloying stench of putrefaction and the damp, wet scent of the river wafting in on a gentle breeze, Eramus had to resist his gag reflex.

Fortunately the canopy ended and fresh air dispersed the foul odors. Hadrius pointed out familiar, open plains several miles in the distance, the silhouetted, snow-capped peaks of the Skytop Mountains even farther. "The canyon's up ahead."

"What do you think?" Eramus asked, his stomach bunching in anticipation. He hadn't eaten all day. His skin hung on his bones like a coat, his feet numb in his stirrups.

"We should get there before nightfall."

"Let's cut into that time," Gavrel said without warning. He whipped his reins and tore into a gallop, mud splashing behind his mare as it gained speed.

Suddenly Eramus could remember the fun he had as a boy, before he accepted the truth that his father's drunken tears meant his mother would never come home, before he lost his father, before his uncle's cruelty. Now nothing could restrain him except for damaging memories. He flashed Hadrius a grin. They abandoned their worries and raced after Gavrel, directly into waning sunlight and refreshingly cool wind.

As the canyon loomed larger and larger, the huge red fireball of sun slipped behind distant mountains and cast sweeping gold and pink shadows over the grassy plains. Before long they reached their destination on sweat-lathered horses. A white moon had already begun its ascent, bleeding shadowy silver pools under rocky outcroppings and swaying grass.

Hair disheveled from the wild ride, Gavrel cautiously dismounted. In the moonlight Eramus could see color flushing his cheeks and vitality brimming in his sea green eyes, an enormous contrast to his sullen, reserved behavior.

"The moon's high," Gavrel said as he peered over the canyon's edge. "Should we rest the horses and go through tonight?"

Hadrius slid out of his saddle. He yanked it off with the blanket and tossed them aside. Ever vigilant, he stalked through the grass with his bow, patrolling their perimeter.

The weight of the last couple of days settled onto Eramus. He leaned forward in the saddle, stroked his horse's neck, eyes closed, and wished for ten minutes of uninterrupted, dreamless sleep. "It's not a good idea to go through the canyon at night. It's watched all the time." He slipped out of reality, his only link the horse's velvety hide. He imagined the contours of Riya's face, smooth cheeks beneath his rough fingertips.

"Watched? By whom?"

"Rebels. Raiders. Whatever they're calling themselves these days."

"Lord Harton hasn't flushed them out?"

"What for?" Eramus asked. He needed Gavrel to shut his mouth, if only for a minute. "There's nothing out here worth protecting but open land." He opened his eyes and jumped down from his horse, immediately regretting it. Pain lanced up his thighs. Heavy fatigue rotted from his heels up to his shoulders. He needed sleep, blissful sleep. "Dawn's the best time to ride through. They'll be asleep."

"Fine," Gavrel mercifully conceded.

With barely a glance at the spectacular moon, Eramus spread out his bedroll and lay back. Gavrel dug around in his saddlebags for food. None of them had eaten for a while. It didn't matter. Riya would feed them if she decided to let them in.

Sleep didn't come. Echoes of voices rose out of the canyon below, men shouting and laughing. Eramus rolled onto his side, angry with himself for being manipulated, incensed about being blackmailed. His emotions had whittled away at his resolve since their departure from the barony. He had to control them or it would lead to distraction.

Distraction would happen whether he fought it or not. The moment he saw Riya, everything else would drift away. He had taken great strides to suppress the anguish that their separation had caused him. She would know that, would cut through his fragile defenses and expose him once more. If they turned around and rode back to the barony, he could plead for an audience to present his case to the baron. Surely the father of two missing children would grant leniency.

Leniency for a coward. He dismissed his ridiculous urges, thoughts of a coward. That night in Grihm had altered the fabric of his perception. Although he still battled his fears, he also did his best to overcome them.

Which, ironically, meant asking a dangerous woman for help. They had shared their bodies and their time, and yet he had never completely trusted her. If she joined them, it would only be for her benefit. Eramus had no illusions in that regard.

Something snapped in the grass. Eramus snatched up his sword and leapt to his feet in time to see a scrawny stranger sneaking around their camp. He appeared fresh, awake under the moonlight. He had only covered a short distance to get here.

"Good evening," the stranger blurted. Weaponless, he positioned his feet to run. He studied the length of Eramus's blade like a man who appreciated life.

Gavrel, hands empty and loose at his side, never took his eyes off the stranger. His escape could seal their death sentence.

Sleek and silent, Hadrius emerged atop an outcropping behind the stranger. He bent his knees, legs shoulder-width apart as he drew back on his bowstring. The creak of the wood whispered in the cool air. Eramus never saw the arrow until it punctured the stranger's right lung and burst through his vest with a leathery smack. The man spilled forward, grass flattening beneath him, the trio wordlessly complicit in his death. Hadrius could have wounded him, they could have bound and gagged him, but Hadrius had chosen to kill him instead.

While Gavrel and Hadrius confirmed the kill, Eramus set his sword down and collapsed back onto his bedroll. He was too tired to worry about his friend anymore. The last thing he heard was Hadrius cursing about the arrow being stuck.

When Eramus wakes on his nameday, he is nine years old. He remains curled up in bed, his eyes filtering shapes as best they can until darkness lightens to gray, until he hears his uncle's grumbling and his hungover father's cursing. He expects a smile, words to celebrate his nameday. Instead he gets a swift kick and a "get up" from his uncle while his father turns a jug upside down like it's the last of their well water.

They eat a cold, quick breakfast. Uncle Reginald orders Eramus to hitch the cart. He trudges outside, shielding his eyes against the glare of the early morning sun, fascinated with the glistening dew on a complex spiderweb. He tugs Uncle Reginald's two stubborn mules out of the pasture, secures them to the cart and waits.

"Where's father?" Eramus asks when only his uncle joins him.

"Feeling sorry for himself," Uncle Reginald says once he climbs into the cart and snatches the reins. "He never takes too long with the self pity. Should be back in a few minutes. We're only going because he says you're too young to work."

The cart bumps and rattles along the dirt road, and Eramus can't help but think something is wrong.

But Loghemit catches up to the wagon with a full jug of ale.

"Better keep your wits about you," Uncle Reginald snaps. "This is for business."

Loghemit ignores him, takes another drink. Eramus hopes his father hasn't forgotten his nameday. Even old Peter remembered.

Eramus decides not to speak to his father or uncle until they arrive in Frehm.

He tossed and turned through the night, unable to manage prolonged sleep despite his exhaustion. He finally sat up and traced blood star patterns with his fingers, wondering how the Blood Eagle had found a man of First Awakening, until the others awoke.

Sore and shivering from the cold, they saddled their horses and galloped down into the canyon, a blinding sunrise at their backs. Shouting erupted. Loose rocks rattled as men scurried for position. They proved to be nothing more threatening than a series of blurs without a single coordinated attack. The trio exited the western end of the canyon moments later, unmolested, their faces caked in dusty sweat.

"I counted thirty-one," Gavrel said, turning his upper body back for a final glimpse into the canyon. "Nobody's chasing."

"They might have eaten their horses already," Hadrius suggested.

They continued on until short tufts of wiry weeds replaced hard dirt, until rich soil and green grass replaced that. After a couple of hours and plenty of turns they spotted the glittering blue-green water of Lake Hastal surrounded by weeping willows and bunched stands of cattails.

"Her estate is that way," Eramus said as he guided them to

looming foothills over the north edge of the lake. His heavy eyes blurred from fatigue as they passed the rickety homes of fishermen. The inhabitants ignored them for the most part, diligently cleaning fish or harvesting what remained of meager crops. Eramus waved to men he recognized, men who had patiently taught him to fish during his stay with Riya. They had encouraged him to join them on the lake with their nets, to learn the sound of the water, the silence of the fish, but mostly to instill purpose in the emptiness they claimed consumed him. Perhaps he would fully appreciate their efforts in Second Awakening.

A familiar acclivity less than a hundred yards from the base of the nearest mountain drew his attention. The gnarled, petrified trees of Blackfoot Forest stretched out before them. "A moment," he called to the others. While Gavrel looked around in wonderment, Eramus unhooked the thin necklace from around his throat and slid the silver band it secured onto his finger. A hidden, inlayed sleepstone ignited with indigo light. His lungs filled with air and his expectations soared. "Let's go."

They plunged into the dense forest, Eramus turning when the ring hummed steadily on his finger, the shadow of the mountains lost to their sight. They covered several miles in a couple of hours, leaping over fallen trees, negotiating unstable slopes, their horses slipping more than once in the rich, black earth until late afternoon sunlight blazed through.

When they came upon a grove of apple blossom trees, Hadrius instinctively took point, spurring his mount up a slope, winding a zigzag path through more trees until they reached a fissure in the nearby foothills. Hadrius had already unsaddled his horse by the time they joined him.

The ring vibrated hotly on Eramus's finger. He would have yanked it off if it didn't also serve another purpose. The fissure's width permitted horses, but they would be dead in seconds if they entered.

"We won't need the horses from here," he said to Gavrel. "We can leave them to graze." They untied their bedrolls from their saddles and slung them over their shoulders, Gavrel never once questioning either of them, a sign of trust on his part.

The thick green carpet of grass beneath their boots died at the concealed entrance in the rocks. A cool stream trickled down from the mountains on its way to the lake, most of it underground, readily apparent as a soft rushing in their ears. Eramus looked back at the grove, remembering the day he had fallen in love with Riya here. It felt like yesterday. He could still hear her laughter.

Gavrel studied the fissure from a distance, mesmerized. "What is this place?"

"She prefers her solitude," Hadrius replied as he disappeared into the rocks.

Déjà vu. Eramus relived a familiar instant, an unquestionable recognition that he had existed here and now at some other time. Reeling with more uncertainty than ever about what he perceived to be his conscious thoughts, he moved closely behind his friend, bracing himself with bare palms on rock until he navigated the claustrophobic tunnel and climbed out into the dale. The ring hummed relentlessly.

The man asked me if I feared anything. I said I didn't.

Rolling grasslands stretched for miles, patches of resilient wildflowers scattered throughout. The Skytop Mountains had formed around this majestic location, their bony ridges bordering the dale until they met up again and continued into the distance. An old, sturdy castle stood in the middle of it all, walls etched with rainwater erosion and overrun with white ivy. A figure leaned on the railing of the jutting third story balcony. Late afternoon sunlight highlighted her slender frame.

Cool sweat squeezed through Eramus's skin at the sight of her. He questioned his true reasons for coming here. Did he hope to reconcile with her, to surrender his emotions to her again?

No.

They had tried to be together. *He* had worked to keep them together. In the end, their relationship had been ostensibly one-sided. He reminded himself of how difficult his days had been after he had left her. He wouldn't submit himself to those feelings again. He wouldn't commit himself to her like that again.

"This place is incredible," Gavrel said with sincere wonder as he absentmindedly ran his fingertips over swaying grass, stiffly twisting his torso to absorb the knolls blanketed in foxglove, lilies, cowslip, and Lady's Mantle. Having woken with neck sprains before, Eramus could empathize with the annoying inconvenience. Gavrel did a surprisingly good job of accepting his ill fortune.

From now on when Eramus felt sorry for himself, he would try to remember the handicap Gavrel lived with every day.

"That ring," Gavrel said, his eyes drawn to the light and color blossoming on Eramus's finger. "How is it doing that? Are you…"

"It's a talisman," Eramus replied. "I know little more than you do. It protects us in here."

"Protects us? From what?"

"You'll understand soon enough."

Hadrius crouched a few yards away, hands dangling over bent knees, eyes locked on movement behind them. "Her wolf's out."

A deep growl.

Eramus bared the ring, their only ward against being shredded and eaten.

"What…is that?" Gavrel asked, fear in his eyes as he deliberately reached for his weapon to defend himself. Hadrius seized his wrist. Even with his speed, the Oshlemin wouldn't get his blade halfway out before his throat was a red stain.

Head low between bristling shoulders, coiled for attack, grisly yellow fangs poking from black gums, a massive gray wolf growled from its gut while it glared back at them. Easily twice the size of an average wolf, Riya claimed this one had lived as a man before he had fallen prey to sorcery.

Regardless of who or what it was, Eramus had witnessed firsthand that the wolf offered trespassers no mercy, its aggressive, feral savagery more dangerous than that of any other creature he had ever encountered.

"It's just a wolf," Eramus said, moving backward one step at a time, the ring casting a sphere of bright indigo light before him. "It's trained to protect. Leave it be or we'll be cleaning you off the grass."

Gavrel didn't relent immediately. Eventually he removed his hand from his sword hilt. Warned away by the magic in the ring, the upset and hungry wolf growled and lunged at them.

Unwilling to show the fear he felt, Eramus stood his ground and thrust the ring in the wolf's direction. The beast slunk back a step in retreat.

Ella.

The wolf bounded away, but not before Eramus heard the name over and over in his head, like chanting, like breathing. Ella. Who was Ella? He shook his head to clear the name, at once realizing that this single thought, this name or idea, felt vaguely familiar, at least in the way it had popped into his head, sudden, brief, and with fearful urgency.

With a deep, relieved sigh Gavrel rubbed sweat out of his eyes. He tried to adjust the kerchief under his jerkin, struggling with shaking hands to fix it comfortably over his shoulder. He finally gave up, clenching and unclenching his fingers to steady himself. "I've never seen a wolf that big."

They waded on through a sea of grass. The castle's flawed stones contrasted sharply with well maintained flower beds and rows of fruit trees, all still colorful and bountiful even this late in the season.

The trio marched up a wide stone stairway to the open gate, where Eramus and Hadrius stopped. The stones of the entryway were covered in indigo runes.

"We're not going in?" Gavrel wondered, all the while checking to ensure that the wolf hadn't snuck up behind them.

In the castle courtyard, a fit middle-aged man and a teenage girl tended to a rich vegetable garden custom-fit into a hole in the floor. After yanking up a handful of milky weeds, the man noticed the three of them patiently standing outside. A grin cracked his weathered face.

"Eramus Pon and Hadrius Uln!" He tiptoed past swollen tomato plants, brushing off his hands. The girl flashed them a shy, halfhearted smile, which vanished when she noticed Gavrel. When Eramus glanced over at Gavrel, he noticed that he, too, had reacted strangely to the man inside. Both men had their guard up.

Annoyed, barefoot, dressed simply in a belted tunic and roughspun pants, Riya Sen descended from the castle's second level on a circular stone stairway. Her once long, golden hair was now nothing more than a dirty blonde tangle bundled at the nape of her neck

The time Eramus had spent apart from her no longer mattered. Even something as simple as her presence filled a void in his existence. He wanted to touch her, to feel her warm body against his. His eyes fell to the black scars on her palms, a disfigurement from the magic she willingly embraced.

"Venard, Lyssa...excuse yourselves for now," she curtly

ordered. They hastily exited through a rear corridor, but not before Venard whispered something to her. She nodded, sighed with blatant irritation.

"Hello, Riya," Eramus said. He searched her expression for a hint of happiness, joy, anything positive about their reunion. She revealed nothing, though her gray eyes sparkled more than he remembered from her pale, thin frame.

"It's a shame the wolf didn't keep you out."

Awkward, uncomfortable silence ensued until Hadrius cleared his throat. "What do you have to drink?"

Eramus had been so caught up in his personal feelings that he had completely forgotten how tired, hungry, and thirsty they were.

"I don't know," she replied. "Venard's been making his own this year. I won't touch it." She regarded Gavrel with more than casual interest. "I assume Eramus convinced you to come here, probably against your better judgment."

Gavrel wiped a sweaty palm on his pants. "I've had my reservations."

"What's your name?"

"Gavrel."

She closed her eyes and massaged the bridge of her nose. "Eramus…"

He swallowed. "What?"

"I'm busy."

He wanted to tell her how much he had missed her, but he couldn't say it. He had promised to guard his emotions around her. "It's in your interest to hear us out."

She frowned. "What? Does another village have a slaver problem? I'm very busy. This is costing me time."

"We've been riding," Eramus said, meeting her protest on middle ground. "Give us a place to rest. I promise that what we have to say will intrigue you at the very least."

"Fine," she relented, sighing. Spreading her fingers in the archway, she concentrated until the indigo runes sizzled, ribbons of the same color leaking out of the symbols to converge into her palm.

Wary, Gavrel stared at the archway, at where the magical defense had hidden. A similar construct had stolen his brother's life.

Eramus could understand the man's trepidations, so he entered first to show him the threat no longer existed, at least not here. Once they had stepped inside, Riya raised her glowing palm, releasing the captured magic to reform the arcane wall.

"You can take it off now," she said firmly to Eramus.

He held the ring in front of his face, marveled at it before he removed it, secured it to the necklace, and tucked it back into his tunic. He immediately missed its warmth.

She led them past the garden and across the courtyard to stone benches bordering a circular fire pit. She waved a limp hand at a pitcher atop a nearby pedestal. "The water's fresh."

While she retrieved a jug from a spirits shelf, they lathered their hands and faces in cool, clean water. She poured a drink for everyone but Eramus, furtively studying the tattoo on Gavrel's wrist when she handed him a traditional wooden *glistas* cup. He swept his eyes around the keep, absorbing the overgrowth of exotic plants. Terra cotta and white marble statuary lined the base of the nearest wall, along with old chests, colorful furniture, and a fortune in unique artifacts, large and small.

Gavrel gulped his drink and slammed the cup down before he realized Eramus hadn't accepted any. "You're not thirsty?" Without waiting for an answer, he squirmed out of his jerkin and discarded the damp, dirty kerchief. He yanked down his sweat-soaked tunic to inspect his mass of scarred flesh. Eramus looked away, unable to imagine how it hindered him.

"Eramus prefers to maintain an illusion of control," Riya said, watching Gavrel as he unbuttoned his tunic. A network of scars illustrated his lean, muscular body. "Don't mind me."

Gavrel ignored her sarcasm, leaned back to relax, his eyes taking in everything and everyone.

This time Eramus refilled Gavrel's cup. "This isn't wine or ale," he said. "It's *glistas*. You don't drink it so fast."

Gavrel gauged Eramus's sincerity. "I drink how I drink."

"Not with *glistas*. Three swallows. That's how you drink it." *Three sips, three mortal Awakenings.*

Without a word, Gavrel picked up the cup and took a quick swallow. Eramus nodded his approval as he recalled the night Rammun had taught him the very same thing. *Part of tradition.* Eramus had never acquired his own set of drinking cups, or a tavern in which to put them. His life had ended up somewhere unanticipated.

The sun threw their long shadows across the courtyard. Eramus felt himself drifting off. A heavy noise rattled him, and he snapped awake from his own snoring, sniffed his nose clean.

"Why are you here?" Riya asked. "I'm waiting to be intrigued."

"You're familiar with Baron Kent?" Gavrel said as he set his cup down. He stood to his full height, stretched his arms out in front of him, favoring his left side.

"Of course."

"And the kidnapping?"

She nodded. "Word spreads with traders and Venard loves gossip."

"We're after the children," Eramus added. "We think we've found the kidnappers' trail in the Coronals.

She leaned forward in her seat, narrowing her eyes up at Gavrel. "Did these two hire you? You're a little much for kidnappers, aren't you?"

He stiffly shook his head. "My reasons for working with them are my own." He pinched his ugly scar, sucked air through his teeth at the contact. "What you have in your doorway…we encountered something similar in the mountains. It's preventing us from following the children."

"A ward," she smiled knowingly. "A protection spell." She turned back to Eramus. "Now you have my interest."

Eramus yawned and shrugged. "There's more. Sir Jacob of Gelofass is blackmailing us."

"Not all of us," Hadrius said as he leaned back for an afternoon nap. If Eramus couldn't sleep, he wasn't about to let Hadrius. He kicked his feet out from under him and knocked him off the bench. "*Kuvos*," Hadrius glared at him while he brushed himself off and sat back down again.

"Look," Eramus continued. "This really doesn't have much to do with the knight. He's connected to it all, of course, but this is just another job. I know you're busy, Riya. You've made that clear. I understand that, but we really need your help. Whatever that is up there, we can't get through it."

Gavrel rubbed his jaw. "We lost two of our party in the mountains. My brother and his woman," he said, nodding at

Hadrius. "You know about magic. We don't. We'll take care of whatever put that there. We just need a way past it. We can figure out a deal, if that's what you want."

She took a swallow of *glistas*. "I already said that you have my interest. Tell me the rest of it."

The three of them described the circle of chalk beyond the bridge and everything leading up to it. Gavrel remained silent when they detailed Lebon's death.

"But the woman died instantly?" she asked.

"That's what my brother said," Gavrel replied, though not without first sparing a glance at Hadrius.

It did not go beyond Eramus's notice that Riya's eyes brimmed with restrained excitement. She thought, planned, calculated.

"Your brother and the woman…"

"Sylvia," Hadrius firmly interjected.

"Your brother and Sylvia," Riya said to Gavrel. "Were they *duba*? Or were they a man and woman of First Awakening?"

"Lebon would never give himself up to Gefil."

"Then he was of First Awakening?"

Eramus didn't understand why Riya was impatiently pressing for information seemingly unrelated to why they were here. Still, when Gavrel glanced at Eramus, he slowly nodded for the man to answer her question anyway.

"I don't know about Sylvia, but my brother always claimed to be of Second Awakening."

Riya turned her head to the side, calculating after his response. She laced her fingers together. "I have a thought, that's all. Venard's heard rumors from my buyers about a desperate sorcerer living in those mountains."

"You know him?" Gavrel demanded, angry. "Is he a friend of yours?"

She rolled her tongue around in her mouth, unintimidated. "Few sorcerers are friends, but this could be an opportunity for…an introduction."

"His…ward or spell or whatever killed my brother. An introduction is not what I have in mind."

Silence followed. Eramus didn't know how much longer he could keep his eyes open. His arms and legs hung heavy on his body.

"I said I've heard rumors," Riya said. "That's all. I won't be a part of your vendetta. I owe you nothing, assassin." Gavrel's face flushed and he self-consciously reached for the tattoo on his arm. Riya stretched, laced her fingers overhead while she arched her back. "Venard's preparing dinner." She glared at Gavrel. "Don't take liberties around here or you'll regret it." Then she pointed a stern finger at Eramus. "Don't disturb me for any reason."

While the three of them watched, she disappeared up the staircase.

"She makes me uncomfortable," Gavrel muttered. Eramus didn't disagree.

CHAPTER 6

Lying on his back in the cart, listening to hundreds of voices chattering back and forth, Eramus imagines himself as the single white wisp of cloud gliding soundlessly overhead against a clear blue sky, guided by a loving breeze. The sun stings his eyes with sporadic spotting yet he cannot look away. He is nine now. Older than eight, and still nothing has changed. He misses his mother. She wouldn't have forgotten his nameday.

No. He is nine now. He is no longer eight. His mother might not have forgotten his nameday, but she has certainly forgotten him. He refuses to shut his eyes, even to blink. He will sear this moment into his memory. Lying in a sea of carts just inside Frehm, surrendering his hope to a fleeting cloud, waiting for his uncle and his father to return with workers. How many hours has it been?

The voices change. A man shouts. People push and shove, excited. Eramus remembers this moment. He forces himself to.

His arm hurts as his uncle roughly seizes him. "Now he's done it." He half-drags Eramus along, elbowing his way through a crowd.

"What about the cart?" Eramus asks. He looks for the cloud but it has already gone. In its place the hazy form of a bird soars, wings spread wide. Its presence feels inherently wrong, and yet somehow familiar.

"Now you'll see what it costs you," his uncle says. He grabs Eramus's other arm, stares at him, and shakes him to emphasize his point. Eramus is terrified that his uncle will really hurt him.

"Now you'll see!"

Before Eramus can ask what he means, a thin, toothless man offers a wineskin at half the price for the execution. Eramus thinks of wine, and then immediately thinks of his father.

"Half the price, eh?" Uncle Reginald confirms.

In his mind, Eramus can once more see the small cloud against the blue sky, and he blinks. His uncle drags him through the crowd. He wonders again about his father, about the strange bird looking down on all of them.

While Lyssa readied guest rooms, Venard set tapers on the table and served plates of garnished quince slices with red and orange nasturtium petals, blackberries piled among dates, figs, and cranberries. He returned with broccoli, cauliflower, and an assortment of winter squash, followed by delicious black bread drenched in butter and honey and a mixed variety of greens.

"Lettuce begin," Gavrel said as he reached for leaf lettuce. "Lebon wasn't much for the green side of the plate. That was his way around it."

The burn of fatigue clung to Eramus's eyes and numbed his muscles, but he felt considerably better after dozing and relaxing for the last few hours. "Let us..." he repeated until the humor dawned on him and he chuckled. Gavrel hadn't yet been able to properly observe his brother's passing into the next Awakening, and now was as good a time as any to begin the recitation of his meaning in this one.

Venard took Gavrel's hand in his own, surprising all of them. "We say words for your brother in true Hamaln." Gavrel didn't resist, though Venard's gesture clearly astounded him. They took each other's hands and bowed their heads. "Seen under brighter sunlight than in life, a man who walked his way through Second Awakening as best he knew how and who left enough of an impression to be missed even after he's left us for his journey to Third Awakening."

"Now we leave him his task," Gavrel finished. They touched their foreheads as a sign of respect and held their palms to the sky to signal that, even after death, Lebon could still be seen by all.

Gavrel hadn't eaten anything yet. He observed everyone else, waited for them to taste something before he put it onto his plate.

"Hospitality applies here," Venard scolded. Gavrel stared back at him for a few seconds, gauging his sincerity and honesty, then tore into the food. Though it was the middle of autumn, Venard carefully poured last season's green summer wine into crystal goblets for Hadrius, Gavrel, and himself. Lyssa arrived late in the meal, smearing colorful squash with butter and nibbling on it. Riya did not join them, but her absence didn't stop Venard from asking about the goings on outside Brudgewan. Gavrel described orchards of golden apples he had passed with his brother.

"You mentioned trading for this wine with a vintner," Gavrel said to Venard. "Was it one of Lord Harton's?"

"Yes," Venard replied. "One of the few with permission to leave the estate. Spirits and food come at a premium these days. That's why I treat the gardens with respect."

"What about the fishermen?"

Venard waved dismissively. "I've had enough fish for a lifetime, and their drink is watered down. Until trade comes back into Brudgewan, we're left to our own."

"This is a different Brudgewan than I've heard about."

Venard shifted in his seat, and at a nod Lyssa cleared the table. "He must not have walked this soil for a while. Lord Harton barely leaves his estate. Baron Kent seems to have an understanding with Keltivar so there's no real need to garrison troops by the Lestwine anymore. Harton's more worried about Moritare crossing the river and burning him out of his castle than anything else."

"Duke or Lord Moritare to you," Gavrel sternly corrected. He let Lyssa refill his goblet, nodding his thanks to her, observing her with more than casual interest. "My brother said My Lord Moritare could have taken Brudgewan if he wanted it."

"Really? Perhaps you forget that Harton used to be a warlord before…Duke Moritare gave in and legitimized his occupation."

Gavrel shook his head and swirled his green wine, studying its depths. "Too much work to hold it. Besides, Keltivar's on the other side. The enemy."

"Maybe your enemy," Venard remarked. "You were never in anyone's army." Gavrel hesitated, sipped his wine. "Keltivar has no reason to threaten Harton or anyone here. We've been sharing a border for years. Yeah, Keltivar could push on our soil, but only to get to Oshlah or Gelofass. Remember, your countrymen put their lips to old scrolls. Brother probably did, too." He bit off the tip of his cauliflower and threw the stem to hiss in the fire. Gavrel glared back, upset but held in check by some unspoken respect.

Hadrius banged his empty goblet on the table. Much to Venard's dismay, as soon as Lyssa refilled Hadrius's goblet he gulped down the remainder of the vintage. He raised the goblet in a halfhearted salute, belching long and loud. "I am...empty," he proclaimed. He turned his goblet over onto the table and burst into song. "I've been riding; I am thirsty; you can get more to drink but first me."

"Get the bard some lake ale," Venard said with a flourish.

With both arms wrapped around it, Lyssa planted a clay jug onto the table in front of Hadrius. She sat at the table with everyone for a while, only smiling politely when one of the men addressed her or offered a clever insight about the origins of the stars or what one could expect from the next Awakening. Hadrius poured himself cup after cup of the brown-colored ale from the heavy jug with ease, ignoring the rest of them while they talked. Lyssa eventually bid them goodnight and retired to her quarters. Gavrel didn't bother disguising his interest in her as he shifted his entire upper body to catch a final glimpse of her on the way out.

"And how are things around here?" Eramus asked as he cleared his throat.

"You mean how is Mistress Riya?" Venard responded with a smirk. His smile faded. "Like before. She locks herself in her laboratory for days. I have to send Lyssa up to remind her to eat. Sometimes she orders us to leave the food outside the door, and when we come back it's untouched. I've ridden out to the lake with her on occasion for meetings with questionable folks. I try not to ask too many questions. I'll never pretend to understand her. I keep the place, and that's all I can do." He drank the last of his wine. "Today is the first time I've seen her in four days."

Eramus was discouraged to hear that Riya had fallen back into her old habits. She had always spent most of her time studying magic, but at least when they had been together he had been able to convince her to enjoy the occasional day in the sunshine or even to accompany him on jobs or trips. Locking herself away as much as she did couldn't be healthy. She needed fresh air.

"I'm glad you're here," Venard yawned. He picked up one of

the candles to light his way. "Long day. Your beds are waiting."

"I won't need one," Gavrel said. "I'll sleep in the courtyard."

"The ground goes colder than ice at night. Don't keep us awake with your chattering teeth."

"I'll be warm enough. There's still a fire going and I prefer the open space. I need to see the stars."

"Then count the stars if you have to but don't try to leave the keep. Do you understand?"

"You think you can make me a prisoner?"

"You're a guest," Eramus reminded him. "Respect the wishes of your host. Don't be ridiculous, Gavrel. There's a wolf out there. The warning's for your safety."

The table clattered as Hadrius bumped into it, knocking a plate onto the ground. "Oops." He scooped up his jug like he would a child, holding it close to his chest with one massive arm. He stopped next to Gavrel and poked him on his good shoulder. "Don't be ridiculous." He waved over his shoulder with a burst of laughter.

With one last look at the vast courtyard, Eramus nodded goodnight to Gavrel and followed the other two by candlelight through the corridors. Their large and comfortable rooms resided on the first floor, the coldest level of the keep, but burning blazes spit in the hearths and the beds were piled high with blankets, a nice change of pace after sleeping outside on the ground. Eramus had spent many nights in this exact room when Riya had been upstairs reading and experimenting. He tossed the blankets aside and fell onto his face without another thought.

Unfortunately he shared a wall with Hadrius, and before long his friend's loud singing woke him from a light sleep. Slurred Uuslefin lyrics died out only to resume, louder, with each new song. Eramus decided to wait him out, and soon enough the singing dwindled into heavy snoring and the empty jug thumped on the floor.

Nine years old. No longer eight. He feels nothing inside his body. His feet hurt. His uncle steers him into the house. His legs fold and he sits at the table, stares down at his hands. Loghemit Pon is dead.

"You start work tomorrow," his uncle says from somewhere far

away in the late afternoon. "I'm paying four men. You'll get meals and your bed for the same work. No more playing."

Something buzzes lazily around the room. Eramus glances up to see a fly join more on the mantel. They pick at a tart. Eramus can't find the strength to shoo them away.

His uncle licks his lips and snatches up the tart when he sees it. He takes a bite and the flies zip away. "Mm. Strawberry and cinnamon."

Eramus feels nothing, not even anger. He has lost his father.

"Your father was weak," his uncle says as he eats the tart. "Afraid to make his own choices, quick to blame others. Who can trust a man like that?" He polishes off the tart, licks his fingers.

"At least I won't get charged for the funeral. They burned the body. A man who doesn't learn in First Awakening has no reason to go on."

Eramus knows he should feel something. Anger. Sadness. Instead he shamefully thinks about how his life might be a little easier without his father in it.

Ten minutes Eramus lay awake, incredibly tired, fueled by a strange euphoria. He tugged the covers over himself, hoping for elusive, dreamless sleep. He sat up and stared at the fire, searching within it for familiar shapes, attempting to read its erratic patterns like Seehlan priests interpreted clouds. The more he peered into the incandescence of the fire's core, the more his eyes watered and blurred the flames out of focus. His eyes turned inward, to memories and impressions of Riya. She would be awake.

He left his room and wandered along the hallway, his stomach a nervous knot. Riya had warned him against disturbing her. He planted his soles firmly onto the cold flagstones with each step, wondering how she would receive him despite the warning.

Soft orange light spilled down the stairwell, accompanied by the stench of wet charcoal and something burning. Eramus stood perfectly still. He could turn back. Gavrel had curled up by the fire on his bedroll. When they were back on the road, Eramus would have to ask him why he had turned down a perfectly comfortable bed.

Eramus crept up the stairs, under an intricate archway decorated with carved expressions of an old man's face, the emotions. Riya once translated the foreign quote at the apex: *"A man who can read the stars is a powerful man indeed."* He ran his fingers over the expressions, unable to remember what all of them represented. He remembered empathy, sadness…

A pair of braziers hung from the ceiling, their heat and light warping the air, casting deep pockets of shadow into the cracks of the stone walls. A square of light revealed the open laboratory door. Eramus peeked in at Riya stirring thick, smoking liquid in a flask. She earned an exceptional living selling potions and magically imbued items to anonymous buyers.

An ancient tapestry hung across the near wall. Upon it a man levitated, cross-legged, in sunlight. Below the tapestry an assortment of stoppered bottles lined the edge of a huge wooden table. Thick yellow candles dripped wax in the foreground, iron rings and contraptions suspending cheesecloth filters full of ground charcoal above them. Intricate runes had been painted across the table's surface in black ink, with titles above each combination. From experience he understood that these combinations represented different potion formulas.

Her open, leatherbound spellbook revealed columns of hand drawn runes and copious notes, her repository of experience. Riya had made it clear to him on several occasions that she would always choose her craft over him. His jealousy had transcended resentment over her declaration, until he realized the futility of competition.

He glanced at an oil painting of an old crone stroking the pelt of a dead wolf on the far wall. She sat beneath a dark tree bearing rich red fruit, surrounded by stuffed birds and other dead animals positioned to appear alive, as if a child had arranged them. No matter where Eramus stood in the room, the crone looked right at him. He had never seen the painting. It made him very uncomfortable, even more so when he discovered a bastard snowthroat among the animal retinue. It was hardly possible for him to distinguish one bird from another, but this one's yellow eye resembled that of the bird following him. He stepped closer, the painting calling to him, as he reached forward with his fingertips, afraid of the contact, unable to resist its beckoning.

"I thought I told you not to bother me," Riya said, startling him out of his trance. His hand immediately fell to his side. Loose strands of her hair had fallen out of the tie behind her head. Candlelight softened her cheeks, added depth to her full red lips, and accentuated the heavy bags underlining her eyes, a sign of sleeplessness that Eramus was all too familiar with. Her expression revealed that she had expected him.

"I can't sleep."

She turned her back to him, raised her hand until a blossom of indigo fire glimmered in her palm. The tiny, fragile flame flickered weak as candlelight in a healthy wind.

"Impressive," he remarked.

Like a spider lowering on its web, she coaxed the flame into a flask half-full of white oak bark. The bark ignited before melting into a lighter colored, syrupy liquid. She stoppered the flask with a cork set around a glass tube and placed it onto one of the iron rings, over a thick candle and under one of the cheesecloth filters. The thick liquid evaporated and the underside of the filter stained with that same unique color. She removed the candle and the flask, replacing them with a small stone mortar containing an unrecognizable, pulpy mess.

The damp odors of charcoal, oak, and other assorted stenches almost made him gag. He had imbibed a few of her potions before, and aside from their awful taste they had always left him uncomfortable once they had worn off. He picked up a human skull from a nearby table. A hole gaped in its forehead. He had never touched a human skull before but the smooth texture was oddly familiar. The rest of the table was neatly organized with a stoppered flask of what appeared to be blood, two sealed scrolls, an intricate sketch of human anatomy, and a moon chart.

"The fishermen killed a deserter who strayed too close to the village. They buried the body without a shroud. I dug it up and stole the head to study the skull."

Eramus put it down immediately. "You cut off the head? That's pretty gruesome, even for you, Riya."

She waited for the filter above the mortar to stop dripping, and then ground the mixture together with a pestle. She used a funnel to pour the mortar's contents into an orderly row of vials. "I haven't descended into the *Rinja Ga*, if that's what concerns you."

"I don't even know what that means."

She licked her lips. "Aefun's cult. Death magic. According to legend, Aefun's mother stabbed her young son fifty-three times and watched him bleed out because he feared to enter the woods alone at night."

Fear. Eramus couldn't recall the details of his conversation with someone who had asked him about fear. Was it a coincidence that the painting on Riya's wall possibly held clues to what was happening to him?

He cleared his throat. "I'm glad to know that you haven't been talking to the dead, or whatever that means."

"I talk to you." The mortar slipped from her fingers, the colored mess rattling on the stone floor, chilling the room. Scents of honey and licorice floated on her warm breath. Eramus forgot everything but the moment. She leaned forward and gently bit his earlobe, quickening his breathing. Her fingers interlaced with his, the burned, dead skin on her palms scratching his hands, the heat of recently used magic tingling over the skin on his left hand where she touched him with her right. "You should visit more often," she said, practically dragging him into the hallway. With a wave of her hand a draft extinguished the candles. Before Eramus left the laboratory, he noticed the acute visibility of the disturbing painting, though he couldn't identify any light source other than the hallway braziers. Fear prickled over his spine. He suppressed it. It was just a painting, a coincidence, and he was just afraid. Again.

The door slammed behind them and Riya twisted free of his grasp. She left a trail of her clothes as she disrobed down the hallway, slipped the tie from hair and shook it free.

When Eramus entered her room, she lay naked under a pile of blankets and furs. A fire popped in the hearth and a selection of apples, cherries, and cheeses sat on a nearby table. A cool wind billowed the decorative curtains over the open windows. Riya extended her hand to Eramus, all the encouragement he needed.

Slick with sweat, they lay together on the bed, most of the blankets on the floor beside them.

"Do you want to go out on the balcony?" he asked, thinking of her nestled close to him, gazing up at sleep stars.

She shook her head. "Too cold." She twirled his hair on her fingers. He closed his eyes, wanting to fall asleep to that feeling, to remain next to her. "You don't smell very good."

He sat up and rolled his shoulders, loosening tight muscles. "I don't imagine I do." He walked to the table and helped himself to some of the cheese with a crumbly texture and sharp flavor.

"It's Medarn," she said as she flopped onto her stomach and propped her chin on her palms.

"Pretty good." He snatched up some cherries and brought them back to bed. Cherries were her favorite, and these were still saturated from canning. "Why did you cut your hair?"

She hesitated. "It got in my way. Don't think you've earned my cooperation just because you seduced me."

He shook his head and sat down beside her, knowing full well she had been the one to seduce him. She opened her mouth expectantly and he dropped a cherry in, their familiar moments of intimacy reminding him how much he had missed her. "This is very serious for me, Riya. I made a mistake and now someone else is in a lot of trouble."

She chewed up the fruit and spit the pit into his waiting palm. "What's new? Your problems always come first." He ignored her sarcastic barb and dropped another cherry onto her waiting tongue.

"Hadrius and I can cover your fee. You'll have to accept what we have on us as a down payment. You know we're good for the rest of it." He paused. "It's my friend, Sadir Nom. Do you remember him? That's who's in trouble. Sadir and his wife and daughter. Innocent people."

She gave him back another pit. "I remember the name. You don't have many friends, Eramus."

She was right. Eramus had a hard time trusting people. "I met him when I was in the IR. He'd been robbed, left to die on the side of the road."

"So you helped him. Now he's your problem."

"He's not my problem. It's not like that. He's a very intelligent man. You'd like him. I escorted him back into the barony after the robbery. It was the first time I felt like I was really making a difference in someone's life. We just kind of got along after that, and now I visit him whenever I'm passing through." *The stone struck Sadir in the face, split his cheek.*

Eramus shook the grisly image of his friend out of his head and tried to feed another cherry to Riya but she waved his hand away, reading the worry on his face. Her gaze didn't waver. She knew him too well. "What did you do, Eramus?"

He looked back at those commanding eyes of hers. They stole his speech, skipped his heartbeat. He loved the way she pronounced his name, stressing all three syllables until she held her tongue on the final sound. He could still taste that tongue. Flecks of indigo glowed at the edges of her eyes, evidence that she had stored more than the normal amount of magic in her body. She had done that before, and the effect enhanced their lovemaking. "The Filthies were beating someone. A woman. I couldn't just watch. I thought that would be the end of it, but they followed me to Sadir's and it got out of hand. They're holding his family hostage until I find the baron's children."

"Did you talk to the magistrate?"

"It's not that simple. I don't know who's involved, and the knight warned me about doing anything other than what he instructed."

"Why would a knight care about the baron's children?"

"He doesn't. Sir Jacob claims the kidnappers are Seehlan."

"Did he ask you to kill them?"

"No."

"But he did send an assassin with you."

"You mean Gavrel, don't you? How do you know he's an assassin?"

She shrugged. "His tattoo. It's the dog head of Twice Unlucky, an assassins guild." She shook her head and clucked her tongue. "You should know who you travel with."

"Sir Jacob sent him along with his brother. I didn't have a choice. He's good in a fight. I don't think he'll murder anyone in cold blood, though. We're only hunting down refugees."

"He could be after them. Nobody hires the Twice Unlucky unless they want to send a message."

"I don't think Sir Jacob hired him. He's in some type of trouble like I am. I think Sir Jacob's using him, too. His brother arranged this to clear his name. His brother was a good man, and I still can't see Gavrel killing refugees without the proper motivation."

"Like money? Guilds have a hard time letting go of men they trained. They're investments. Maybe he has to pay the guild back."

"I don't know. Maybe. He's caught up in all sorts of trouble and he won't answer any of my questions." He dropped his head in his hands and groaned. "It just doesn't make any sense. Sir Jacob has soldiers at his disposal. He could send them to kill refugees, or he could just do it himself."

"Why is it that you can stand up for a stranger but not for yourself? She must be quite a woman." He ignored her sarcasm. She scratched a dormant itch along his bare back with her scarred palms, allowing the slightest hint of magical warmth to seep through. He missed that wonderful, unique feeling. "There's something inherently flawed about you."

"So says the woman who collects human skulls."

She laughed at that, and he laughed with her. She didn't laugh often. It was the wrong time for humor but he couldn't be solemn and angry all the time. He settled his head into her lap and let her comb his hair with her fingers, the sensation washing away his worries.

"Once we find the children, I'll take them directly to their father and tell him everything."

"And what's that?"

He thought about it for a second. He had no proof of anything, and no idea if the baron had sanctioned this mission. "I suppose I'll know what to say when it's time."

"If the baron cared about his children, they wouldn't have been taken in the first place." Riya's mother had sold her to a sorcerer when she was still a girl. Her hasty judgment in this matter might be unfair, but could he disagree with her? The baron really should have done a better job of protecting his children.

And what Sir Jacob had said about Loghemit Pon had been bothering Eramus for the last few days. *Your father's irresponsibility led to the deaths of four men.* Even if the knight had twisted the story to suit his own perspective, Eramus had no doubt that Loghemit Pon had indeed carelessly put himself into a bad situation, the result of which had left Eramus without a father. The father had made the mistake but the son had been forced to carry the burden of the consequences.

Riya was right about the baron.

With a heavy sigh, she tossed a pillow at his head. He easily dodged it, pulled her down onto him, and they kissed, him searching for her tongue while she playfully kept it from him.

When she withdrew her lips from his, he felt unusually lonely. The outside world did not exist in here unless he brought it with him. He wanted to stay in this room with her forever, but he knew he couldn't.

He hesitated, wondering how out of the ordinary his next question would sound.

"What is it?" she asked as she caught her breath, a raw smile still spread across her beautiful face. She read him too easily. Perhaps he wanted that. Perhaps he needed it.

"I…sometimes…do you really believe in animals forming connections with people, I mean besides something as simple as having a pet?" It was a strange question coming from him, one which immediately raised her defenses.

"Why do you ask?" She had claimed that the spirit of a man resided in her wolf, and it wasn't until today that Eramus had begun to believe her.

Then again, he could just be losing his grasp on reality. Perhaps the absurd notions had manifested when he had seen the wolf, or even when he had noticed the strange painting in her laboratory. Ella was a common name. He could have heard it anywhere.

"It's just…strange things have been happening to me, things I can't really explain, and you once told me that the wolf used to be a man." He struggled to tell her, struggled to make sense of his words without coming off as too ridiculous.

"It is a man."

"That's what I meant to say." She waited for him, but he couldn't seem to formulate any coherent questions about his recent experiences. He knew what he considered saying would sound utterly absurd, even to her. Frustrated, he pulled away from her to get dressed. "I'd better get some sleep. Are you coming with us or not?"

She pulled a blanket over her head. "I'll tell you in the morning." She threw off the blanket and rolled onto her back, her breasts rising and falling ever so slightly as she breathed. "You can sleep here, you know."

If he didn't leave the room now, he would never be able to, and he desperately needed sleep. He stood still, unable to excuse himself.

She rolled her eyes. "Good night, Eramus."

He crept back downstairs into a courtyard stained a cold, bloody red by early morning stars, frustration churning within him. Riya's way of making him feel foolish could be part of his attraction to her.

Her room had been hot. Now he shivered with cold. When he reached his room the fire had already faded to glowing embers. He lay on the floor and wrapped himself in blankets. The bed would be too comfortable for him. He tried not to think about Riya, about how he felt so alive and unimportant at the same time in her presence.

The petals of a perfect daisy bend in golden sunlight. Eramus reaches for it, flinches when a winged shadow passes. Again, he knows this presence does not belong. His stomach tightens when he understands that he cannot wait for his mother. Arms spread, he leaps as high as he is able and soars on a strong current.

Faster than he anticipates, he glides down a hill, running clumsily as he lands until he stands in front of the tavern in Grihm, mere feet away from a well. There is no brace for the well, no crank for a bucket to pull from its depths. It is a circle of stones. It is sunless daytime. Aside from the tavern and the well and the trees of the woods, Eramus is alone. There is no longer even a whisper of wind.

And yet he hears the water in the well lap against the stones like waves on the beach. He walks to the edge of the well, and is surprised to see that it isn't a well at all but rather a pool of some kind with reflective red sand resting beneath placid water. How has he come to be here? He recalls the sounds of the water moving and yet the water is as still as ever. He sees no reflection of any kind, not even his own. He instinctively knows touching the water is forbidden, and yet he reaches for the surface with his finger.

A bird shrieks, startling him. The indigo and white bird has appeared on the edge of the pool, its black feet scraping on stone. Eramus knows only that he might belong here, but the bird certainly doesn't. Yet the bird exists somewhere, and Eramus ponders its presence. It shrieks at him again, this time with greater concentration, this time with sounds he knows are words but which he cannot understand, vaguely familiar words.

"Are you afraid?" he hears his mother ask from nowhere. Before he can answer, cold steel punctures his flesh and she stabs

him over and over and over.

Eramus awoke, disoriented, to dust motes floating in a bright beam of sunlight shooting through his room's high window. His bones ached from the cold. He closed his eyes and tried to fall asleep again without success. He sat up and ruffled his hair, clinging to the vestiges of his strange dream. It was damn cold but finally he crawled out from beneath his blankets. He padded out into the courtyard, where Venard attended to morning chores. The aroma of fresh bread wafted out of the fire pit, where plenty of it cooked over embers. His senses felt powerfully alive.

"Feel free to refresh yourself," Venard said. He pointed to the pedestal where fresh water had been set out. "Breakfast will be served shortly." As he walked away Eramus noticed the tattoo on his arm that he had always taken for granted, the same as Gavrel's: a dog's skull. That would explain the bond between the men. No wonder Riya knew what it was. She had once told him that Venard and his daughter had been in trouble before they came to work for her. Now Eramus had an idea what that trouble might have been. Assassins walked beside him and he was oblivious.

He shivered through his ablutions. Riya hadn't yet agreed to join them. Without her, he didn't know what his next step would be. He tried not to worry too much. He hoped the lure of a sorcerer would be enough to tempt her.

Gavrel already sat by the fire pit. He nodded a greeting to Eramus. When Eramus finished washing he joined him, holding out his palms to warm up. Lyssa emerged from the kitchen and set bowls of sweet cream butter, warm honey, and spiced apples onto the table. She pulled the bread out of the fire pit and they followed her to the table. She was a kind, quiet girl with a good heart.

Hadrius strolled up and tore into the breakfast. Lyssa returned with cheese and warm milk. Gavrel flashed an uncharacteristic smile at her, and she shyly returned it.

"What did she say?" he asked Eramus. "Will she help us?"

Eramus could only reply with a shrug.

"I slept better than I have for a long time," Gavrel said, changing the subject. He almost spit out his bread it was so hot. He gazed sideways at Hadrius. "Even after the performance."

Eramus wished he could say the same. He felt tired, on edge. His eyes and his body had sagged under fatigue and sleeplessness for days. He might have gotten sleep last night but his unusual dream had sped the time into mere minutes.

Hadrius said nothing, not even in response to Gavrel's remark about his drunken antics. With slumped shoulders and bloodshot eyes he quietly ate. Normally reserved, he seemed even more so since Sylvia's death. He sopped his bread in disgusting amounts of butter to soak last night's binge, the stink of which sweat through his pores even in the seasonably cold morning.

Riya appeared at the foot of the stairs in a nondescript brown cloak and matching leather boots. Eramus almost collapsed with relief at the sight of her. Numerous pouches hung off her belt and a satchel strap separated her breasts. Though he couldn't see it, Eramus knew that she had an enchanted dagger bound to her upper arm and that the satchel swinging behind her, under the cloak, contained her prized spellbook.

"Venard," she called out. Her assistant hustled back into the courtyard and she handed him a wooden potions case and a document sealed with indigo wax. "I trust that all is in readiness?"

He bowed slightly to her. "Your horse waits in the village."

"Good. You're master until my return. Make the delivery at the usual time and place, and don't take anything less than the amount marked under the vials."

"And this?" Venard asked, holding up the document.

She quickly glanced back to Eramus to see if he was paying attention, though he had no idea why. "Take that to Lisbeth. You remember where she lives, don't you?" He nodded, though his expression revealed that he did not much care for the woman Riya had named.

Riya joined them at the table. "I'm going with you." She snatched bread from his plate and nibbled at it. Eramus found himself still overwhelmingly attracted to the physical scars of her scorched palms. Her scent excited him. She had a way of invading his dreams, no matter how much distance lay between them. He slipped his hand onto her thigh under the table, and she gently nudged it away.

She stood up and brushed crumbs from her hands.

"We should get moving," Eramus said, following her lead.

Gavrel took longer than usual to pack his gear. Eramus couldn't understand why until he saw him stop Lyssa for an awkward goodbye.

Riya removed the magical protection from the entryway, reminding both Lyssa and Venard to keep the heavy iron gate closed and locked in her absence. Eramus knew from experience that Venard also possessed a talisman to protect him against the wolf should he need to leave the grounds.

The four of them left the castle minutes later, crossing the colorful meadow, their boots crunching frost on the grass. A freezing wind rolled off the mountains even as bright sunlight burned off wispy clouds to reveal even more ebb stars. The wolf circled them from a distance, and Gavrel clenched his already colorless fists.

Riya ignored the animal, her eyes locked on the sun. "I'll never understand," she said cryptically.

Eramus glanced back, and could have sworn that the wolf watched only him, though this time no names flashed into his head.

They found their horses where they had left them. Hadrius quickly saddled his mount and swung up.

"Ride with me," Eramus said as he helped Riya up to settle pillion. When she wrapped her arms around his waist, the warm press of her body banished the cold and dissolved the wind into a throatless whisper. He wanted to ride away with her somewhere, to leave everyone and everything else behind.

Instead he kept a steady pace through the dense trees, turning whenever and wherever she indicated. He wanted to tell her that his feelings for her had never waned, but when he imagined the words aloud they only sounded pathetic. They would need to work together for the next few days and he didn't need any more complications between them.

She clutched him a little tighter when they rounded a series of sharp turns to emerge on the bank of the sparkling lake.

Riya pointed to the fishing village on the far shore. "My horse is stabled there. We'll have to buy some supplies."

Hadrius trotted ahead without waiting. Eramus and the others eventually arrived at one of the fishermen's homes, where a boy hastened to saddle Riya's horse at their approach. When she dismounted and released her hold on Eramus, he felt the void of her absence. He dismounted as well and headed to a trading post for dried goods and grain for the horses. The owner whistled for his son to help load them up.

Riya's horse had already been led out. She sat astride it, reins wrapped tightly around her hands. Eramus instructed the boy on how to properly pack their saddlebags. When the boy got to Riya's horse, she shooed him away.

"There's no more room," she told him.

Eramus glared at her before he flipped the boy a silver. He whistled at Hadrius to finish up whatever he was doing, and soon they were on their way.

They rode four wide for the next mile. "We can camp half an hour up the road, until sunset," Gavrel said, his eyes straight ahead.

"We're not going through that canyon after dark," Riya said, swinging her satchel forward.

Gavrel glanced at Eramus and Hadrius for support, his reins in his left hand as he held his bandage in place with his right while he turned. "Deserters are waiting to ambush us. I've seen them myself. We can put the sun in their eyes again."

"Don't worry about them," she said.

"So what do you plan to do?" Gavrel asked, his face marked with concern as she opened a wooden case she had pulled from the satchel. "What's in those vials?

She selected eight vials from the case. "In my saddlebags," she said to nobody in particular, "are padded boots for the horses." She glanced over at Gavrel. "Heresy is in these vials."

"I don't kneel before any temples," Gavrel snapped. "Don't bother with the cheap theatrics."

Eramus found the thick cloth boots and tossed them to Gavrel and Hadrius. "Just do what she says."

"Put them on," Riya said as politely as she could. "I'll take care of the rest."

Gavrel looked as if he was about to refuse, but he changed his mind when Eramus slipped the boots onto his horse.

"And which potion is on the menu today, milady?" Eramus asked sarcastically as they coaxed the horses into the boots.

"Obscurity."

"Ah. I remember that one."

Gavrel waited for an explanation.

"Yes," Hadrius added as he clawed at his scalp for effect. "This one is fantastic. I can't see you, you can't see me...at least we know what the cute little horse boots are for."

"You're so hungover I could have gotten you to wear them," Riya said. She tapped at her potions case. "If that ale's too slow for you I have an alternative."

"No thanks. I remember the last time you tricked me."

She shrugged. "Your loss."

Gavrel climbed back up into his saddle. "Obscurity. What exactly is it?"

Riya flipped a pair of the corked vials to Eramus. He caught them and held them up for Gavrel to see. "Obscurity." He inspected the vials himself, watching the indigo-tinted, translucent liquid inside it as it spun around and around. "Have you ever imbibed a potion before?" he asked.

Gavrel shook his head. "Tell me exactly what that is."

"Obscurity. At least that's what I remember. That and the fact that it tastes terrible, makes you ill in your stomach, and leaves a unique hangover behind once it's worn its course."

"Yes, yes, yes," Riya said impatiently. "And bandits gather flowers and lace up each other's jerkins. The darker ones for the horses' tongues and the lighter ones for each of you."

Eramus uncorked one of the vials and took a whiff of the oaky charcoal. He waved the awful stench away from his wrinkling nose. "I'll go last." He accepted three more of the darker potions and seized the horses' bridles one at a time, overcoming their resistance to pour the potions into their mouths. One at a time, they faded from sight.

With more courage and less reluctance than Eramus expected, Gavrel watched Riya and Hadrius melt out of sight until he waved his own vial under his nose, quickly turned away, and finally closed his eyes and gulped it down. "Odd indeed," he said from his invisible saddle, his lower body a blur of smeared color where it touched the horse. His eyes widened and he clutched at his vanishing legs. "The effects…"

"They're temporary," Riya said in anticipation of his question. "You're not going to lose anything. Ride straight through at a trot, no faster. Keep two lengths in front and behind, single file. Don't close your eyes for too long or you'll feel like you've been out to sea for a week."

Eramus fumbled up into his saddle as his horse whinnied and

shuffled beneath him. He uncorked the last potion and swallowed it, the oily texture and foul taste almost gagging him as he felt the warm liquid racing to his heart. Soon he looked left and right to a landscape as bare as it was before their arrival. Where his hands had been he saw only dirt. In his horse's place he saw yielding grass and hoof prints stamping into the ground.

Out of nowhere, Gavrel unloaded a barrage of questions. "What will happen to us? How long will we be like this?"

"Let's go, let's go," Riya said from somewhere in front of them.

Gavrel cursed, panicked. "Oh…I closed my eyes for too long." A horse whinnied nervously with a brush of contact.

"Calm down!" Eramus ordered. "She warned you not to do that. You'll just have to follow us the way you are."

"Follow you…"

"I made the instructions clear," Riya said sternly. "The potion's effects won't last long. Accelerated heart rate and adrenaline will burn it off. You can either pull yourself together or stay here. I don't really care."

Eramus knew they would have to hurry to take advantage of the potion. He wrapped his arms around his horse's neck, sucking down deep breaths to regain his sense of balance. Unlike Gavrel, he had experienced the obscurity's vertigo before. Still somewhat disoriented, he grunted out that he would follow immediately behind Riya. He focused on the tracks appearing in front of him. He heard horses moving, but the cloth boots muffled their steps well.

He followed the tracks into the canyon. Wind howled through the enclosed space, stinging his eyes. He heard the ragged, thin deserters off to his left, laughing about a dice game. In these circumstances they were simply men like him, who enjoyed a game and a conversation with friends, but he had to remind himself that they would open his guts for a coin.

His saddle creaked and his stirrups jingled under his heels, enough noise to alert the men. They peered into the canyon, relying on deceitful eyes. A couple of them inched forward, sniffing the air, twisting their ears toward faint sounds with no identifiable origin.

After what felt like forever, Eramus eased up onto the plateau overlooking the canyon, overcome with nausea. He hadn't closed his eyes for any extended period of time. His body simply didn't agree with what had happened. "Riya?" he called out. She didn't respond. The ground here was much more convoluted with thick grasses and bushes, the earth not as telling. He couldn't see any traces of her passing. Dizziness flooded into him. Despite his better judgment he clutched his horse around the neck again and squeezed his eyes shut.

"Wait for them," Riya's voice said.

"We're through," Hadrius said from a short distance behind him. A hoof floated into the air and dropped. It was connected to a leg, connected to a shoulder.

Eramus's stomach lurched. He grabbed the pommel of his saddle just to stay on the horse.

Gavrel wasn't as fortunate. He slid right off his horse and vomited on himself. Hadrius at least landed on his feet, but stumbled backwards until he hit the ground, laughing. He lay there, eyes closed, laughing and laughing.

Only Riya hadn't reacted to the reversion.

"We can rest here for now," she said calmly.

Like Hadrius, Gavrel lay on his back, eyes closed, mouth wide open. "Almost like a hangover."

"Food and water will help," she said.

"A liquid did this? How?"

"A potion, and you wouldn't understand."

"That was…amazing." He opened his sea-green eyes and self-consciously wiped away at the vomit on his chest with the hem of his tunic. Riya hid a smirk at his embarrassment.

"How are you doing?" Eramus asked Hadrius. "Okay now?" Hadrius nodded from his supine position without opening his eyes. Eramus handed him a waterskin, and his friend drank greedily.

A gentle breeze lifted Riya's hair as she stared off into nothingness.

"What's she doing now?" Gavrel asked Eramus quietly as he leaned on his elbow and looked over the tops of his boots at her.

"You can always ask her," Eramus said. He shielded his eyes from the sun and looked east at the distant Coronal Range. If anyone could help them get past what was up there, it was Riya.

CHAPTER 7

When next they stopped to rest it was to allow the horses to graze in tall grass and to drink from a pond off the road. Riya ignored the others. She sat cross-legged and opened her spellbook, silently mouthing words while she read, dipping a quill into an inkpot over and over again as she filled a page with notes.

Eramus paced in a wide circle, nibbling on salted pike from their supplies, wondering how much he could trust Gavrel or Riya. Hadrius lay on his back, eyes closed as he napped in that typical worry-free fashion of his that infuriated Eramus to no end.

Gavrel stripped off his jerkin and tunic, squatting beside the pond to splash water over himself. Eramus couldn't help but notice the ugly latticework of grooved and puckered whip scars decorating his back. Raised white flesh resembling deep cuts or arrow punctures dotted his arms and chest. The man carefully removed his shoulder bandage and traced his fingertips over the colorless mass of skin. When he had scrubbed most of the trail dust and dried vomit from his jerkin, he replaced the old bandage with a new one and negotiated his way back into his tunic and jerkin.

"What's she doing?" he asked Eramus as he nodded at Riya hunched over her spellbook.

Eramus swallowed the bite he had been chewing. "Figuring out how to do things better. Probably writing down how much of the potion we took, how long it lasted, how many steps we took, the force of the wind, the height of the sun. Specific details."

"All in that book? It would fetch a fortune in the black market."

Eramus glared back at him. "Trying to get your hands on that would cost you your life. It's not worth consideration."

"Geflin missionaries say that all sorcerers should be reported."

"To whom? For what purpose? I don't see anything on your forehead. Are you *duba* or Hamaln? Be grateful she's on our side and leave it at that."

Gavrel stared up at the darker ebb stars in the clear blue sky. "What if the Ismah's right? What if the Forgotten Prophet really will return?"

Eramus had often wondered about the same thing. "You're asking the wrong person."

With a sigh Gavrel dug through their supply pouches, turning up his nose when he found grayling gone bad. Eramus chuckled to himself. He had purposely left the rotten fish in there for his own entertainment.

"How did she become a sorcerer?" Gavrel asked as he tossed out the fish. "I was told these people are cursed from birth. It seems like such a strange path to walk."

"A middleman called a calex came to her village and tested the children there for certain abilities. When she passed the tests, the calex bought her from her mother and promised to give her a better life."

Gavrel's face darkened. "Her mother sold her? That's slavery."

"The calex already had a buyer lined up," Eramus said with a frown. "She ended up apprenticing to a sorcerer."

"She survived what her mother did to her," Gavrel said with a hint of admiration. "And now she's a sorcerer. It's just another occupation, like a blacksmith or a wheelwright."

"It's hardly the same thing."

"She won't get pity from me," Gavrel replied. "I have my own bad memories." He glanced at Riya again. "Is this why she agreed to come along? Does she know this sorcerer?"

Eramus shook his head. "That man is dead."

"Lebon always told me that if you do it to them first, they can't do it to you." His hand dropped to his belt. "Is Lyssa…is she her apprentice?"

"No. Her father works for Riya. That's all."

"Venard."

"Yes, Venard. An assassin like you, or at least I think he used to be."

Gavrel nodded, not surprised at all. "I'd heard of him before. He was very good. When he disappeared, we assumed someone had made him disappear. Nobody claimed credit, but that doesn't mean anything. In the guilds, the better you get the more of a target you are. People go missing all the time. It's part of the job."

"Is that why Sir Jacob chose you to join us?"

Gavrel looked away. "You're not going to give up, are you?" He found edible pike in a pouch. "I'm not in the habit of explaining myself."

Eramus angrily shook his head. "I've had to put my life in your hands once already because of your past. Be honest with me. I've been pretty straightforward with you. You're an assassin. Were you hired to kill someone?"

Gavrel's lip twitched. "You accuse me of bringing trouble down on you. Have you forgotten what brought us together?" He stuffed an entire fillet in his mouth, barely chewing it.

"Of course not. Answer the question."

He swallowed his food, thought for a span of heartbeats and scratched his jaw. "I'm not squeamish."

"I've seen that already," Eramus said as he pointed to the tattoo on his arm. "You're a member of Twice Unlucky. I'm grateful we have your skills to complement ours. Don't misinterpret my concerns."

Gavrel didn't respond.

"You might have endured hard times," Eramus continued, thinking of all the physical scars he had seen, and how some would have come with even worse psychological damage.

"You have no idea."

"You're right. And I won't unless you tell me."

Hadrius's eyes fluttered open. He looked at the two of them as if he didn't recognize them. "We should get moving."

Gavrel regarded Eramus briefly but remained silent, his walls back up. Eramus would have to try again another time.

It didn't take long for the party to resume riding. Hadrius refreshed himself with ale, generously offering some to Gavrel and Riya along the way, though neither accepted. His interactions with the others indicated that his grief and depression over Sylvia's loss had lessened.

They rode until the horses tired, then walked them for a while, over the bridge and outside Brudgewan. As they headed south, they passed travelers on the way north to Keltivar. Gavrel had donned his cloak, wearing his hood low enough to conceal his features in shadows. Eramus paid special attention to bodyguards hovering near caravans. If any of the hired men recognized Gavrel and knew about the reward, things could quickly escalate. One man in particular, slender, with a few days of facial stubble and woolen gloves sans fingertips, had been pacing them for the last several minutes from a considerable distance, his gait too casual to imply anything other than an attempt to "appear" casual. Eramus made a mental note to keep track of him just in case.

"What are you thinking about?" Riya asked him, interrupting his thoughts. Her face glowed pleasantly in the sunshine.

"Nothing," he lied. His thoughts had drifted back to Alina. If he hadn't interfered in her troubles, he and Hadrius would be at the festival already. But then Eramus wouldn't have met Gavrel, and Riya wouldn't be with them. Amidst everything else transpiring, though, Eramus had begun to wonder how Alina fared. He shouldn't have left her alone.

He shielded his eyes from the setting sun and studied the barony walls looming before them. Sadir, Kathryn, and Raisa were depending on Eramus, possibly enduring torture every moment he failed to find the missing children. He had tried to push those thoughts to the back of his mind so he could focus on the task at hand.

Hadrius had suggested a rescue attempt. Eramus glanced over at Riya. With her help, the idea became even more possible, but that was only if he could convince her to try it, and he doubted he could. He also doubted that he could trust Gavrel to do something like that. The assassin was trying to clear his name, not add another charge to it. Regardless, the plan would ultimately prove to be too risky, and even if it succeeded they would all be forced to live as outlaws, including Sadir and his family.

Eramus glanced at the mountains, focusing on what lay ahead of them. What if Riya couldn't get them past whatever was up there?

"Eramus," Gavrel said as he discreetly fell into step beside him. Riya had fallen back a bit but Hadrius, still within earshot, feigned disinterest while paying close attention.

"What is it" Eramus asked.

"I know...I'm..."

"Whatever it is, just say it."

Gavrel swallowed, appearing almost ashamed. "I must ask a favor of you, something which would place me in your debt."

Eramus stopped walking, felt the reins tug in his hand as his horse stopped, too. "I can't help you if you don't tell me what it is you want."

Gavrel stopped his horse, too, and slowly pet its neck as he spoke. "I have no shroud for Lebon. I do not have the proper materials for the ritual." He immediately looked up, slipped a coin purse from his waist. "I have some money I scavenged from the men who attacked us. I don't know if it will be enough, and I—"

"Can't go into the city," Hadrius finished as he snatched the coin purse from him. He uncharacteristically patted Gavrel's good shoulder in reassurance. "I'll take care of it. I have to purchase a set for Sylvia anyway." He climbed up into his saddle, nudged the horse to face the barony's gates.

"Thank you," Gavrel said with genuine gratitude.

"Thank you, *prophuug*," Hadrius corrected before he drove his heels into his horse's belly and galloped off, leaving dust in his wake.

Gavrel said nothing. He and Eramus simply resumed their trek down the Lestwine. It was only then, as Eramus ticked off a mental note of the location of the man with the woolen gloves who had been pacing them, did he notice out of his peripheral vision that Gavrel deliberately unlaced the top two holes of his jerkin. It was a simple act, one as routine as anything, a man wanting cool air on his skin, but the man with the woolen gloves veered directly toward the barony's gates as soon as it occurred, and never looked back. Had that exchange been a coincidence? Was it even an exchange at all, or simply a product of Eramus's overactive imagination?

As he continued walking, reminding himself to at least mention his suspicions to Hadrius at a later time, he rubbed at the fatigue in his eyes, wishing that he could just ride as far away from everything as possible. If it had been only his life in danger, he would have. He and Hadrius had plenty of spending money, but money couldn't solve the problems facing them now.

He scanned people on the road, hoping to spot a familiar face, maybe someone he had met before whom he could ask for recent news. He was very surprised when he spotted Alina.

"Go on ahead to where we camped the first night," he said to Gavrel without waiting for a response. He turned around. Alina was safe after all, heading north, away from the barony. He had feared the worst, that the Filthies might have found her. He swung up into his saddle and trotted toward her. She kept walking without looking his way. "You there. Alina."

She froze as he came up beside her and marveled at her black hair, striking in contrast to the mostly blonde and brown heads shuffling past.

"I remember you," she said, looking up at him. "What do you want now?"

She stood there alone and vulnerable. He couldn't stand the thought of her being hurt. He wanted to protect her, the urge more insistent since their last encounter.

"Are you travelling alone?" When she didn't respond, he asked, "I thought you had plans to leave days ago."

"My plans changed."

He cleared his throat, thinking of anything to keep the conversation going. "Are you hungry?"

"No. What do you want?"

He didn't care that his attention irritated her. The perils of the unsafe Lestwine Road outweighed his usual courtesy. He wanted to protect her, and the best way he knew to do that was to keep her in sight. People moved around them, surreptitiously noting their conversation.

"Going to Keltivar?"

She nodded. "It's not so bad up there. Nobody will bother me too much, and I can find work."

He couldn't just leave her. He felt responsible for her somehow. "My friend and I will take you up there in a few days. We were going that way anyway, but we have something to do first. Are you interested in working with us until then?"

"I don't...I can get there fine on my own."

"The Lestwine isn't safe. You know that. We'll be going that way anyway. Plus, the soldiers may be looking for you." As an afterthought, he added, "I can offer a wage. A silver piece a day to handle campsite duties. Please at least consider the offer."

She gauged him instead of his offer. "Why are you so interested in me?"

The direct question startled him, and he didn't have an immediate answer. "I don't want to see you in danger again. You seem like you need a friend. That's all."

She seemed to process his response, and then her shoulders slumped in resignation and her eyes fell to his sword. "I can't fight."

"We have plenty of warriors in our party. I need an extra set of eyes, someone to tend to the horses, things like that." That wasn't the complete truth, but he couldn't expect her trust when he hadn't earned it. He held out his left hand. She looked at it and recoiled, staring up at him in alarm.

His horse shuffled and spun around until she faced his other side. This time he extended his right hand. He held it out for several seconds, about to withdraw his offer when she set her much smaller and more delicate hand inside his. He gripped her wrist tightly and flung her nearly weightless body into the saddle behind him.

Once she settled, he caught up to Gavrel and Riya, unsure if concern or an unadmitted physical attraction had prompted him to ask Alina along. He doubted that her mysterious beauty had been the cause. No, he saw a fellow human being in need.

"Who are you?" Gavrel wondered.

"Yes, Eramus," Riya asked, eyebrow cocked. "Who is she?"

"Her name's Alina. She's a friend."

The reason we're all here.

Riya peered past Eramus and intently studied Alina. The woman's demeanor and physical features warranted attention, but not Riya's overt scrutiny.

"*All this over her?*" Riya asked bitterly.

"Maybe this isn't such a good idea," Alina said. She moved to dismount.

"Don't worry," Eramus said over his shoulder. "They'll get used to you. She'll be nicer once she gets to know you."

Where at first Riya's extra attention could be attributed to petty jealousy, it soon became apparent that something else about Alina bothered her.

Eramus felt Alina's hands tightening around his waist. He had a strange feeling that this third meeting of theirs was more than coincidence. Could he be setting himself up for failure again? He couldn't leave her by herself this time.

Twilight greeted them at their old campsite. While Gavrel searched for anything they could burn, Alina tentatively gathered the horses.

"Can I borrow the tinderbox?" Gavrel asked. He had dumped a small pile of kindling into the fire pit.

Tucked in her cloak off to the side, Riya ordered him to stand back. She pointed an outstretched palm at the pit. Her hand glowed with indigo light, the only warning Gavrel had before a fire of the same color erupted in the pit. He backpedaled, raising his arms to ward off the immediate, intense heat from the eldritch blaze. He cautiously eyed her, then carefully braved the heat before settling in to a comfortable spot near the fire. He gazed into it, lost in thought and wonder.

Riya's magic surprised Alina, but when she looked around at the others and noticed they had taken it in stride, she regained her composure. "Are you going to cook?" she asked Eramus when he dragged out a pot and pan from his gear and set them near the fire. She couldn't look away from the colorful flames. None of them could.

"Unless you want to. My friend will do a little hunting when he catches up with us," he said.

"I'll cook."

Eramus regarded Alina's smooth bronze skin and layered eyes, physical characteristics which he could better study in the light of the magical fire. From his peripheral vision he noticed Riya glaring at him from under her hood and he pretended not to notice.

"Aline," Riya said as the woman dropped a flat rock into the blaze as a cooking surface. "How long were you in the barony?"

"Her name's Alina," Eramus answered for her.

"Let her speak for herself."

Alina emptied her waterskin into the pot but hesitated before she set it over the fire. "Is it...safe?" she asked, unable to make eye contact with Riya.

"It's hotter than a normal fire, but of course it's safe," Riya said. "Now look at me and answer my question."

Alina cautiously set the pot over the fire, raised her eyes to meet Riya's. "Not too long. Maybe a week."

"And the soldiers? You had some trouble with them. What was it about?"

"I don't know. I didn't do anything to them. I didn't break any laws." Her eyes began to water. "They just started yelling at me and hitting me and laughing about it."

"That's enough, Riya," Eramus said when he saw the other woman growing upset.

Alina rummaged in the community food bag for carrots and leeks. She crouched in front of the fire, quickly trimming the vegetables and adding them to the pot.

Riya watched her work. "No meat. I don't eat it."

Alina nodded and that seemed to satisfy Riya for the time being.

"Walk with me," Riya said to Eramus. He strolled after her, baffled by her unusual behavior. Riya hardly cared what others thought.

"What is it?" he asked, grabbing her wrist and spinning her around to face him.

She stared down at his hand until he released her. *"Where did she come from? Has she told you why she's here?"* she began in Uuslefin.

"Alina? Riya, what's this all about?" he asked, planting his hands on his hips. Was she this jealous?

"Eramus, she's Kortheen."

He put a finger to his lips. "I think she knows Uuslefin. Lower your voice." Eramus recognized the name but he couldn't remember exactly what it meant. "Korth—"

Riya waved in his face to interrupt his fumbling. *"I think she's a bastard or a cast-off. Her skin tone's too light for her to be of a pure bloodline, but her indigo eyes leave no doubt."*

"Riya, I—"

She shook her head at him. *"She's dangerous, Eramus. Centuries ago the Kortheen made a bid to conquer the Five Nations. Warriors of legend barely, and I mean barely, drove them into retreat at the Battle of Korthas."*

Eramus rubbed his eyes with his hands and let his memory reconstruct the story Riya had told him before. The legendary warriors Riya spoke of had vanished after the battle, never to be seen again. *"She can't be. I mean, I would know, right?"*

"She looks like an exotic woman, that's all, but she descends from a race of powerful warrior sorcerers."

"No," Eramus said in disbelief. *"You don't understand. When I met her she was being attacked. She couldn't even defend herself. You're wrong."*

Riya smiled menacingly. *"Even if her people didn't raise her, she would have inherited their abilities."*

"Like what?"

"Enhanced senses, sensitivity to magic. Her blood's worth a fortune on the black market. It contains magical qualities." She pursed her lips. *"She could be a herald, a spy."*

"And you're the only one who knows this? If she's so dangerous, why hasn't she been arrested?"

"Who's to say she hasn't been? You told me the soldiers were after her. Maybe they know. Maybe the knight knows."

"I doubt it. They don't seem too concerned about her anymore."

Riya had to be wrong. Even if Alina was related to the Kortheen, and Eramus wasn't even sure if that was true, she hardly seemed threatening.

"You're wrong about her," he said. *"Besides, if she is what you say she is, her heightened abilities could prove to be of value."*

Riya sighed. *"You ask me along for my skills and experience, yet ignore my counsel?"*

"I asked you to join us because of what awaits us in the mountains, not to persecute a helpless woman. She's just having a rough time and needs help. We all need help sometimes."

"Watch her, Eramus, and not just her ass," Riya said. *"I'll certainly be watching her, and not the same way you will. Make no mention of her heritage."*

"I'll keep that in mind," Eramus replied, disgusted at Riya's insinuations.

Unfortunately Eramus regarded Alina differently after his conversation with Riya, which could have been her intent all along. He cleared a space near the fire and lay back, lacing his fingers behind his head to relax. The sounds of Alina's cooking lulled him into a comfortable, half-awake state. Then Gavrel shuffled a bit and Eramus sat up to see Hadrius enter their campsite. He quickly dismounted, handed a traditional burial set to Gavrel, and strung his bow, loping off into the long grass, arrow nocked. Alina watched him melt into the darkness. Hunting the baron's game incurred a hefty fine, but it was just money.

Hadrius soon returned with a pair of hares. Alina skinned them on the side of a large rock, eventually skewered them and set them over the blaze.

"Give me your bowls," Alina said when the smell of rabbit saturated the cool night air. Eramus and Gavrel politely held out their bowls, stomachs growling, while she served the boiled vegetables and hunks of hare.

She smiled and handed a bowl of vegetables to Riya. "I don't eat meat either."

Hadrius waved his portion away. He had already begun drinking his meal out of a jug.

"This is very good," Gavrel commented as he licked grease from his fingers.

Alina shrugged. "I've worked in kitchens here and there."

The food was good, and without Hadrius eating there was enough of it for seconds. Alina had already contributed to the mission, justifying Eramus's decision to ask her along. She had handled the care of the horses, had cooked a meal, and was already cleaning up the campsite for the night.

"We're going straight up the mountains come first light," Eramus said to everyone as his meal settled. "Try to get some rest." He needed sleep more than the others, but he volunteered for first watch anyway. As he bounded atop a boulder on the edge of the camp, a nagging in his mind that he forgotten to do something, he let the night air hit his face and refresh him. He pushed away at the impulse rattling around in his head in favor of a worry-free night. Though intelligent and resourceful, Riya could be difficult at times. Still, he felt much more confident about almost everything with her around.

He closed his eyes for a second but time had passed when he opened them. The surrounding landscape glowed a soft silver and indigo under the sleep stars and moonlight. The fire continued to burn as strongly as it had when Riya first cast her spell. How long had he been asleep? He looked down to see Alina, curled up in her cloak, staring back up at him. How long had she been watching him? In the tint of the firelight her scintillating irises shone with even more indigo brilliance. She turned away and pulled her hood over her head. It seemed odd to him that they were complete strangers and yet he felt as if he knew her, or at least knew something about her. His inability to forge the connection frustrated him. He decided not to think about it anymore or it would be one more thing rattling around in his head.

His mind wandered to Sadir, to the last time he had seen his friend, being dragged away unconscious and pulped by Filthies. It wasn't fair that his friend was in such danger, but Eramus had learned long ago that things were rarely fair. Sir Jacob had already proven that Sadir's life, and the lives of his family, mattered little to him. Like it or not, Eramus had to go back into the mountains and face whatever had taken Lebon's and Sylvia's lives. His eyes grew heavy with the strain of the day and his gnawing thoughts. He fought to keep them open but they resisted. He surrendered.

He is back in Grihm, peering through the fog of his own breath. He can't see the tavern but he knows it is close. The Filthies will be waiting for him in the woods, eager to set upon him as they already did. He has been deceived, though how or why he has no idea. The Filthies will be waiting for him in the woods, but he has to go in there anyway.

He stops where the trees begin and sets his hand on a nearby branch and pets its rough feathers. It isn't a branch at all, but rather a bastard snowthroat which takes flight without disturbing the air. His curiosity compels him to chase it rather than question its appearance, and he runs faster and faster until his feet no longer touch the ground and he glides nearly weightlessly, deeper and deeper into the woods, farther away from the tavern and the lack of certainty which lies behind. An eerie backlight coalesces into a dilapidated wooden structure lit from the interior. Its door creaks open and shut as if by the wind, even though there isn't a breath of air. The shadow of movement comes from within. Are the Filthies waiting for him inside? The bird flies inside, timing its entrance perfectly with the opening and closing of the door. He instinctively knows it wants him to follow it inside, but he won't. He jams his heels into the ground to skid to a halt, cowering in fear outside. He has followed the bird this far but now he doesn't trust it. He could stay here, where the Filthies wouldn't find him, where he could stay far enough away from the structure to be able to run at the first sign of trouble. He can see the bird's large shadow cast along an interior wall. He no longer believes Filthies are in there with the bird, so who is inside with it? Someone whispers something he cannot understand, something in Medarn. He hears his heart in his ears, hoping the shadow doesn't notice him…

His eyes popped open to a dark sky, his ears adjusting to the call of a night bird and the others sleeping soundly. Perspiration dampened his skin. He drank long from his waterskin as his dream faded. Unable to understand its message, he clenched his fists, breathing deeply to calm his racing heartbeat. Whatever had happened in his head, in his dream, had passed, but there was no doubt he had heard Medarn. What did that mean? How could he dream in a foreign language?

When they broke camp the next morning, Riya extinguished the magical fire with a single gesture.

"How are you able to do that?" Alina asked her.

"Years of practice," Riya offered with a rude stare. She whisked her cloak around in dramatic fashion to emphasize her point.

Before they began their climb, they unsaddled the horses and left them to graze in the woods like they had done on their first endeavor. Hadrius removed a shovel and mattock from his saddlebags and strapped them to his back with the rest of his gear.

The second time up they made haste, putting themselves well up the mountains by midday. The warmer than usual temperature combined with the labor of moving uphill forced everyone to strip off their cloaks and open their armor and tunics for better circulation.

Eramus noticed how easily Alina moved up the mountain while the others struggled, her silent steps and easy grace very similar to Hadrius's. He stole glances at her even, bronze skin. Could this woman really be as dangerous as Riya warned?

"I can't believe I agreed to this," Riya said as she wiped her damp face with a wadded cloth and swatted away insects. Sweat stains circled her neck and underarms. Scrapes and bruises covered her bare skin where she had slipped and fallen along the way.

When they came across a stream running over rocks, Hadrius dropped to his knees and splashed his face. The water appeared to rejuvenate him, despite the fact that he still seemed a bit hungover.

Gavrel kicked off his boots and waded into the stream with red, raw blistery feet. "We didn't come this way before," he said over his shoulder to nobody in particular.

"You're right," Hadrius said as he wrung out his hair. "This trail intersects the route we took the first time."

"I never thought I would see the day when you converted to the Temple of Gefil," Riya said from behind Eramus's left ear. *"You're running the knight's errand for him."* He didn't turn around. She spoke Uuslefin to irritate him, not for privacy, but her whispering reminded him of his dreams and the bird. He was too uncomfortable to reveal his fears about the bird to her. He hadn't even told Hadrius. He'd considered it, of course, but he'd also considered what it would sound like.

"There's more to it than that, and I haven't converted," he replied in Oshlema.

"Obviously."

"Listen…since you're in a talking mood…"

"Am I?" she asked with amusement.

"You're good with Medarn, eh?"

"There's no Medarnay," she replied, twisting his word separation. "It's not Oshlema. You don't change it to suit your needs."

"No, no, I meant…you know how to speak it."

"You want to know about this now?" she chuckled.

"Well, I've been putting off the learning for a while. A jobah made an impression on me, tried to teach me a little bit. Nothing against Sadir, but I was more interested when this man took time with me. I wish I could have learned more from him."

"Why can't you?"

"He's dead now, Riya. He's dead." He took a deep breath and looked down at his clenched fists. Carden had seemed to be a good man, and he had died because of him. Eramus believed that honoring the man's memory was as good a reason as ever to learn Medarn. Like Lebon had said, people had to make time for what they considered to be important. "I can't get the pattern down, Riya. I tried and I tried and I tried. I can remember the words. *Toh*, and *di*, and *pedap*—"

"And *o* and *I*."

"Right, right."

Hadrius walked over and stared at them, his wet hair staining his shoulders with damp. "*What are you talking about?*"

Then Riya broke into laughter and Eramus felt his face flush. She had just been holding in the laughter the entire time. She always thought he was stupid. Maybe he was. He stormed off, angry at her again, like he always got when she treated him like that. He would never master patience, especially not around her. Maybe in some ways he let her get that far with him. He shouldn't be so upset. He had been expecting her derision. He set his mind right, reminded himself that Riya only wanted a reaction out of him. He calmed his thoughts.

They soon resumed their ascent. Alina pointed out circling carrion birds far up and to their left before anyone else, supporting Riya's claim that at least the woman's eyesight exceeded Eramus's own.

"We must be dead already," Riya huffed, cursing when sweat stung her eyes. The arduous, unforgiving mountains were already chipping away at her composure.

"Our welcoming party," Gavrel said. He and Hadrius pressed on, Alina a few paces behind them, as Riya and Eramus brought up the rear.

"Trouble?" she asked him under her breath as she dragged her scraped forearm across her damp brow to wipe away more sweat.

"We took care of it. No problem at all."

"Nothing like learning Medarn?" she asked with a serious face, maddening him even further. She would have fun with this for a while.

"No, Riya, nothing like learning Medarn."

She sighed, shifted her satchel on her shoulder. "How much longer until we're there?"

"A while still."

Questions popped into his head but he suppressed them. He didn't feel like being mocked again.

"You act like a child sometimes," she said, getting closer to him and running her fingers through his dirty hair. When she touched him he lost track of everything else.

"Only because you treat me like one." He looked over at her dusty cheeks and bloodshot eyes. "You look terrible."

She wiped her cheek with the back of her hand, leaving a clean streak of flesh in the dusty sweat. "Nothing a bath with you couldn't cure." She regarded him carefully. "Of all the skills a peeran would want, why Medarn? Who cares about a language that's only spoken in one little place?"

Why did she always need a reason for something? Why wouldn't she just help him? "Forget I asked."

"They're not talking about you, Eramus," she smiled.

"What do you mean?"

"The people in the barony."

He couldn't help but roll his eyes. "I always tell myself I'm going to learn Medarn and I never do. Now I want to. Now I want to take the time."

"Fine. I guess I don't know what you know. I have a feeling you're going to be very confused about what I teach you. You're always confused about what I teach you."

"No surprise in that."

"*Picture possibilities*," she said. "*That's the key to Medarn.*"

"In Oshlema," he said. "I'd like to learn it that way. So, possibilities?"

She nodded. "Words are easy, like you said, but Medarn is predicated on the future possible. What is going to happen dictates what is said."

One, pause, *one, one*. Could it be that simple? "Wait. Not on what's happening now? It's about what's going to happen?"

"No," she said curtly. "I haven't even started and you're already lost." She planted her palm on his chest. "Stop."

He stopped and waited, sweat trickling down his temples and his cheeks. His forward motion dissolved in an exhalation. Where was he going? What was he doing? He was in the mountains, risking his life, facing irritation and frustration at every turn. Outside forces had rendered him powerless, a puppet.

Riya snapped her fingers in his face, jarring him from his self-pity. Her face so close to his brought him comfort, her beauty evident even through caked filth. "Pay close attention, Eramus. Medarn's a mix of Oshlemin, Keltivarin, and an eastern trade language."

He nodded, ashamed that her face alone had the power to distract him.

"You are completely motionless now. *Odupi*."

"*Odupi*? What's that? Here? What does that mean?"

She snapped her fingers in his face again, focusing all of his attention.

"Don't ask me who attached a transition to a word which defines 'at rest'. I can't answer that. What I do know is that *odupi* is what you are."

One, pause, *one, one. Odupi*. He felt *odupi*, whatever that meant.

"Do you understand?" she asked, peering into his face.

"Yes."

She sighed. "No you don't."

"I do," he argued. "*Odupi*. At rest. Where I am." *Odupi*. He took her hand, gently squeezing her fingers, tracing the rough outline of the scar on her palm. "*Odupi*." He bit her lower lip. Her hot breath and the stink of her sweat aroused him. *Odupi*.

She returned his kiss briefly and pushed him away, wiping his saliva from her lips. "I can tell where this is going. Take time to process what little I've taught you. At this rate you'll be fluent in a decade."

"I can do that." He wanted to whisk her away, to hold her in his arms. He wanted to pour his cares and worries into a river and let them wash away.

She left him standing alone. *Odupi*. He closed his eyes and listened to her footsteps for a minute before he caught up to her and the others.

They hiked until Hadrius warned them that their path had merged with the original and that they approached the bridge. Riya already seemed to know. She had also said that Alina would be sensitive to magic. The woman fidgeted, her odd behavior supporting Riya's earlier claim.

Eramus felt his stomach drop as a thought occurred to him. If Alina truly was a descendant of this magical race, could she have been responsible for casting the spell that had killed the others? Magic users weren't very common. There had been signs of magic at the base of the mountains. The Filthies had been involved in that, just like they had been after her in the barony.

"Are you okay?" he asked her. His hand rested on his sword hilt, just in case.

She shook her head. "My skin's upset. I don't know a better way to explain it. It's trying to tell me something."

"Like what?"

She rubbed her arms and shivered. "Like a thousand ants in my blood. They say not to go that way."

"Why?"

"I don't know," she said, shaking her head, discomfort evident on her expression.

"You don't know what's over there?"

She shook her head again. "Why would I?"

Eramus glanced at Riya with a silent question. Her cheeks and nose were pink from the sun. She saw his hand near his sword and slowly shook her head.

"Everyone, behind me," she said, pointing back down the path. She reached into one of her pouches, removed a sleepstone the size of a pebble, and closed her fist over it. Slowly, gradually, her hand glowed with light of the same color, and the veins along her arm darkened visibly beneath her skin. When the light disappeared, she tossed the now colorless stone to the side. She closed her eyes and concentrated, her palm outstretched.

"How long is this going to take?" Gavrel wondered as he paced behind her, kicking at the ground. "We already know where this thing is."

She ignored him, extended her arm, fingers spread wide. Seconds later, five equidistant dots of indigo light, similar to buzzing insects, materialized in the air in front of her. She opened her eyes, each of her fingers still manipulating the points of light.

Eramus scratched at his left arm, which had suddenly begun to itch, but the more he did the quicker it pulsed with dull, throbbing pain. He endured the discomfort, a likely side effect of the spell.

"I know what the sorcerer has done," Riya replied. "But what I must determine is the extent of his work. Follow these, quickly," she said as she released the dots of light. They zipped along the trail, through undergrowth, soundlessly vanishing. She chased them at a jog, and the others raced after her.

Eramus remained in place, unable to move as one of the glowing dots of light floated back his way. The burning on his arm approached agony. Forgetting everything else, he frantically yanked up his sleeve. The hovering dot of light dove into his forearm. He shuddered as an eerie symbol the same dark blue of ebb stars seared to existence just below the surface of his flesh. Something had gone drastically wrong with Riya's spell. He panicked, wondering if magic would consume his arm. Only Riya would know.

He bolted through the bushes, dodging rocks and trees in an effort to cut the others off before they reached the bridge. Leaves whipped into his face as he narrowly avoided tripping over vines more than once. "Riya!" he shouted as he ran. He struggled to keep the panic out of his voice.

He saw the path ahead, through a doorway of forked tree branches, heard the scuff of boots on the ground. When he saw Riya, he burst out of the trees and grabbed her by the trailing hem of her cloak.

She reacted with the speed of a snake, her left arm chopping down to break his hold while her right arm, dagger already in hand, arced skyward for a fatal stab, but years of experience had honed his skills. He moved much more smoothly than she did, his hand catching her wrist in midair.

"Riya!" he yelled at her. "It's me. Calm down."

Her mouth hung open in surprise as she realized what had nearly happened. Her eyes glowed with flecks of indigo. Her dagger disappeared as quickly as it had appeared. He didn't have time to apologize for his behavior.

He rolled up his left sleeve, frightened by the foreign symbol beneath his skin. Riya's cheeks flushed hot with blood, her face overcome with confusion at the sight of it.

Suddenly the others arrived. Eramus barely had time to roll his burned and blackened sleeve down, startling Riya back into the moment. They exchanged worried glances, though her eyes couldn't disguise her fear and concern.

Alina pointed at the twinkling dots of light as they rushed past the skeletons of trees off the path and vanished into the fog spreading past the rock bridge. Beyond that bridge lay the bodies of Lebon and Sylvia.

"And now I will learn what we are facing" Riya said, sparing one last look at Eramus before she turned her back on him, dismissing his dilemma for the moment, proving once again how unimportant he was to her. She closed her eyes and held her palms out. Four of the original five points of light emerged from the fog, pulsing like a single heartbeat, their flight sluggish and unpredictable. The lights found their way to Riya's palms, burrowing into her burn scars. She opened her eyes in visible enlightment.

"That's disgusting," Gavrel said, glancing from Eramus to Hadrius for support they didn't offer. Too consumed by the fact that the pain along his forearm had ceased, Eramus cautiously peered under his sleeve. The symbol had vanished. He studied the others to see if they had noticed. They appeared oblivious, much more interested in Riya.

But Alina purposely avoided eye contact with him. He recalled their fortuitous meeting back on the Lestwine. She had spurned his left hand when he had offered it to her, but embraced his right. She knew something. Riya had been right after all. The woman was more than she let on. He would have to watch her carefully. He checked his arm one last time. Whatever had been there was gone. He had no idea what purpose the symbol served, or why it had appeared when it did, but he was relieved it had gone.

The fog spilled out of the ravine like a living entity. Too much happened too fast for Eramus. He felt himself caught up in a current and could only splash his arms to stay afloat. "We should go back," he said, wondering if the fog had somehow sensed their presence, or had been attracted to the mysterious mark that had been on his arm. "At least a little ways. I don't want to get caught in that." He backpedaled as the creeping fog swirled around his boots.

Riya shook her head. "The fog is harmless. The gift of a Seehlan priest."

"Then Sir Jacob was right after all," Eramus said. "Seehlan did take the children. If this fog is the work of one of their priests, then the construct has to be, too."

Riya looked back at him as if he was a child. "Seehlan priests aren't capable of what you described."

"This fog isn't harmless to me," Hadrius said. He looked at Eramus, and Eramus knew his friend was aware something was different about him. He could feel sweat beading on his face but he chose not to wipe it away. Hadrius finally turned back down the path and Alina followed him closely, as if she couldn't bear to be alone.

Gavrel watched them go, then peered into the fog. "Can you get us past it?" he asked Riya. "Can you free my brother?" His hand closed around his sword hilt, his jaw tight with conviction and pride. He probably felt just like Eramus did: powerless. They had to depend on Riya now. This was why she was here.

"Go back with them," she said as she, too, looked into the fog, then back at Eramus's arm. "You too, Eramus. We'll talk later."

Gavrel nodded in his unique way and walked back down the path. Eramus's stomach fell when he saw the way Riya looked at him. Whatever she wanted to tell him wasn't going to be good. How had he been marked like that? Was it the spell? Had the others been marked as well? He took a deep breath to calm himself. One more problem. He just wanted to be rid of everything.

But Riya wasn't the only one who had an idea of what had happened to him. Alina knew something as well, and Eramus wouldn't accept any lies from her. He had his life to think about, after all.

CHAPTER 8

"Alina, come here," Eramus demanded.

She approached him, reluctance in her unusually colorful indigo eyes. When he thrust out his left arm she tripped over her own feet trying to get away from him.

"What's wrong?" he asked. Only blackened edges of the mark's manifestation remained, yet she had been wary of it, on the Lestwine, before he had even seen it.

"I...I don't know."

"You do know!" he growled, drawing concerned looks from Gavrel and Hadrius. He stared back defiantly until they broke eye contact.

"I know there's something wrong. I can feel it. I don't know what or why or anything like that. You have to believe me. I can just...sense it."

He studied her frightened face. When he covered the flesh on his arm she breathed a sigh of relief and got back to her feet.

"It's like ants in your blood, right? Isn't that what you said before? Is this the same thing? What are they telling you?"

"I'm so sorry for whatever's happened," she said, resting her fingers on his right arm.

When she didn't elaborate, he snatched his arm away. He could tell she didn't know much about any of this, and it wasn't her fault or anything to do with her, but he didn't want her hollow comfort. "It's not your problem," he snapped. "It's mine, right? You don't need to concern yourself with it," he said coldly.

He didn't need pity. He needed answers. He needed to know how to get rid of the mark. He needed to find out why someone or something had put it there. He drew his sword and chopped at overgrown groundcover in frustration. Everyone watched him but he didn't care. He cursed and hacked until his arm ached. Then he noticed the inscription along the crossguard. It calmed him, centered him. He sheathed his sword and brushed his hair out of his eyes just as Riya rejoined them.

She looked at his sweat-lathered face until he casually shook his head to indicate it wasn't a big deal. As if she really cared. She sat down cross-legged and dropped her head into her hands.

"What is it?" Gavrel asked. She ignored him, and beneath her hands she spoke quietly to herself.

"Let her do whatever it is she has to do," Eramus said as he wiped sweat out of his eyes with the back of his hand. "She needs to focus. Quit asking questions."

Gavrel huffed away several paces, still observing her. Eventually he sat on a large rock, set his sword across his thighs, and began to clean it with a rag.

Eramus sat near Hadrius and Alina, wondering what the future held for all of them. What lay beyond this magical construct? What, exactly, did Riya know about the sorcerer who had put it there? Could this sorcerer also be to blame for what had happened to him? After all, Alina hadn't reacted to his arm until after they had come down from the mountains. But then why hadn't Hadrius and Gavrel also been marked?

Eramus pulled at his hair in frustration. He rapped his knuckles against his forehead. He could only think about the mark on his arm. He wanted to grab Riya and shake her for answers. He had seen the shock on her face. Did she know what the mark represented, what the consequences were for him? Did she know how it had gotten there? He shivered at the thought of magic controlling him, or influencing his waking moments at the very least.

Waking moments. Could the bird be connected to the symbol? Is that why it had taken an interest in him? And what about his dreams? They had been pieces of his memories at first, but slowly the bastard snowthroat had begun to assert itself within them. Did magic have something to do with that? The bird had only begun to follow him around the time he reached the barony. So when and how had the mark gotten onto his arm?

He glared at Riya. If she wouldn't tell him, and Alina didn't know, he would have to get his answers from the sorcerer, if one existed. He needed answers before he went mad.

He rolled up his sleeve and jabbed at his flesh, at the dormant mark. He wanted to scream, to vent his frustration. He scratched at his arm. When he did, Alina shifted uncomfortably.

Had she felt that? He kept his eyes on her and dug at his arm until it bled. She doubled over and emptied her stomach.

He stared at her for a second, wondering if he had really caused her reaction. He rolled his sleeve down. With a pale face she glanced his way, flecks of vomit on her lips, and forced a smile. He simply got to his feet and kicked dirt over her mess.

"Are you okay?" Hadrius asked her with a glare at Eramus. She nodded and wiped her mouth with her sleeve. "Where exactly are you from, Alina?" He sloshed the remains of mead around in his jug, offered it to her, then eased it back a bit when he looked at where she had vomited. She politely declined his reluctant offer.

"Here and there," she said distractedly, her eyes straying in the general direction of the bridge as she absentmindedly scratched her arms over and over with shaking hands.

"What do you mean?" Gavrel asked. He examined his reflection in his polished blade.

She fidgeted under their attention. "I've been moving from place to place for a long time."

"Well, where have you been?"

"Lots of places," she answered noncommittally.

"Like where?"

She took a moment to answer. "I lived in the forest on the edge of these mountains for a while."

"These mountains? You've been here before?"

She shook her head. "Not on this side. I never went up the mountains, just in the forest, during spring and summer. I would make things and sell them when I needed food. Nobody bothered me there."

With a look of longing, Hadrius considered her words. "I always wanted to live in the forest."

"Why didn't you?"

He shrugged. "I don't know how to make *glistas*."

Despite the situation, Eramus couldn't help but grin at his friend's most likely honest humor.

"So how did you end up in the barony?" Hadrius asked her.

Her cheeks flushed and she broke eye contact with him. "I met a man in the forest. I usually don't want people to know I'm there, but he played music, beautiful music, and he was so handsome. I wanted to find him again."

Eramus rolled his eyes and chuckled. "I think I know where this is going. You had sex with him, didn't you?"

She looked almost ashamed at her admission. "We shared something."

"I'll bet," Gavrel muttered.

Alina looked embarrassed now, uncomfortable about revealing too much. "It meant something important to me."

"It's only special for people who don't do it all the time," Hadrius remarked. "It's just pleasure for the rest of us. People get emotions mixed up with physical satisfaction."

"And which kind of person are you?" she demanded.

Hadrius had no reply. Less than a week ago, Eramus had no doubt how his friend would answer that question. The events over the last few days had proven that Hadrius might be a different person now, that his relationship with Sylvia had mattered beyond the physical on at least some level.

"Have you considered what may be waiting for us?" Gavrel asked, changing the subject, giving voice to their thoughts. They might soon have to see their fallen comrades.

"Of course," Eramus said. If Riya could get them past what had killed the others, he wanted to find the sorcerer who had put it there. He wanted to ask about the mark on his arm. He would make the sorcerer talk.

"It could just be a trap," Hadrius said. "Like what hunters leave. Someone may come back and check it from time to time. If a Seehlan priest could put that fog there, a sorcerer could have done the same thing with the circle."

Alina shook her head. "There's someone beyond it, close. I know."

Gavrel scoffed. "There's no way you could know."

"I have a feeling."

"Hey," Eramus said. "If she says she knows, I believe her."

Gavrel muttered under his breath but didn't argue. Instead he asked Eramus, "What if your woman can't get through that? Do you have any other ideas?"

Gavrel's words didn't penetrate Riya's focused preparations.

"She's not my woman. But if I had another plan, I wouldn't have spent the time getting her here," Eramus snapped. "What kind of question is that? It's a dumb one. A dumb question." He had consolidated all of his worries and fears into one straight line, and that line led across the rock bridge. His answers were past the bridge. He had to be patient.

"If she does get us through," Gavrel continued, undaunted, "then I want the person who put it there."

Eramus shook his head. "She gets first shot. That's part of the deal." He had no intention of letting Riya hurt the sorcerer. He had too many questions.

"And what about us?" Hadrius asked. He nodded at Gavrel. "We have a right."

Gavrel sheathed his sword. "We're all here for different reasons, but we all want the same thing."

"My friend and his family are in considerable peril," Eramus said as he rose to his feet. "That's why I'm here."

Gavrel stared back at him. "I had nothing to do with that, if that was a veiled accusation. In case you've forgotten, I lost my brother up here."

Eramus waved away his words. Gavrel hadn't created this situation. He had done it himself. "I just want to find the children and get them back to the baron. Once that's done we can go our separate ways." He pointed at Hadrius. "*And you. You know you can't fight a sorcerer. Don't do anything stupid.*" Hadrius only glowered back at him. Eramus knew what was on his mind. Gavrel was right. They all wanted the sorcerer. Hadrius and Gavrel wanted revenge. Eramus wanted answers. Riya wanted whatever she wanted. And then there was Alina, whom Eramus had coerced along. He had brought her for selfish reasons. He claimed he wanted to keep her safe. There was nothing safe about any of this.

Silence hung in the air until Riya abruptly said, "Get ready." She pulled a sleepstone the size of a robin's egg out of a pouch and closed her fingers over it, draining the stone until it lost its color and the veins from her arm to her heart darkened with magic. She tossed the used up stone away just like she had done with the other one, but this time the color of the indigo stone leaked out of her eyes and palms.

Eramus rolled his neck, loosening up for action. He jimmied the dagger on his hip to ensure an easy pull. He pushed all distracting thoughts away. He wanted to channel his frustration and anger for the mark on his arm and for what the knight had done to Sadir and for the bird that insisted on pestering him in a language he couldn't grasp. He needed to face what lay past that bridge.

"We should cooperate with a purpose," Gavrel said.

"I have a plan," Riya said. "Eliminate the sorcerer as quickly as possible."

"Eliminate?" Eramus asked in disbelief. Riya nodded. "We need answers. I'm not for killing right away if it can be helped."

"I might not kill anyone right away, but I will kill them. The plan works for me," Gavrel said as he scratched at the lump on his left shoulder. The more he scratched the more he kept scratching.

"Stop that," Riya said.

He stopped in mid scratch, self-consciously lowering his hand.

Everyone removed their excess gear and tested their weapons. Alina stood nearby, her pack still on her shoulders, her eyes brimming with anxiety and fear.

"Eramus…" Hadrius said, nodding at Alina. "*Maybe she should hang back?*"

She looked so nervous that Eramus couldn't help but agree. She had told him she couldn't fight. His carelessness could get her killed. Sleeplessness and anger prevented him from thinking straight. He had to pull himself together before he put everyone at more risk. He remembered the line he had imagined. His answers lay over the bridge. He took a deep, calming breath. He was supposed to be finding kidnapped children.

"I should wait here," she offered. "I don't want to go up there."

Eramus placed his hand on her shoulder. "That's an excellent idea. If anything happens to us, head back down as fast as you can."

"The sorcerer," Gavrel reminded everyone. "I'm not worried about her right now." He hissed at Alina. "Get moving."

"He's right, Riya," Eramus said. "We need to work together

here. Tell us what to expect."

"Expect anything. Everything. The sorcerer and I will be using magic at the same time. His is different than mine."

"Is that all?"

"I'll need the two of you to keep him distracted," she said to Eramus and Gavrel.

"What does that mean?" Gavrel wondered. "Attack him? What else should we expect from your magic? What should we expect from this sorcerer? We need to be better prepared."

"Draw the sorcerer's attention," Riya said very clearly.

"And what about me?" Hadrius asked, stepping forward, bow strung, arrow in hand. He could end all of their troubles before the fight even started, but then Eramus wouldn't get his answers.

"You're going right at him," she said. "I'll give you another taste of the obscurity to cloak your presence."

"Don't kill the sorcerer," Eramus said. "I want information." He looked from face to face, realizing that the others probably didn't care what he said. If he wanted to keep the sorcerer alive, even for a little bit, he would have to personally ensure the man's safety.

"Wait. Why not give all of us a potion?" Gavrel asked. "With magic like that, we could end the fight immediately."

"Leave the magic to me," she snapped. "To a sorcerer, the potion Hadrius consumes will shine like a white light."

"Then why..." Gavrel trailed off as realization dawned on his face.

"He's the real target," Eramus said, pointing at Hadrius.

Riya licked sparking, barely contained magic off her palm. "Be ready for anything. The sorcerer might not be alone."

"Wait," Eramus said, holding up a hand of caution. "What exactly are we doing here? We're getting rid of the spell or ward or whatever, right? That's the priority?"

"No," Riya said. "The priority is to deal with the immediate threat. The sorcerer won't parlay, Eramus. He knows we're here. He knows I'm also a sorcerer. He will attack us. He will kill us." She handed a potion to Hadrius and he plugged his nose and gulped it down, shaking his head in disgust.

"Riya, I need information."

"The sorcerer won't cooperate. In case I didn't make myself clear, he will do his best to kill us." She took an exasperated breath. "Follow me."

Gavrel sniffed defiantly, sheathing his sword. "I'm not following you. Forget it. This whole thing sounds sloppy and ill-prepared. It's a game of odds. We need something more thought out than misplaced trust when we haven't even assessed our opponent. We'll be the ones doing the fighting. We need more to go on."

"This is all we have," Eramus said. "This is why she's here. We'll work together on this, fight as a unit like we did before. Just don't kill the sorcerer." He turned to Riya. "We don't kill the sorcerer."

The air around Hadrius twisted and bent with light until he disappeared. Eramus heard shuffling feet where he had stood.

Riya glared at Gavrel until he threw up his hands in surrender and drew his blade. She closed her eyes and raised her palms, releasing a wave of slow moving indigo magic that disappeared on the other side of the bridge. Eramus cringed when he thought of what had happened the last time she had used magic, but his arm did not react this time. Nothing made sense anymore.

"Prepare yourselves," she said, her satchel still strapped over her body, the outline of the spellbook she never left behind clearly apparent. They tentatively stepped onto the bridge.

Eramus squeezed his sword handle. He didn't feel comfortable about the way things were happening but they were already in motion. He exhaled quickly a few times and flexed his arms to kick his heartbeat into gear. He needed to be ready for anything.

"I'll take the lead," Gavrel said, pointing his blade at the fog as they stepped inside. Visibility stretched to no more than a few inches in any direction, and an ominous feeling hung in the air like they plodded through a nightmare.

"Wait until you can see," Eramus warned him, remembering the bodies. "And stay away from the sorcerer. We have to be smart about this or we'll all end up dead."

Gavrel muttered something unintelligible as he stepped off the bridge and onto the ground beyond.

"I mean it. I want him alive."

Suddenly Riya screamed in agony. She clutched her head and dropped to her knees on the middle of the bridge, clenching her fists as she fought to remain conscious. Black, indigo-tinted smoke wafted out of her palms. Eramus tried to reach her but a powerful wind shoved him back. He concentrated his weight into a lower center of gravity, the leather of his soles scraping against rock while he still slid back from the unseen force.

And then Riya sprang back up, arms thrust before her, and the air exploded with intense indigo and a thunderous boom. Blue light, obscured by the fog, erupted from the magical circle, followed by a sound similar to breaking glass. Riya collapsed, fighting for breath. The force that had been pushing against Eramus vanished as quickly as it had arrived.

"It's gone," Riya panted.

In response, the fog flushed away like a fast moving river and men wrapped in black and tan bandages leapt out of trees, crescent shaped swords raised over their heads as they screamed and attacked. Eramus's first instinct was to put himself between them and Riya, but then he remembered what she intended. He needed to find the sorcerer before her.

He launched himself at the closest attacker, parrying the first blow, which was immediately followed by more with even greater force. Eramus looked back at a pair of diseased yellow eyes. Was this a man?

Gavrel yelled from somewhere up ahead. It was hard to think about much else besides survival. They had to regroup. This wasn't a smart way to fight. Gavrel had been right about the lack of any real strategy, and Eramus had discounted his opinion. Eramus cursed Riya's name as he launched a hard kick into his attacker's stomach, enough of a blow to create a gap of space. He could hurt these things, whatever they were. He would cut through them and get to the sorcerer. If he reacted quickly enough, he could get there before anyone else.

Something burned.

Eramus turned around to see if Riya had recovered yet. Where she had been, a wisp of black smoke dissipated. He scanned around for her quickly, and when he didn't see her he uttered a string of curses, now confident that she intended to beat everyone to the sorcerer.

Three of the mysterious opponents had overwhelmed Gavrel. He was on his heels, only his compact fighting style keeping him alive. He needed help soon or he would be killed.

Atop a boulder at the peak of the path, the sorcerer, a thin, black-bearded man with hollow eyes, barked orders at the mysterious warriors. Eramus merely needed to charge up the path. With enough speed and luck, he might even be able to frighten the man into making a mistake. The line had led here, to this point, and the sorcerer was within reach.

But Gavrel could barely swing his sword anymore. His attackers surrounded him. He couldn't extend his arms far enough to take the offensive or even to break free. The sorcerer's warriors were stronger, faster, and smarter than the men they had beaten the other day. This time Gavrel needed help, and only Eramus could get to him in time. He spared a last look at the sorcerer, then abandoned all thoughts of going after him. His answers would have to wait.

Only a shadow warned him that his original foe hadn't yet quit. He twisted to the right, feeling the sharp burn of steel as it screamed into his hip. He faced his attacker just in time to receive a roundhouse punch to the jaw. In an instant his head had turned in a completely different direction without his permission. He staggered back, shaking black spots from his vision, knowing that loss of consciousness on a battlefield led to death.

Then his opponent charged. Only his reflexes and years of repetition enabled him to block the flurry of blows. His opponent didn't have much technique, but he compensated for that with relentlessness. Eramus couldn't gain an advantage. He could only react, defend himself. He finally found his opening and risked ducking beneath a swipe and rolling to his right. He spun up on one knee and swung as hard as he could with both hands. He didn't hit bone but he did sever his opponent's Achilles tendon to incapacitate him. The creature collapsed, shrieking as it clutched at the back of a useless foot, struggling for balance on a leg that wouldn't respond.

Eramus leaped over him and sprinted straight to Gavrel. He was halfway to him when an arrow zipped out of nowhere and miraculously deflected off the sorcerer's body, causing no damage at all.

Amused, the sorcerer snapped his fingers and Hadrius appeared, exposed. The sorcerer raised glowing blue hands, an angry scowl on his face. Eramus froze, unable to do more than watch.

But Hadrius furiously pumped his arms and legs and raced in the opposite direction. He was fast, very fast, but no cover presented itself, and the sorcerer's magic worked much more quickly. The black-bearded man patiently watched him zigzag across open ground. Hadrius risked a glance over his shoulder just in time to see the sorcerer thrust his hands forward, spittle flying from his lips as he unleashed a violent ripple of blue magic. Hadrius leaped into the air like a giant rabbit to escape the spell. It barely grazed him, but the impact whipped him around like a rag doll, spinning him through the air and smacking him into the ground in a tumble of dirt and bushes.

The sorcerer raised his glowing palms again, his focus directed entirely at Hadrius's still form. Eramus shouted obscenities at the sorcerer to distract him. Somewhere he could hear the clash of steel and Gavrel yelling for help, but he didn't care. Hadrius, his friend, was about to die. They should never have challenged a sorcerer. Eramus shouted again, his voice lost in the cacophony of battle.

A deafening thunderclap ripped across the air, forcing Eramus to his knees. No longer concerned about Hadrius, the sorcerer stiffened and frantically scanned his surroundings as if he sensed a threat but couldn't determine its origin. Riya materialized behind him, yanked his head back by the hair as she dragged her dagger across his exposed throat. The blade's acid etched surface blazed with indigo light. "Hello, Gourak." He never even saw her. A red line blossomed across his throat and she let him fall to the ground like a flopping fish while he choked on his blood. She watched him die from only a couple of feet away.

Eramus felt his heart skip a beat, the sorcerer's death bittersweet. Eramus wouldn't have the answers he had wanted, but at least Hadrius still lived. His friend sat up, stumbled once while he got his feet beneath him, then snatched up his bow from where he had dropped it, his movements slow and clumsy from the sorcerer's attack and the aftereffects of Riya's potion.

He dropped to a knee, closed one eye, settled, held his breath, and released an arrow at one of Gavrel's attackers, a perfect shot through the back of the lung.

Eramus had been so caught up in unfolding events that he had become a bystander. Without wasting another second, he exploded into action. The leather on his sword handle became an extension of his hand. When one of the creatures turned to face him, Eramus ducked and sliced into it. Gavrel made short work of the last creature with a stab through the chest. He yanked his sword out and leaned forward onto it to rest. One of his hands had been badly cut and there were tears and slices all over his arms and chest, more scars for his collection. He took a while to catch his breath, glaring at Riya while he did. One of the creatures wheezed from his fatal arrow wound. They left him to suffer and die.

Hadrius jogged over to them, uncharacteristically stumbling more than once, obviously injured.

"Good shooting," Gavrel said, slapping him on the back. He wiped sweat from his face, managing to leave streaks of blood and dirt where his wrist passed. He glanced at Eramus. "You took long enough, but we're all alive and that counts for something."

Eramus sheathed his sword. "Your brother was right. We do fight well together." He clasped wrists with Gavrel, who nodded in acknowledgement. This second time Eramus had seen Gavrel in action, he had been even more impressed with how well the man handled a sword. He had held off three of those things, while only one had given Eramus a lot of trouble.

"And your friend?" Gavrel wondered with an angry face. "She deceived us. I don't take that lightly."

"I'll deal with her," Eramus promised. He checked his hip where he had been cut. The bleeding had already stopped. Thankfully it was only a superficial wound.

He found Riya rifling through an encampment several yards off the trail, her eyes and hands still glowing with magic. She disappeared into a tent and emerged seconds later, clutching a midnight blue leather tome to her chest. The surface bore a painted white eye in the center of a moon. In her left hand she held a makeshift leather pouch containing four corked vials of dark blue liquid. "No stones of any kind," she complained. Starstones were more valuable to sorcerers than precious gems, and an entire network of savvy collectors and dealers profited from their trade and sale.

"Did you get what you came for?" Eramus asked, startling her. The dead sorcerer's bloody fingerprints had stained the hem of her cloak. Eramus's hands shook in anger.

She scoffed at him. "You were never in any real danger."

"Hadrius was. You should have told us more, that you never intended to let the sorcerer live." Though still breathing hard, his adrenaline had mostly worn off. "I need answers from him!"

"It was too dangerous to let him live. I told you that. You say Hadrius was in danger? Who saved his life? I did. You begged me to help you, and now you don't like the way I do it?" She held the spellbook out. "Do you have any idea how valuable this is?"

"I almost found out!" he shouted. He pointed back at Hadrius. "He almost found out."

"I told you what I wanted. Don't take the high road on me. You have no idea what the sorcerer was capable of."

"The sorcerer might have known about what happened to me," he said. He shouldn't have been surprised by her behavior. Her words rang true and he knew it.

"No he wouldn't have, Eramus. Your affliction surpassed his skill."

"Really? And how would you know that? Why don't you enlighten me? Why won't you tell me what you know?"

"Don't take your anger out on me. I will tell you what I know, but there's nothing you can do about it now. Why don't you calm down? Why don't you wait to ask questions like these when you aren't so upset?"

He took several deep, calming breaths and glanced back at the bodies of the bandaged attackers. Riya's condescension contained more common sense than he was willing to admit. He was very angry. What she didn't understand was that she was the one making him angry. "Who were they? What were they?"

"Morgta. A disease rots away their flesh, something dormant from birth that surfaces later in their lives. These people tend to live in seclusion, stealing and robbing to survive. You did them a favor."

"You've seen them before?"

"Once or twice," she shrugged, still hugging the tome close to her. "But never with a sorcerer. How odd."

"Riya, I—"

"We can talk later, Eramus. When you're calm."

"I am calm," he said through gritted teeth. He was upset right now and he knew it, but so what?

"Later. Now stand back," she said as she lowered her arm and aimed her palm at the ground. Slowly, expertly, she burned into the earth with a beam of magic, steadily increasing the force until it dwindled and sputtered out. Exhausted, her shoulders slumped and she fell to her knees. "Help me up."

They returned to the killing ground to see Hadrius scouring the perimeter. "So where are the children? Everything led straight here but there's no sign of them."

"Sir Jacob said refugees took the children," Gavrel said. "They must have gone a different way."

"Or come through here before the sorcerer and the Morgta did," Eramus suggested.

"So that's what those things are called? And what of the circle over there?" Gavrel asked Riya. "Is it safe now?"

She nodded. "The sorcerer imbued a cube of chalk with magic, then crushed it into powder before charging it. I've never even heard of anything like that before. Brilliant idea."

"I'm so glad you're impressed, Riya," Eramus said snidely.

Gavrel glared at Riya. "You stole my kill. Try anything like that again and I'll end you."

Riya stared back unflinchingly. "You're not that good."

The two locked eyes for a moment. Eramus thought they were going to kill each other. He didn't know for sure if he would stop Gavrel. Then Gavrel turned back to him. "Do you think we should keep going forward?"

"I don't see why not. At least for the rest of the day, to see if the trail runs cold."

Hadrius, bow still in hand, walked through the carnage of dead foes. Finding mercy for enemies intending your death often proved difficult, but as Eramus regarded the diseased flesh of his foes, he wondered if what he and his companions had dispensed truly was mercy. "I'll go and get our stuff." He shot a parting scowl at Riya but she was too caught up in her new spellbook to notice.

Gavrel's face visibly saddened. He looked at Hadrius. "I'll see to my brother and your woman." He pointed away from the campsite, under the trees, at traces of chalk on the grass.

Hadrius nodded once. "I'll join you in a minute." His jaw clenched and he wandered off to find Alina, unstringing his bow as he went.

Gavrel walked toward the bodies. Eramus followed him. He spotted Sylvia first, her red hair standing out among the corpses. There were at least a dozen in varying states of decay. Tears glistened in Gavrel's eyes. Eramus followed them to the twisted, unnatural angle of Lebon's body. There were four Filthies among the dead, as well as six or seven men and women who appeared to be hunters or unsuspecting pilgrims. A merciless use of magic, the death trap had sucked its victims in and then sapped their life force. At least the dead could find solace in the fact that Riya had killed the sorcerer behind it. He couldn't harm anyone else.

Eramus walked outside the circle, which still existed but no longer glowed, its power drained. He studied the lines within to see if the symbol matched the one on his arm. It did not. This one was a combination of parallel lines and a few quarter circles, but nothing like the twisted serpent shape he had seen in his own forearm. At least it appeared that these two marks were not from the same source. The revelation didn't ease his anxiety.

Gavrel reached out with a stick and raked a line through the chalk circle. He tossed the stick aside. "Will this work? She said it would work."

"Wait a minute," Eramus said. He stepped into the circle, covering his mouth with one hand to keep himself from gagging, and nudged at the bodies with his toe as he searched through them.

Gavrel shoved him away when he neared Lebon's body. He must have interpreted Eramus's actions as disrespect.

Hadrius joined them. He had brought his shovel and mattock. "What's going on?" he asked, confused. "There are dead people here, Eramus. Stop it."

"No children," Eramus said, his hand waving at the bodies. "Not a single child among them." Hadrius listened, but the man's concentration wavered when he saw Sylvia among the dead. Eramus grabbed him by the shoulders and looked him squarely in the eyes. "They must have come through before this was here or had a way to get past it." He looked beyond Hadrius. "Where's Alina?"

Hadrius shook free of his grip. He didn't seem to care about anything. "I took her into the camp, *prophuug*. She had a problem." He didn't say *with the dead*, but he might as well have.

Eramus left Hadrius and Gavrel to their mourning, comforted

that Gavrel adhered to Hamaln customs. Eramus remembered what Gavrel had told him about Lebon being one of the last to surrender. He would definitely not have converted to the Temple of Gefil, even if the Ismah himself had ordered him to. There were some things that still mattered to men beyond mortality. If Lebon had told his brother the truth, he would be on his way to Third Awakening after a proper burial.

Alina huddled outside the sorcerer's tent, crying quietly. "So many," she said, looking up at his approach. Tears only made her colorful eyes that much more exotic.

"They have gone beyond us now. Some will return."

He thought back to that night in Grihm. He hadn't been ready to die. Someone had saved him. Did he want to save Alina? Had he asked her along for this reason? She didn't seem cut out for a place like this, for circumstances like these. Why had he brought her? Why was he subjecting her to this? It didn't matter. He couldn't send Alina away now, at least not alone. It was too dangerous.

"I'll never be ready for what comes next," she said with a sniffle.

"Your day will come. Best be ready for that. It's inevitable for all of us."

She nodded at his arm. "Did you get any answers?"

He shook his head. "Nobody wants to tell me. Riya killed the sorcerer before I could ask him. She said he wouldn't have known what it was anyway." He searched all around the tent, even inside it, for clues. He found nothing more than old blankets, clothes, and moldy bread.

"What are you looking for?" she asked.

"We know the children came this way but we haven't found them. Help me find them."

They searched well beyond the camp but could find no sign of the children. If they had somehow gotten past the sorcerer, they could still be alive. The sweat had dried on Eramus's body. Cold seeped into his bones and his new wounds ached. He shivered uncontrollably. He found his cloak and threw it over his shoulders.

Hadrius had already dug Sylvia's grave, and knelt near the base of a tree with her body, gently washing her for interment in traditional Hamaln fashion, while Gavrel, nearby, sweating and stripped to the waist, dug Lebon's grave. Gavrel's shoulder was a disgusting pile of scarred flesh, chafed and raw from his jerkin, though almost lost in the rest of the assassin's scars and fresh cuts. He took a quick look at Eramus before getting back to digging. Eramus briefly considered offering to help. After all, digging had been his job for years under his Uncle Reginald, before he became a messenger and then a peeran. But he reconsidered. Gavrel alone needed to bury his brother.

Eramus looked through the bodies again, specifically at the Filthies first. He wrapped a handkerchief over his mouth and nose to block out the ghastly odor of putrefaction. He turned the soldiers over one by one, examining their goatees until he found one missing his turquoise beads, and it looked like part of his goatee had been ripped off. They had found loose beads down at the base of the mountains. This soldier had been involved in that skirmish. He and his comrades would have pursued the sorcerer up here.

But if the sorcerer proved capable of casting something as powerful as this circle of death, why hadn't he simply done that at the bottom of the mountain? Maybe the Filthies had escaped the first onslaught and followed him up here with reinforcements. Maybe they had surprised the sorcerer and had him on the run, and he had gotten enough of a head start to work this particular spell up here, just in time to catch the Filthies and any other unwitting victims who happened into it. Other than the fog which Riya had said was from a Seehlan priest, this seemed to be a logical enough conclusion, given that Sir Jacob had come to Eramus for help when he could have used Oshlemin soldiers. The knight saw an easy way to blackmail Eramus and to send desperate men with him. The knight lost nothing if they failed. If they succeeded, he could easily have them imprisoned or executed. The Filthies had reported in after the fight with the sorcerer and then never returned after their second attempt.

Second attempt at what? That would explain the sorcerer's head start, but why would the Filthies chase the sorcerer up a mountain? Why would they fight him in the first place, and what were they even doing in the trees at the base of the mountains to begin with?

Eramus continued his inspection, examining the boots of all the men, searching for the special boot Hadrius had described days earlier. That man should have been among the dead, but Eramus didn't find the special boot anywhere. He even went back and checked the Morgta and the sorcerer, but they were all barefoot. From what he could tell, the first group, the one with the children, had somehow continued on. Their pursuers, the Filthies, had died in the sorcerer's trap, just like Lebon and Sylvia.

He looked over at Hadrius. He wanted to talk to his friend, but Hadrius just kept drinking and drinking, cursing loudly at the tree at his back.

Gavrel finally finished his brother's grave. He took Lebon's tunic from him, whispering to his brother as he set it aside, before he set to sprinkling water over his brother and wiping the filth of this Awakening from him so he could pass freely to the next. When Gavrel finished, Eramus walked over to where Lebon lay, his body clean, waxy and pale, and without words the two of them hoisted the stiff corpse up and laid it gently into the hole facing east. Gavrel nodded his thanks.

"He was a decent man for trying to make things better for you," Eramus said.

Gavrel shrugged. "I always looked up to him. I was always proud of him. It's a shame there is no priest here to usher him along to the next Awakening. He deserves better than this."

"And he'll have it," Eramus comforted him. "We'll say the words together, aye?"

"Aye. Thank you."

They gathered over Sylvia first, reciting the Passage of Awakening together while Hadrius slowly covered her body with an indigo, silk shroud.

"Unhindered passage and the promise of hope," they said in unison. *Gohlay-gohlay*, Eramus thought. *Could be happy.*

Hadrius stayed to fill Sylvia's grave and guard her spirit until the appearance of the ebb stars. Without a sentry to protect her spirit, it would fall prey to the summoning of blood stars.

They moved to Lebon's grave next, and Riya surprised them by participating in the ritual to some extent. Though silent through their recitation of the Passage of Awakening, she paid close attention to what they did, her eyes constantly drifting to the night sky, her lips moving with unspoken words.

Once Gavrel began to shovel dirt over his brother, Eramus and Riya left him to stand guard. She headed to a small spot she had cleared several yards away, while Eramus paced around for a bit, lost in thought. But the more he tried to make sense of everything, the sleepier he got. His thoughts tripped over themselves. Where were the children? How had they defeated magic that had killed so many others? Where would they be going? Trying to get to Keltivar along a pilgrims' trail? There were too many unanswered questions.

Eramus was drawn to a fire Alina had lit close to the sorcerer's tent. He walked past her, and it, and into the tent without a word. He lay down on fur that had been used for a bed, just to close his eyes and clear his thoughts. Unfortunately they turned back to the mark on his arm. Was it connected to his nightmares? His sleeplessness? He wanted it gone. He wanted to be back in Riya's bed. He would forgive her. He always did. He cared for her, despite how she treated him. Everything fell away.

He stands in the dark, in front of the rundown structure he is too afraid to enter. He feels the heat of a fire. It is too dark to see anything but the edges of trees and the building. A wind picks up, and with it comes flapping wings. No, the wind originates from the flapping wings. It gets hotter. He can barely make out the heat's source. There is a fire inside the structure now and he can see the bastard snowthroat's wings flapping through cracks in the wall. It is so hot. Eramus wipes his forehead. It is drenched with sweat and fear. It is so hot and he is so afraid. He squeezes his eyes shut against the heat, holds his hand in front of his face to shield it.

The next thing he knows, he lies in near darkness in the sorcerer's tent, his mouth incredibly dry, his body sweaty and damp. For the space of a few heartbeats he listens to chanting, terrified that something or someone would burst in and shred him to pieces. He hears the roar of the fire just outside, sees the silhouette of a figure as it passes in front of the flames.

With unfamiliar courage he opens the tent to see Alina naked, ceremoniously dancing around the fire, oblivious to his presence. Her bronze skin glows in a shimmering indigo hue, a pair of large feathery wings sprouting from her back. The flames spark and snap as her wings furiously flap. Smoke stings his eyes, forces him to shut them as they squirt tears. A strong wind threatens to lift him off his feet and whisk him into the night sky.

Before he opened his eyes again, Eramus lay in the sorcerer's tent, wondering what had inspired his latest bizarre dream. Hadrius snored somewhere in the distance, a true anchor to reality. Exhausted, Eramus sat up and rubbed his eyes with cold fingers, longing for decent, dreamless sleep.

He stepped out of the tent to the warmth of a fire. Alina peacefully dozed next to it. What had he seen? What had his imagination created? Riya had warned him about the mysterious woman. Had the strange dream been her doing? He doubted it. His dreams had worsened even before his first encounter with her.

He looked off to the left and noticed for the first time that the sorcerer had built his own little flowerbed of purple and yellow mountain pansies, a spot of beauty flourishing in a harsh environment.

The strong red glow of blood stars marked the time as hours before dawn. Hadrius had passed out next to Sylvia's grave, an empty jug discarded on its side a few feet away. Gavrel sat cross-legged, attentive and wide awake over Lebon's grave, his brother's tunic set out beside him. Eramus gave him a quick nod, wondering even as he did if Gavrel would follow through on his word to abandon his thoughts of revenge now that his brother was buried.

Still awake, Riya knelt within a perimeter of candles while she scribbled notes into her spellbook. Eramus found his gear and took long drinks from his waterskin until his belly swelled. He kept enough room between himself and Riya so as not to disturb her. It didn't work. She turned at his approach. He couldn't read her face well enough to see what kind of mood she was in. Though still upset with her, he didn't want to let his anger create a rift between them. The more he tried to change her, the more she resisted. That was part of his attraction to her.

"Do you do this all the time now?" he asked.

"It's not every day I get a new spellbook," she said as she held her hand out for his waterskin. She only took a quick sip before handing it back. She flipped through pages. "He wrote everything in code. He moved hard sounds to the end of words and left soft sounds at the beginnings. It only took me a few minutes to make sense of it."

Despite the fact that Riya studied the dead sorcerer's spellbook, Eramus also noticed the blue potions he had seen earlier and a few sheets of parchment off to the side containing several notes and a precise illustration of the moon and at least two unfamiliar constellations. It reminded him of the moon chart he had seen in her laboratory. He wondered about a possible connection, or if the moon was just a similar magical interest.

He turned back to Riya and the spellbook. "What does it say? Is it more magic?"

"He earned the name Gourak the Mad for a reason. I already know about much of what I've found in here so far but he also experimented with amplifying and maximizing magic in ways I could never conceive of. The trap he created back there is just one example." Her face lit up with excitement. "But his theories are what truly interest me. There are pages and pages of his speculations about starstone origins and rebuilding magical effects from trace elements."

Unsure of what any of that meant, he nodded to the potions. "And those? What are they?"

She pulled them closer to her. "I haven't figured that out yet."

"So what now?" Eramus wondered, deciding it wasn't worth pressing the issue. She had done what she came here for. He didn't care about any of this unless it related to him.

She pointed to the spellbook as if he was a child. "I have a lot of reading to do."

"I was talking about you." He swallowed. "With us, I mean. With all of us. What are your plans?"

She stared back at him. "I'll have to head back to Brudgewan very soon, if you really need an answer right now." He rolled his eyes and turned back to the campsite. "Come back here," she said, her eyes straying to his left arm. He made a fist, a reaction to his self-consciousness. "I want to see it."

He rolled up his sleeve. "I don't know what—"

"Have a seat," she encouraged, patting the ground next to her. He had finally found a way to attract her interest. A debilitating weakness overcame him as he gladly surrendered to her whims. He tried to convince himself that he wanted to find out what afflicted him, that this interaction had nothing to do with his need for attention, to feel like he mattered to her, like the way she mattered to him.

He sat down and held out his arm. It was covered in cuts and scratches from his attempts to physically remove the supernatural mark. She seized his wrist with one hand, unafraid, and spread her fingers wide with the other hand. A small indigo light from her palm bathed his skin and the symbol on his forearm flared to blue life.

"What are you doing?" he growled in horror. He tried to pull his arm back but she had a surprisingly strong grip on his wrist. "Riya, it really burns."

"Hush."

The curved line of the symbol appeared similar to a slithering serpent, with short, double lines intersecting the center and another pair of short lines running perpendicular to the ends. His stomach turned when he saw it under his flesh but curiosity inevitably outweighed his physical reactions to it. She copied the lines in her spellbook with incredible speed and accuracy.

"Hold still," she ordered. He continued to squirm as though a hot iron brand blistered his flesh. "It will fade in seconds, when my magic wears off."

He looked at the smoldering blue symbol while she did, unable to make sense of what it meant or how it had gotten there. He had no memory of it before earlier in the day. Had it always been there? Alina had been cautious of him back on the Lestwine. She had known something of its existence before he did. Two, three days at least he had had it for sure.

"It's a curse," she murmured as her magical light and the symbol vanished. If he hadn't felt the pain, seen the symbol, he would never have believed it existed, the only evidence a mess of lines he had carved into himself. She sprinkled sand onto the fresh ink in her book and quickly blew it away.

"What does that mean?" he demanded as he peered at the symbol on the page. "Why would someone curse me? What does that mean?" Panic flooded through him, more from the unknown ramifications of being cursed than anything. "This is your craft, Riya. I expect answers."

She regarded him carefully, like she sought what he couldn't see. "I don't deal with this branch of magic. You'll need to find a *cseripta* to get your answers."

"A what? What...where..." he swallowed painfully, cold fear clogging his throat.

"What you carry is called a *cseript*," she said.

"What?" he said, his voice cracking.

"Say-ript. It's a Kortune term. It means 'sight of the old one', but not like you think. The old one in this sense is probably another sorcerer."

"How did this come to be on my arm, Riya? On my flesh? Infecting me? Where did it come from?"

His first thought was of Gourak the Mad. Next he thought about Riya. And, finally, he considered Alina. He recalled the sense of helplessness his dream had left him with, recalled Alina's ceremonious behavior. He couldn't rule her out, even if it had only been a dream.

He had come into contact with only two sorcerers in his life, one right in front of him. She had to be wrong.

"So if I find out who this mark belongs to or what it means, I can find who did this?"

"I don't know much about *cseript*."

His muscles tensed. He straightened up. "So you say, and yet you've just made it appear."

"You're overreacting. I cast a reveal spell, which uncovers traces of magic. I used a variation of the same spell before the fight."

He slipped out his dagger. He would remove it himself. No more cuts. He would take the surface of the skin right off his arm. He would spit in the face of whomever or whatever had done this terrible thing to him.

She eyed the steel. "That won't work. You already tried, remember? Put it away."

He sheathed it, and immediately thought of her dagger, covered in magical runes. Maybe it would work.

"What about—"

"My dagger won't work, either," she said as if she had read his mind. "A *cseript* is a true name. To invoke it correctly invites the one who placed it there to access your mind and body. You should be thankful that you became aware of it before that happened."

He broke out into a cold sweat. He couldn't feel his legs, even though he knew they were there. "Access…what…is this?"

"The *cseript* is unique. Only a *cseripta* can tell you for sure. They dedicate their lives to studying this branch of magic."

Cursed. He thought about the wolf roaming Riya's grounds. She was lying to him. "Then why do you think your wolf was once a man? He carries a *cseript* as well, right? You told me before that he was marked. You said he's a man." Up until now he hadn't fully believed her about the wolf. Now he clung to any shred of information he could get.

He drew several deep breaths, wondering if he should tell Riya about his dreams, about the bird.

"I paid a *cseripta* for that information," she continued. "For the *cseript* on the beast's flesh." She narrowed her eyes at him. "The mark on him is different than what you carry, Eramus."

"And the *cseripta*? Where is he?"

"I poisoned him. The knowledge of what he saw was too tempting to allow him to live."

Now Eramus was more than a little wary. He had never known how Riya had come to discover what she knew. He had always assumed she had used her magic to find out, and he didn't always trust that. Did she really kill someone when she got her answer? He blinked and the decrepit building from his nightmares flashed under his eyelids. He shuddered. The image vanished as quickly as it had appeared. Was he cursed like the wolf, doomed to live the rest of his existence in the body of a beast? Would he become Riya's slave?

"*Cseripta* are expensive," she added, bringing him back to the moment. "A good one, an authentic one, is not easy to come by. The secrets they uncover tend to make them targets. As a result, they usually travel with protection. And they'll leave with the secrets, if that's the case."

"And yours?"

She didn't flinch. "Someone who trusted me. I used that trust against him."

Riya continued to prove what she would do to someone if she felt she had to.

He felt physically drained at the thought of what might happen to him. Would this mark keep him from ever reaching Second Awakening? He paused, took a deep breath to calm himself. He thought about when this curse had manifested itself. "What will it do to me? Will it control me? Who does this *cseript* belong to?"

"I already told you I don't know, Eramus. Yours is only the second I've ever seen. You'll need to find a *cseripta* for the answers you want. Please...I have to finish my work."

He plopped down onto his rear end, emptiness gnawing away at his insides. "I guess what happens to me just isn't important to you right now." He waited for her to say something, anything, hoping she would console him, knowing she wouldn't. That was part of his strange attraction to her. He knew he would never have to make any commitments, and could expect none in return, even if he was cursed.

Riya wrote in her spellbook, transferring notes from the other one. She read through select pages, skimmed through others. She finally looked up at him, shaking her head.

"I had a feeling that his codes couldn't be that easy to decipher," she said. "Some of the words in here don't make sense. He shifted whole sections of text to unrecognizable patterns. I need the peace and quiet of my laboratory where I can work without distractions."

Eramus stared into the flame of one of her candles. He felt like a moth, eager to dive into the finality of the harsh, beautiful light. "What makes you think I care about your spellbook?"

"You're not going to give up, are you?" she asked.

"It's not on you." He dropped his head between his knees, hoping for a word or touch of comfort that never came. "Strange things have been happening to me lately, and I'm not just talking about the mark or *cseript* or whatever. I'm having...dreams..." he said cautiously, thinking it wouldn't be a good idea to tell her everything, about the bird or about how Alina had appeared to him. She would just call him paranoid or label the dreams as his own strange fantasies. Most of the time he knew he was just worried for no reason. Still, it felt good to unburden at least some of what he had experienced.

"We all have dreams, Eramus."

"Riya, please help me."

"I'm sorry but I don't know much more than what I've told you."

He kept his forehead on his knees until he heard Riya settle in, until her steady breathing indicated that she was asleep. He wouldn't shut his eyes for fear the nightmares would return. He looked up at an orderly cluster of blood stars, watched the moon as it arced across the sky, and wondered why he loved a selfish woman. He reminded himself that people were all inherently selfish.

At some point it got a little lighter out and Alina appeared and offered him dried beef. He hesitated, peering back into her eyes for any indication that she bore responsibility for his supernatural predicament. He supposed it wouldn't make much sense to curse him and then offer him food. He took the beef and chewed absentmindedly, watching daylight splash color on trees and bushes. Would he soon grow feathers? Be watching the sunrise through a bird's eyes?

Hadrius and Gavrel stood over the graves, heads bowed under the first twinkling ebb stars as they released Sylvia and Lebon to their next Awakenings. Eramus knew he should join the ceremony, but his eyes were so tired. He had to close them, rest them for a minute. Then he would pay his respects.

He jolted awake to everyone packed and telling him it was time to get going. He had fallen asleep again.

He inhaled burning cold morning air, angry at himself for missing the funerals. He spared a glance at the graves, bowed his head for a moment and asked the Hamal for wisdom to aid them on their way.

Riya hugged her new spellbook close. He wanted to light it on fire so she could watch it burn.

"You're going the wrong way," he told her.

"Hadrius told me what happened to you on the way up here the first time," she said. "I don't want to deal with robbers and the like alone if I can help it. That's your line of work. I'll stick with you for now."

He sighed, knowing his mission would prove even more complicated with her near, as she cast doubt on his choices and distracted him. Still, he was glad to have her along. He enjoyed her company, good or bad, and he wanted her to help him understand what was happening to him. She had to know more about his curse than she had told him. Was she trying to protect him from something or was she just lying to him?

His neck hurt. He rolled it around, collected his things. He noticed Gavrel staring at him. He wore his brother's tunic, a dead man's shirt.

"And what about you?" Eramus asked. "Are you going to follow this thing through with us?"

"I said I would. I'm in no hurry to get back down there anyway. I'm a wanted man. If the militia doesn't throw me in prison, I'm bound to end up facedown in an alley. Somebody in the *culipi* network will get lucky sooner or later."

"Your odds aren't much better up here."

"At least up here there's a purpose and people are watching my back," Gavrel said over his shoulder as he set off after the others. "Even if they don't want to. I go back to civilization, I'll have to figure out what to do next. That's a choice I'm not ready for yet."

Eramus couldn't argue with the man's logic. He would have to make some tough decisions as well. He had also been thinking about what would happen if the children couldn't be found, or even worse if they were dead. What would he do then? The entire mission hinged on the knight's word that Sadir and his family would go free if the children were returned unharmed.

"*And you?*" Eramus asked Hadrius.

"*I told you I would finish this with you,*" Hadrius replied. "*And I will. You wouldn't make it ten feet up here without a tracker and you know it.*"

There was too much to think about, too many decisions. Eramus followed the others up the trail, taking one last glance at the scattered corpses and fresh burial mounds. He couldn't keep track of the dead anymore. It wasn't supposed to be like this.

After only a short while, Hadrius found smaller, lighter child tracks in among the adult prints. Eramus hadn't seen him take a drink all morning. He wondered if laying Sylvia to rest had helped him to cope with the grief of her loss. He felt guilty for not talking to his friend about what had happened to her, but Hadrius had essentially shut him out after her death and they had all been dealing with so much.

"What if these children live up here?" Riya asked.

Eramus let the question hang in the air. They were going the right way. He could feel it. The bird had shown him the way. *Roua.* He thought back to the mercurial sensations of his dream, where the bastard snowthroat had tried to lure him inside the rotted building. He hadn't followed it inside, though every other sign the bird had provided along the way had proved useful. Could he continue to believe in its omen only as it suited his needs?

Riya cursed. She pulled her dripping black hand out of her

satchel.

Eramus froze and stared. The form of a dark bird coalesced, feather and beak. The black blood of a bastard snowthroat stained her hand. He had given in to the enigmatic summons too soon. "What…"

She smeared black into the dirt. "My ink."

He let out a nervous breath. She had thrown a fit over ink. He squeezed his eyes shut, clawed at his scalp. He needed to withdraw from this half-wakeful dream state of obsession and rejoin reality. He just needed a couple hours of sleep. He watched the ink spread into black wings. He whimpered and wrung his hands together.

Alina leaned against a nearby tree, staring at him, making him more uncomfortable.

Riya's eyes shifted slightly toward the mysterious woman. "Bring me some of your water."

Alina took her waterskin off her shoulder and held it out, eager to please, her eyes never leaving Eramus. He wanted to shake both women until answers fell out. He walked over to the spilled ink and smudged it with his boot until the image blended away. The bird wouldn't get him if he could help it.

Hadrius and Gavrel took the cue to remove their packs and rest.

Riya scrubbed dirt between her palms while Alina dribbled water onto them. Some of the ink bled away but most remained. Riya carefully removed the damaged inkpots and tossed them away.

"Were they all ruined?" Alina asked.

"What difference does it make to you?"

Alina slipped her pack off and rifled through it. She pulled out an inkpot that looked a little older, though still sealed and full. "I have this."

"What do you want for it?" Riya asked suspiciously.

She handed it over. "Nothing. I can't even write. I hunted rats for a blind man. He gave it to me as payment."

"Why did he give you ink?" Eramus wondered.

"Why would he need it?" Alina asked.

"Why indeed?" Riya said. She pinched her middle finger against her thumb, her eyes closed while she concentrated. Her fingernails glowed indigo, then her fingers, until a flame of the same color licked over her hand and consumed the ink stain. She made a fist and doused the flame. She held her fist closed, her brows furrowing, eyes squeezing shut even tighter, until sparks leapt off her fingers and quickly burned out. Out of breath, she opened her eyes and let her hand fall to her side, disappointment visible across her face.

After that she opened the new spellbook and traced her index finger down lines of runes as if nothing had happened. Eramus remembered her saying something about rebuilding magic. Had that been some kind of attempt on her part?

Alina studied the scars on Riya's palms. "What happened to your hands?"

"Magic has to burn through something," Riya said without looking up. "My hands are the best conductors I can control." She held up a scorched palm, and Alina took hold of it to get a better look. Riya snatched it back. "What are you about?"

Alina looked down shamefully. "I only wanted to see."

"Never touch me again."

As Alina picked herself up and walked away, Riya flipped through her old spellbook until she found loose sheets of parchment, the pages with complex illustrations of the moon.

"Let's keep moving, Riya. You'll have time to do that when we stop for the night."

She packed up the spellbook and carefully wrapped the inkpot Alina had given her. "Like I said…distractions."

Eramus took point for the next hour, the trail taking them down below the tree line once again, just above a thick valley of evergreens. Though they were heading down and not up, sleeplessness eroded his endurance along with the rough terrain. He concentrated on the present, on picking up his feet and putting them down, on making sure he didn't lose his footing and roll down into the valley.

Close behind him, Alina plucked small white flowers from a bunch of late blooming heath bedstraw she had found beside the path.

"What's that for?" he asked her.

She had already begun to twist and braid the green stems together. "It's one of the ways I make money." She slipped a newly constructed bracelet on her wrist and removed it. Satisfied with her work, she started on another one.

Riya brought up the rear, perspiration spotting her rosy cheeks. "I need to rest." She leaned forward onto her thighs. "I can't believe we haven't caught up to anyone yet." She flexed her writing hand while she caught her breath.

Hadrius ran his fingers through his sweat-matted hair as he slowed. "They're days ahead of us."

Eramus lay down on his side, intent on catching a brief nap, filthy with his own sweat but too tired to care. His mind had quieted for a change. He heard his breathing in his ears, rough and gasping.

Suddenly Gavrel shook his shoulder to wake him. "Come on. Time to move."

Disoriented, he blinked several times to get his bearings. His back ached and his muscles throbbed. The impromptu nap hadn't helped. His recent sleep resembled unsafe blackout spells. He fell into step behind Hadrius, holding his sword against him so it didn't slap his thigh.

They didn't press themselves so hard this time. The trail leading down into the valley was even more dangerous to navigate once the sun passed overhead and the canopy blocked almost every light source but scattered ebb stars.

As it grew darker, they all stumbled mindlessly along, including Hadrius. Only Alina didn't trip over anything. Even in the dark, she seemed to know exactly where to step. The rest of them cursed and kicked at overgrown tree roots and animal burrows.

"I can't keep going," Gavrel said, grimacing, hands on his hips as he panted. "I can't see anything."

Riya glanced through a hole in the trees at the full moon, translucent against the colorful wash of sunset. "And if you could?"

Gavrel, suspicious, straightened up as much as his shoulder would allow. "We don't have any torches. We could try to make some, but we need to rest first. At least for a little while."

"There will be time to rest later. I have something other than torches in mind."

"More magic," he said with a frown.

"Yes." She opened her potions case and withdrew the blue potions she had taken from the sorcerer.

"What's that? Colored fire?"

"No. These vials should contain moon vision."

"Should contain moon vision?" Eramus asked. "Are you sure? You said this sorcerer, this madman, wrote everything in code. What if that's poison?"

She shrugged. "I'm confident this is moon vision. Gourak's notes explain how it allows one to see the night as the moon does. We could close the gap on the people we're after. Hadrius said they're days ahead of us. They will be just as tired. They'll have to stop at night when it's too dark to see."

More than anything Eramus wanted sleep, but navigating in the dark would allow them to make up lost time. It was worth the risk if it worked. Riya's business was to know about magic. He had to trust her. The sooner he finished this job, the sooner he could secure Sadir's release and see about finding a *cseripta*. Everything else had become secondary to his fatigue but he could stay awake for a while longer if he had to. If he stayed awake he wouldn't have to deal with any more nightmares.

The others looked to him for leadership. He briefly wondered how the moon could see before he snatched a vial from Riya and gulped down its oily contents. Whereas Riya's potions consisted of warmth, this one whisked into his bloodstream like a cool breeze. When he didn't choke or collapse, the others followed suit. It was only after the four potions had been consumed that Eramus realized Alina wouldn't have one. The others would just have to help her along.

They stood perfectly still, hearing only the sound of their own breathing, until their circular irises shone bone white in the darkness.

"Incredible," Hadrius said, his wide eyes absorbing the new world that appeared before Eramus. Gradations of weak silver and gentle blue existed, just as the sharp contrasts of color did in daylight. The unique form of sight offered much less color variety but much more contrast with what was available.

"The effects aren't permanent," Riya said. "Gourak's notes indicate that he infused his potions with heavy doses of magic. The consequences will be severe once they wear off. We'll have to hurry."

The companions descended deep into the forest, pushing themselves for the next several hours until the declines flattened considerably and every step wasn't potentially a twisted ankle. Eramus forgot his troubles and again lost himself in the moment. He marveled at the clarity with which he could see nightlife. Bats fluttered through insect clouds. A fox stalked through tall bushes, its glowing eyes observing their every move. It was a familiar world but he had never seen it like this.

They took time to adjust to this world of wonder. If Eramus hadn't known any better, he would have thought Alina had imbibed one of the potions as well. She moved at the same pace as the others, never faltering. "I don't think we should go any farther," she said when they reached a stretch of thinning tree cover.

"Why not?" Gavrel asked. "You heard the sorcerer. The magic will wear off."

"We're going to keep moving," Eramus said. "Unless you have a reason why we shouldn't." He had plenty of his own but he kept them to himself. The nightlife had already started to disappear. "Dawn's not too far away. Stay close." Alina hung back anyway.

Eramus couldn't have been more correct. When they rounded the next bend, the sun broke through the spotty evergreens, bright light stabbing their eyes. He fell to his knees, rubbing at the pain. He heard the same reaction from the others.

"I knew I would regret this," Gavrel seethed.

Footsteps pounded all around them. Eramus struggled to open his eyes but couldn't see past blurry tears. He wiped at his eyes and blinked them as rapidly as he could. Shapes and colors coalesced, no longer ethereal silvers and blues but mundane primaries of normal vision. Seehlan refugees in ragged clothing had them surrounded. He fumbled for his sword and managed to draw it. *"A good Hamaln does not solve problems with violence."*

As his eyesight returned, he noticed how thin and desperate the refugees were. He also noticed that, unlike Seehlan he had encountered before, these men were armed. He looked around for the children. They were nowhere to be seen.

"Everyone calm down," he said to his companions, hoping they wouldn't have to fight. His skull throbbed from the potion, nauseau had begun to overtake him, and his limbs felt heavy.

"Oshlemin!" one of the Seehlan yelled as he pointed his short sword at Gavrel. Some of the others grunted and then they charged.

Riya didn't wait for them to close the gap. She pulled her elbows back and opened glowing palms. When she straightened her arms, violent wind shrieked past Eramus, blowing up his hair in its wake. It ripped five of the refugees off their feet and dashed them against rocks and trees. None of them got up.

Someone shouted in another language. A bowstring twanged and an arrow hit soft flesh. Riya's scream followed as she fell and curled up on her side, teeth gritted in pain, tears welling in her eyes. She grasped for the feathered shaft poking out of her calf. Riya wasn't one to show weakness, but Eramus could see her fear for a heartbeat. Then her confidence returned.

"Do something!" she growled at Eramus. He turned slowly, sword ready. He heard more footsteps, dry leaves and branches snapping as refugees closed in.

One of the refugees threw a rock and hit Gavrel in the side of the head. He cried out, staggered. Then men attacked him, beat at him with sticks and spit on him. Others swarmed around him to kick and punch, rats fighting over a carcass. Someone dropped a sack over his head and tied his hands behind him. He squirmed like a wounded animal, but there were too many of them and he was dazed. The quick, brutal assault rendered him unconscious.

And still Eramus hadn't moved. Sweat stung his eyes and he wiped it away with his free hand. He clutched his sword, vowing to himself to cut down anything that came close. Hadrius was also armed with his sword, and the two of them stood back to back, protecting each other from the same attacks that had disabled their comrades. One of the refugees threw a rock at Eramus but he saw it coming and easily dodged it.

Thinking Riya easier prey, one of the Seehlan crept up behind her, his hands ready to seize hold of her. Eramus flicked his eyes to warn her. She waited until the man moved within close range, then slid out her dagger and stabbed him up to the hilt in the femoral artery. She tried to pull her blade back out but he tripped backwards, gasping as blood sprayed out of him and soaked the forest floor.

Eramus nudged Hadrius, and they inched closer to Riya. The majority of the Seehlan stayed where they were, waiting expectantly, but one of them ran to help his wounded comrade, his own hands red and wet as he tried to stop the blood. The man died in seconds from the mortal wound.

Eramus glanced around, his eyes settling on the bowman hidden in the trees, his arm drawn back, one eye closed as he aimed at Riya.

Unwilling to watch Riya die, Eramus cursed, roaring as he stupidly broke his protective formation and rushed through the bushes at the bowman. Before he could reach the man, though, the bowman slackened his string and melted into the trees. Confused, Eramus spun around to see that the refugees had gathered around Riya and were tying her palms together and gagging her. One of them punched her in the face until she blacked out. The arrow in her calf probably hadn't been meant to hurt her as much as disrupt her concentration. That kind of pain would interfere with the focus required to summon magic. These men knew what Riya was, and they also knew how to deal with her. That made them extremely dangerous.

Eramus held his sword in front of him with both hands, trying to decide what to do. Nine armed men bore down on him. They had smartly filled the space between him and Hadrius, separating them. Someone had trained them well.

A burly man with a ruddy complexion shouted an order and one of the men lunged in at Eramus. He stabbed the man in the arm and he dropped his club. There was no room for error here. They were severely outnumbered and still recovering from the disorientation of the potion, and the leader acted with enough experience to not waste his men by sending too many of them in range of Eramus's sword. That was his only advantage at the moment. He wiped more sweat from his eyes and peered into the trees for the bowman. He didn't see him anywhere.

The men surrounding Gavrel slipped a noose over his neck and threw the other end of the rope over a tree branch. As they lifted his unconscious form upright and heaved on the rope, they pumped their fists and cheered. Eramus couldn't get to him. There were too many of them in the way.

The men shouted as they hoisted Gavrel up to hang him. He was still unconscious, his left side bunched up from the old wound on his shoulder. Eramus couldn't make out most of what they said, but he did hear the Ismah's name and something that sounded like

Gefil.

"Circle around my side when I attack," Eramus said to Hadrius in Uuslefin. Eramus swung down in a mighty overhead blow that scattered the men. Hadrius spun around, zigzagging through his own attackers as he cut around Eramus and raced toward the makeshift gallows. Three men cut him off and tackled him. They tried to pin him but he twisted one man's arm around and put his boot in another man's face. There were three of them, though, and with all six arms they eventually managed to hold him down and secure his wrists.

As men closed in on Eramus, he took a punch with the weight of a sword handle behind it that almost took his head off. He spit blood but remained conscious. He drove his forehead into the man's nose for payback, regretting the reactionary blow when his skull felt like it would shatter. His fears and nightmares didn't exist right now. He would fight. He would make these men regret ambushing him. He ignored his physical pain, gripped his sword tightly in both hands. He wanted blood.

"Put him down!" someone shouted in a clear, commanding voice.

When Eramus followed the voice through the trees at the top of a hill to its owner, he recognized the face of the man who had saved his life in Grihm all those years ago. He was much thinner now, but still wiry and even more intimidating, his sword strapped to his back. Eramus had never expected to see him again.

The men yanking on Gavrel's rope let it slacken just a fraction.

"Oshlemin," someone grumbled.

Rammun shouted back in rapid Seehlan and the refugees lowered their heads and followed his orders, taking the noose off Gavrel's neck.

A brown and black dog hastened past Rammun, through the trees, and trotted up to sniff Eramus. Just like Rammun, the dog looked familiar. Eramus lost his bloodlust in an instant, even though his chest continued to rise and fall with heavy breathing.

"Unni!" Rammun yelled. He slapped his thigh, but Unni had decided to lick Eramus's hand instead. Eramus scratched the dog's ears and his tail wagged. Eramus was so happy to see that the puppy had survived that night. As Rammun approached, his boots crunching dry leaves, his mismatched eyes glimmered with recognition. The man appeared weary, and streaks of gray cut the blond hair along his temples. "Don't touch my dog."

Eramus ignored him and continued to pet Unni, but he threw his sword down, so happy to see the dog. The fight had lost its purpose. "We didn't come here for trouble."

Rammun glared at Unni until the dog's tail went between his legs and he came to his master's side. Then Rammun stared at the bloody mess that had been one of the refugees and his cheeks flushed. "I don't care what you're here for. Now you owe the Missing Brothers." He turned to the refugees and said something in Seehlan.

Eramus got to his feet and surrendered, letting himself be bound, submitting to the rough treatment, knowing he and his companions would be much better served if they didn't resist. Rammun was a fair man. The refugees took the dagger strapped to Eramus's thigh, and also found the concealed dagger in his boot. As he wondered who exactly these Missing Brothers were, he looked around and realized for the first time that Alina wasn't with them. He had assumed that she had been overpowered like the rest of them. How had she gotten away? She had warned them not to keep going. What had she known? He should have listened to her. At least one of them had evaded capture. That, in and of itself, reassured him. It gave them a chance. Then someone grunted and something heavy hit him on the back of the head and everything turned to darkness.

CHAPTER 9

Eramus's head thumped. Tiny insect legs tickled his cheek. His stomach jostled from movement. Boots shuffled in the dirt. He tried to lift his arms but his wrists were tied, his hands numb from lack of circulation. He eventually determined that he hung upside down from someone's shoulders. He groaned as recent events returned to him. At least nightmares hadn't disturbed his unconsciousness. The refugees might even have done him a favor by granting the respite, however long it might have been. For once he hadn't thought of the bird.

The lungs of the man carrying him filled with air and he yelled in Seehlan. The world rushed by in Eramus's ears as he was unceremoniously dumped onto his feet. His legs couldn't support him. He fell down hard, twisting at the last second to absorb the impact with his shoulder. His mouth opened in a soundless scream at the agonizing impact. Rough hands hoisted him upright and held him steady. Foreign chatter droned around him, as did constant movement. Strong sunlight forced his eyes shut. More hands steered him forward, barking unclear orders.

They plodded up a scree-littered path for a while. Eramus walked for what seemed like forever while he squinted at the Seehlan in front of him and the blurry bushes and trees walling them in on both sides. At first he wondered if the moon vision potion had permanent side effects, but the landscape around him gradually sharpened. The greens and browns of the trees, the gray of the rocks, and the sporadic bursts of red and yellow flowers on bushes were becoming that much more recognizable. Finally someone placed a hand on his chest to stop him. "Where are we?" he asked.

He blinked rapidly when they emerged from the shadowy maze of trail they had traversed into crisp, clean daylight. Cool air washed over his sweaty face. A motley assortment of tough, rangy men had gathered around him. Only a few were armed with swords, but all of them had weapons of some kind. One of them relied on a walking stick for support. He limped along, sour face struggling through each step.

Her hands tied awkwardly behind her, her body dragged by a rope leash cinched around her waist, Riya looked furious. A dirty rag had been stuffed in her mouth. They had confiscated her cloak and her satchel along with all of her stone pouches, jewelry, spellbooks, potions, and anything remotely associated with magic. At least they had pulled the arrow out of her. She was limping, a blood-soaked tourniquet knotted below her knee.

Gavrel was conscious, his face a battered collection of dried blood and bruises. They had stripped his armor, taken his sword and boots, but they had begrudged him Lebon's tunic, most likely as a reminder of who he was, or who they thought he was. If anything, he was less of an Oshlemin than most claimed to be.

They had disarmed Hadrius as well, but he appeared otherwise unharmed. Alina, thankfully, was still missing. Eramus could only hope that they hadn't caught her, hadn't even seen her. She had hung back a little, had even warned them not to proceed. She may have avoided their captors altogether. Had she known something the others didn't?

Rammun was also conspicuously absent. There was a chance that Eramus could talk to him, reason with him. The Seehlan hiding in these mountains wouldn't care about Eramus's story, especially because of his affiliation with an Oshlemin like Gavrel. But Rammun might listen, and these men seemed to respect him.

"Where's Rammun?" Eramus asked the man next to him. When he didn't answer, Eramus asked another one, with the same result.

"Dey nonunstan you," Gavrel slurred through a fat lip.

"What?"

"Nonunstand you."

Eramus moved through their captors until he caught up to

Gavrel. "They don't understand me?"

Gavrel nodded in frustration.

"Do you know where they're taking us?" Eramus asked.

Gavrel shook his head, his right eye swollen shut, the bruises on his face appearing much worse this close up.

"You're lucky to be alive," Eramus said. He leaned in a little closer. "I know one of them. He's a mercenary. I'll try to talk to him."

Gavrel didn't respond, but his left eye betrayed his thoughts. If he had a weapon and a chance, he would fight. He didn't look like he wanted to negotiate.

The Seehlan separated them, shoved them, herded them, just like Eramus had once seen the Filthies herd the Seehlan. They crested a hill and descended into a clearing bordered by rocks and trees, a concealed mountainous haven of crude huts and a series of tents. Eramus would never have found this place on his own. He had no doubt, however, that Hadrius was busy memorizing every curve of the terrain, every subtle shift and incline, should they need to attempt an escape or even to find their way back at some point.

Seehlan were everywhere. Children played while men and women toiled in gardens and repaired livestock fences to keep the handful of goats and pigs from running off. A stone-ringed well sat off to the side, and Eramus wondered where the water came from. The functioning village served as a last home for a people with nowhere else to go. More than fifteen years had passed since the Seehlan had been driven out of Gelofass, and this was what had become of some of them. If Sir Jacob knew about this place he would raze it to the earth.

"Seehan," one of their captors proudly boasted.

"What does that mean?" Eramus asked.

The Seehlan scratched at his stubble and repeated the word. When Eramus shook his head to indicate he didn't understand, he was shoved in response.

Angry shouts welcomed Eramus and his companions throughout the village. Most of the anger originated from younger adults. Elders simply looked concerned. They had already seen enough hate in their lives.

But Gavrel seemed unworried about the epithets hurled his way. Instead his attention fixated on a boy and girl working with others in a vegetable patch. Their light hair and pale complexion marked them as outsiders.

Eramus couldn't help but gawk. He had begun to think that the baron's children didn't exist.

Suddenly Gavrel angled his shoulder into one of their captors. He managed to knock him down before others restrained him. It was a desperate act, not something Eramus would have expected from an experienced, intelligent fighter like Gavrel. One of the Seehlan punched Gavrel in the face three times until he ceased struggling.

The children stared at the commotion. The girl watched with more interest than her brother until one of the women in the garden gently coaxed her back to work.

Eramus and his companions were led beyond the village to a cave just outside a stand of firs. A pair of refugees hauled Gavrel's limp form to a small entrance barely wider than two men and only a few feet high. Guards sat or leaned on a boulder off to the side. One of them twirled a thick branch in his hand.

Eramus groaned. "Our new home."

Unni barked furiously, the noise echoing in the still air, as he and Rammun appeared atop the cave and looked down on them.

"I don't know why," Eramus said, "but you're holding Baron Kent's children as prisoners. Release them. Release us."

"Shut up," Rammun said. He signaled to the Seehlan, who shoved Hadrius and Gavrel into the mouth of the cave. They left Eramus and Riya alone. Hadrius easily crawled inside on his belly. He dragged Gavrel, groaning with exertion until the barely conscious assassin vanished into the cave after him.

Rammun leaned on his thigh, one knee bent on a rocky ledge. The expensive jewelry he had flaunted years ago had been replaced with a simple emerald bracelet of braided stems, but he still projected the innate confidence Eramus had envied.

Eramus and his companions were in trouble that only seemed to worsen. He glanced at Riya, who appeared lost in thought.

"You'll have a chance to speak," Rammun assured him as he motioned to the men around Eramus. They pulled him and Riya back and worked together, one using his branch as a lever, to roll the boulder forward and seal Gavrel and Hadrius inside.

"There had better be air in there," Eramus warned.

Rammun bounded down from his perch, landing gracefully among the others, Unni at his side, always expectantly looking up at him. "Yah?"

"I'm just here for the children. I don't care about the rest of this."

"Really? That why you travel with an Oshlemin?" Rammun whistled and Unni bolted ahead. With an escort of armed men, Eramus and Riya were taken back to far side of the village. Rammun pointed to a weathered tent. "You can wait there for now," he said to Eramus.

"You said I would have a chance to speak," Eramus argued.

Rammun's mismatched eyes brooked no argument. "Just get in the tent."

"At least let us stay together," Eramus said, nodding at Riya. "She's hurt. Someone needs to look after her."

The Seehlan threw Eramus into the tent and sealed it behind him. Dust motes fluttered in the dim light, the stink of mold heavy. Outside the industry of the village carried on, bits of foreign conversation and clattering tools.

With no better plan, he lay down to rest. Flies buzzed all over him but he couldn't swat at them because his hands were tied. They walked on his face and arms while he tried to assess his predicament.

The tent flap opened. He had fallen asleep again. He was hoisted up and taken outside, where his bonds were cut. He rubbed at his chafed wrists and sore neck.

Cold mountain air encroached as the sun set. Returning hunters carried small game with them, their catches little and less. Most of the villagers had gathered in front of their huts, smoking pipes or drinking tea, watching as Eramus was guided to the village center where a pair of women threw logs onto a growing blaze. Thick wooden benches, hewn logs lashed together with vines, surrounded a great stone fire pit, and seated on them were older, distinguished Seehlan, Rammun among them. The refugees had done well enough up here in the mountains to survive, but winter breathed down their backs. The first snow would change everything.

Eramus was directed to an empty bench. The heat of the fire reached him immediately, a small comfort to combat the frigid wind beginning to howl down the mountains and through the trees.

Once he sat, a boy brought him a bowl of cabbage soup.

"That's all you'll get," Rammun said.

Watery, hot, and with a hint of meat, it was enough. Eramus sucked it down, coughing and choking as he drank too quickly. He dropped the bowl, wiped his mouth with the back of his hand, and cleared his throat. "And my companions? We have some dried goods in our packs."

"That food is now Seehan's property."

"You mean you're stealing it, like you've stolen our weapons and the rest of our supplies. Seehan...what does that mean? I heard it on the way in."

"It means 'New Seehla'," Rammun replied, unfazed by the accusations. "The Ismah forced them off the land they had owned for generations, claimed it for Gelofass and his Forgotten Prophet, and built the Temple of Gefil there. Yah, so this is their new home, and anything on it belongs to them." Unni sat beside his master, paws crossed in front of him, head down, ears flat, eyes up. Rammun scratched his head and pointed to the others sitting around the fire. "Tell them your name and where you're from."

"Is this a trial?"

"Just do it."

Eramus looked at a grim-faced boy with rough hands who couldn't have been older than sixteen, a woman with dark hair tied back tightly, hands clasped in front, who never took her eyes off him, and an elderly man in the sky blue robes of a priest with a milky white eye who peered from a face of etched leather, tilting his head to the side to hear better.

"I am Eramus Pon of Uuslef."

"Friend to Oshlem," the woman with the dark hair said in a heavy accent.

The elderly priest slammed his hand on his bench and shouted. Tears streamed out of his good eye and he pointed to the sky.

"He called you a murderer," Rammun translated, "and said that the Seehli's ashes weep for you."

Eramus looked around at the accusing faces. He wouldn't allow himself to be judged by people bent on revenge. "I'm here on behalf of Baron Kent," he lied. "Do you fail to recognize his authority?"

"Another friend to Oshlem," the woman with dark hair said.

"His personal guest is a knight of the Temple of Gefil." There was no need to elaborate. Eramus knew what they thought of the Ismah and his knights. Did they know he was here because of Sir Jacob? They couldn't know that.

He glanced at Rammun. Why was the mercenary among these people? Were they paying for his protection, his training? How could they afford to hire him? Maybe he led the Missing Brothers he had mentioned.

"Baron Kent's children were kidnapped," Eramus said. "And now they are here." He held up a hand before the woman could protest. "I'm only here to bring them home."

"Guilty again," the woman said. "The Seehlan are guilty again."

"I'm not saying that—"

"Enough!" the boy shouted. "The Missing Brothers should execute the Oshlemin immediately. We'll decide the fate of the others later."

"You can't be serious," Eramus said. He turned to Rammun. "He's not a *duba*. He's not responsible for any of this. You have to stop them. Say something."

"Why should I? What do I care?"

"The baron once offered asylum to Seehlan. Only when the Ismah sent Sir Jacob did they have to leave. Baron Kent didn't have a choice." He sighed. "The man I'm with--the Oshlemin--his name is Gavrel. He came here to find the baron's children," Eramus said as he turned to the men and women around the fire. "To reunite them with their family. He believes in Hamaln. He's from a small village called Kluhm. It's far from Oslah. Things are different there. He didn't come looking for you. He didn't come to hurt anyone." He kicked the bowl in frustration. "This is a mistake. You can't condemn the man because of his birthplace."

"Like us?" the woman asked.

"That's…different," Eramus said unconvincingly. The looks from those around the fire were unforgiving, unsympathetic, the faces of those who had been condemned for that very reason. They had already made their decision. They had listened to him as a courtesy, nothing more.

"His name is Gavrel," Eramus said, swallowing a lump in his throat. He turned to Rammun. "I would expect you to show sympathy at the very least." Men moved in to restrain him but he shoved them away. "I told Sir Jacob that Seehlan wouldn't steal children. At the time, I believed that. All I find before me are child thieves and killers of innocent men. Are these the Missing Brothers? You're no better than the knight."

"No man is innocent," Rammun said, his face darkening. "Especially not one allied with a knight."

The men started to drag Eramus away. "What about me and the others?" Eramus demanded. "Will the Missing Brothers come for us, too? Will our fate be the same?" He glared at Rammun. "You should never have saved my life."

Rammun stared back menacingly as Eramus was hauled away. Instead of being taken back to the tent, he was shoved into the damp, frigid cave with Hadrius and Gavrel. Eramus slumped up against a wall and crossed his arms over his chest. A single shaft of moonlight already illuminated the cave's interior.

Gavrel looked rigid. At first Eramus thought he was dead.

"He said he doesn't like the walls," Hadrius said.

"I could say the same thing," Eramus said.

"I spent one hundred seventy-one days in a labor camp outside Prehm," Gavrel said. "I suppose there's no more reason to keep secrets."

"Prehm. I know that town. Ten leagues south of the Hereton, in Antonay. We delivered a fugitive there once. There were nothing but hopeless eyes and broken bodies trapped between walls."

Gavrel grimaced as he touched the bulging scar on his neck. "Yeah. I was one of them. I got this right before my arrest. I lost myself to madness in there after a while. Being trapped again like this brings it back."

"I don't think the Seehlan intend to release you after one hundred seventy-one days."

Gavrel coughed, his swollen features visible in the silvery-blue moonlight, his teeth chattering from damp and cold. "This isn't my first funeral. The men who gave me this nasty remembrance on my neck were Missing Brothers. Four or five of them went to work on me. The authorities didn't have a problem catching me after that."

"Missing Brothers again. Who are they? I've never heard of them."

Gavrel coughed several times, hawked and spit deeper into the cave. "One more name. One more group. I asked around about them in the labor camp. Seehlan don't approve of violence. Their Seehli or clouds or whatever they are…abhor it. But there are those among them who take a vow to protect their people. They know they won't receive the same treatment after they die. It's worth it to them to help as many of their brothers and sisters as they can. The fellows I ran into were hiding off the road, waiting for me."

"Doesn't seem very honorable."

"No, but who is these days? I thought the attack had been random at first, that I was targeted just for being Oshlemin. Later I found out that it was retaliation. I had been hired to assassinate a miller who had been selling them delivery schedules so they could steal supplies. They found out about it and came after me."

"How did they find out?"

With a groan, Gavrel moved into a more confortable sitting position. "Somebody from the Twice Unlucky told Prince Luc. The miller happened to be part of his network. I had already taken contracts on some of his other lieutenants and he didn't like that."

"So much for the guild's protection," Hadrius remarked.

"Yeah. Well, it's the younger ones, the newer ones. That's how assassins take out competitors. It's not common practice but it happens when there's a weak guild leader."

"No wonder your brother didn't want you to go after the people who betrayed you," Eramus said. "There are too many of them."

"Definitely. The guild leader, if he still is the leader, for letting it happen. Prince Luc for selling me out to the Missing Brothers. The Missing Brothers, if the men who did this are still alive. The rat who sold the information to Prince Luc…"

"Don't forget the extra man with the patrol."

Gavrel tapped his temple with a forced smile. "He's in there."

They all laughed at that, Gavrel wincing from the pain but unable to stop. Eventually he caught his breath. "I heard the Missing Brothers used to be knights a long, long time ago…good knights who stood up for their people. Not like the ragged group hiding out up here with a vendetta against Oshlemin."

"You're not worried what these men will do to you?"

"What will worrying help?" He coughed some more. "People have been trying to kill me for years. I'm used to it. Starving refugees who think the clouds cry don't frighten me."

"They're more organized than you think."

"Are they? Is that why they hide up here?"

"We have to find a way out," Hadrius said, interrupting them, his hands feeling along the cave walls. "Where's Riya?"

"I think she's fine for now," Eramus replied. He considered what Gavrel had said about most of the Seehlan believing in a life of non-violence. Perhaps he had something in common with these people after all. His father had tried to teach him to be a peaceful person. Could it be that his father, who had taught him nothing but Hamaln, had also asked the Seehli for guidance?

The two had untied each other in Eramus's absence. Gavrel sat upright, his left arm cradled close to his stomach, his deformed shoulder bunched up, as he mumbled to himself. Hadrius paced impatiently in the cramped space, his boots splashing in mud Eramus couldn't see. Water dripped from the ceiling and puddled onto the ground. At least they wouldn't die of thirst before the Missing Brothers stretched their necks.

Without thinking about it, Eramus's hand strayed to his necklace. The Seehlan hadn't thought to take it, and it wasn't until this moment that he had even remembered it. If he could somehow get the ring to Riya, she would be able to use the magic left in it to aid their escape. But how could he do that?

And what would be the point? The odds were against him. Riya was hurt. Gavrel was hurt. How could the four of them get the children away from the Seehlan and back to the barony? He didn't have any idea.

The pressure of his burden nearly crushed him. He couldn't rescue Baron Kent's children. He couldn't save Sadir's family. Why was all of this up to him? Why was he the only one who felt guilty for not saving these people? He slumped onto a natural stone seat, full of hopelessness and despair.

Gavrel negotiated into a crouch, panting as he waited in that position to catch his breath. He held out a hand. "Help me up, would you?"

Hadrius took hold of his hand and helped him lean against the wall. Gavrel winced and held his side.

"Are you going to be okay?" Eramus asked, only half-concerned.

"The beating they put on me doesn't come close to the aches of prison labor," Gavrel said. He nodded at the entrance. "Can we push our way out?"

"Doubtful. At least we know the children are here."

"They may be harmed if we try to escape," Hadrius added. "Our first priority should be to get them to safety."

Eramus shook his head. "No, we're better off waiting in here. I don't think they'll hurt the children."

"They kidnapped them, didn't they?" Gavrel asked in disbelief.

Eramus considered the question carefully. "Yes but other than being here they don't appear to be in any immediate danger." He shook his head. "I had an opportunity to talk to the Seehlan. I tried to reason with them but they won't listen."

"They did steal children," Hadrius reminded him.

"I know."

"'*They are borne of stained soil,*'" Gavrel said.

"What is that?" Eramus asked. "What does that mean?"

"It's from the *Otauh*. I learned it in the labor camp."

Eramus shook his head. "I don't read from the *Otauh*."

"But the result is the same, isn't it?"

"Do you truly believe that or do you say it to yourself so you can ignore what's happening around you? Don't tell me that you want all Seehlan dead, too. I argued about how you weren't a part of all of that."

Gavrel stood up to his full height and let his arms hang at his sides, his neck tilting to the left. Even that simple act seemed to sap his energy. He took a moment to compose himself. "You know one of them, right? The mercenary?"

Eramus nodded. "I met him a long time ago. I don't know what he's doing here."

"What's his name?"

"Rammun."

"Rammun," Gavrel repeated. "Have you ever seen him fight?"

Eramus scowled. "You might think you're good with a sword. This man's been carrying one for a lot longer than you have. Besides, I don't think he's anything more than an advisor here."

"He seems like one of the Missing Brothers to me. Doesn't he give them orders?"

"Maybe in battle. They have some kind of council that makes their decisions. I don't think he's anything more than a hired sword."

"It has to make you wonder why anyone would agree to help these people, even if they're paying well, which I doubt," Hadrius said.

Eramus settled back against the wall and closed his eyes. "Try to get some sleep. We can come up with a plan when we're rested."

"You sleep," Gavrel said. "And you wait, if you want to. I'm going to think of a way out of here before they kill me."

Eramus can't stand the heat coming from the structure anymore. He can't tolerate the bird's shrieks. He creeps away, walking over soft beds of fallen pine needles, until he returns to the center of Grihm. The tavern is gone. The well is gone. Refugees pass him on their way into the woods, heading to the burning wooden structure, their faces hidden in the shadows of their lowered hoods.

"Don't go that way," he pleads.

"But we must. We must sacrifice ourselves for redemption."

"No. You have to turn around. You can't go."

An old woman says, "The Ismah will save us and deliver the Prophet."

Eramus tries to stop them, but he can't. He hears Sir Jacob laughing behind him. He feels the intense heat of the fire. Steel hews through bone. The Seehlan keep coming.

Above him, the jagged silhouette of the bastard snowthroat dives and snatches at the majestic, soaring form of a red eagle. When the bird has driven the eagle away, it drifts on unfelt air currents, slowly descending until it is able to settle onto his wrist, its clawed feet tearing into his skin as it struggles for balance. Fear roots him to the earth.

His Uncle Reginald's warm, wet hands hold his head in place. "You're going to watch and see what happens. You're going to watch and see what a big mouth gets you."

The bastard snowthroat stares back at him with its yellow eye. "O shun uven demafen."

Eramus bolted awake, shivering. Damp and mold irritated his nostrils until he sneezed. Details of his dreams or nightmares or whatever they were tended to slip away from him, so he repeated the bird's Medarn words, fairly confident he could translate at least part of the sentence, if not all of it, with a little help. Some of those words had been familiar, even if he couldn't immediately recall them. *O* was the easiest. It was *I*.

Then what? Riya had mentioned the future possible when it came to Medarn. He imagined the bird settling onto his wrist. Could the language and the dreams be connected? Was it possible?

Gohlay-gohlay. Could be happy.

The dream had reminded him of the day Loghemit Pon had been executed. For the most part, Eramus had grown up without his parents. His uncle had taught him the value of discipline, but hadn't given him any love along with it. Instead, loneliness, emptiness, and doubt defined Eramus. He clutched the ring around his neck, and thought again about how he might be able to get it to Riya. Hope surged through him. Maybe there was a way out of this dilemma.

He heard distant singing.

"The hymns," Gavrel explained. "Must be sunrise. They take off their damn boots and sing at sunrise." Eramus remembered the hymns from his time in the IR, when he had traveled alongside the Seehlan on occasion.

After a while the singing stopped, and a short time later the boulder barricade shifted with the grunting of men. Gavrel and Hadrius cautiously stepped back as if they expected an arrow barrage.

"I'll go," Eramus said as he dropped to his belly and wiggled his way out. He needed to find an opportunity to locate Riya, to get the ring to her, to attempt their best chance to escape. Strong hands yanked him upright. The boulder was already moving back into place. A trio of Missing Brothers motioned him toward the village. He recalled the phrase from his dream. Sylvia had spoken the words of a prayer to him on their first trip up the mountain. *Kreest demafen.* The stars above you. *Demafen.* Above you. He now understood what more of the phrase meant, even if it had only been a meaningless part of a meaningless dream. "I *shun uven* above you."

As the men led Eramus into the village, he furtively searched for any signs of where Riya was being held, but instead noticed the old priest crouched down next to a skinny boy with a focused expression on his face, the same boy who had brought soup to Eramus at the council proceedings. As the priest pointed to thin clouds strips, the boy recited something in turn. Then the old man raised both hands to the sky and tendrils of silvery air dashed up and penetrated the clouds. They darkened, swelled, and sprinkled raindrops and a light scattering of snow. With a single gesture from the boy, the rain stopped. Now Eramus knew where the village got its water. He also realized that this could have been the priest who left the fog further down the mountain. It made sense.

The old man had begun to pass his wisdom on to the boy, and it reminded Eramus of the time his father had spoken to him at the edge of the rain, in sight of the rainbow. *"I'm sure life has been difficult without your mother, Eramus. You'll see her soon."* Eramus could still feel the elation of relief at his father's reassurance, quickly followed by the sting of the lie. The boy glanced back, acceptance in his eyes, and that was when Eramus knew that this entire mission was never about him, or even Sadir. It was about the children. About Raisa. About Baron Kent's son and daughter. About this boy who had begun to embrace his tradition, to see the old world through new eyes, to interpret the wisdom of those who had come before him.

Rammun sat alone by the ashes of the fire pit, his forearms resting on his thighs as he tightened strings on a lute. It seemed such an odd thing for him to be doing.

"I've gotten better," Rammun said, setting the instrument aside at Eramus's approach. It wasn't the same lute Eramus remembered from the tavern long ago. "One of the villagers made it for me. He used to make these in a little shop before the Ismah burned it down and replaced it with a rose garden." He motioned for Eramus to sit and the guards left them. "I wanted a chance to talk to you. To find out when you started carrying a sword and traveling with dangerous people."

Eramus shrugged, knowing that Rammun had been playing the lute because he missed his mother. "I have questions of my own, too. You were headed off to some campaign or other the last time I saw you."

"Yah. Two long years for Suraam. That's how I used to make my fortune. That's also when I used to think about who I was."

"And now?"

"Fine things and a reputation aren't as important to me anymore."

"Why?" Eramus asked. "Are you one of the Missing Brothers?"

Rammun glared at him. "I would expect a better question than that from you."

"This isn't fair, and you know it."

Rammun scratched at the back of his head. "Why? Because you don't agree with it? Because you don't understand it? You called them child thieves."

"Isn't that what they are?"

"The Ismah calls these people heretics. He stole their land. They've been hunted down and murdered, treated as less than animals, because the Ismah believes their genocide will incarnate his prophet. I sculpted the Seehlan into fighters when they didn't want to be. The Seehli doesn't condone violence but these people are learning what the alternative is."

Rammun's passion for the Seehlan cause defied reason. Mercenaries worked for money. They typically didn't care about morality. Why was Rammun so different? Why did he care? Were the villagers really paying him that much?

"You have to let the children go," Eramus insisted. "Please help me. I spent most of my life without my mother and father. Every day I feel like there's something wrong with me, like I'm missing a valuable piece of myself and I don't know exactly what." Eramus thought about Kathryn, about the look on her face when Sir Jacob had been suffocating her daughter, about how she had begged Eramus to help her. "Children need their mother and father."

Love yourself.

Rammun lowered his chin onto his fist. "It's not that simple. You *know* that."

Know.

What had the man with the crossbow said to Gavrel on the road? *"O shun fen."* Sylvia had told him the man recognized Gavrel. *I shun fen.* I know you. I know *uven* above you. So Eramus could learn Medarn after all. Why did his mind so eagerly attack this little mystery when there was so much else going on?

"It is. Let them go. They're children."

Rammun refused to look at him. The mercenary held his head in his hands. He sniffed once, exhaled, and raised a blank, emotionless face. The man was hiding something.

"They're children," Eramus repeated.

"No," Rammun said, shaking his head. "They're much more than that. Life in the mountains is different. The mountains demand survival. We don't sign treaties here. We give our word." He wiped his mouth with the palm of his hand and sniffed again. "I gave mine to a sorcerer."

We? Rammun had included himself with the Seehlan. Was that intentional?

Uven. What did *uven* mean? Eramus couldn't recall ever hearing that word. Was it another compound? Pieces of something else? Why did his mind relentlessly insist on translating the phrase?

The sorcerer. Rammun mentioned the sorcerer.

"He's dead," Eramus blurted.

"Shame that. Whatever else he was, Gourak was fair. He saved those children. You should know that."

Gourak the Mad. Riya had said his name right before she murdered him. "What?"

Rammun nodded. "Yah. Filthies dragged the children into the woods to bleed them out and leave their little bodies to the buzzards."

Puzzle pieces interlocked, established more connections. The knight would have access to the children, and the Filthies at his disposal. The soldiers had attempted to murder the children. Why?

It stood to reason that only Sir Jacob would be bold enough to order the execution. When Gourak had rescued the children, the Filthies would have reported their failure to Sir Jacob, who could have easily claimed that refugees had been responsible. So the sorcerer had protected the children until he could hand them over to the only person he knew could keep them safe: Rammun. Then the sorcerer had returned to the bridge and cast his spell, most likely with the help of the Seehlan priest, knowing that someone would come after him, after the children.

And Riya had opened Gourak's throat for no better reason than to get her hands on his spellbook. He had been barefoot when he died. Some of the tracks Hadrius had pointed out were from bare feet. Who else would be barefoot in the mountains but the sorcerer and the Morgta?

Eramus thought back to the other tracks, and he remembered the Missing Brother with the limp who had brought him into the village. He would have been the one with the modified boot.

Eramus heard his heartbeat, felt it pumping inside his chest. No wonder the Seehlan wanted them all dead. Eramus and the others were nothing more than Sir Jacob's pawns. Even Riya, who tried so hard to isolate herself from others and their manipulations, had unwittingly eliminated a powerful Seehlan ally. No matter how Eramus looked at the circumstances before him, the Seehlan guilty label still applied to him. He might as well have been one of the Ismah's knights.

Rammun pointed at Eramus's head. "I can see things moving in there. You think you know something, yah?"

I know uven *above you.*

Eramus's head hurt. The clues had all been there. "You didn't steal the children. You saved them."

"Yah. Gourak brought them to the village. He didn't know what else to do with them."

The children. Could all of this really be about the children? Something else nagged at Eramus, something beyond his mission to rescue the children. Riya had told him that the knight would do whatever it took to rid the world of Seehlan. So he had ordered his soldiers to murder the baron's children.

But to what end? To eliminate his heirs? To blame refugees? It seemed like an elaborately unnecessary step, and one that didn't concern Eramus. He had a job to do.

"Let me take them home," he said. He would have to figure things out later, when his head cleared, when he wasn't so tired, when his nightmares didn't control him, when he had determined what the *cseript* on his arm meant. "I can explain what I know to Baron Kent. I won't mention the Missing Brothers. You know you can trust me. There are other lives tied into this as well. My friend and his family…"

Rammun shook his head. "These people here have nowhere else to go. I'd like to think I can trust you, but it's not my decision to make."

Eramus looked around at fathers, mothers, sons, and daughters, at the boy learning to interpret and to speak to the clouds. "You have to do what's right," he said weakly. The Seehlan wouldn't allow them to leave. Eramus couldn't blame them. If their situations were reversed, he would make the same decision. He still had to think about Sadir and his family, though. That was his burden, his responsibility.

"I am doing what's right," Rammun said. "Just like I did five years ago."

Silence followed as Eramus remembered that awful night. He owed this man his life. Rammun had saved him, even though he hardly knew him.

Rammun stood up and hitched his thumbs in his belt. "I have something else to tell you now, but I promise you won't like it."

So Rammun told him and his stomach shrank with shame and guilt.

"This can't be possible. It has to be a coincidence."

"There's no coincidence, just as there's no denial. It is what it is. There's nothing to be done for it now. There's no way we could have known."

Dejected, full of despair, Eramus stared at the ashes in the fire pit, wondering if the world would be better off without him. How many lives had been lost because of him? His eyes glazed out of focus as he wondered what others would think of him if they knew. What would Sadir say? How would Hadrius and Riya react?

Rammun's comforting hand rested on his shoulder. "It's not as if we were the cause, my friend. We were merely the excuse. I didn't think before. I am thinking now. I want to help these people."

"We should...we should..." Eramus said, unable to even form a simple sentence. He couldn't face these people. He couldn't reveal that his cowardice, his weakness, had brought Sir Jacob to the Barony of Medar. If the rumors were true, the knight had been responsible for the deaths of over three hundred men, women, and children since his unofficial occupation.

How could Eramus live with the guilt? "What do I do? What...can I do?"

"You move on. You learn from your mistakes and you move on. There's no way to take it back."

Seehlan eyes were riveted to Eramus. The pressure squeezed him. He lurched forward and vomited the paltry contents of his stomach. A cold sweat broke over him. He fell to his knees, wanting to beg forgiveness.

"Get up. You're frightening them."

Eramus wiped his mouth with the back of his hand and sat in the dirt. "They should fear me. How many brothers and sisters, sons and daughters, fathers and mothers have I cost them?" He kicked at the dirt in frustration. "How many?" he shouted.

Rammun stood over him, glowering. "Enough. The Ismah's dog did this, not us. Not intentionally." He held out his hand.

"That doesn't make a difference."

"It does to me. How many people have you helped since that night?"

Eramus looked up at a capable, honorable man who tried his best to make amends to these people.

Rammun pulled him to his feet. "You'll be taken back to your friends now."

"Thank you, Rammun. Thank you for telling me the truth."

Rammun stood there while Eramus's escort led him away. Eramus tried to memorize every face he passed. He would remember them.

As the cave loomed ever closer, a familiar face peeked out from behind a tree and vanished as quickly as it had appeared. Had he imagined it? He had almost completely forgotten about Alina with everything else that had transpired. He decided to trust that her appearance had not been a trick of his mind. Just as in combat, he had to sieze an opportunity when he found it. He might not have another one. He deliberately yanked off his necklace and flung it to the ground, out of sight of the guards but clearly enough so that Alina would be able to see what he had done. If she was even real.

He snaked his way into the cave as the boulder ground back into place, reminding him that he was a prisoner. From this day forward, he would always be a prisoner. His conscience would see to that. He didn't need a boulder to remind him of the future possible, of the branch from which the rest of his decisions would spread, just like the expectations of words in Medarn. It struck him as odd that he had only now begun to understand what had eluded him for many years.

But it wouldn't be as simple as him surrendering to pity, would it? Sadir and his family still needed his help. Nothing had changed. He couldn't do anything for these people here, but his friend's life depended on him.

"What happened?" Hadrius asked.

"I…I don't know," Eramus said. "I honestly don't. I'm trying to talk sense into Rammun. I think he's listening." He didn't want to tell them about what he had learned. He didn't want to tell them about his hopelessness.

"We're going to need a better plan than that," Gavrel said.

"I saw Alina hiding in the trees. I dropped my ring for her. There's magic in it. Maybe she can get it to Riya."

"Are you sure it wasn't your imagination? She would have to be pretty stupid to come here."

"I doubt I imagined her," he lied.

"She's not in here," Hadrius said. "I'd say that's our best plan yet."

Gavrel's stomach growled. "Do either of you have any food? It's not the hunger that gets me." He rubbed his throat. "It's the burn in there when you don't eat, you know?"

Hadrius waved his hand around the cave. "Plenty of mud." It was hard to tell if he was joking. It didn't matter. Gavrel lost his stoic cool and laughed. He had to calm himself quickly, though, because of his injuries. He let out half chuckles along with winces.

Eramus closed his eyes, drowned out their voices while he slipped in and out of wakefulness, feeling sorry for himself. Twisted, incomplete images from that night in Grihm flashed through his mind: the Filthy, his eyes wide open, white light on his dead face; Rammun's silhouette looming over him like a demon.

He snapped awake. His memories had attempted to deceive him. That was not how it had happened. It didn't matter. Eventually Eramus would have to make amends for what his weakness had caused. He would have to make himself stronger, in both flesh and thought. He would have to labor for forgiveness, strive for redemption from a people to whom he had barely given much consideration beyond general disdain.

He would have to stop being weak.

He would have to stop being such a coward.

And how could he do that? He had to figure out how such a thing would be possible.

His eyelids sunk, and this time he succumbed to his body's need for sleep. He begged his thoughts to rest with it.

A profile hidden in shadow. A bastard snowthroat perches on his arm and someone whispers to the impatient indigo and white bird. The bird glares at Eramus with its glowing yellow eye and says, "O shun uven demafen." Eramus pulls his hand away. The bird disappears. Déjà vu clouds his free thinking. He has experienced this moment before, though he is unsure if he was present at the time.

Eramus woke so violently that he slammed into Hadrius's shoulder.

"Eramus!" Hadrius whispered, holding him steady. "What was that all about?"

"What do you mean?" Eramus asked as he fought for breath, panicking. *Future possible.*

"You kept saying something about a sound," Gavrel said with a concerned look.

"What do you mean?"

"*Uven* is Medarn for sound. It's not a common word but I've heard it before. It refers to the origin of a voice, its source."

"Sound," Eramus whispered to himself. "Voice. *O shun uven demafen.* I know the voice above you." It didn't entirely make sense but at least he had some kind of translation for the phrase. Could it be wisdom from the Hamal? A reference to the origin of a voice, of words? But why would they communicate in Medarn, of all languages?

"Pull yourself together," Gavrel said. "There's something going on outside."

Eramus noticed a distorted moonbeam spearing the cave's interior. He followed it to Riya's face peering down through the hole in the ceiling. He couldn't reconcile his emotions at the sight of her. Happiness? Relief? Sadness? Now he would be forced to act. Now he would have to conceal his cowardice.

"What?" Gavrel asked, clearly surprised at the sight of her.

She disappeared and moonlight poured back inside. Seconds later a yelp of surprise preceded a heavy weight crashing into the earth with a wet thud. An indigo glow washed into the cave, fading as quickly as it had appeared, the boulder gone.

Alina's face appeared at the mouth of the cave. "Come on."

The image of a bastard snowthroat flashed in his mind. He couldn't escape it. *I know the sound above you.* What was this sound? What did it mean? Why did the bird even talk to him?

He considered the bird he had seen in his waking moments and in his dreams. Supposedly the Blood Eagle had told the Forgotten Prophet a great many things after the man had lost his memory.

Suddenly everything made sense to Eramus. The bastard snowthroat was trying to tell him something. Did he lack the faith necessary to interpret the signs and the words? His head hurt at the possibilities.

They quickly crawled outside, shaking away the cold and stiffness of the cave until they were alert and on their feet. Alina couldn't help but stare at Gavrel's battered face. A trio of unconscious Seehlan lay just off to the side, the boulder several feet away.

"Time to go," Riya said. She appeared close to exhaustion, her shoulders slumped, her breathing clipped, her face pale even in the moonlight.

I know the sound above you.

Eramus looked at the fallen men. He would be blamed for this. They could only run now. They could get the children, get a good head start, and then maybe he could rest and think of a better plan. He didn't know if the Seehlan would follow them once they found out. They might not think it worth the risk. Rammun would probably have them pack what they could carry and leave Seehan, their home.

Moonlight vanished in a heavy bank of ominous storm clouds that boomed with thunder. The dark sky roiled above him, possibly the work of the priest.

"Do you have anything that can help us?" he asked Riya. He glanced down to check her leg but it was covered. It was clear from her limp that she hadn't recovered, and possibly never would because of where the arrow had hit her.

"My potions and sleepstones are being guarded along with your weapons. The only magic at my disposal will have to come from the ring, and I've already drained what I could."

"What about Gourak's spellbook? Wasn't there anything that can help us escape this place without costing more lives? What was the point of killing him if you didn't learn anything?"

Riya didn't respond.

"I know where they're keeping the children," Alina interrupted.

"What about the mercenary?" Gavrel asked. "Where is he?"

Alina didn't seem to know to whom he referred.

"Don't try anything," Eramus warned. "There's no point to it. You're good with a blade, Gavrel, but he's better, and he's my friend. You'll lose. We can't afford that. We need your help. You made a promise to your brother, remember?"

Gavrel glared back at him. "Of course I remember."

Hadrius stripped swords from the unconscious sentries and handed them to Gavrel and Eramus, keeping one for himself.

"We'll have to fight our way through in some spots, but no killing," Eramus warned them. He wouldn't have any more deaths on his conscience.

I know the sound above you. The phrase wouldn't leave his head.

Gavrel stole the worn boots off of one of the unconscious men.

"Wait," Riya said as she shifted her weight. "You're right, Eramus. There was something I learned. Perhaps I can rebuild the effects of one of my potions, something familiar we've been using like obscurity. It could be unfiltered, stronger. You could be very sick when it wears off. Normally I would test the magic, take samples in my laboratory…"

"We don't have much of a choice," Eramus said. "If you think you can do it, then do it."

"I tried it before, with my own fire, but that was different. This time I'll have to pull from the traces in your blood."

"Riya…"

"This is what I do, and you said so yourself that our options are limited."

His eyes drawn to Riya's ring, Gavrel asked, "How will you make the magic work?"

She eyed Hadrius' sword. "Small cuts. I'll have to draw it out first, and in order for that to happen more magic will need to reach your blood."

Nobody appeared overjoyed at the idea. Gavrel eventually raised his arm, already scabbed over and bruised, and flicked his blade over the top of his forearm to create a small red line. "A little blood or a noose? I'll take blood anytime." Hadrius followed suit.

"The magic will be unpredictable," Riya added. "Without the proper components to create the obscurity, I will have to pinpoint the vestiges of the potions you consumed, and attempt to reconstruct them. This will put incredible strain on my own body."

Eramus held his blade just over his right forearm, conscious that he needed to keep his left concealed from the others in case the *cseript* flared to life. "And what of Alina? She hasn't touched one of your potions."

With suppressed excitement, Riya regarded the other woman. "We will be sharing blood, Eramus. What's yours will be hers, and I've already told you her blood contains special qualities. Now we must hurry."

"She's right," Eramus said to Alina. "This might be our only chance to escape." He nicked his own arm, and hers next. She appeared overly frightened but didn't resist.

"Your arm," Riya demanded. He thrust his arm out and Riya pressed her palm onto it. She closed her eyes, focused. Nothing happened for over a minute, and then he felt warmth seeping out of him. Her hand glowed with indigo light even as her breathing grew more and more ragged. She removed her hand, nurtured the light in her right palm before placing her left palm over his cut. Warmth leaked back into him and he knew her spell had worked.

"Are you okay?" he asked as her body sagged. Even if she could use this spell on the others, he wondered how much her injury and her fatigue would slow her down.

"No." He started to say something else but she silenced him with a look. She seized Alina's arm next, taking twice as long to execute the process, and when she finished, Riya's posture had straightened and her breathing had returned to normal. She emptied the magic into the others and ordered everyone to join hands.

Eramus took Gavrel's sweaty hand in his own, surprised because of the man's usually calm composure.

They linked hands, disappearing one by one. Eramus felt alone, even though he could feel the others. "Alina, take us to the children."

"I'm going to get my things," Riya said in a firm voice.

"Riya...we can't split up," Eramus cautioned, but she broke away. She valued her possessions more than her life, more than the lives of her companions. She was on her own now, the way she always wanted it. He couldn't count on her. She had probably freed them just so she could use the distraction to her advantage.

They shuffled and switched hands until Alina reached the front of the line. The only sounds they made were the occasional scuff or grunt as someone stepped wrong.

Most of the villagers slept, but Rammun sat awake by the fire with Unni.

While Eramus and the others passed, Unni's ears perked up and he stared right at them. So did Rammun when he noticed his dog's reaction.

Alina froze, and Eramus bumped right into her. He forced down the curse that sprang to his lips, instead whispering in her general direction. "What are you doing? We have to keep moving."

"The man," she whispered back.

"What man?"

"The man I told you about," she hissed more insistently. "That man I sought. That's him!"

Eramus thought back to her story, about the music and where she had met him and it all made sense. "We have to keep going," he reminded her.

For a handful of heartbeats he expected her to pull away like Riya had, but she reluctantly tugged them forward once again. He looked around him to see if Riya's spell had worn off, but he couldn't see anyone. Rammun couldn't have known they were there but he trusted Unni's instincts.

Finally Eramus relented and they shifted ahead cautiously, their steps blending into the crackling of the fire. Unni let out a half bark.

Suddenly Gavrel slipped his hand free of Eramus's grasp. Unni bolted upright, his ears flat, his teeth bared as he growled. Rammun, still unsure of anything but Unni's concern, reached over his shoulder and drew his sword from the scabbard on his back in one easy movement. At least Eramus finally understood why Gavrel had asked questions about Rammun, and why he was so nervous. Gavrel had never intended to recover the children. He had come to assassinate Rammun, and Eramus had led him right to him.

Eramus owed Rammun his life. He wanted to stay and help him, but he couldn't. Rammun could take care of himself. Eramus had to think about everyone else involved. This could be his only chance for escape, his only chance to help them. He grabbed Alina when he felt her try to do what he had been considering.

"We can't stop him," Eramus whispered to her. "It's too

dangerous."

A commotion erupted behind them, but Eramus wouldn't look back. Gavrel had made his choice and would have to deal with the consequences. Was this what his brother had wanted him to do all along? Was this why the knight had selected him? Of course. Sending an assassin made sense. The knight must have known the Seehlan had a leader. The very thought of being manipulated by Gavrel angered Eramus to no end, but he had to focus on rescuing the children now. Everything else was only a distraction.

Unni barked repeatedly. Someone shouted.

There was no point being quiet anymore. Villagers rushed outside their huts. Unni kept barking.

"The children are just up here," Alina said from the front of the line.

"*Keep your sword ready,*" Eramus said to Hadrius in Uuslefin. "*Remember...nobody dies.*"

Half dressed men hustled past them, running to the fire to help Rammun, who ordered them to check on the children. He still lived. Gavrel had failed. Eramus found a hint of solace in that, even though he had also begun to like Gavrel in some ways.

Alina took them right where they needed to go. She ripped a tent flap open to reveal the baron's children huddled among others. Eramus grabbed them both and dragged them outside while they screamed.

"Give me the girl," Hadrius said. Eramus shoved the girl out until Hadrius seized her and clamped his hand over her mouth. His friend flashed into existence before vanishing again. The same thing must have happened to Gavrel before he could kill Rammun.

"The magic's wearing off," Eramus said. "We need to hurry!"

The rest of the children poured out of the tent, running to the village center as they yelled for help.

Eramus shook the boy, who kicked like a rabbit in his grip. "Keep still and quiet, boy!" He hoped the child spoke Oshlema. He was too excited to remember much Medarn.

"Come this way," Alina said from off to the left. They stumbled along with the children in tow until Alina took Eramus's hand. It was visible for a second and then it was gone. Riya's magic hadn't lasted long, but they had to try to coax its remaining value anyway. Eramus hoped Riya had escaped, even if she had abandoned them just as quickly as she had helped to free them.

They left the village, jogging along a wide path for the next twenty minutes, using a fixed blood star to navigate in a southwest direction. They sporadically appeared and disappeared. Eramus kept looking back over his shoulder to see if Riya followed them, or if any of the villagers had discovered their trail, but they were alone. Alina steered them onto a game trail littered with undergrowth to conceal them from any pursuit. The sky lightened as dawn forced its way through from the east, hazy sunlight punching through storm clouds.

Heavy footfalls crashed in cadence, but not from the village's direction. They ducked into a depression off the trail and lay on their stomachs, unwilling to further depend on the weakening magic.

Ground birthed the ghastly head of a silver and red eagle, an apparition which coalesced into the familiar shape of a man in decorated armor bearing a sword nearly two thirds the length of his body. A score of Filthies marched behind him. Sir Jacob descended on the village.

"I would not remove a blighted branch to accomplish this, but rather the entire tree, from its roots, and burn the soil upon which it failed."

Eramus forced the others low to the ground, covering the boy's mouth with his hand while they observed the martial procession, his gut frozen when he considered what the knight's appearance meant. Sir Jacob had come to slaughter the unsuspecting villagers, the same as he had their kin. He would stab the hearts of the men, disembowel the women, and smash the children's heads on rocks. He would wipe out their existence, all in the name of his faith.

And when Eramus thought of Sir Jacob, the final clue to the mystery presented itself. Sir Jacob hadn't sent Eramus after the children simply as a pawn. The knight, whose memory was concise enough to remember the specific execution of Loghemit Pon, could surely have read the public records in Drohm and learned of Eramus's involvement with a sorcerer. Sir Jacob had counted on Riya just as much as he had counted on Eramus to seek her help.

And Eramus had cleared the way for the knight.

But Eramus had no means to stop him. Even if he warned the Seehlan, they weren't strong enough to fight that many soldiers and a knight. Not even Rammun. Eramus knew he was good with a sword—the fact that he still lived proved that—but he was only one man.

I know the sound above you.

Nobody could save these people. They had been driven from their land and hunted to the edge of extinction. The Ismah wanted to erase them from history. That was why Rammun was with these people. He had made a mistake and this was his redemption.

Eramus's dream had to have been a sign, an exhortation of sorts. *I know the sound above you.* Could he be speculating too much? Trying to interpret images and impressions that could mean nothing, trying to make sense of his own madness, trying to do anything but face the reality that now lay before him?

The soldiers were barely out of sight when the magic completely wore off. The children appeared relieved to see that people, and not spirits, had abducted them. Eramus was almost complacent in his suffering of the spell's after effects. He pitched forward, his stomach trying over and over to vomit what didn't exist. The world spun around him.

He remembered the smiles of the children in the village. He remembered the boy on the council, forced to become a man out of circumstance. He drew on those thoughts and regained his equilibrium. The Seehlan wanted to live. This was their opportunity to prove it. Their existence was no different than that of any other village or community.

"Impossible," Hadrius said in awe. "They couldn't have found us."

"Yes they could,"Eramus replied as the memory of Gavrel's signal to the man on the Lestwine outside the barony came rushing back into his head. "And they had help." When Hadrius appeared puzzled, Eramus said, "Gavrel."

If his friend's disgusted expression was any indication, they both felt the same sense of betrayal and guilt.

"Let's go," Eramus said, his back to the village as he started up the mountain. He would have plenty of time to think during the long trip.

To think about how much of a coward he was. He had left innocent people to a murderer's mercy, had even brought the murderer to them. They would die without his help.

He reminded himself that they would die anyway. If Sir Jacob didn't kill them, the Ismah would just send another knight. These were not Eramus's people, not his problem.

The little boy started crying. His sister said nothing, simply wiped her own runny nose with the back of her hand, chin held high, more concerned about her own pride than her brother's suffering. Alina stroked the boy's head, soothed him with gentle words.

"Be quiet," Eramus ordered. "There might be a rearguard and we don't want to alert them."

The girl half-inhaled a series of dry sobs, her best attempt at silence given the circumstances. Alina put her arm around the girl to comfort her.

The boy turned back to Eramus, his jaw set firmly in his best stoic expression. "Did my father send you?" When Eramus didn't answer right away, the boy's eyes watered. The two children had been separated from their parents, and aside from each other, their only comforting thought would have been that their mother and father were desperately trying to find them.

"I said be quiet," Eramus snapped. He didn't want to talk to these children. He didn't want to know anything about them. They were a means to an end. Saving them meant saving Sadir and his family. Eramus knew Raisa. He knew Kathryn. He didn't know these children. He didn't know the Seehlan.

He stopped and waited while Hadrius crouched to study the path and Alina helped the children over a series of thick bushes at the base of an incline. His eyes drifted out of focus as he thought about the day his father had died. He had been just a boy, around the same age as the baron's son was now. He had trusted others to care for him.

"You're going to watch and see what happens."

His uncle had made him watch his father's death. Eramus had been helpless then. More than anything, he had needed comfort, the same comfort Alina had shown these children. Instead he had been taught to live with the pain of his father's death, to endure what he had no control over. He had been taught to accept, to carry his despair with him, and to move on. And he had taught himself to give up, to accept certain losses rather than risk even more. He had assumed, until this very moment, that the internal acceptance was a lesson of First Awakening.

He couldn't have been more wrong.

He couldn't leave the Seehlan to die like this. He just couldn't. He hoped Sadir would be able to forgive him. He heard the chaplain's words in his head. *"Your brothers and sisters need your example. They need your courage and your aid. They need to learn from you."*

"I have to warn them," Eramus said to Hadrius before he could stop himself. "Take the children back to the barony."

Hadrius shook his head, clearly struggling with the same internal conflict. "If you go, I go."

"This has nothing to do with you."

"There are children in that village and I know what the knight will do to them. They need warriors."

"You're willing to fight a knight?"

Hadrius's stubborn expression proved he would.

Alina regarded both of them as she pulled the children close to her. "I'll take them as far as I can."

Eramus nodded. He remembered the way the bird had been agitated when he had interfered with the Filthies who had been harassing her, how he had felt inexplicable encouragement in her presence. Riya was wrong about her. She wasn't dangerous at all, just as lost as the rest of them, and she was offering to help others in their time of need.

He crouched in front of the children. "I want you to listen. This woman will take you home. She will take you to your mother and father. It's going to be a long way, but you've already made the trip once. Please go with her. If you don't, you'll die."

The children seemed convinced enough. The boy extended his hand to his sister. The girl took it, visibly relieved, and the two of them followed Alina.

"I will never see you again, Eramus Pon," Alina said matter-of-factly.

Eramus spared her and the children a last glance, wondering about the woman's prediction.

"Let's go," he said to Hadrius. They ran low, through the thicker portions of the surrounding trees to reach the village before Sir Jacob could. Eramus thought about himself, how he had been sent off to risk his life for Uuslef while still a boy. Hadrius had experienced the same thing. And Riya had been sold by her mother when she was still very young. They had been children, and someone should have protected them from those dangers.

"This is the worst idea of all the lost causes you've ever had," Hadrius said as they cut through the brush. "We're going to die with them."

"I'm only going to warn them," Eramus lied. He wasn't ready to die, but he would protect these children who couldn't protect themselves. He would make that sacrifice, the one that nobody had made for him. The Seehlan had seen enough hardship for one lifetime. "But I don't think you would have insisted on coming if you thought you were going to die." He tried to forget about Sadir and his family. He tried to forget about the *cseript* and his strange dreams. He had to stay focused. He had to deal with the present.

When they arrived, Gavrel was on his stomach, trussed hand and foot. Bowmen had Riya surrounded. She looked thoroughly upset. It served her right for what she had done.

"Rammun!" Eramus shouted. He looked everywhere for the mercenary. The villagers were already coming at them, but he didn't care. "Rammun!" he shouted again, shoving some of the Seehlan aside when they tried to grab him. The mercenary emerged from a nearby tent, blood on his left arm from a deep gash.

"Take them," Rammun said, pointing at Eramus and Hadrius.

The villagers charged in at them. Eramus threateningly raised his sword and they stopped. "There isn't much time," he pleaded. "A knight is on the way."

A ripple of fear spread through the villagers. They all knew the reputation of the Ismah's knights, and what the arrival of one would mean.

Rammun's eyebrows shot up as he pointed at Gavrel. "You did this!"

"There's no time for that," Eramus said.

"And you brought him!" Rammun shouted at Eramus, silencing everyone.

"I did bring him. I had no idea this would be happening. You know me. You know me. Blame me if you have to, but we have to work together now." He pointed at the village. "We have to protect these people." The entire village had stopped. Everyone, including

Hadrius and Riya, were staring at Eramus. What was he doing? "In five minutes they will be here. Rammun, if we don't act quickly everyone will die."

"Where are the baron's children?" Rammun asked.

"On their way back to their father. They're safe, with someone I trust."

A woman began to sob. Her daughter consoled her. Many of the Seehlan children were braver than their parents. Maybe they didn't understand the impending doom. Some of the men looked to their families, wanting to protect them. The refugees were strong. They had to be in order to have survived this long. They needed help, though, and Eramus could help them. He could protect them.

Rammun regarded Eramus for a handful of seconds before motioning to the bowmen around Riya. "Lower them." He turned back to Eramus. "Is the knight alone?"

"No. I counted at least twenty soldiers with him."

The priest shoved his way to the front of the group, his young apprentice beside him, the boy brave in the face of danger. "We'll delay them."

Rammun nodded to the old man, who took the boy to the front of the trail with him. Together they dragged clouds out of the sky, forming a fog they could send down the trail. Riya watched in fascination.

"Give them their weapons," Rammun ordered. He whistled sharply at the bowmen and directed them into a crossfire arrangement on opposite sides of the village. He barked orders at the rest of the men and they sprang into action. It wouldn't be enough.

"I can help, too," Riya said, surprising Eramus most of all as she limped over. "But I need my things. Now."

"Good," Rammun said, eyeing her carefully. "Because I won't allow these people to die today." The fighters stepped to the front of the group. "The Missing Brothers will honor their vows. Do you hear me? Do all of you hear me?"

Eramus nodded, agreeing with the mercenary. He didn't intend to let them die, either. He meant to protect them.

CHAPTER 10

Sir Jacob did not arrive in five minutes or even ten. The bowmen fidgeted behind rocky cover, peering into the fog while they waited.

Eramus had recovered his daggers and his own sword. The former he returned to his thigh and boot, while the latter fit comfortably in his hand, a weapon he could trust. He ran his finger over the inscription, wondering how he would fare in battle against veteran soldiers. Would his word hold true? Would he protect these people?

His throat tingled from the potion he had imbibed. His stomach hurt as if a pile of snow rested inside it. Indigo ice in liquid form, Riya had told them, a cold, necessary draught, with only enough for two. Eramus the fool had volunteered to be the first, Rammun the second. The two of them had already made their share of mistakes. What was one more?

The potion clearly disturbed Rammun as well, as was evident by his generally uncomfortable expression, but he didn't complain. Out of the refugees, the younger men seemed to be the most anxious, their bodies glistening with sweat, their pale blue eyes alive with fear. They whispered one name: Sir Jacob, the monster who stole old age and kin, the beast beyond reason, their finality.

But unlike the refugees, Eramus longed to meet the knight in combat. He wanted revenge. Medarn law and authority would fail to support the knight in the mountains. What had Rammun said? *"The mountains demand survival."* Out here Sir Jacob would be just another man. Eramus had no illusions about the knight's abilities. His reputation would be well deserved, but whom had he slaughtered aside from the helpless and the weak? Eramus couldn't recall a tale where the knight had vanquished an equal. Perhaps he hid behind his men, raising his sword only to murder defenseless women and children. After all, he had brought a small army with him.

Eramus lowered his head and closed his eyes, wishing for the wisdom of Second Awakening. He didn't hate the knight. He hated himself. His lack of judgment had been the catalyst for this single moment in time. Neither Sadir nor these people would be in danger if not for him.

It didn't matter. He couldn't change any of that now. He had to steel his resolve and prepare for the inevitable confrontation. The knight had plenty of soldiers and his reputation, but Eramus had his trusted friend, an experienced mercenary, a sorcerer, and superior numbers, the best odds he would most likely ever get.

When half an hour had passed without attack, Eramus wondered if his imagination had conjured the knight and his Filthies. Had they been part of one of his dreams? No, Hadrius had seen them, too.

A scream split the silence. A sentry fell, his hand raised in helpless defense as a Filthy chopped into him with a crunch of bone and splattering blood. Reapers rose from the village perimeter and hacked at the refugees established on the rear defense. The fog slowly melted away as the slaughter began.

"Help them!" Rammun shouted as he vaulted down from his vantage point, sword raised high. He landed on a Filthy's chest with enough force to smash him into the dirt with a screech of metal. He sprang to his feet when the Filthies collapsed on him like scavengers on a carcass, as if they had expected his aggressive assault. His eyes glimmered with the realization that he was the intended target, and he immediately switched to a defensive stance, utilizing wide, overbearing strokes to fend them off while he tactically retreated. Even their number advantage couldn't prevent him from quenching his steel's thirst. In three seconds, he had disabled or killed as many men.

Eramus launched himself into the fray as well, cutting into soldiers who swarmed around Rammun. He had to keep the mercenary alive, and not only because of the debt he owed him. The Missing Brothers looked to Rammun for leadership. If he fell, they would most likely retreat.

Arrows hissed through the air, some sticking into flesh, others glancing off armor. Eramus shielded his face with his arm before he felt the biting sting of an arrow grazing his shoulder.

"To the middle!" he yelled, whipping around his free hand in a rally while he weakly parried a blade on the flat of his sword. His opponent had the look of a wild dog, spittle smeared across his lips, nostrils flaring as he closed in. There were too many of them to fight fairly, so Eramus used the man's momentum to keep him off balance. He punched him in the mouth, hoping to generate distance and more options. The Filthies smothered him, coming at him in waves as they pressed him on his heels, making it difficult for him even to breathe.

Rammun barked at everyone to drive the soldiers into the village center, but there were simply too many of them. There were bearded faces, dented armor, and bloody swords everywhere.

Their plan to funnel the soldiers had turned against them. The Seehlan outnumbered the soldiers almost two to one, but the soldiers fought as a unit. Some of the villagers retained a loose formation, but the younger men broke ranks and fled.

And still there was no sign of Sir Jacob, which worried Eramus more than anything. Why did the knight hold back?

A blade sliced into Eramus's lower back and he screamed in agony. His inattention had cost him. Something else hit him in the side of the leg, just below the knee, and offered a taste of real pain. He tripped and stumbled forward, landing in the dirt with disorienting impact.

He heard a yell and the clashing of blades as Rammun appeared, beating back one soldier with a hammer of bone-crunching elbows, kicking another one in the groin so hard he collapsed. More soldiers closed the hole. The Filthies were smarter than anyone had given them credit for. They feinted on one flank, powered in on another when villagers took the bait. Their target always appeared to be Rammun, but he used his entire body as a weapon when he couldn't bring his sword to bear, and the Filthies didn't have the numbers or skill to disarm or kill him.

"I can stand!" Eramus shouted over the din of battle. He had no intention of being a hindrance to the man who had singlehandedly kept the Filthies from their goal. He shook off his dizziness and planted his good knee into the dirt, bracing his weight on the pommel of his sword as he regained his footing. Rammun had provided him with the valuable seconds he needed to recover his bearings.

He didn't have time to check the seriousness of the damage to his leg. Though it hurt, he could still use it. That would have to be good enough. His back still stung, too, but he hadn't passed out yet.

More soldiers came at them, more familiar faces from the first wave of repelled attackers. The Filthies were conserving their numbers and the effort made them twice as strong. Their tactic had whittled away the Seehlan number advantage. He and Rammun shared a look of understanding. They wouldn't yield, no matter what. Eramus was already exhausted. Despite the spattered blood and filth on his clothes, armor, and exposed flesh, Rammun's breathing came slowly and evenly.

The soldiers attacked again, this group more precise with its blades. Eramus switched to a single-handed grip, relying more on his footwork than his sword, until he found his opening in a man's stomach. He almost felt sorry for him when he yanked the blade out and watched him, eyes watering, drop to the ground. Then he remembered why they were here.

"This will have to do," Eramus said through gritted teeth to Rammun as he accepted another single combat challenge from a soldier who filled the hole left by the man he had just slain. Eramus parried a strike and risked a quick glance toward the trees on the other side of the village. Riya sat cross-legged, her skin shimmering indigo with contained magic, waiting for a signal, Hadrius beside her for protection. The tracker rose to his feet, pointing beyond Eramus.

Gavrel had escaped his bonds. He came in hard and fast with a sword, slashing through anyone in his way to get to Rammun, an unforeseen deviation of their plan.

"Look out!" Eramus screamed.

Rammun spun and caught the first blow, his quick reflexes enabling him to deflect the angry attack. Then the two engaged in full combat, furiously slicing and stabbing at one another. Eramus couldn't get to them because he still had to hold the line. Too many Filthies stood in the way, as if purposely keeping others from this particular fight.

"You have to die!" Gavrel shouted, his face a mess of blood and snot.

Eramus channeled his own anger to beat back as many swords as he could, but his sword arm felt dull, tired, and it seemed impossible to get to Rammun, to help him out of the center of battle. Part of their plan hinged on Sir Jacob being caught in that same spot. Where was the knight? If they sprang the trap now they would never get him.

"Help him! Get him out of there!" Eramus shouted at the few remaining villagers, hoping they could make sense of his words. They tried to cut through the Filthies as well, but they were overmatched. One was decapitated and the other two were stabbed and chopped into the dirt. No matter what Rammun had tried to make them, they had never become fighters.

Rammun fought on valiantly, keeping his cool. "Do it!" he shouted up at Riya. He had Gavrel's wrist in his grip to stop him from using his sword, and he stabbed a Filthy in the ribs with his own sword at the same time, quickly swinging his blade back up in an arc to parry the thrust from Gavrel as he jerked free of the hold. It was some of the most impressive fighting Eramus had ever seen, especially considering Gavrel's skill level, but Rammun wouldn't last forever. One man would eventually tire if the odds against him proved great enough.

Eramus looked up at Riya and nodded assent. They had no choice. The cold in his throat and stomach had spread. Riya raised her hands over the battle. The Filthies surrounding Rammun were so congested that only the flash of his blade proved he still lived.

Eramus blinked and the world turned indigo.

Intense and beautiful, a ripple of fire consumed steel and flesh. Filthies shrieked before their throats scattered into ash. The inexorable, living flame hit with the impact of a falling tree, obliterating everything in its path save Eramus, Rammun, Gavrel and a Filthy. The draught of indigo ice had protected Eramus and Rammun, and the others had been behind Rammun when Riya had unleashed the magic. The concussive force of the spell had thrown everyone to the ground, but Eramus could still see the fire eat itself until the final, indelible spark vanished into the air.

I know the sound above you.

Eramus regained consciousness to the single sound of his own breathing inside his head. His fingers came away from his face sticky and wet with blood. Smoke rose off his forearm where the *cseript* sizzled as it faded. He looked through a swirling ash cloud at a tangle of bodies. Riya had warned him about the aggressive fire, but even that hadn't prepared him for the carnage before him. He inspected his left arm again, where the mark had been. Despite the lies of his eyes, the curse still existed. He struggled to his feet, searching for survivors.

He found Rammun on his back, his wide, mismatched eyes staring up at the sky, his hand pressed against his bloody left side, just below his heart. Eramus felt tears well in his eyes at the loss of such a great man.

He surveyed broken pulps of human flesh, twisted, dismembered, and scorched beyond anything he had ever seen. Slowly his hearing returned. The Filthy who had miraculously survived gasped sobs of grateful relief.

Eramus unsheathed his dagger and cut the man's throat. He could think of no reason for him to live. He looked a few feet away at Gavrel, whose chest still rose and fell with life. Eramus clutched his bloody dagger, wanting nothing more than to take the assassin's life. He had betrayed them. He had tricked them, deceived them so that he could kill for the knight. So why hadn't Eramus killed him yet? Perhaps because he felt Gavrel had been like him, caught up in a current, and wasn't a complete monster.

"Don't..." a voice rasped. At first Eramus thought Gavrel was begging for his life. Then he realized the sound had come from Rammun. A surge of hope coursed through Eramus, and he wiped the grateful tears from his eyes.

"He has to die for what he's done."

Eramus crawled over to Rammun and lifted his fingers to reveal a gaping stab wound oozing with dark blood. Hadrius jogged up, his right arm bloody and dangling uselessly at his side. Riya hobbled behind him, her satchel hanging over her shoulder. She glanced at Rammun's wound and quickly looked away. Eramus, however, with Hadrius's help did what he could to clean and bind it.

"Thank you," Rammun said, the man's impressive strength still evident as he gripped Eramus's hand. Blood had shot through the white of his blue left eye. "My friend." His eyes rolled into the back of his head.

"What…" Eramus began as the mercenary's grip slackened.

"There's still a faint heartbeat," Hadrius responded, his fingers pressed against Rammun's thick neck.

"I'd better at least tie him up," Eramus said to the others as he pointed to Gavrel.

"Why is he still alive?" Riya demanded. She looked more energetic than she should have after exerting herself to this extent. She had told him that Kortheen blood contained magical qualities, and he had no doubt that Riya had somehow manipulated the means of their initial escape to take what she could from Alina.

"Where is Sir Jacob?" Eramus asked, skirting her question as he bound Gavrel's wrists and ankles.

"I never saw him," Hadrius said.

"And the rest of the villagers?" The priest, along with Unni, had led away the older men, the women, and the children. Eramus and the others had stayed behind to give them a chance at escape.

Riya shrugged. "They had a good head start but the knight could have gone after them."

"That's what I'm afraid of," Eramus said. He had been considering the possibility since the fight had started. He looked down at Rammun. The mercenary had sacrificed everything to keep these people safe.

"We'd better get going," Hadrius said. "We gave them a chance. We've done all we can."

"Have we?"

Hadrius gave him a long, hard look. "I've had enough of the killing. You don't have to keep doing this. You can never let anything go." He held up his wounded arm. "I don't know how bad this is. Besides, the baron's children won't be safe until they get home."

"They weren't so safe the last time they were there," Riya snorted. Hadrius silenced her with a glare.

"Let's go, Eramus," he said. "If we hurry, we can catch up to Alina."

Hadrius and Riya started toward the mountains, a pair of

ragged, battered survivors of a brief and brutal battle that would attract any ear over an ale and a fire.

He tried to follow them but they were going the wrong way. "I'm going after Sir Jacob," he whispered to himself. They continued down the path, Hadrius running a blood-stained hand through his mess of hair, Riya muttering curses while she limped along.

He watched them take a few more steps.

"I'm going after Sir Jacob," he repeated, quite clearly this time.

They stopped.

"What?" Riya scoffed as she turned around. "We did what we could for these people. It's time to leave, Eramus. It's not your problem."

"Yes it is. The knight's only here because of me."

She crossed her arms over her chest. "I know that. He's here because you think the rules don't apply to you. You think you can do what you want."

"And what was I supposed to do, Riya? Let the Filthies hurt a helpless woman? Stand there and watch it happen?"

For a moment she said nothing, further frustrating him. Then, "Look at the consequences of your actions. Instead of one person in trouble, you've cost many their lives. The assassin's brother, the woman Sylvia...do I need to keep going?"

"You think I don't know what I've done?" he asked, balling his fists. "You think I haven't thought about that?"

"Have you?" she snapped. "Do you think you're going to make everything better by running yourself through on a knight's sword? Do you think that he'll even listen to you? Do you think there won't be consequen--"

Without thinking about it he closed the distance between them, leaned in and, forgetting his anger and irritation with her, kissed her dusty lips. *Conceal your emotions*. She frustrated him so much but he didn't know if he'd ever see her again, and he didn't care what she thought about him anymore. She didn't resist, which confused him even more. He wiped a smudge of dirt from her cheek.

"Leave. I have to fix what's broken. I have to make things right again."

She limped back a couple of steps, glaring at him. Eramus

hoped the arrow hadn't crippled her. "You'll never learn. Typical Eramus. Leaving one mess to clean up another."

But this was not typical. This was about redemption. He had to prove to himself that he wasn't afraid. He had to separate himself from those he cared about to keep them safe. "Thank you, Riya," he said with the utmost sincerity. He decided to stop being mad at her despite her flaws. He loved her. She had given him that feeling without even knowing it. He had so much more to tell her, to give her. Would she ever give him that chance? Would he live to have it?

She just shot him another angry look. Did he see something else in her eyes? Was she worried about him?

Hadrius tightened his belt, checked his blades.

"She's right, you know," Eramus said. "I'm always dragging you into these things. Sir Jacob's here because of me. You don't want anymore killing. I understand."

Hadrius shrugged. "Maybe, but you need my help. You can't do anything alone, and you know it."

"You're right, but that doesn't mean I can't try." He gripped his friend's good shoulder firmly. Eramus didn't want to face Sir Jacob alone but he couldn't stand the thought of Hadrius risking his life even one more time for him, and his friend's injury would be a liability in combat. "Please help Riya get home safely."

Hadrius wouldn't look back at him.

"There is no Second Awakening," Riya said. "There will be no light to guide you, Eramus, no holy warmth to protect you from harm. You will die up here the same way you came into this world: confused and helpless, even more so now that you've breathed and felt your heartbeat. Trust yourself, Eramus. You've been smart enough to survive this long. You have to know this is a mistake."

She was afraid for him even if she wouldn't come right out and admit it. Though Eramus understood why she had said what she had said, her words still cut to his core and left him with doubt. "You ask me what I stand to gain from all of this? I don't have the answer to that question." He pointed in the direction the Seehlan had gone. "I think the answer is that way."

"You're a fool."

"Please go with her," he told Hadrius, "even if she's miserable and rotten to you the whole way, even if she slows you down and it would suit you better to leave her behind." At this he earned a grumble from Riya. "Catch up to Alina if you can and get the children home to their father. I need you to help Sadir. I can count on you, can't I?"

Hadrius relented with a shake of his head. "If this is what you want, then I'll see you some other time, *prophuug*," he said, grasping Eramus's forearm in his own.

A cold knot tightened in Eramus's stomach. A part of him had hoped that Hadrius would insist on going with him, no matter what he asked.

Eramus was afraid of being afraid again. His decision to pursue the knight had most likely condemned him to the same finality as his father. There would be nobody to recite his Passage of Awakening, nobody to stand guard over his spirit until the ebb stars arrived. This would be it for him. His final moments. He squeezed the dagger in his hand for reassurance. Maybe he was ready.

"I'll see you soon," Hadrius said.

Riya slipped her arm over Hadrius's shoulders for support. "You won't feel so noble when you die alone up here, Eramus."

Soon they were gone from sight, but Riya's words still echoed in his head. He was resigned to go after Sir Jacob, but that didn't mean he hadn't considered the consequences of his actions. He wiped his dagger on his pants and slipped it back into its sheath. He didn't want to die. He surely didn't want to die alone. Part of him wanted to race after them, to leave Sir Jacob behind. The old part. The coward part. The part he had lived with for years.

He hadn't told Riya about how he had been in the cold and dark for a long time. He would always be alone. Every day brought a new acceptance of this for him.

"Heh," came a wet chuckle. Eramus looked down to see Rammun looking back up at him. "You look sad, Eramus." Damn but this man was hard to kill!

He knelt down and made sure the mercenary's bandages were secure. "What's funny?"

"It's the guilt, yah?"

Eramus nodded. "Sure."

"It got to me, too." He coughed a bit then licked flecks of glistening blood off his lips.

"I'm going after the knight."

Rammun wouldn't last much longer. He needed care and Eramus couldn't leave him in the dirt, alone.

"I'll get my friends."

"Forget it," Rammun said, gripping his fingers tightly. He still had plenty of strength. "I would have ended the knight, if I could have."

"What do you—"

"Listen…I'm running out of words and I still have one more thing to tell you before you go, but this is only for you." Rammun was closer and closer to leaving his mortality behind, to discovering the secrets that escaped the living.

Eramus nodded. "I understand." He tried to be patient for Rammun's sake, but he wanted to go after Sir Jacob. Was he in that much of a hurry to die? He glanced over at Gavrel, still bound and unconscious.

"My mother," Rammun said. "She was Seehlan, one of the first pilgrims." Eramus just stared back at him. No wonder he had come back to help these people. No wonder he wanted to protect them. He was one of them. Rammun didn't look like a Seehlan at all. Did the villagers know? Did anyone else know?

"I would never have guessed."

"That's how we were able to find this place. I kneel before dawn and sing hymns to the Seehli, too. That's how we touch the True Mother's tears. How do you see me now?"

"I see the same man I have always seen. I see Rammun who treads in the strongest light. Nothing changes that."

"You don't think me wrong for postponing the return of the Forgotten Prophet?"

Eramus shook his head. Perhaps he was learning lessons in First Awakening after all. "It's not my faith."

"Then there's something else I must confess. My mother told me that my father is Baron Kent." He said it so fast that it almost didn't register.

"Then the children…"

"Would be my half brother and half sister, yah, but they don't know. Nobody knows. I have only my mother's word. She left the barony when she found out she carried me. She didn't want to ruin my father's reputation."

Eramus squeezed the man's hand. "Your brother and sister are safe. They're with someone I trust, on their way back to their father."

"My father."

"Yes."

"Thank you. Thanks for helping a bastard. Sorry to confess all of this to you, Eramus Pon, but there is no Seehlan priest in sight and I'm not much longer here. I know your feeling. The emptiness. The loneliness. Never belonging. I have it, too. You have to move on. You have to take what little pleasures you can out of living."

Eramus scooped up a nearby water skin, dipped his head in a small bow and raised it above the other man. "*Gohlay-gohlay.* Could be happy." He dribbled some of the water onto Rammun's lips.

"Yah. *Gohlay-gohlay.*"

Eramus released Rammun's hand, tried not to think about his dying friend, about the time they could have talked to each other, shared stories. "I have to go."

"Yes," Rammun sighed, worry in his mismatched green and blue eyes. "You should have come with me, Eramus." He spoke of that night in Grihm, when they had split up. What would Eramus's life be like now if he had followed Rammun?

"I really have to go." What happened to a man who believed in the Seehli after he died?

"After the knight."

"Yes."

"Remember that he's only a man."

Rammun drifted back into unconsciousness, possibly forever, but he seemed content, ready for death, with whatever he faced after, and resolved to rely on Eramus.

Eramus wished he had the same courage. He stood up, his muscles protesting the effort. He pushed the pain away and jogged after the villagers, his injured knee slamming agony up his leg with every impact, as he remembered what Rammun had said about Sir Jacob being just a man.

Exhausted, Eramus cut through the forest, sword raised, feeling more alone and frightened than he ever had in his life. His adrenaline had worn off to the point where his sword arm was so heavy that he had to jam the blade in his belt. His acute awareness of his body extended to every fresh wound, blood pumping furiously into injuries to tell him of their exact locations and thresholds. But he didn't have time for pain. Dark clouds swelled overhead, threatening rain. The Seehli would weep.

Unsure of the villagers's route, he followed a narrow path, scouring the tall grass for signs of passing. Grass had been pressed down and there were footprints in the earth. The signs were there, but he couldn't be sure how old they were. He always relied on Hadrius to do that sort of thing but his friend wasn't with him. He was alone now, just as he had always been. He had been foolish to ever think otherwise. He kept going.

When he couldn't jog anymore, he walked for over an hour, too stubborn to surrender to his physical limitations. He had to stop a few times to lean against trees and catch his breath, even once to rip the pants away from his bulging knee. He wished the sun would break through the clouds and show him the way. He wished he didn't have to rely on himself. He wished he wasn't so weak. He wished he wasn't so afraid. His eyes brimmed with tears when he thought about Rammun dead back in the village. Eramus sobbed for a bit, his body shuddering as he stood helpless and alone, wishing he had begged Hadrius to come with him.

Suddenly he woke up. He had fallen asleep on his feet, pressed against a tree. He rubbed dry, red flakes from his face and hands, wondering if it was his blood. A light snow began to fall, evaporating on contact, stinging open wounds he had tried to ignore. The Seehli had begun to weep, but at this altitude the rain froze. He wasn't sure he was going the right way. Frustrated, he drew his sword and hacked at a nearby bush. It didn't help. He had to stay composed. He had to stay focused. He had to fight against the blackout spells, against the exhaustion, against the fear that he might actually find the knight. He looked at the engraving on his sword, the flowing script which reminded him of who he was. Now he had no excuse. Now he wouldn't forget.

He prayed to the Hamal for the wisdom of Second Awakening, for the caretakers of the Eternal Fires to send him a sign, something to aid him, something to instill him with confidence. Nothing came. Nothing ever came. Riya had been right about one thing. Faith was largely about belief and interpretation, about what one chose to see and what one chose to make of what one saw. But just because Eramus didn't interpret the signs correctly did not mean they weren't there.

He recalled the words of the chaplain in the barony. *"Though the path through First Awakening may not always be clear, it does not mean you are left alone without faith. Believe in yourself and wisdom will reveal the way."*

He prayed harder, begging this time. He asked for anything, anything at all.

But nothing came, and he found it hard to believe in himself.

Love yourself.

Eramus Pon decided to pray to what had illuminated his perception, what had aided him in the strangest of ways. He prayed to *Uven Dema*, though at what cost he did not know. He closed his eyes and reached out to the bird haunting his sleeping and waking moments, allowing his consciousness to expand beyond his scope of reality.

Nothing happened. Exhausted, deafeated, his shoulders slumped and his body grew heavier. He thought of his father, and how Loghemit Pon had created a fantasy in which his wife would one day return and love him, and had turned to drink as a way to hide from reality. Loghemit Pon had been weak. He had given up.

And Eramus almost had, too.

He concentrated harder now, ignoring his physical fatigue, his thoughts flashing through a series of images from memory, sensations, until he found the impression of danger the bird had pushed his way back in the barony, that he hadn't clearly identified before, and he stretched this to the bird he had seen in his recent dreams.

Nothing.

Still nothing.

And then he felt a presence drawing nearer, summoned by him, a predatory bird tearing through the sky, dropping like a stone, intent on a target, frightening Eramus.

A yellowish tint leaked across the insides of his eyelids. His eyes snapped open and he saw a sharply defined version of himself, tired and defeated, leaning against a tree with his sword in hand, fields of sparkling energy floating above the ground and flickering around the metal of his weapons. Even through the clouds he could see an infinite number of stars pulsing brightly in the sky, a blur beside each one as its movement coincided with a greater celestial rhythm, one he had never known existed until now. The beauty of its reassurance nearly drove him to tears of happiness.

Another consciousness directed him, causing movement of his head and not his eyes, turning the sweeping vista in the opposite direction to trampled grass. Eramus tried to make sense of what he saw. White hot pain lanced through his head and he fell to his knees, clutching his skull in agony. When the pain subsided, the colors and focus of his own eyesight had returned, the world white with a thin blanket of snow, the stars hidden behind the clouds.

Something fluttered overhead and he looked up to see a bastard snowthroat on the bough of a fir tree, shrieking noisily. *Caw, caw, caw! Uven, uven, uven! Roua. Ah-roua. Ah-roua.* It tilted its head to the side, staring at him with a single eye, before flapping back into the air and disappearing into the trees.

He stands in the dark, in front of the building he is too afraid to enter. He can see the bastard snowthroat's wings flapping through cracks in the wall.

The paralysis of his own fear awaited him. Cool snow melted on his cheeks and reminded him this wasn't a dream. He closed his eyes and raised his face to the snow's cleansing power.

He stood there for a span of heartbeats before understanding, trusting that he had indeed summoned the physical form of the bird, though what he had seen through its eyes had been signs of passing, signs revealed to him by *Uven Dema*: the Sound Above. The dreams were merging into reality. Riya was wrong about faith. It did serve a purpose. His faith had manifested itself. No longer did he fear to enter the structure. The spirit inside, trapped and dangerous, was his.

I am a prophet, he told himself. *I am to deliver the Word of the Sound Above, just as the Forgotten Prophet revealed the words of the Blood Eagle.*

He briefly wondered if he would ever see Riya again. He had never met a woman quite like her.

He imagined himself a bastard snowthroat, gliding on the wind, looking down from higher up, as he jogged in the wake of the disturbed grass. *I am a prophet.* Soon he had to stop. His legs burned with fatigue. *I am a prophet.*

He came across the body of the priest. The old man's head had been smashed in and Eramus could see the spongy brain inside the skull. A trail of blood marked the grass where he had tried to crawl away. Eramus might not have ever found this spot if it hadn't been for the bird, if it hadn't shown him the path, if he hadn't given himself over to the Sound Above. He wondered about the priest's apprentice. Would the boy become another casualty?

He kept on for a while until he arrived at a clearing. Reed grass and dead flowers surrounded a pond in the center.

He stands in the dark, in front of the structure he is too afraid to enter.

No, this is where I have been led. This is where I am supposed to be. This is where the Sound Above has brought me.

He stiffened when he noticed Sir Jacob crouched, drinking from the pond like a lion in his prime. The knight looked completely guiltless and fresh, pieces of his armor set neatly off to the side. Eramus had the element of surprise. The knight was too far away for him to strike cleanly, but he could charge in or even follow him while he waited for the perfect opening. He couldn't make any mistakes. He tried to reassure himself that the knight was just a man. *I am a prophet.*

Then Eramus noticed the priest's apprentice hiding in the distance, watching both of them. The boy had survived, and now drew upon his training to summon clouds to the clearing.

Eramus thought of the massacre back in the village, about how he had been manipulated, and his anger consumed him. He raised his sword.

"Sit there and do not move," his father says. Eramus almost can't contain the rage in his trembling body. He wants to hit something, to release his anger. Sitting still is near impossible.

"For how long?"

"Until I say so."

Eramus would kill Sir Jacob now, when his back was turned. He would decapitate him with one clean cut. He would deliver the justice that the Seehlan could not. He would strike a blow for them. He would champion their cause when they could not. He would strike where Rammun couldn't. No longer a coward, he felt the wings of the bastard snowthroat filling his arms and shoulders, pouring strength and courage into him.

"A good Hamaln does not solve problems with violence."

Loghemit Pon had been wrong about what violence could and couldn't do, but only now did Eramus fully understand the implications of his father's lesson. First Awakening mattered because a man of First Awakening made his own decisions, imposed his own will. Loghemit had chosen to be a victim, had turned to drink as a way to hide from the truth, and Reginald Pon had chosen to watch his own brother die. Perhaps the Hamal had shown wisdom to Eramus after all. Or perhaps he had found the answers inside himself. He wouldn't make the same mistakes. He would be a man of First Awakening on his own terms. He wouldn't let others decide his fate. He would deliver the only message every man could understand: submission through physical pain.

He cautiously stepped into the clearing, holding his breath, appreciating how the snowflakes left ripples across the pond. He saw no bird, no signs from *Uven Dema*. For a heartbeat he doubted his present. Had his dreams deceived him?

Sir Jacob slowly stood up, looking at Eramus more as an annoyance than anything. The knight could not have heard him.

"And what do you intend to do?" he asked. His eyes weren't the same brown with golden flecks that Eramus had noticed the first time he had met him. Now they were black and empty, the pupils completely dilated. His combination of red, black, and silver armor ranged from chainmail to heavy plate over his torso, a likeness of the Blood Eagle in the center of his breast. *He's just a man.*

The Blood Eagle had always been Eramus's enemy, though he hadn't known it until now.

"I'm here to kill you," Eramus replied. He must have been tired or even still dreaming. Nobody's eyes were black like that. Then he remembered that *culipi* had that effect on its users. He saw the open pouch, the dregs of the hallucinogenic fungus, and realized that the knight had succumbed to its influence. He heard the taunt of his childhood bullies condemning his mother. *"Mushroom head! Mushroom head!"* He heard his father's warning, inescapable despite his realization. *"A good Hamaln does not solve problems with violence."*

Eramus would decide what he could and couldn't do. He couldn't blame his father for his inaction anymore. He couldn't blame anyone but himself.

Deliver the message.

I am a prophet, sent from the Sound Above.

"You can hardly stand."

"*I am a prophet.* Defend yourself."

Sir Jacob's brows furrowed in anger, and his booming voice echoed across the clearing. "The Holy Temple of Gefil would have me punish you for such heresy. There is only one true prophet, and you are not him." He drew his bastard sword with a gauntleted hand. It scraped leather for an eternity before sliding free, and required both of the knight's hands along the hand-and-a-half hilt. Still armored, he left his helmet beside the pond, the eagle's beak intimidating even from this distance, along with the vambrace and gauntlet from his left hand. Eramus recalled an image from one of his dreams, the bastard snowthroat attacking a red eagle in flight. Eramus was a bastard snowthroat. *He's just a man.*

The knight stood his ground while Eramus advanced. When Eramus was close enough to strike, he slashed in at his enemy's waist. Sir Jacob easily turned the blow, as Eramus expected. He slid his blade up the length of the knight's, relying on the flat surface and friction to gather speed and momentum for a killing chop to the knight's face. The knight deftly twisted his arms to manipulate the massive bastard sword's crossguard into an intersecting block, easily anticipating the desperate tactic. He kicked Eramus full in the stomach, the force of the blow launching Eramus onto his back several feet away. The sudden, brutal attack knocked the wind out of Eramus, and he lost his grip on his sword.

The unforgiving steel of the knight's gauntleted hand closed around his throat before he could recover. He fumbled and clawed while he choked, his strength a fraction of what it should have been. He had underestimated his opponent. He shouldn't have challenged him. He shouldn't have surrendered to emotion and delusion. His fear had tried to warn him, but he hadn't listened this time.

I am Eramus Pon, and I am a coward.

Sir Jacob loomed over him, face cleanly shaven, black eyes terrifying. They locked onto Eramus's left arm. The knight's head twitched and he moaned with frightening happiness and excitement. "I see you, *ahzis!*"

Did the knight know about the *cserip*t? How could he?

Eramus scratched futiley at the vambrace over Sir Jacob's wrist with both hands but he couldn't break the righteous grip. The knight squeezed hard enough for Eramus to think his windpipe would collapse. Intense pain accompanied his need for air. *I am a prophet. I am a coward.*

"The *Otauh* demands that those who are marked must be cleansed, " the knight said. He chanted and opened the palm of his left hand until it glowed with bright light. He hummed louder and louder until the dark blue sigil on Eramus's forearm flared to life and seared brighter than it ever had beneath his flesh. Eramus tried to scream against the excruciating agony but he didn't have any breath in his lungs. Dark spots threatened to smother what little he could see. A high-pitched ringing had overtaken most of his hearing, and his entire body felt numbingly cold except for the unbearable scorching of the *cseript*.

"You must renounce your heretic ways," the knight ordered from somewhere far away. "You must present your impure soul to His Excellency Ismah Carleton for salvation."

Eramus couldn't concentrate on the knight's words. He could only see the man's fanatical face directly in front of him. The world slowed. Eramus felt incredible pressure on his chest along with a dull pounding in his left wrist. Thunder boomed somewhere far away.

He didn't want to die. He knew that now, more strongly than he had ever known it before. He remembered happy moments of his life, moments with his father, with Riya. Moments worth living. Moments worth remembering, worth fighting for.

He reached for his dagger. Although he knew in his mind that it was a simple matter to slip it free and stab his enemy, his fingers wouldn't obey him. The task's complexity exceeded them.

I know the sound above you.

A man crushed him, shouted into his face, but he forgot why and forgot to care. He ceased struggling. He closed his eyes and felt snowflakes on his forehead. That simple sensation reminded him of living. He loved Riya. He would miss her.

A bird's wings engulfed the insides of his eyelids and grew to unimaginable size. His fear had gone. *Uven Dema* waited for him.

He found peace.

Then awful pain consumed the pressure he had forgotten. He coughed icy air into the same lungs that had surrendered. Every breath hurt. Had *Uven Dema* saved him from death? Or had he somehow passed on to another Awakening?

He opened his eyes to discover Sir Jacob in the grass beside him, dazed, struggling to his hands and knees, his sword many feet away in the snow.

This was not an afterlife. Eramus reached for his own sword with clumsy, numb fingers. He eventually managed to snatch it up.

He was disappointed to see a trail of footprints in the snow leading to Gavrel hovering over Sir Jacob, glowering, his own sword in hand. "You told my brother that you just wanted the men and the mercenary. You never said you would murder the children."

Sir Jacob spit blood. "And he believed me? The Forgotten Prophet will never find his way back as long as a single Seehlan survives."

Gavrel leaned over him and clenched his fist. "You lied!"

Eramus stood up, his sword at the ready. He hoped that neither man would see just how weak he really was. "You were a part of this," he said to Gavrel in a hoarse voice that scraped his throat raw.

Gavrel screamed in rage and punched Sir Jacob across the jaw. The knight laughed. He hadn't even tried to dodge the blow. Gavrel stumbled backward when he noticed the knight's eyes.

Before either of them could react, the knight had sprung to his feet. "I intend to finish my purification."

Gavrel raised his sword. "You're not going anywhere. You don't even know what you're looking at right now, do you?"

"I see disease." The knight flicked his gaze down for a heartbeat, shoulders relaxing, and Gavrel's sword lowered a bit.

Sir Jacob tackled him at the waist, stealing his momentum enough to prevent him from properly using his blade. The knight moved with grace, speed, and frightening ferocity, even in his armor. The two hit the ground hard, Gavrel taking the brunt of the impact. Eramus wasted no time. *Uven Dema* wanted him to fight. He had led him here and spared his life, had even delivered an ally. Eramus ran at Sir Jacob, intending to stab him in the neck. But he hesitated at the last instant. This man knew something about the *cseript*. Perhaps he had the answers Eramus sought.

The knight took advantage of the hesitation. He turned, grabbed Eramus's blade with one hand and squeezed until it shattered. Eramus had never seen such strength. He stared at the sliver of steel still jutting from his hilt, at what remained of his identity.

Gavrel lunged at the knight again. He swung his blade in a downward, diagonal arc. The knight dodged with preternatural reflexes, and the steel missed him by mere inches. Sir Jacob stunned Gavrel with a slap across the face, then closed his gauntlet into a fist and hammered on his scarred shoulder once, twice. Gavrel shrieked in agony and dropped his sword, and Eramus couldn't help but cringe at what had sounded like a butcher pounding raw meat. Gavrel had taken a ridiculous amount of physical abuse in just the short time that Eramus had known him. What the knight did to him must have been unbearable. Dazed, Gavrel wobbled on his feet.

Eramus summoned the last of his strength and launched himself at Sir Jacob, slamming the hilt of his broken sword against the knight's armored back. He clawed for a grip on the armor as he slid free, but the knight shrugged him off and swung a lazy backhand at him. Eramus hit the ground, tasting his own blood. His legs refused to respond to his commands.

The knight laughed and jammed his boot heel down hard on Eramus's exposed side, breaking something inside him and filling him with more pain than he had ever known. Once again he struggled to breathe, wishing he could just rest for a few seconds, thinking of how he had been as vulnerable as this five years ago, and all of the time between then and now had been wasted because he had come right back to that moment of cowardice. He needed time to understand what he had done wrong.

Sir Jacob didn't give him time. He shoved his face in the ground so hard that Eramus swallowed snow and dirt. He tried to cry out but instead gagged on more dirt. The knight ripped him up by his hair and threw him aside. Eyes closed, he felt around for a weapon. His fingers found only snow and dirt. He opened his eyes to see the knight looming over him, snowflakes sizzling as they touched his armor. A hole in the thunderclouds had opened up. The sun shone down, sparkling off his armor in a powerful wash of holy light. His faith protected him. He had offered salvation to

Eramus. Had the knight already been granted that salvation himself?

Then steel hit steel and the knight pitched forward, tripping over Eramus. The clouds sealed the opening, blocking the sunlight. Gavrel walked over him a second later and kicked the knight across the face so hard that Sir Jacob landed face first in the snow and grass. He didn't move after that.

"Is...he...out..." Eramus wondered through ragged, painful breaths, unsure of exactly what he had seen. *He's just a man.*

"I think so," Gavrel said. He held his sword with both hands, ready to swing it again. His legs buckled beneath him and he jammed his sword into the ground, leaned on it for support while he recovered. A long dent creased the back of the knight's armor where Gavrel had struck him. "Check him. Do it!"

Eramus crawled, his side splintering in pain with every breath, and it felt like forever until he reached the knight. He swung his leg around and kicked him a couple of times. Sir Jacob didn't move. "I think he's out."

Eramus looked for the boy among the trees, who had already disappeared. Sir Jacob would have slit his throat given the chance.

Filled with rage, Eramus scooped up a fist-sized rock and held it over the knight's head, debating on what consequences killing a knight would bring down upon him.

"You can't kill him. If you do, Ismah Carleton will send other knights. Better for him to be disgraced. Better for Lord Kent to decide his fate."

"Just one blow? It will make me feel better." He couldn't tell Gavrel what he had seen. He couldn't tell anyone. He really had no intention of killing the knight, at least not yet. He was ashamed to think that he had finally managed to come face to face with Loghemit Pon's killer, and couldn't avenge his father's death.

Gavrel shook his head.

Tired, angry, Eramus tossed the rock away. "What difference does it make? You've already interfered."

"I wouldn't have killed any children. You must believe me."

"How am I supposed to believe you? You led the soldiers here."

After checking one of his loose back teeth, Gavrel leaned forward and half-spit, half-drooled blood into the snow. "I didn't know the refugees would have children with them. I didn't care about the others. It made no difference to me at the time. I didn't know any of them. It wasn't personal."

"And now?" Eramus asked, wondering if what Gavrel had witnessed had changed him.

"It's…different."

The two of them sat in silence for a few moments until Eramus recovered enough strength to crawl on hands and knees to pick up the handle of his broken sword. He used a handful of snow to wipe away red mud, revealing Trixie's beautiful engraving. She had looked past his façade, had shown him a semblance of compassion. Why?

Gavrel stood over him. "What does it say?"

"*Prophuug*."

Gavrel plopped down on his rear and tossed his own sword aside. He looked just as exhausted as Eramus felt and he had another fresh bruise on his jaw. He favored his shoulder where the knight had struck him, wincing every time it had to move.

"It means that I've acknowledged that my father failed to teach me what I needed to survive. That's what the engraving will always remind me."

"So you taught yourself. And yet here you sit," Gravrel said with a half smirk.

"Yes, because of my own decisions."

"Decisions…I just wanted to do what was right for my brother. This was the only way I could clear my name. That was more important to Lebon than anything. He wanted me to start fresh, to help him on his land. " Gavrel swallowed hard, and his next words seemed difficult to him. "I'm sorry for betraying you, Eramus Pon. You have been nothing but a friend to me, when you had every reason not to be. I am ashamed. Lebon would not have approved of my actions."

"I know you're sorry. It's not easy to remember that what's right for you isn't right for everyone." Eramus wondered if he spoke of himself. He had no right to give advice. Even after all that had happened, after the brutality he had witnessed, a part of him still wondered if the Ismah really could grant him salvation, could save him from the curse that infected his body and quite possibly his soul. Could there be an end to his nightmares and his fears? And what would he have to give in return? He couldn't believe he even considered this. *Uven Dema,* and not the Ismah, had aided him when he needed guidance.

Gavrel looked up, away from Eramus, and wiped some of the grime and blood off his face. "It isn't always clear what needs to be done, is it?"

Eramus sat down as well, and sighed. The way was never clear. He had always believed that Second Awakening would grant him the wisdom he needed. Now he wasn't so sure. At least he knew the Seehlan would be safe for the time being. That alone was a small consolation. He thrust the shard of his blade into the earth. He wouldn't be taking it with him. "No. Sometimes it seems like whatever you do is wrong."

"Lebon knew what to do. I miss him. I miss my brother."

Eramus glanced over at him. "How's your shoulder?"

"No worse off than it was two days ago. It just hurts."

"I wanted to kill you, you know."

"And do you feel that way now?"

"Not really, but stopping the knight doesn't absolve you of guilt."

Gavrel sighed. "I know. I'm kind of in the middle somewhere now, you know? What's that word? Profog?"

"*Prophuug,*" Eramus replied. "Pronounced pro-foog. In Uuslefin we leave the stress on the beginnings and ends of words."

"Pro-foog. Pro-foog."

"The translation is to be caught up in a current, like in a river or something. Hadrius likes to remind me of how easily I let myself get caught up in the current around me. My father was like that. Always said it was bad luck. It's a coward's way of letting things control you."

Gavrel looked over at him. It was difficult to read the man's sincerity. "You should learn how to swim."

Eramus thought back to his days in the IR, when he let others choose where he went, what he did. He considered the events of the last several days. He had been nothing more than the knight's puppet. Eramus intended to choose his own way from now on. He wouldn't simply accept things, like his father had tried to teach him to do.

"I'm going back to Kluhm," Gavrel said after a long pause. "At least to check on my brother's wife and make sure his land is in good hands. I promised Lebon I would."

"But you won't stay there? Is it because of his ugly wife?"

Gavrel smirked. "Lebon wouldn't have married an ugly woman." The smile faded. "It's not a home for me without him there. I don't know. I'm doing my best to let go of the revenge. It's difficult, like it's eating away at me. There's a part of me insisting on paying back those who have wronged me. That would take me to many places."

Eramus shook his head. "Then you're like us, you know? That's what we do. We move from place to place."

"Pro-foog," Gavrel repeated to himself several times. "I guess we all have to go our own way sometimes."

Eramus checked his arm, unable to see the *cseript* he knew was there. He could feel it. Could the Ismah really help him? They sat for a few minutes, and eventually Eramus looked up and watched the clouds roll by overhead. The snow had stopped falling. He wasn't sure what happened next. They couldn't stay in the mountains. He knew that for certain.

He closed his eyes, tentatively probing with his mind the same way he had done earlier, until he saw filmy yellow versions of himself and Gavrel in the clearing from somewhere up above. Closer and closer he appeared, and he lifted his left arm and clenched his fist.

When he saw through his own eyes again, the bastard snowthroat circled them before tentatively lighting on Eramus's forearm, just as it had in his dreams. He let the bird move around with complete freedom while Gavrel stared at it. It eventually settled on his shoulder, and he felt as if he and the bird were a little closer to understanding one another. He had to bear the curse for now. Condemned by the temple or condemned by the madness, he saw no difference. Either way, he belonged to someone, something else, and this bird was the key to it all. Was he really a prophet?

"I'm not going to be able to explain this to you," Eramus said.

Gavrel nodded his acceptance, grimacing at the simple action. This was one more odd circumstance in a sequence of many. "The bird my brother spoke of. Is it a sign?"

Eramus shrugged. "I really don't know."

"I've seen so much over the last several days that, strangely enough, your pet bird seems almost normal."

"How did you get here?" Eramus asked, quickly changing the subject. The bastard snowthroat was not his pet.

"The mercenary—"

"Rammun."

"He told me I had made a mistake but I could fix it. He trusted me to do what was right. He showed me something most men don't."

"And what was that?"

"Mercy."

Eramus moved closer and put his arm around Gavrel's shoulders. "It took me a while to come around, too."

"The lessons…First Awakening…I suppose part of it is learning about other people."

"What do you mean?"

"I haven't trusted anyone since Lebon for a long time. I used to blame it on my profession, but I don't think that's all of it."

"Then what is it?"

"I'm finding out that I can't do everything alone. Every once in a while, I need to ask for help. That's not easy for me to admit."

Eramus had no response. Maybe Gavrel was right. After all, he and Rammun had both helped Eramus in his time of need. Like Gavrel, though, Eramus had trouble asking for help. He felt it made him a burden to others, made him appear weak.

Gavrel looked back at him. "But it's not enough."

"Then what do you have in mind?"

They stripped the knight of everything but his undergarments, revealed a mutilated body covered in runes that had been tattooed and branded onto his flesh. They tossed his expensive armor into the bushes, and bound his hands before tying his arms to his waist as well. He woke after they had tied him up.

"You have interfered with my mission," he said in a calm voice. Thankfully his eyes had returned to normal. "The Temple of Gefil sanctioned my work. By interfering, you have condemned yourselves."

"Are you sure we shouldn't kill him?" Eramus asked Gavrel.

Gavrel shook his head. "I have people after me anyway. Holy warriors don't scare me, especially butchers of women and children." When the knight opened his mouth to respond, Gavrel stuffed a gag into it.

After Eramus and Gavrel had rested for a while, they passed through Seehan, knight in tow on a leash of knotted rope, as they searched for survivors. They found none. When they reached the spot where Rammun had been, they discovered that he had vanished. Eramus felt relief. The mercenary was a survivor, and a friend.

Eramus and Gavrel gathered what food and supplies they could find and followed the trail the soldiers had left on the long trek back to the barony, all the while Eramus wondering exactly what his death warrant would mean. Would he be just like the Seehlan now? He wondered if his curse would be the greater of two evils or if he could save himself trouble by surrendering to the Ismah. Could he truly grant salvation to Eramus like Sir Jacob had promised?

EPILOGUE

Hadrius, arm in a sling, awaited them at the base of the mountain with horses, a pair of Medarn soldiers, and a suppressed smile. The bird who had accompanied Eramus down the mountain immediately took flight, and Eramus forgot about it for the time being. He and Gavrel were tired from the trip and from having to constantly watch the knight.

"*A rescue party?*" Eramus asked Hadrius.

"*I didn't want to part with my money. These two were free.*"

As Gavrel bid both peerans a terse farewell, the soldiers spoke in hushed tones to one another. One of them said something to him in Medarn but Hadrius and Eramus both waved the soldier off and hurried Gavrel on his way. The assassin galloped off, not waiting to be identified. He already had a dangerous enough trip ahead of him. With the help of the soldiers, Eramus threw Sir Jacob over the back of one of their horses and they hauled him into the barony.

According to Hadrius, Riya had crossed to the Hereton and Alina had doubled back much sooner than that. Now Eramus knew how Rammun had managed to survive. She had gone back for him. It had been Hadrius alone who had returned the children and explained events. He had been arrested on sight and thrown into a dungeon until Jobah Soames, of all people, had corroborated at least part of his story. He still had both of their names on record, and he had remembered Hadrius's face when the guards had hauled him away.

Eramus was introduced to Baron Kent, who thanked him for saving his children. Eramus could easily see the resemblance

Rammun bore to his father. He wished he could tell the man about his son. He would be proud of him.

The Medarn militia had already stormed the Filthies' barracks and overpowered them to free Sadir and his family. Eramus personally spoke out against Eamon and the men who had harmed his friend. Every soldier involved in the crime was eventually hanged in the public square, one by one, on a gallows specifically built for the occasion. Eramus attended the hangings, and was particularly pleased when Eamon's neck didn't break straight away. The Filthy kicked and squirmed while he slowly strangled.

The baron held the knight in custody for several days. His crimes were read, his punishment decided. His property confiscated, he was banished from the barony, as were all knights and representatives of the Temple of Gefil.

Eramus and Hadrius were invited to observe the sentencing. A militia captain led them to a balcony in the back of the throne room and ordered them to remain quiet.

"I'll remember this day," Sir Jacob said.

"I should hope so," Baron Kent retorted. "Otherwise your memory would be subject to question."

"Your actions constitute an act of war."

"This is hardly an act of war."

"You've hanged Count Sevelah's men and denied me entry to your barony. Count Sevelah and King Willum will be upset to say the least, and His Excellency surely won't treat this latter offense as lightly as you do. You must remember that I am an extension of His Excellency's will."

"I have no control over anyone's feelings. I've said enough to you as it is." He nodded to his guards and they escorted Sir Jacob from the throne room.

The captain nodded to Eramus. "Let's go. His Lordship has asked you and you alone to assist in escorting him from the barony." They led the knight from the city in chains. Even in defeat, he retained his resolve.

"There's a chance for your salvation. I'll rest in Frehm," the knight told him. "Where your father left you. The villagers believe in the work I do. I'll be there for ten days, awaiting word from His Excellency Ismah Carleton. Ten days, Eramus Pon, but no longer."

"Are you implying that you'll be waiting for me?" he asked the knight in surprise. "Why would you do that? You've already condemned me, remember?"

Sir Jacob's wrists were chained so he nodded his head at the invisible *cseript* on Eramus's arm. "You are an *ahzis,* visible by the *hzis* on your flesh. Despair, madness…these are merely symptoms of what will come. The *hzis* will eventually seize control of you. Renounce your heresy and embrace the Temple of Gefil. I will speak to His Excellency on your behalf."

"You don't know anything about what's happened to me. You don't know anything about me, either."

"There you are wrong, brother. I know more about you than you think."

Eramus ignored him as they continued ahead, unwilling to believe that the knight told the truth. Riya had already called the mark on his arm a *cseripta,* had said that it had come from a sorcerer of some kind. The knight's words were a trick, a deception to force Eramus to surrender to the Ismah. He would never accept the Temple of Gefil. He would never ally himself with murderous zealots, would never ally himself with the man who had murdered his father.

"Do you know what your father died for?" Sir Jacob asked.

Eramus did not, and that question had eaten away at him for years. "You have no idea who I am," Eramus said. "You have no idea who my father was."

The militia unlocked the knight's shackles and left him in an empty field with nothing but the roughspun clothing on his back. He grinned arrogantly. "Ten days!" the knight shouted at Eramus as he turned his horse and trotted away.

Eramus stopped at the bound parchment shop and made a single purchase once he returned to the barony. He found Hadrius in the baron's courtyard a short while later. "This is where we part ways, *prophuug*," his friend said. "I'm going to find Sylvia's sister and let her know what happened."

"And then what?"

"I truly don't know. Maybe find some honest work."

Eramus could go with him, could try to catch up to Trixie. And then what? Put her life in jeopardy? No, he had to stay as far away from her as he could.

Future possible. Could he determine what this would be?

Possible. Nothing more than a synonym for the word "guess" in his mind, a variable he wasn't altogether comfortable with. *What do you stand to gain?*

"I almost forgot," Hadrius said as he reached into his pocket. He produced a folded letter. "She made me promise to give this to you."

Eager and nervous, Eramus unfolded the page and read Riya's handwriting. His heart sunk. He shook his head, wondering why he should have expected anything different.

They left under fading ebb stars late in the afternoon, without saying goodbye to Sadir, their saddlebags a little heavier with an unexpected reward. The baron had also gifted them with letters of passage endorsed with King Willum's royal seal. They said their farewells outside the eastern gate, Hadrius heading north. Eramus felt an emptiness in his stomach while he watched his friend ride away.

Eramus had given a lot of thought to Gavrel's suggestion that he learn how to swim, and Sir Jacob's promise that the curse, or what he called the *hzis*, would consume him.

But Eramus would never embrace the Temple of Gefil. He wouldn't let events control him. He wouldn't be a victim like his father. He had the power to make his own decisions, to shape his own path.

Ten days. No more.

The bastard snowthroat came down and landed on his shoulder. It preened itself, as completely comfortable with him as he was with it. He had an idea what its purpose was after all, and his as well.

"Tah, roua."

A pair of hearbeats followed before he heard *Se fen demduli? Poh gur o frel fahl gur* inside his head. He pulled his recently acquired leatherbound copy of *Practical Medarn* from his saddlebags, licked his thumb and forefinger, and flipped through the pages until he could translate at least part of what he had heard.

Yellow haze leaked into his eyesight, the road sharpened around him, and the sky opened up to starry magnificence. *I am Eramus the coward.*

He turned to the bird. *"O duli."*

"Caw, caw, caw!"

Look for book two of the *Eramus Pon* novels

Eramus the Foolish

By Vincent R. Hagman

ABOUT THE AUTHOR

Vincent R. Hagman was born in Southern California during the United States Bicentennial. He received a degree in English from CSU Sacramento before accepting full time employment in the medical supply industry to fund his true passion: writing. He spends one night a week competing in league bowling and partakes of the occasional cup of *glistas* with good friends. He currently resides in Northern California. ***Eramus the Coward*** is his first novel.